DRAGONBOURNE

The Wyvern War

WRITTEN BY A.N.ATTEBERY

ILLUSTRATED BY
Adrian Davies-Ratcliffe

Chapter List

Una Puella,

Unus Puer,

Caeruleosque implexae animabus illorum,

Draco et Sedebat,

Unum pro Pugnans.

2018 Amazon Direct Publishing

A loving gift for Irene and Paul

Chapter 1

Wyvern Academy

Two Kingdoms rested side by side, the only thing dividing them being the Plain of Fire. Gailoiyn was ruled by brother and sister, the royal Ricco and Veronica Gailoiyn. The nation had a reputation for its peaceful nature. They used to get on with their neighbour, the kingdom of Brozanta. However, when the old king died, the throne was succeeded by his ruthless brother, King Stephan. Stephan Brozanta craved power above all else, and he hungered for it with every waking moment. He would take control of Gailoiyn in a second given the chance...but the Gailoiyn's wouldn't allow it. He was cruel and corrupt, and even his own people feared him, as did his orphaned nephew, Lucas Brozanta. Lucas had not been seen since Stephan's succession. Stephan was a tyrant, but Stephan was also special...for he had the blood of the Dragon. He was Dragonbourne. A human, with the blood of a Dragon. Dragonbourne's can turn into a Dragon at will, with practice of course, and their scale colour would resemble their human eye colour. There were also humans who had perfected the art of riding these beasts of war. And that is where our story begins! Wyvern Academy is a school in Gailoiyn's capital city of Algora. A child may enlist in the school at the age of thirteen, where they will be trained in the art of riding with a partner. A Dragonbourne child will automatically receive a letter inviting them to join, but not all do. In the school, they learn to fight, ride and work with their partner to protect the kingdom from any threat they may face. The Brozantan equivalent of Wyvern Academy is Bloodbourne Academy, but even that has been corrupted by King Stephan's influence. But I am not King Stephan, nor am I a Gailoiyn royal. My name is Xandario Sykes.

So, a little about me. I'm just a short, fourteen-year-old, golden haired orphan. I often wear my hair in a ponytail, and I have these bangs that curl either side of my face. My eyes are weird. Because my left eye is green and my right eye is bright blue. I got pale skin, so pale that I always look unwell because I never tan, no matter how bloody sunny it is. My parents aren't around...they left when I was young, and I never really knew the truth as to why. All I had left of them was their wedding rings on a golden chain. I always wore it around my neck. Somehow, it made me feel close to them. Their names were Alphonse and Kirani Sykes, but I hardly knew anything about them. My Grandparents didn't like to talk about their son or daughter-in-law. So yeah...I wasn't raised by my parents. I was raised by Grandma and Gramps. Harry and Beatrice Sykes were the best grandparents ever. I couldn't ask for a better upbringing. Come to think of it, I didn't really know much about their past either. Anyway, back to the day in question. It was a hot, sunny day, and I was excited but scared as I was leaving my small village of Lightwater for the capital Algora to attend Wyvern Academy! No, I am not Dragonbourne, but I have always been fascinated in them, and have wanted to become a rider for as long as I can remember. The day I had been accepted at Wyvern Academy I was so surprised! I mean I hadn't really expected to get in. My grandparents were worried sick, but they were happy for me. Grandpa was the village blacksmith, and I had been learning his trade...but he always knew I wasn't happy. I didn't have many possessions of my own, and the only thing I really had of sentimental value was the necklace with my parent's rings on it. Anyway, I was finishing packing my bag. It felt strange...leaving all this behind. It was all I had ever known. My thoughts were swirling around inside my head as I began to imagine what direction my life was about to take. Suddenly, I was pulled from my thoughts as there was a knock at the door. I heard the grainy voice of my grandfather through the door as he spoke. "Xanda, are you dressed?"

I quickly zipped up my bag and turned to face the door.

"Yeah!" I replied.

He opened the door, painting a small smile on his face. He was a tall man, with grey hair around the side of his head. The top of it was bald, which I always thought looked rather odd...kind of like a monk. However, his deep grey eyes were always comforting to see, and he had somewhat of a calming presence.

"Look at you..." He said in a rather sentimental tone.

I chuckled a little. "I look the same as I always do, Gramps."

It was true, I mean nobody in our village really had a wide variety of clothes. We were simple folk after all. Gramps was always covered in dirty black dust as he was always working. I was wearing an outfit I wore a lot. I wore heavy, fingerless brown blacksmith gloves, and a long sleeved light blue undershirt. I had a brown leather jacket on, which had white fur draped over the right shoulder and leather straps holding it together crossing over my chest. I had a thick brown belt on, and light brown trousers...which some found strange as not many girls wore trousers. I also wore dark brown boots. As I looked at my grandfather, I saw he had something behind his back. I then added to my previous statement, a question.

"What you got there?"

It was then Grandma walked in. She was a small lady, not much taller than me. She had white hair always worn in a bun, and bright blue eyes that matched my right eye. She smiled sweetly as she spoke.

"We couldn't let you leave without giving you a going away present!" She said.

Gramps then moved his hands, and presented me with a scythe, just big enough for me to use. My eyes widened as I looked it over. The craftsmanship was extraordinary! I gasped happily.

"Grandma! Gramps! Awe man you shouldn't have!" I suddenly hugged them both, and Gramps moved the scythe away to keep me safe. They both smiled and hugged me back tightly.

"We wanted to, sweetheart." Gramps said softly. "I made it myself. It's one of my best pieces. It's yours. Just the weight you like, and easy to swing around."

"You're the best!" I pulled back and held it proudly after he handed it to me. He was right, it was perfect for me.

"Well." Grandma started. "It's time for you to go. Your coach is waiting for you outside. Come on." She smiled weakly and they both started to lead me out of the cottage, after of course I had picked up my bag and fastened my scythe to my belt. I took a deep breath, and took one look around my childhood home, before pushing open the front door. I felt a rush of excitement, and my hand went up to my mouth as I saw the entire village standing outside, cheering and wishing me good luck. They had all come to wave me off. It was a small village, but everyone looked out for one another. So naturally, it meant a lot that they had all come to bid me farewell. I smiled as I hugged people goodbye. After all, it was one of those villages where everyone knew everybody else. I felt grateful that they had done this, but now a little sad that I was leaving this all behind. I mean not for good, I knew I'd be able to come back in the holidays. Still, I was gonna miss the place. I was ushered towards the carriage that awaited me in the village centre. It was drawn by a simple brown horse, which to be fair was really cute. I loved horses. In fact, I loved animals of any kind. I put my stuff into the carriage before climbing in and shutting the door. I opened the window, leaning my head out. I smiled, seeing that Grandma and Gramps had made their way to the front of the crowd. They both took my hands, and I smiled at them as I simply said. "I love you."

"We love you too." Grandpa said.

"Now go, before I start crying!" Said Grandma with tears in her eyes. "Go enjoy yourself and we'll see you soon."

"That you will. As a Dragon Rider!" I grinned, letting go of them slowly. I took a deep breath, sitting back in the carriage, waving my old friends goodbye as the carriage began to move. I allowed a single tear to fall, but I quickly wiped it away. There was no going back now. I may fail...the thought did cross my mind. I may be a hopeless student. But I felt deep down this was something I felt I had to do. I didn't know why, I just knew this was where I needed to go. I closed my eyes, not daring to look back as the carriage carried me away.

I had fallen asleep on the coach. To be honest I hadn't gotten much sleep the night before, as I was so excited but also extremely nervous. I had my feet resting on the seat as I lay across it, my head resting against the side of the carriage. I was half and half right now, and I could feel a soothing breeze sweeping over me through the open window, and the sun beating down on my face. My body felt warm, and I felt at peace. I hadn't felt this way in a long time. Thinking about where I was heading made me think of my parents, and what kind of people they were, what they did for a living...stuff like that. As I said before, I knew next to nothing about them. I suddenly heard a change in the sound of the horse's hooves, like now they were walking on stone and not a dirt road. I rubbed my eyes with my hands and let out a big yawn. Stretching out, I put my feet back onto the floor. I rubbed my eyes again, and I turned my head to look out the window, suddenly finding myself wide awake. "Whoa…" was the only thing that escaped my lips. I leaned out the window, feeling the city breeze blow through my golden hair. I gazed upon the grand city of Algora. It was huge! And uphill. We were riding through the marketplace, which was flat. The carriage stopped, and I gathered my things and stepped out into the square. I didn't even notice the driver ride off almost immediately, as I was too much in awe at the sight before me. I had never seen a city so big! Standing in the marketplace, my nose was overcome with the strong smell of freshly baked bread, and I could see stalls around the edges with all sorts of colourful items for sale. There was fruit and vegetables, cake, books and antiques! There were more stalls than I had ever seen in my life! In the centre of the marketplace was a large, round fountain. The water sparkled like crystals as the sun shimmered on its surface. There were shops behind the stalls made from tanned stone, which looked weird to me because all the buildings in my small village were made of wood. I hadn't really seen many buildings made from stone before, except from the tavern back home. Looking upwards, there were houses, which were a lighter shade of stone. All of them seemed to have pretty, neat and pristine front gardens with loads of different types of flowers. I wouldn't know any of the names because I'm not really into gardening, but they did look beautiful. I craned my neck back a little to look towards the top of the kingdom, which was higher up. To the far left, I saw the royal palace. I could only see the top of it, but I had never seen anything so wonderful in my entire life! The stone was white, and it looked huge! I envied the King and Princess…what I wouldn't give to have a place like that to call my own. The turrets were so tall, and the roof a mystical shade of light blue. I then turned my attention to the far right, and there it was…Wyvern Academy! It was basically another castle, yet it looked different from the palace. For one, it was shaped squarer than the royal palace, and I could see things flying overhead in the distance. Were they Dragons?! I couldn't wait to see one properly up close! My heart buzzed with excitement as I gazed upon the school I would be attending. I took a few steps forward, when I was snapped out of my thoughts by a soft voice. I stopped, turning around.

A girl, looking about my age, was walking towards me. She was so beautiful. Her skin was so fair and smooth, and she had pale hazelnut eyes. Her hair was long, thick, and curly, and it fell perfectly in place. She had a braid draping the top of her head, like a headband. Her hair was a gorgeous shade of silky lilac. She held a wooden staff in her hand which curled at the top majestically. She wore a green dress, and a fabric belt draped around her thin waist. The dress was short, and towards the bottom it was layered with light green thin ruffle material contrasting beautifully with the other shades of green. Her sleeves came to just above her elbow, but she wore long, thin fingerless gloves which went up her arms and even under her sleeves. She also had on white tights, and light brown over-knee boots. She looked stunning, but also timid. I could tell she had had a completely different upbringing to me. I must have looked like a proper commoner compared to her.

"Excuse me." She said softly.

"Yeah?" I said nervously. "S-Sorry...were you talking to me?"

"Yes." She chuckled softly, which put me at ease. "Do you know the way to the Academy?"

"No." I replied. "But I'm heading there myself. Your welcome to tag along."

"Thank you. I didn't really want to walk in there by myself."

"Nah me neither. I'm Xanda by the way. Xanda Sykes." I smiled holding out my hand, which she took gently, shaking my hand as she introduced herself.

"I'm Irina Rozanna. It's nice to meet you Xanda." She smiled sweetly and began to walk through the streets, using her staff like a walking stick, even though she clearly didn't need it. In a way, it made her look more majestic. I walked at her side. There were a few moments of silence before I finally struck up a conversation.

"So, Irina...are you Dragonbourne?"

"No." She said looking at me. "Are you?"

"Nah. Although sometimes I wish I was."

"My cousin Pippa is. In fact, she's the reason I'm here." Irina explained.

"Is she your partner?"

"Yes. We are the same age, so she automatically got accepted to the Academy last year when she was thirteen. You can't have an official partner until you're fourteen. The Dragonbourne's spend a year learning how to transform into their Dragon form efficiently. Some learn quicker than others. I've been riding Pippa since we were little, but I was too shy to join the Academy last year. She came home at the end of last year and convinced me to go...she hadn't found a partner. She didn't feel compatible with any of the first-year students at the time. So, she asked if I would come and be her partner...and I agreed."

"That's so sweet." I smiled gently, thinking on what she said. "You're so lucky to have a partner already. I have no idea who mine will be."

"You'll know."

"How?" I questioned.

"You just will." She smiled reassuringly. "So...tell me about yourself."

"M-Me?" I was a little taken aback...I hadn't really been asked this before. But then again, living in such a small village, everyone knows your life story better than you do. "There's not much to know about me. I'm an orphan from Lightwater. My Grandma and Gramps raised me. He's the blacksmith, and was teaching me the trade but...well...I'm not that good at it. In fact, I'm...not much good at anything."

"I'm sure that is not true." She smiled softly at me, and I smiled back. She made me feel more at ease. I hoped I would find a friend in Irina. She really was lovely to me. We continued towards the academy, and I started to wonder what kind of people I would meet while I was there. Thankfully, I had already made one friend, so at least I didn't have to walk in like a loner.

We talked on the way to the Academy, and I learned she came from a Nobel family in a town called Kazura. She was the youngest child in the Rozanna family. I didn't really pry much more, she seemed like a private person, although that may have just been her shyness. What we both did share, was the admiration we felt upon arriving at the Academy gates. We both stopped, gasping in awe as the iron gates took the form of two Dragons. It was amazing craftsmanship, and I wasn't sure even my Grandfather could forge something like this. The castle was huge! It made me feel so small. The oak doors were open and welcoming students in, as were the gates. Old students were walking straight through. However, sitting at a small table to the right of the gates was a middle-aged man, who was signing in first years and giving them keys to their rooms. He had muscles, and looked quite intimidating. With piercing blue eyes and long white hair in a ponytail, he really isn't someone I would mess with. Irina and I began to make her way over and we joined the line, which wasn't that long right now. Irina was in front of me, and we talked a little more about how amazing the place looked until she was front of the cue. She approached the man nervously, who looked at her. "Welcome to Wyvern Academy. What's your name?" He spoke with a hint of boredom in his tone, like he had already said this line a hundred times today. "I-Irina Rozanna." She swallowed nervously.
"Irina!" Just then another girl ran over. She had piercing yellow eyes and dark red hair. Her fringe fell to the right in front of her eyes, and she wore the back in two messy buns. She wore a deep purple jacket, which had eight buttons on it, four on either side. The jacket had a rim just below the waistline but then carried on, down a little way draping over her short skirt. The skirt was layered a little like Irina's, with different shades of pink and purple. She also wore deep purple gloves which were spiked at the end, and had a pink rim. Her legs were slender, and she wore over knee, black tights, with pink and purple short boots. I swear I will never get used to the elaborate colours rich people wear. Anyway, from the way she embraced Irina, I realised she must be her cousin, Pippa.
"You made it!" She smiled at Irina, clearly more outgoing than she was. She then looked at the teacher. "Hiya Mr Davandrin!"
"Ah, Miss Capell." The teacher smiled a little at her. "This is your cousin I assume? And the new partner you're so eager to start working with."
"You bet!"
"Pippa." Irina smiled, looking more at ease now she was with her cousin. I could tell just by looking at them they were a good match. "Meet my new

friend. This is Xanda."

"Hiya Xanda!"

"Um…hi." I smiled back a little nervously. The teacher found Irina's name and ticked her off.

"You will be sharing your room with Pippa, Miss Rozanna. Riders and Dragons share a room. There will be a welcome meeting in the great hall tonight. Do not miss it. And you are?" The teacher then looked at me. Pippa and Irina stepped aside, but stayed there waiting for me, which I was grateful for. I cleared my throat and told him my name.

"Xandario Sykes."

"Xandar-……." He stopped looking for my name, and slowly looked up at me. He just stared at me. I instantly felt uncomfortable and looked behind me, then back at him. Nope. He was defiantly looking at me. "Xanda Sykes…" He repeated. Irina and Pippa exchanged a confused look between each other. Mr Davandrin then cleared his throat, snapping out of his thoughts as he ticked my name off. He handed me a key. "Room 305 Miss Sykes." He said.

Pippa excitedly took my arm, and began dragging me away excitedly, Irina jogging a little to keep up.

"That means your next door to us! Come on Xanda!" Pippa exclaimed.

"I'm coming!" I chuckled softly, feeling welcomed and…happy.

As I was dragged across the courtyard, my eyes caught the glimpse of a boy around my age, sitting on a bench. There was something…I couldn't explain the feeling. We were instantly connected, like when we crossed our souls intertwined. It was just for a second that we met eye to eye before I was dragged inside…

When I entered the Academy, I had no idea the danger I was throwing myself into. Little did I know that my decision to join the Academy would leave me in the centre of a war that I could not escape…

Chapter 2

Turrets are High

My room was incredible! It was so much bigger than my room at home. In the upper right-hand corner was a bunkbed, with deep red sheets and white pillows that looked so silky and soft. The beds themselves were bigger than a standard size bed too. Ahead of me was a large window, which opened onto a short balcony, the stone railings perfectly sculpted. The balcony looked over a cliff and a sandy beach below, and of course the ocean. Draped either side of the window were deep red curtains that matched the colour of the bedsheets. In the left top and bottom corner of the room there were two wardrobes. I assumed one would of them would be for me and one for my Dragonbourne partner...when I finally got one. They were a lovely deep shade of oak wood like the front door, and a strong smell wafted from them like they had recently been varnished. In between the wardrobes, in the middle of the wall, was a magnificent dressing table! It was made from white wood, and the wood around the big mirror was carved into the shape of two thin Dragons. I had always wanted a dressing table! I felt so posh right now. In the bottom right was a small door that led into a bathroom. Anyway, I had been in there a while, and had unpacked all of my bags. I sat on the bottom bunkbed, fiddling with the rings around my neck, just like I always did when I wanted to feel close to my parents. I often wondered if they were proud of me, and proud of the decision I had made. Now though I admit, I hadn't done much to make them proud. I was suddenly pulled from my thoughts as I heard a knock at the door.

"Heya Xanda! Can we come in?" I heard Pippa shout from the other side. I stood, hiding the rings back under my shirt.

"Yeah." I smiled as Pippa opened the door, walking in with Irina.

"Hello Xanda." Irina smiled sweetly at me. "Do you like the room?"

"Are you joking?!" I chuckled, beaming. "It's amazing! Its huge! I can't believe I got this to myself for now!"

"For now." Pippa grinned, moving over and putting an arm around me. It felt strange, but somewhat nice...I mean, I'd never really had girlfriends before. "There are dormitories in the cellar where the Dragonbournes sleep until they find partners. When you have one, yours will move in with you."

"The cellar?" I raised an eyebrow. "Really?"

"It's not that bad." Pippa answered. "In fact its lovely down there. So cosy. The rooms are big too. There's usually four of us in a room, and it's so warm down there! Just the way we Dragonbourne's like it."

"So why move up here?"

"To help with bonding. When you have a partner...there's a lot more to it than just riding them. You have to work together. If there is no bond, they can have real trouble working together. You'll learn more about that in History of Dragons class, Riding Class and Partner Bonding class. You'll also learn to fight together on land and sky in combat class."

"I see. So, what's with this meeting tonight?" I queried.

"Just 'Welcome to our school, have a great time here' stuff. There's also a huge feast. That's the best part. While you're down there someone will put your timetable through your door so you know what classes you have tomorrow. You're rooms next to ours, so you should be in class with us."

"That makes me feel better." I sighed in relief. Just then, I heard a voice I didn't recognise.

"Yo Pip! Irina!" I turned to look in the doorway as two boys entered the room. Neither one of them was the boy I had seen on the bench earlier, but they seemed to know Pippa as they came in and high fived her. The boy that had spoken had scruffy, pure white hair, and his eyes were a deep shade of purple. He was a little tanned, but not too much. He wore a loose grey jacket, and baggy light tan trousers with dark boots. He looked simple, and a little rough around the edges. The other boy had brown hair swept over his brow, and blue eyes. His skin was pale like mine and he wore a sleeveless dark yellow jacket, and a white shirt underneath with baggy sleeves. His trousers were a light grey and like his friend he wore brown leather boots. They looked quite the pair.

"Hiya boys!" Said Pippa.

"H-Hello again." Said Irina, a little nervously.

"Taz, Joey, this is Xanda Sykes. A new Rider! Xanda, this is Tazmin Periwinkle and Josef Danaris." Said Pippa as she introduced us.

"But please, call me Taz." Said the white-haired boy.

"And call me Joey." Said the other.

I smiled gently at them and nodded in appreciation. "Nice to meet you. So...are you two partners?"

"Yeah." Said Joey, grinning at the other boy. "We've been best mates since like...forever. Taz joined last year being a Dragonbourne, and I got a place, but I couldn't attend cos of...um...family issues. But I'm good to go this year!"

"This is going to be so fun!" Irina smiled, clenching her hands over her chest in anticipation.

I smiled weakly at what she said. It was going to be fun with these lot. But...they both had partners already. I didn't. What if nobody wanted to partner with me? What if I was training to be a rider with no Dragon?! That would be so embarrassing.

"You bet!" Said Taz, grinning widely. "Anyways, we were just heading down to the Great Hall. You three coming?"

"Sure." I nodded.

"You bet! The feast better be as good as last year!" Pippa said excitedly. And so, the boys lead us out and I locked my door, putting the key inside my pocket. I took a deep breath as I followed them through the halls, thinking about what lay ahead.

The Great Hall was...well...very long. Like everything here, the doors to the room were huge. However, when I finally stepped into the Great Hall, I couldn't believe my eyes. The walls were decorated red, with a swirly gold pattern which shimmered in the candlelight. In the four corners of the room, were candles burning more brightly than I had ever seen. The sticks the candles were placed on were tall, and the top was in the shape of a Dragon head, with the wax inside the Dragon's mouth. At the top end of the hall, were three steps leading to a little higher section where the teachers sat, and there was a long white wooden table stretched out across it with fancy chairs behind it. There was also one big chair in the centre for the Headmaster. The rest of the hall contained large circular tables, with a small Dragon statue in the centre of each one, all in a different colour. At the back of the room, behind the teachers' chair was a huge, colourful stained-glass window. The picture in the glass appeared to be that of a large green Dragon with a male rider, who was blonde of hair. I stood still upon entering the hall, not noticing others walk past me. Something about the image intrigued me, or seemed familiar. However, I couldn't put my finger on what it was.

"Um...Xanda?" Irina stood in front of me, pulling my gaze away from the window. "Are you alright?"

"Yeah..." I looked at her a little dazed "Sorry. Deep in thought."

She smiled back at me. "That's alright. Come. The others are waiting." I nodded, and followed her as she began to walk towards one of the middle tables. Pippa, Taz and Joey were already sitting, Pippa with an empty seat either side of her.

"Hey Xanda!" She yelled. "Sit here!" Pippa beamed brightly, patting the seat between herself and Josef. I sat down, looking at the blue Dragon statue in the middle of the table. I couldn't wait to see one for real! The table we were sitting at wasn't as big as some at the back of the hall, and there were only six seats around ours, and five were already taken up. Nobody seemed to be joining us though, but that was because Taz kept telling people the remaining seat was taken. I began to wonder by whom. Nobody was coming over to us as the hall filled up more and more.

I watched as the Academy's teachers began to walk towards their table, and Pippa and Taz told me who they all were as they walked up towards their seats. First there were two young women, looking completely opposite to one another. They talked enthusiastically, and I could tell they were very close. The first had tanned skin with bright blue eyes. Her hair was green and in dreadlocks, pulled back into a ponytail. She had big breasts too, which were scaled down by her tight-fitting suit, which was pale green and black. It was low cut, but some of the material spiked over her chest giving her a more menacing look. She wore dark green bracers with electric green crosses going down it. Her suit was all in one, and black leather crossed over her legs. Around her waist, she wore a drape attached to a black rope. It was the same shade of green as the rest of the outfit and fell to just passed her knees. On her feet, she wore long, dark green over knee boots, which had quite a big heel on them. To be honest I'm not even sure how she managed to walk in those things. The other woman was light blonde of hair, which curled beautifully near the tips. Her lips were as pink as a summer rose. Her clothing was more simplistic, wearing a plain orange dress with a thin yellow strip at the bottom, reaching just above the knees. There were six buttons on her waist, three on each side which were also yellow. She also wore a thick golden necklace. The sleeves on her dress were a little odd, as the fabric draped under her arms and was tied on around her wrist. She wore pale gloves which reached up to her forearm. Also she wore light brown, heeled boots which were so long as you couldn't see them under her dress.

"That's Ivy Wellworn, and her partner Cassandra Nebilia. They teach partner bonding. They only take three sets of partners per class so it's more intimate." Pippa explained. "Been best friends since they were little apparently. Cassandra's Dragon form is pink. It's pretty cool!"

Then I saw the white haired, muscly man from earlier, the one at the gates with a ponytail dressed like a hunter. He looked at me again as he passed in the hall, which made me feel even more uncomfortable than before so I looked at Joey and pretended I hadn't noticed him. Joey leaned closer to me and spoke. "That's Zadlos Davandrin. He teaches combat. He looks pretty tough but once you get to know him he can be a laugh outside of class, so Taz says."

"I don't think he likes me already..." I whispered to myself, gulping hard.

Then, there was another woman who walked up. She looked around the age of mid-forties, and she had shoulder length red-brown hair, with dark brown eyes and rectangular glasses. She had a long black and dark purple dress on, and she carried a book in her hand as she talked to a man at her side. The man looked younger than her, and had spiky blue hair and piercing purple eyes. He wore simple clothes, but his pale brown jacket looked of good quality.

"That's Monica Madana and Jasper Ventus." Said Pippa.

"Mrs Madana teaches History of Dragons." Taz added. "Mr Ventus teaches flying."

"That sounds amazing..." I said. Flying on a Dragon...wow. That's the thing dreams are made of.

"Yeah...its breath-taking." Joey smiled. "When I'm riding Taz...I feel like I'm free. We still haven't mastered it yet though...we have so much to learn. It's tough...but the first time you're in the air it's so worth it."

A few more teachers sat down, then when they did, the hall went quiet. A very tall man walked down the centre of the room. He was extremely intimidating, and his skin looked...grey. It was very pale, and an odd colour. His hair spiked directly upright, and was dark purple in colour. His outfit was black and white, and it looked like it was some sort of armour. His presence was overwhelming, and I couldn't take my eyes off him.

Pippa whispered to me, finally revealing the man's identity. "Drevin Drogon. The headmaster..."

I watched in silence as he climbed the steps, and turned to face us all. He spoke in a deep, entrancing voice.

"Welcome to another year at Wyvern Academy. For those of you who are just joining us, I hope you have a pleasant stay, and manage to achieve your full potential while here. I look forward to getting to know more of you. Now…I must warn each and every one of you. Dragon Riders from Brozanta have been seen patrolling the area of late. While riding with your partners, do not go too far from the school, for your own safety. That said, train hard, grow stronger, and prosper. And as our school motto states, 'Embrace the Fire'." At this, the students began clapping him. He may have looked scary, but I could tell he was well respected. "Now! Let us feast!" He raised his arms, beaming. At this there was a roar of excitement, and people clapping louder. Just then there was a gasp, as the tables were covered in a ring of fire! It didn't last for very long, but when the fire died down, there was food on the table! More than I had ever seen before! There were meats and fruits and vegetables and cakes and puddings! I couldn't believe my eyes! There was also a silver plate before each of us, and I was so spoilt for choice I didn't know what to eat first! Everyone else had already tucked into their food, and I licked my lips, reaching over for a piece of chicken. I stopped dead in my tracks.

He was there. Sitting next to Tazmin. The boy from earlier! I felt my heart stop as I noticed him. When had he gotten here?! I didn't even see him come in! He was talking to Taz…but glancing at me. He had black, spiked hair, with a white stripe on his left side, which hung in front of his face. His eyes were emerald green, and he wore a long sleeved white shirt, with a green Jacket over it. I shuddered, leaning over to Pippa, whispering.
"Who is that…?" I asked curiously, fidgeting with the rings around my neck.
"Leon Raphael Drogon." She answered. "The Headmasters son. But I wouldn't bother trying to partner with him."
"Why not?"
"Loads of people tried last year. He refused all of them. Said he didn't feel anything. He's a good ally to have though."

Leon Drogon…something about him made me feel different. Like before, when I felt like our souls were entwined, the feeling came again. There was a connection between us and I couldn't figure out why…

Well, I was stuffed! I had never eaten so much in my entire life! The meal was incredible! I had never tasted food that was so full of flavour before, and I savoured every last morsel that trickled down my throat. And the drink…oh wow. We had this smooth, silky, deep pink shake called Dragonberry Juice. It was the most wonderful thing I had ever drank in my life. It was so much better than the weak rubbish served in 'Ackerman's Tavern' back home.

According to Taz, there is a Tavern he likes just off the marketplace called 'The Dragon's Eye', which also serves free Dragonberry Juice to Wyvern Academy students. We were so going there at some point. Anyway, dusk was approaching, and I had decided to have a look around the castle until I headed for bed. The place was so big...and I felt so small as I walked through the winding corridors. I tried to memorize where the classrooms were, but I wasn't too worried as I had compared timetables with the others and we were in the same classes after all. There was a courtyard in the centre of the castle, which I had taken a stroll through. It was really pretty, like a mini maze with low shrubs and flowers but plenty of places to sit down. After my walk, I decided to head back up to my room. I walked down the corridor, as my room was the last one in the hall. However, it was then I noticed a door at the end of the hallway, next to mine. I moved over to it, and opened it slowly. There was a winding stone staircase leading upwards, and as I stepped onto it, I could feel a breeze sweeping down from above. I shut the door behind me and slowly began to climb the stairs, being careful not to trip as they were clearly old and uneven. I kept my left hand on the rough stone wall to help keep my balance as I climbed higher and higher. The staircase opened upon to a turret, and I stepped out into the centre, looking round. I was so high up! I felt like I was practically in the sky. I moved over slowly towards the edge and leaned over the side, my hands firmly against the stone wall. I looked down, the wind rushing through my golden hair. I felt a sense of panic surge through me, and my legs began to shake. Suddenly, there was a rush of wind flying past me, and I stood upright. My eyes widened, and I couldn't believe what I was seeing. A Dragon flew past! I watched in awe as a blue Dragon swept through the air. It wasn't overly big, but it was still huge to me! He was just the right size for the rider, (who was male in this case), to climb on. He looked so secure as they twisted and turned through the evening sky, which was painted with splashes of cool orange and pink. The rider and Dragon looked at ease with one another, and I could tell they had already bonded deeply, despite the rider not looking that much older than me. The rider, from what I could see had dirty blonde hair, but other than that I couldn't really make out much more. I felt a sense of awe just looking at them, thinking how amazing it must be to soar through the sky without a care in the world.

It was then I sensed somebody else...and it was like my body froze. I turned around, and saw a figure walking up the stairs. I watched, and to my surprise, it was Leon. He seemed as equally shocked to see me. We both stared at each other nervously. I wanted to talk but nothing came out of my mouth. Again, that strange feeling overcame me. In the end, it was him that struck up a conversation.

"Um...hello."

"Hello..." I smiled weakly, adding on nervously. "What are you doing here...?".

He walked over to me by the edge, leaning against the wall and watching the

Dragon and rider in the sky.

"I come up here a lot. Nobody else comes up here so I like to come here to clear my head." He said. I felt awful, as I began to feel like I was invading his space.

"I'm sorry. I'll leave."

"No!" He said, standing abruptly, which I was a little taken back by. He took a deep breath and continued. "I mean...I could use the company. Me and you, we just keep running into each other don't we." He grinned, leaning against the wall again. I did the same, raising an eyebrow.

"What do you mean by that?"

"Well, I saw you first in the front gardens when you came in, then at dinner."

"Oh right. Well we haven't actually struck up a conversation until now." I chuckled.

"Well now we have." He smiled holding out his hand. "Leon Drogon." I smiled back gently, taking his hand and shaking it politely.

"I know." I giggled. "Xanda Sykes."

"I know." He laughed. Well that was a weird introduction, we both already knew each other's names. We may as well have just not introduced ourselves, but it did kind of make our meeting official. I mean, it was better than just staring at each other across a room like we had done until now. There was a moment of silence, before Leon looked towards the Dragon and his rider soaring through the evening sky. "Cool, aren't they?"

"Do you know them?" I asked.

"Yeah." He said. "Naia and Seto Ventus. Identical twin third years. It's so rare for identical twins to have one born Dragonbourne and one not. But I know that Seto the Dragon wouldn't want any other partner than his brother."

"That's sweet when you look at it like that. Although I don't know how they cope flying so high..."

Leon raised a brow. "You're afraid of heights?"

"No!" I answered almost instantly. "Just not used to them."

"Where you from?"

"Lightwater."

"Oh. That little village at the bottom of the valley with the Simmon River running through it? Yeah. I can see why. But there's really nothing to it. It's not the height that's scary, it's the falling down part."

I chuckled a little at this. "Yeah, I pretty much had that figured out."

"Take my hand." He said suddenly. I turned to look at him, confused as he held out a hand to me. What was he doing?

"What?"

"Come on. Trust me." Trust me. Those words rang in my ears. It was strange, but I did trust him. I hesitantly gave him my hand. "Now step on the ledge."

"Balls Leon, are you insane?!" I said a little louder than I had originally intended.

18

"Hey, you trust me, right? I'm not going to let you fall. I promise."

"Well...alright then." I felt my heart pounding against my chest, and my legs felt so wobbly I thought I was gonna fall over any second. I swallowed hard, as Leon helped me stand on the thick ledge, then climbed up next to me. He put his arm around me, holding me with a firm grip. I looked down, feeling faint almost instantly and I became unsteady, but Leon kept me close. To be honest right now I was too scared to feel anything.

"Whoa steady. I've got you." He spoke softly, reassuring me.

"Can I get down now?" I panicked.

"Nope." He chuckled softly. "Now...close your eyes." I didn't respond to him. I looked up slowly, dead ahead into the sunset. I felt numb, but I wasn't sure why. "Close your eyes..." He repeated, softer than before. His voice calmed me, and I took a deep breath before I shut my eyelids. His grip loosened, but he kept me in his arms, probably in case I fell. Then he began to speak...slowly...softly...

"Don't think of falling. Think of floating. Of flying. Feel the wind as it rushes past you, not knocking you down, but inviting you to join it. Smell the air...the fresh air, not polluted by smoke, or fumes, or soot. Imagine, you're on the back of your Dragon, holding onto his neck. Then slowly, you let go. But you don't fall. You raise your arms, and you are free. Free to go where you please, free to fly with the singing birds. Free to swoop down, and soar next to the running water. You're free. You and he, you glide upwards again...into the clouds, as soft as candyfloss. You can touch them, but they slip through your fingers as you fly onwards. You're at one with your Dragon, and he is at one with you. The sky is not your enemy, it is your friend. You greet it. You welcome it. It is a part of you and always has been. You reach back down, and you can feel your Dragon's scales. It's rough, but comforting to you. He is your friend. The two of you are one with the sky. Do not fear falling...for he will catch you. Always. You feel your soul and his intertwining...they are one. They are together. Partners. The sun shimmers on his scales, and beats down upon your face. It's so warm, and you both ride towards the ocean. The sun beams down on that too, and the water sparkles. Turrets are high, but you can fly higher. For you are one with the wind. You are one with the sky. You are one with the world. At last."

I opened my eyes slowly, coming back into reality. I felt so calm. So at peace. So relaxed. I had never been so calm in all my life. I turned to look at Leon, staring into the deep green of his eyes. He gazed at me softly.

"Feel better...?" He asked.

"Strangely...yes. I don't feel...so on edge anymore. No pun intended." I looked down at the world below me, and my heart rate was back to normal. I no longer felt like I was in danger. Leon jumped down back onto the safety of the turret and I followed after him.

"I would have helped you down y'know." He blushed a little, chuckling nervously.

"I'm not completely helpless." I laughed with him. "But I appreciate you helping me like that..."

"It's no problem. I'm glad I could help." He yawned. "I'm shattered, so I'm gonna go to bed. Let me walk you to your room...make sure you get back safe."

"There'll be no issues there. My rooms 305. The one right next to the door to here."

"Oh well. All the same, I really would feel better knowing you were alright." He said. Wow. Nobody had ever done that for me before.

"That's really kind...thank you."

So he did as he said, and he walked me back to my room and wished me goodnight before heading off. By now, I was yawning too. It had been a long day. I moved over to my window, looking out towards the ocean. I had never seen the sea before. This was all new to me, and hard to take in. But I was finally doing something with my life. However, I still wasn't sure if this was where I was supposed to be. My life had been rocky from the start...ever since my Grandparents told me my parents weren't coming back. I was three years old, but I still remember it like it was yesterday. But just, Leon made me forget everything. This connection between us...maybe we were meant to be partners. Maybe not. I couldn't put my finger on it. I was hopeless at dealing with emotions, but he calmed me. I couldn't dwell on it anymore, I was so unbelievably tired. I closed the curtains, got changed, and went straight to bed...

The night started...and I slipped into a dream. That was the first time I dreamt of Leon. I was falling through an endless sky, and it was so dark around me. I struggled to breathe, reaching out frantically to try and grab hold of something to stop me falling. My stomach churned and I began to feel sick. Just then I saw a light above me, and Leon fell through hurdling towards me! There was a flash and Leon was gone, but replaced with a green Dragon! He flew towards me and I reached for him. We were just about to touch when suddenly-

Chapter 3

A Team is born

"ARGH!" I awoke suddenly, sitting up abruptly. I was sweaty and breathless. I took a deep breath, calming slowly as I ran my fingers through my hair. It was just a dream. I got up slowly, making my bed before having a quick wash in the bathroom and getting changed while in there. After that, I moved over to my dresser and picked up my hairbrush, and began to brush my hair. I growled a little, starting to get frustrated when my brush got stuck in my thick golden locks.

"Xanda?" I looked round, seeing Irina walk in slowly. "Are you alright?"

"Yeah...sorry...just...having hair issues." I smiled weakly.

"Here." She walked over to me, taking the brush gently and beginning to brush my hair for me.

"Thank you Irina..." I spoke, a tone of sadness in my voice. To be honest, I was nervous about starting lessons, so I was a bit quiet.

"Are you alright? Pippa and I heard you screaming this morning..."

"Hm? Oh yeah...I just had a nightmare. That's all." She was so gentle with my hair, and managed to brush through it with ease. She then began to braid my hair expertly. After she had finished, I turned to her and smiled, feeling a little more awake.

"Thanks."

"Your Welcome." Irina smiled.

"Yo! We're gonna get some breakfast. You two coming?" We both turned to see Pippa in the doorway with Taz and Joey.

"Of course!" I smiled back. "I'm starving!"

The five of us had eaten breakfast in the Great Hall. Again, eating until we could eat no more. My grandparents weren't bad off money wise and we always had food on the table, but just enough to get by. We were simple folk...but nothing compared to the others. My new friends were probably used to eating like this all the time. Y'see, people like me from small places didn't get into a school like this. It was so rare. I guess that's why my whole village had turned up to wave me off. Anyway, I was here, and my first lesson was History of Dragons with Mrs Madana. I must admit, it was a subject I had been looking forward to. As I said before, I loved all animals, but Dragons had always fascinated me. Dragon's themselves were extinct, or at least nobody had seen one in over a hundred years. I always wondered how the Dragonbourne's came to be around. Human's tainted with Dragon blood...the idea seemed amazing. We had entered Mrs Madana's classroom, which was very simple, but clean and very tidy. There were four rows of wooden desks, each desk fitting two people on each. I sat on my own in the middle of the first row by the wall. Irina and Pippa sat behind me, and Joey and Taz sat next to me in the second row. My back was leaning against the wall, and I had my feet resting on the empty chair next to me. The teacher hadn't arrived yet and people were still walking in. We had been early to be fair. So, we were just talking.

"Man…" Said Joey. "I slept like a log last night!"

"I always wondered who came up with that phrase." I said. "I mean, do logs actually sleep? I know trees are supposed to be alive and stuff, but that saying still never made any sense to me."

"Good point." Taz chuckled. "Anyway Xanda, where were you after dinner last night?"

"Yeah!" Joey looked at me curiously. "Taz and I came to see if you were alright, but you weren't in your room."

"Oh! Sorry. I went for a walk and got chatting to Leon." I answered.

"Leon?!" Pippa exclaimed surprised. "As in Leon, Leon? Leon Drogon Leon?!"

"Yes. Leon Drogon Leon."

"Wow." Said Taz. "You're special. I mean, Leo's our mate, but other than that he doesn't really talk to people he doesn't know."

"Who you on about?" Said a voice from behind. And sure enough, there he was. Leon standing behind us.

"Leon!" We all exclaimed, looking at each other for help.

"Oh nobody!" Irina chuckled nervously.

"We were just talking about dinner last night." Pippa said calmly, like we hadn't even been speaking about Leon. I never knew she had such a poker face.

"Oh right." Leon said, turning to face me. A smile spread across his face, and he gestured towards the empty seat that my feet were resting upon. "Mind if I sit next to you?"

"N-No! Of course not!" I was quite taken aback, and rather shocked. I instantly moved my feet from the chair and sat upright. I could feel the others watching, bewildered that Leon was talking to me. Strangely, what they had said, I didn't see in Leon. He had been so kind to me, and caring. He sat down next to me, smiling at me gently, and I smiled back.

"Sleep well?" He asked.

"Yeah."

"Liar." He said, his face blank.

"What?! How do you know that?!" I was so shocked I just kind of blurted that out. How did he know I hadn't slept well because of that nightmare? It was like he could tell what I was thinking.

"Just…intuition." He answered, smiling. The others looked at each other, and I knew as well as they did it was more than just intuition. We didn't have time to continue the conversation however, as that was when Mrs Madana hurried in. She shut the door behind her. She was very cheery, and she trotted to the front of the classroom, smiling down at us with her big smile.

"Hello!" She beamed down at us. "I am Mrs Madana. Now, there's only one of me and twenty-six of you so if you wouldn't mind passing round this parchment and writing down where you sit that would be wonderful to help me learn your names." With that she handed a piece of parchment and a quill to the people on the front desk, and we all did as she asked, writing down our names on the seating plan as she began her lesson.

"Now, in these lessons you will learn all about the history of Dragons. From the first Dragon's to have lived, to how people first began riding them, and the bonds formed between Dragon and Rider. We will also be learning about famous Dragon's and Riders. You may not think this beneficial, however, learning about the past will better help you understand the future, and as you learn with your partner, the stronger your bond will grow."

As she said this, Leon and I looked at each other out the corner of our eyes. This bond we felt...these feelings I'd been having...were they because we were meant to be partnered together?

"Thank you all." Mrs Madana said as the last person handed her back the parchment. "Now...Miss Rozanna?" She looked over towards Irina. Irina flinched a little, clearly feeling nervous about being put on the spot. Mrs Madana moved over towards us and chuckled softly. "No need to be nervous, dear. Now, is there any part of history you are interested in, or wish to know about?"

"Um...D-Dragonbourne's. H-How they came to be I mean." Irina stuttered.

"Excellent." Said Mrs Madana. "What better place to start than learning about your fantastic partners. I know not all of you have partners yet...but don't worry. When you find a partner, you will be in classes together if you are not already. So, you probably will go over this again with them. And for those of you in here who are Dragonbourne, feel free to ask any questions, and I will answer best I can. Now...can anybody tell me who was the first known Dragonbourne?"

"Pevrel the Fierce." Said a geeky looking girl at the back of the class.

"Correct Miss Ocrina." Mrs Madana said, as she had checked the girls name on the parchment. "Not much is known about his past, but Pevrel the Fierce is the first known Dragonbourne. As Legend tells it, Pevrel was a mage who befriended a Dragon, and became her Rider. When the Dragon was killed by a rival sorcerer, Pevrel used a spell to try and give her a part of his soul to bring her back to life. The spell however, failed. But, the two souls mixed together and he instead gained the ability to turn into the late Dragon's form. He later married and had many mistresses, which continued his legacy. Nowadays, a child may have two human parents, and still be a Dragonbourne." Now I must admit, that did sound a little hard to believe. I mean, a mage binding his soul to a deceased Dragon? Sounded completely balls. I wasn't sure how much of that I believed, but I did believe that Pevrel the Fierce was truly an amazing Dragonbourne. Just then, my attention turned to Leon, who raised his hand to ask a question. He had a weird look in his eyes, and I could tell something was bothering him.

"Yes, Mr Drogon?" Mrs Madana smiled at him, noticing his raised hand.

"I was wondering if you could tell us about the last Dragons." He spoke plainly, lowering his hand. I turned my head to face him, but he just looked dead ahead at Mrs Madana. Madana looked at him for a few moments, before adjusting her glasses and clearing her throat.

"Very well." She started, pacing up and down the classroom as she told the story. "As you all know, Wyvern Academy and Bloodbourne Academy were founded by identical twin Dragonbourne's. Astrid and Aurora Drago lived in a time when the last two Dragons were known to have lived. Figro and his son Fergo lived in peace with humans, until a sickness of the mind consumed Figro. He became insane, destroying all in his path. Dragons were much bigger than Dragonbourne's in their Dragon form, and much more deadly. Figro became a monstrosity, and many people died. The Drago twins founded the two Academy's to train young human's and Dragonbourne's to bring Figro down. They recruited Fergo, who stood by them. The day of the final battle came, and they stood against Figro on the Plain of Fire. The battle raged on well into the night, and much blood was spilt. It is said Fergo was scratched by his father down his left eye, and was scarred. In the end, Aurora distracted Figro, so Astrid could deal him the final blow. Figro was vanquished, but Aurora had been mortally wounded. She died, and was buried in the catacombs in Bloodbourne Academy. Astrid came here, and became headmistress of Wyvern Academy until she died, and was buried in the catacombs here." I thought that was really sad. I mean, the twins should have been buried together in my opinion. It was a tragic tale, but an interesting one. Leon didn't seem to care much about the twins though, he was more interested in Fergo. He spoke up, keeping eye contact with Mrs Madana. "And Fergo?" He asked.

"He went into hiding after the battle." She replied. "And he has not been seen since."

Leon had been acting strangely since that lesson. He'd been quiet, and deep in thought. I mean it's not like we were partners so I didn't really bother him about it, although I was worried about him. To be honest, I was beginning to wish he was my partner. There was something between us, but I couldn't put my finger on what it was. It was like, every time we were together or I even thought about him, I felt connected right to the soul. I know it sounds odd, but it's hard to explain. Anyway, our next class was Combat with Mr Davandrin. He's the big, muscly guy with the white ponytail that kept staring at me for some reason. Of course, I wondered why this was. Did he know something that I didn't? The thought had crossed my mind, but to be honest he scared me so I wasn't gonna ask him about it. So, we had gone up to our rooms to get our weapons. We all had one, as it was a requirement to bring a weapon of your choice if you were a Rider. I of course grabbed my scythe, Irina her staff and Joey had a bow. Pippa told me that all Dragonbourne's had the ability to bend fire while in their human forms. I thought that was incredible! I really admired Dragonbourne's, and had always wished I was one. But there was nothing I could have done about that...it's something that's determined even before you are born. So, we had headed down to Mr

Davandrin's indoor classroom. The room was big, and there was a large storage cupboard at the back of the room. In the centre of the main room, was a circular raised stage. Mr Davandrin stood proudly, a sword in his left hand. He watched us all as we entered, gazing down at us like a hawk. We all took a stand, in single file around the stage. I was standing in between Irina and Taz. I watched slowly as Leon walked in, but I had seemed to have sensed his presence even before he had entered the room. He moved over and looked at me, before standing next to Joey. Once we were all there, Davandrin spoke with his booming and strong voice. "Welcome to combat. For those of you who don't know me, I am Zadlos Davandrin, and I will be your teacher. Now, since this is your first lesson and not all of you have partners yet, we will be learning to fight on the ground. When you do have a partner however, you will need to work together not only on the ground, but in the air as well. A piece of advice...know your weapon, and know your enemy. Miss Sykes!" He looked directly at me. I swallowed hard, feeling a lump in the back of my throat. This was the last thing I wanted. All the attention turned to me.

"Balls..." I whispered nervously under my breath. Davandrin strutted over to me, holding out his hand to help me up onto the stage.

"Would you join me, Miss Sykes?" He added. I found myself looking over at Leon, and I saw a small smile spread across his face. He nodded his head, as if telling me to go ahead. I looked back into Davandrin's deep sea blue eyes, and took his hand. I was shaking as I climbed up, and he managed to smile a little to try and put me at ease.

"For those of you that don't know, Miss Sykes is the granddaughter of Lightwater's blacksmith. Now, Miss Sykes...I'd like you to tell me what you know about my blade." I looked at it, and I must admit the blade intrigued me. The craftsmanship was wonderful. I held out my hands, gesturing for him to hand the blade over.

"May I?" I asked gently. He nodded and handed me the sword. It was quite heavy, so I used both hands to hold it. The last thing I wanted to do was drop his sword. I think he'd kill me. I examined the blade, trying not to cut myself, and told him what I could work out.

"It's made from steel. Forged in Brozanta...I'm guessing in a big city, probably the capital Eruznor."

"Very good." His mouth tugged into a smile. "How old would you say it was?" I looked at the blade closer. There were no engravings, but there was a fair few scratches. This sword had seen battle, that was clear.

"I'd say around ten years." I answered. He nodded in approval as I returned the sword to him.

"I'm impressed." He grinned. He then turned his attention to my own weapon, looking towards the scythe on my back. "That's a nice weapon. Draw it." I felt myself becoming afraid again. Was he actually gonna ask me to fight him?! I mean, I could fight, but that's not the point! There was no way I

26

could take on an elite like Zadlos Davandrin! Not wanting to anger him, I slowly took my scythe into my hands, gripping it tightly in my sweaty palms.

"Now." Said Mr Davandrin. "I want you to fight me as if your life depended on it."

"What?! Are you insane? There's no way I could win even if I tried!" I protested. I gasped as he swung his sword, and I raised my weapon quickly to block his attack.

"Concentrate!" He said sharply. I flinched a little, the pace of my breathing picking up. "Keep your feet grounded at all times, Sykes. Your balance is crucial. Flow with my movement!" He then began repeatedly swinging his sword at me, and I blocked as best I could, moving around the stage to try and avoid him. I wasn't sure whether he was actually trying to kill me.

"Balls man! Stop it!" I finally swung back, and once I had an opening, I spun round, kicking him in the stomach and throwing him off balance. He let out a chuckle, barely hurt, but rubbing his stomach.

"Good good!" He exclaimed, regaining his balance. I could feel the suspense fill the room, and heard a gasp of surprise from the class as Davandrin swung his sword back at me. I ducked quickly, my heart racing.

"Balls! You nearly took my head off!" I shouted, gripping the scythe tightly in my hand.

"Great reflexes though." He grinned, pushing me. I gasped, almost falling off the edge of the stage. I desperately tried to stay on the stage, trying to keep my balance as Davandrin came towards me. Suddenly I felt a hand push on my back, and I was shoved back onto the stage. I jumped to the side when Mr Davandrin tried to attack. I panted, looking over to see who had pushed me out his way. It was Leon. He stood at the edge of the stage, nodding encouragingly. I looked at Davandrin, and he was glancing between me and Leon. I took this moment to catch my breath, as I was breathless at this point. As Mr Davandrin looked between the two of us, he seemed to sense the connection between me and Leon. His eyes finally rested on Leon, and spoke sharply.

"Mr Drogon! You just included yourself in this battle. Come!" He said. Leon looked over at me, before climbing onto the stage. I could feel the anticipation in the room begin to rise as the headmaster's son joined the fight. He moved over to me, standing next to me protectively.

"Thanks..." I said quietly.

"You're welcome..." He whispered back.

"Well!" Mr Davandrin said swinging his sword around. "Isn't this getting interesting."

"Enough small talk." Said Leon. "What are the rules?"

"Simple. You disarm me, and you win. I disarm Miss Sykes, then I win." Said Mr Davandrin. I glanced over at our friends. Irina looked nervous, like she wasn't used to this sort of environment. However, Taz, Joey and Pippa were just loving the drama. I'm sure I would have too, were I not on the receiving end of it. It was then Davandrin charged towards us, and swung his blade at Leon. I felt a rush of adrenaline, and swiftly jumped in front of him, blocking the attack. I quickly ducked down, swiping at his feet. As Davandrin jumped over my blade, Leon leap-frogged over my back and pushed Davandrin backwards, throwing him off balance.

"Xanda!" Leon yelled, bending over. I got up and rolled over Leon's back, swinging my scythe at Mr Davandrin. As he was already off balance, his sword flew out of his hand. The sound of it clanging on the floor rung through my ears as I helped Leon stand upright. We were both breathing hard. There was a roar of applause from the class, and even Mr Davandrin joined in. But we didn't see it, we were just staring at each other. I had that strange feeling again...the one from before. I looked down nervously, then back up at him, smiling gently.

"Thanks...again..." I said swallowing hard.

"Your welcome. Again." He chuckled. "Don't look so nervous, I won't bite." It was a good job he was in his human form, because if he wasn't, I don't think what he said would have put me at ease.

Davandrin had been very impressed with us, and quite right too in my opinion. He nearly took my head off in that spar. I swear, he doesn't pull any punches that one. He was fearsome in combat. I still wondered about him though. Like how he knew Harry Sykes, the Lightwater blacksmith, was my grandfather. I wasn't gonna ask him about it though...not yet anyway. I mean, he still scared me a bit. So, after the fight, we had all gone into the storage cupboard with Mr Davandrin and helped him bring out some training dummies, which we spread out across the room. We all split off into small groups and began practising the basics of attack, while Davandrin walked around the room and helped people out individually. I admit, he was very hands on, and a good teacher. I had learned a fair deal in my duel with him. I was sharing a dummy with Pippa and Irina, and I was helping Irina out with her stance. Once she had it sorted I stood back, watching. Just then, I noticed Leon out the corner of my eye. He was sitting alone, against the far wall. He looked deep in thought, and I was beginning to worry about him. All the time I had known him...he'd seemed lonely. Pippa grinned, putting an arm around me, noticing me watching the boy.

"You should go and talk to him!" She said excitedly.

"No." I replied. "I don't want to intrude. Besides, it's not like he's my partner."

"I think you should go." Irina smiled. "You seem to make him happy. And I can tell he cares for you." She did have a point, that was obvious. I had come to care for him also. I did want to go over and make sure he was okay, as he did seem very withdrawn.

"Okay okay..." I sighed, and took my parents rings in my hand once more, grasping them tightly. I took a deep breath, and began to make my way over.

I stood before Leon, and he slowly lifted his head to see who it was. I smiled down at him gently.

"Hey Leon."

"Hi." He smiled back up at me. I leaned against the wall and slid down it so I was sitting next to him.

"Something on your mind?" I asked.

"Nah." He replied. "Well...there is, but I'm not sure what to make of it." To be honest, I hadn't got a clue what he was going on about, but he was my friend so I tried to comfort him in any way I could.

"I'm not sure what you mean by that, but you know you can talk to me about anything." As I spoke, I saw his smile brighten. He gently punched my arm, and nodded in appreciation.

"Thank you." He said. "I'm alright, honest. But I would like to talk to you at some point. Maybe later?"

"Oh!" I said in surprise. "Yes, of course. Whenever you want to talk, I'm ready to listen." I smiled at him gently, and punched his arm back. I stood, and began to make my way back over to Pippa and Irina. I didn't see Leon watching me as I left him. I began to wonder what he wanted to talk about. We were becoming extremely close, considering we had only known each other a short time. I thought back to the 'partner bonding' that kept being mentioned. Is that what was happening? I needed to know about how the bonding worked to be sure, but that would have to wait, as I had one last class...flying.

After helping Mr Davandrin tidy away all the training dummies, we headed off to have some lunch in the great hall. As always, the spread was amazing! And of course, I had my fill of Dragonberry juice. I swear, I couldn't get enough of it! I didn't eat too much though. I wasn't that hungry, and I wanted to save some room for dinner. Anyways, flying lesson took place on a huge field at the back of the school, with a large pond at the far side. We headed down there after lunch. I was really looking forward to the flying lesson. I knew I probably wasn't gonna fly in that particular lesson, considering I didn't even have a partner yet, but seeing the others fly was gonna be just as breathtaking. Those twins from before, the ones I saw from the turret, they were incredible! They made flying together look so easy. I admired them so much. I could have stayed up there that night and watched them forever.

So, we headed out through the back gardens, and out the back Dragon inspired gate to the flying field. As we left through the back gate, we skipped excitedly down some stone steps and onto the lush green grass of the field. Most of our classmates sat in the middle of the field, laughing with the teacher, Jasper Ventus. His light blue hair shone and his purple eyes glistened in the sunlight. We moved over and sat with the group. The grass was warm and soft under my fingertips, and the girls smiled as they sat with me. The lads sat behind, and were passing around some sweets in a paper bag. Pippa and Irina took one, eating them with delight.

"Here Xanda!" Taz grinned, practically putting the bag in my face.

"Cheers!" I smiled happily, looking into the bag. I pulled out a blue liquorish stick, and instantly pulled a piece off, popping it into my mouth. I began to chew, laughing with the others. Suddenly, we all stopped as Mr Ventus looked over.

"Oi Periwinkle!" He said. We all froze thinking we were in trouble, until he said, "where's mine?!" We all chuckled at this as Taz threw him the bag of sweets. He caught it and dipped his hand in, pulling out a weird shaped green sweet before throwing it into the air and catching it in his mouth. There was a cheer as he caught it, and he moved it to the side of his mouth to chew. He swallowed it down as the last members of our class joined the group.

"We all here?" He asked. "Good! We can get started!" By this point I had finished my sweet as well, and Taz had put the remaining ones away. "So." Ventus said. "You all know why you're here. I'm going to help you all learn to fly with your partners. Now, don't stress if you don't have one yet. Some people don't partner up until their second year. Those of you without partners, we can experiment with different Dragonbourne's in my lesson just to see if you connect with anyone. Sound good?" There was a response from the class, people agreeing with him as we listened. Just then, I saw two boys walking towards the class. Then I noticed they were the twins from before! They were completely identical in every way, both sharing the same scruffy, dirty blonde hair and bright blue eyes. It boggled me how anyone could tell them apart. They both moved over and carried a rather large saddle between them.

"Ah!" Mr Ventus smiled brightly as the twins walked over. "For those of you that don't know, these are my sons! Naia and Seto. Seto is a Dragonbourne, and Naia is his rider. These two are an incredible team so pay attention, you can learn a lot from them."

"Papa..." One of them said under his breath, blushing deep red with embarrassment. We all laughed at the boys' reaction. He did look pretty cute blushing like that, whichever one he was. Jasper Ventus stood, and stepped back. I suddenly felt my heart stop, and my mouth gaped open with amazement as a bright white light surrounded the teacher. We watched as he expertly changed his form into a beast of legend. I couldn't believe my eyes! I never thought I would ever witness something so incredible. He was a majestic, deep purple Dragon. His scales glistened in the sunlight, and his claws were short, but sharp. He roared loudly, and it sent a shiver down my spine. I was in awe. He was amazing. Jasper took off into the air, and we were blown back by the sheer force of his wings as he ascended into the sky. He flew high and soared around effortlessly. I gasped in amazement as he began to breathe fire. The fire formed perfect rings in the sky. He drew twelve fire hoops in the sky, before swooping down and landing by us. Jasper Ventus landed perfectly and light on his feet, as if he were as soft as a bird. Now, I had no idea Dragonbourne's could talk while in Dragon form, but it was then I learned that apparently, they could.

"The rings above you will not harm you. The challenge is simple! Fly through all the hoops. Today, I will choose people who are partnered together to have a go at the course, and we can observe and discuss technique, and talk about improvements etc. etc. you get the jist. Sound good?" We all nodded, as Ventus turned his head towards the twins. "Seto, Naia, if you wouldn't mind demonstrating." Seto nodded, and stepped back. We watched him take his blue Dragon form, and he looked just as splendid as he had the other night. Seto wasn't as big as his father was, but he still looked awesome. The other twin, Naia, didn't look at his brother...he looked at the ground. It was obvious something was upsetting him. Mr Ventus leaned over and nuzzled Naia's cheek with his snout, and the boy smiled weakly at his father. Seto moved over to his brother, and Naia climbed onto his back, not even using the saddle. He held on to the spikes on his brother's neck, and they took off into the air. They flawlessly soared towards the first hoop, and glided round the course with ease. They were so precise and so in sync. Mr Ventus began to give us advice as we watched the twins effortlessly swoop through the course. "See how in tune they are with each other. Watch how Naia moves his body in sync with Seto's to ease around corners. They trust in each other completely, and that is what makes them work so well together." He was right...you could see the bond between them was incredibly strong. They were a brilliant team. The two finally landed, a little more heavily than Ventus had. Seto waited for his brother to jump down before changing back into his human form. We gave them a round of applause, everyone entranced by the two of them.

"Thank you, boys!" Mr Ventus beamed. "Right! Who wants to go first? Ah! Tazmin Periwinkle!" He said looking towards Taz. The white-haired boy stood, walking over to the teacher. "I hear your partner is here this year."

"Yup!" Taz said happily. "Joey's never let me down." At this, Joey stood, and took his place beside Taz. He looked a little nervous, but he took a stand next to Tazmin.

"You have a strong friendship, I see. Good." Said Jasper Ventus. "Tazmin, you know what to do."

"Jeez, I keep telling you, its Taz!" Taz said in annoyance, which made us all laugh. He stood back, and the white light surrounded him. It was a wonderful sight, as I watched my friend take the form of a purple Dragon. He was smaller and lighter in colour than Mr Ventus, but no less extraordinary. Naia and Seto picked up the saddle and began to fasten it to Taz's back. Mr Ventus looked at Joey, who was still looking a little nervous.

"Mr Periwinkle tells me you have been flying together a long time." Said Ventus.

"Yeah." Said Joey. "But never that high. I did own a saddle, but it wasn't that safe so we never trusted it."

"You've known Tazmin a long time. All your life, so he tells me. Trust him." Ventus said calmly. "Keep your body in sync with his."

"Got it..." Said Joey. I must admit, Joey looked terrified as he moved over to his partner, and climbed onto his back. I guess no matter how much of a daredevil you are, flying that high for the first time would make anybody nervous. He held onto the handles at the top of the saddle, and took deep breaths. It looked as if he were holding on for dear life!

"Calm yourself, Mr Danaris." Said Mr Ventus. "I will be remaining in my Dragon form should anything go wrong. You are in safe claws." Joey nodded, and took one big, deep breath.

"Ready, Joey?" Asked Taz, craning his neck back to look at his partner.

"Always." Said Josef, his mouth tugging into a grin. Suddenly, Taz leaped into the air, and began to fly higher and higher. There was a roar from the class, and we all cheered encouragingly for the pair. They weren't graceful, to say the least, but that was just Taz and Joey. They had their own unique style. They were quite a pair. The two stopped just before the first fire hoop, hovering in the air.

"Are you ok?!" Asked Taz.

"Yeah. I'm good." Replied Joey.

"Don't worry." Taz laughed. "We'll probably be rubbish, but in my view as long as we don't die we've nailed it."

Joey laughed back. "C'mon. Let's go!" And with his words, Taz flew forwards, and the two passed through the first hoop with ease. They carried on around the course, a little wobbly as they moved around the corners. They missed a few hoops, but not many. In fact, I think they did better than even they thought they would. We continued to cheer for them from the ground, but I had no idea whether or not they could even hear us from down there.

They reached hoop number ten, which was on a corner. We all gasped, my heart stopping in fright as Joey lost his balance and fell!

"Joey!" Irina screamed terrified, as she watched Joey hang onto the saddle for dear life. Taz stopped, calling his name as he desperately shifted to try and help Joey get back on. Mr Ventus wasted no time in soaring into the sky. However, before he could even reach them, Joey had managed to sit back up! He was panting hard, probably through shock.

"Joey!" Taz said worriedly. "Are you ok?!"

"Y-Yeah..." Joey said breathlessly, holding on tightly. Mr Ventus hovered next to them and sighed in relief.

"You good?" Ventus asked Joey, to which the boy nodded. "I'm impressed, the way you managed to regain your balance was extraordinary. You've done well today, Mr Danaris."

"Gee thanks!" Joey beamed.

"Your welcome. Just remember, you need to work on your body alignment with your partner, and defiantly work on your corners. However, you are a brilliant team. Well done, boys!"

"Cheers man!" The boys said in unison. Taz began to glide down back towards the ground. We cheered them once again as Taz landed heavily, and Joey jumped down, clearly glad he was back on land. Taz changed his form back, the saddle falling around him. He jumped over it, and put his arms around Joey as he walked back to us. Pippa and Leon patted them on the back as they sat back down with us.

"Well done, guys! That was amazing!" I smiled at them.

"Thanks Xanda!" Taz grinned. Mr Ventus had now landed and walked over to us.

"Well done again, boys! Now, who's next?!" He grinned, and his beady eyes scanned the class. His eyes then finally fell upon Leon. He stayed quiet for a moment before speaking lowly. "Mr Drogon." Without a word, Leon stood, and stepped over us until he stood in front of Mr Ventus. "I sense your soul has at long last connected with another. Who is your partner?" Asked Ventus. Leon turned slowly, and he stood in front of me. I gazed up at him, and watched as he extended his hand out towards me.

"Xanda Sykes."

"Me?!" I said in surprise. I was so shocked…I mean, yes, I had felt a connection, but I had always remembered what Pippa had told me about Leon turning down everyone who wanted to be his partner. Yet here he was, extending his hand towards me. I took his rough hand in mine and he pulled me up onto my feet.

He looked into my eyes and spoke. "C'mon Xanda, don't tell me you haven't felt the same."

"I have. But are you sure? I mean…me?" I asked nervously. His mouth tugged into a smile and he squeezed my hand in his.

"I've never been so sure of anything. It's strange I know." Leon stated. "But you and me…it feels right."

"Aye…that it does." I grinned happily and pulled my hand back, as did he and we high fived.

"So what do you say?" Leon asked. "You wanna be my partner?" I simply nodded and he laughed happily, like a weight had been lifted off his shoulders. Leon then took a few steps back, and the same bright white light surrounded him. I watched in amazement as he began to take his Dragon form. He roared playfully, as the sun glistened off his deep green scales. I couldn't stop smiling. I finally had a partner! Mr Ventus came beside me as the twins began to hoist the saddle onto Leon's back.

"Miss Sykes." Mr Ventus began. "You have never flown before, correct?"

"That's right…" I said a little shamefully, now starting to feel nervous at the thought of being so high in the air.

"Keep cool, and remember what I've told you. Analyse Leon's movements, and make sure you are in sync with him. In the sky, you are one." You are one...those words lingered in the air around me for a short moment. They were very close to what Leon had said to me upon the tower.

"Got it." I swallowed hard, looking towards Leon who was moving over to me now he was all saddled up. I chuckled weakly as he nuzzled my cheek with his snout.

"Climb aboard!" Said my partner. I took another shuddering breath as I began to make my way around him. As I walked slowly, I brushed my hand against Leon's scales. They were rough, like his hands...but they were comforting. One of the twins stood beside Leon, and he helped me onto the saddle. I put one foot in the foot holder, and hoisted myself over, making sure I put the other foot in. I felt my breath pick up as Leon stood, and I heard the class shout towards me encouragingly. I went pale and I started to feel sick. I was beginning to think this wasn't such a good idea after all. Just then I jumped as I felt a hand on my leg. I looked down, seeing the twin that had helped me up smiling at me.

"Good luck." He said.

"Thank you...um...whichever one you are."

"Naia." He giggled. "Don't worry, Leon will look after you. You're in safe claws." I looked down at Leon, who craned his neck slightly to look at me. I took another deep breath, and wrapped my hands around the handles on the saddle. I could feel my heart smacking against my chest and at this point I actually wanted to throw up.

"Ready?" Asked Leon.

"No!" I yelled back in fear.

He just laughed. "Too bad!"

"LEON!" I screamed as he flapped his strong wings and we ascended into the air! The people down below were cheering, but I couldn't hear them. The wind brushed ferociously against my face, and my golden hair waved in the breeze. My hands tightened around the handles as Leon hovered in the air level with the first hoop. I decided it was best not to look down just yet, or I may have fainted. I took deep breaths, trying to calm myself down.

"You alright back there?!" Asked Leon.

"No."

Leon just chuckled at my response. "Remember what we talked about on the turret the other night. Stay calm. Up here, with me...you're free. You and I are one. Don't fear it, embrace it." I'm not sure how, but his words seemed to calm me. I took one more deep breath, looking ahead at the first ring of fire.

"Alright...I'm good to go." I said, with a newfound determination.

"Good!" Leon grinned. "Okay, remember what Ventus said. Keep your body in line with mine. Even stand up around the corners and while descending if you must, it'll help you balance."

"Okay, I think I've got it."

"Great." He laughed. "Because you and I are gonna be the first pair to complete this first time!"

"Woah, pressure!" I laughed nervously.

"Well, what is life if you're not living on the edge?" Those words rung in my ears. The more I thought on them, I realised how true they were. I chuckled with Leon, and gripped the saddle even tighter.

"Let's go!"

"That's more like it!" Leon grinned as he soared forward. The first ring was pretty straight forward and we glided through it with ease. The second hoop was a little higher, so Leon flapped his wings while I stayed close to him, keeping focused on the ring as we flew through it. I quickly scanned for the third hoop. It was downwards and at a cornered angle. My eyes widened as Leon shouted. "Stand up!" I quickly pushed myself upright and felt the wind whoosh past as Leon soared downwards. He then turned sharply to fly through the hoop. I felt a sense of achievement as we zoomed through the sky. I had never felt more alive than I did at that moment. We worked together, making our way through the hoops as we focused on one after another. The crowd cheered below us, but alas I couldn't hear them. Before we knew it, we were on the last hoop. But I couldn't see it. I looked around curiously, when I saw it in the sky above us. It was horizontal, meaning we had to fly vertically upright to get through it.

"Leon! Up there!" I pointed as we flew towards it, and he followed my gaze. "I see it!" He said. "Stay close to me, and hold on tight!" I nodded, and pressed my body against his, changing my grip and holding onto the spikes around his neck. I felt a rush of adrenaline surge through me as Leon shifted his body upright, soaring up towards the target. My heart was pounding with sheer excitement. We were gonna do it! There was a huge cheer from the crowd below us as we ascended through the final ring of fire! I started to believe this was where I was meant to be. This was what I was meant to do. I punched the air triumphantly as Leon began to swoop down towards the class. We watched them as they got onto their feet, clapping and cheering with excitement. Finally, at long last...I belonged somewhere. But this is not where my story ends...in fact, this is where my story truly begins.

My name is Xanda Sykes, and my Dragon...is Leon Drogon.

Chapter 4
The Ambush

I slept like a log that night. My first day had really taken it out of me. I was shattered. As soon as my head hit my pillow, I was fast asleep. I was so proud of myself! I had a partner, and I had done things I never even thought I would ever do! Such as spar with a veteran knight and then soar into the sky on the back of a Dragon! And, I partnered with the best partner in the world! It was the best day of my life and I was filled with excitement! This was the stuff that dreams were made of. Speaking of dreams, I slipped into another one that night. Or more specifically, a continuation of the last dream...

Leon was in his Dragon form as I fell through an endless abyss. He was desperately reaching out towards me. I tried hard to grab onto him, but to no avail. Suddenly, I heard a chilling roar from below me. I looked down, and saw a huge red Dragon beneath me! It was much bigger and more ferocious and on a larger scale than any Dragon I had seen so far. Its teeth were like swords, and its scales looked as hard as nails. As I fell towards it the Dragon looked up at me, and began to open its huge jaws. I saw nothing but a gaping black hole at the back of its throat. I was just about to plunge into his mouth when-

"Xanda! Xanda wake up!"
My eyes shot open, and I sat up quickly. I was breathing hard, but I soon calmed down when I saw Leon sitting on the bed beside me. I sighed in relief, running my hand through my thick golden hair.
"Leon..." I gasped. "What are you doing here? I didn't think you were moving into this room until tomorrow."
"I'm not." He said. "I felt your soul becoming unsteady...I came up to check that you were okay." He felt it? I must admit, this puzzled me. It's true, I had felt a connection, but I didn't think you could sense that the other person was in danger or scared.
"What do you mean?" I asked.
"When two people bond their souls physically entwine with one another, becoming one. It doesn't usually happen so fast...you and I are a rare exception I guess." It was then I realised that this is how Leon had known I was lying about sleeping well the night before. What he said did play on my mind a little. I mean, even I knew it usually took time for the bonds to form...so why was the bond between Leon and I so instant?
"Why do you think we have bonded so fast? I don't remember meeting you before I came here."
"Who knows?" He replied. "Maybe our paths have crossed and we just don't remember. I don't suppose it matters anyway. We are partners now, some would say with a head start. We need to work together. I mean, there's some cool stuff you can do when you strengthen your bond." He grinned.
"Oh Yeah. Like what?" I asked intrigued.

He just grinned wider. "Well, they say that when your souls truly become one, you can actually speak to the other person through your mind! We'll learn more in partner bonding classes, but that won't start for a few weeks until more people have partners." Wow. Now that did sound cool! I mean, who wouldn't want to do that? I also imagine it would be very useful. I knew the path ahead of me was not an easy one, but it was the path I chose. It was wondrous and exciting, and I couldn't wait to properly get started!

A few days' past, and it was clear winter was on its way. Summer bid a harsh farewell so the bitter air of winter could take its place. It was getting colder outside, which heartily agreed with me. I'd take the soothing sting of winter over the sweaty summer heat any day. We were sitting in the library, researching some stuff for History of Dragons lesson. The head of the library was Miss Olivia Ackerman, a young bookworm. I knew of her before I came here. Mr Ackerman owned the tavern back home. Miss Olivia was his niece, although I'd never met her before. She had skin as pale as snow, with long midnight black hair and hazel eyes. She wore a pretty, pink dress and had a slender figure. She was a quiet girl, but incredibly knowledgeable! She knew loads! And if you asked her a question about anything you read in a book that you didn't understand, she would be able to explain it to you so easily. She really was clever! Part of me wished I was as intelligent as her. While we sat in the library, she sat at her own private desk in the corner with her face practically buried into a large book. The rain smashed against the large windows. To me, the sound of it was rather soothing. We were sitting on a long, wooden table, cosily enclosed by two long bookshelves. I sat in between Leon and Pippa, with Taz and Joey sitting opposite us. I was reading about Pevrel the Fierce, but I wasn't learning much more than I already had in Mrs Madana's lesson. I sighed hard, closing the book. I leaned over Leon, and saw he was reading a book about those Dragon's...Figro and Fergo. The Dragon's he had asked about in Mrs Madana's lesson. I raised an eyebrow, looking at him.

"You're still reading about those two? Why are you so interested in two Dragon's that don't even exist anymore?" I asked curiously.

"No reason." He smiled weakly, closing the book. "It's purely academic."

"Well, who wouldn't be interested in a fire breathing beast of legend?!" Said Joey excitedly. "Y'know, it's said that Dragons were at least three times bigger than Dragonbourne's in their wyvern form, if not bigger!"

"Imagine if they were still around!" Taz beamed. "I bet they were so cool!"

"Yeah." Said Leon quietly. He had a strange look in his eye, like he was deep in thought. Pippa on the other hand was being unusually quiet. I turned to her asking.

"Is everything alright, Pippa? Where's Irina anyway?" I queried. Pippa just sighed, closing her book sadly.

"We had a fight this morning..." Said Pippa.

"Irina?!" Said Joey surprised. "I mean, she doesn't seem like the fighting type."

"She isn't." Said Pippa. "It wasn't really a fight I guess...she got upset saying that I could have a better partner than her. But I don't want another partner! I want Irina. I tried to tell her that she wasn't useless but she just wasn't having any of it." Poor Irina...she really had no confidence at all. Even if she didn't see it, we all thought she was wonderful! She was kind and compassionate, and she was a wonderful mage. The magic she cast in combat lessons seemed effortless, and it was so beautiful to watch.

"Irina is many things, but useless isn't one of them." Said Joey. "I've seen her in lessons...I mean, she needs a little push, but she can defiantly hold her own."

"Would you like me to go and talk to her?" I offered.

"You'd do that?!" Pippa smiled warmly.

"Of course." I replied.

"Thank you! You may be able to talk some sense into her. I sense her soul is near the ocean. You should try the beach...she always liked looking out to sea when we went on family holidays."

"Alright." I smiled back, standing up and taking my book with me. I quickly moved over to the shelf I had gotten it from and slotted it back where it came from. I smiled as I walked back past them on my way out.

"See you later, Xanda." Said Leon.

"Yeah." Said Taz. "See you at dinner!"

"You will indeed." I grinned at them, walking backwards as I waved at them before turning and walked out of the library.

So, I had left the academy and was making my way down through the city, towards the beach. It was still raining, so I had put my hood from my brown jacket over my head to avoid getting my hair wet. Not that it was working. I finally found the side gate that lead down to the beach, and I walked through it. I started making my way down the wet wooden steps down towards the sandy beach. I looked out towards the ocean. Despite it raining, the sea still looked beautiful. Even at this distance I could see the light rain creating ripples on the ocean's surface. This was the first time I was even stepping foot on a beach. I felt my boots sink into the soggy sand as I stepped foot onto it. It was a strange feeling. I mean, I hadn't walked on anything this soft before. I stopped for a moment as I saw Irina standing in the middle of the beach, gazing out to sea. Even as it waved in the wind and the rain, her lilac hair still seemed heavenly and perfect. I sighed gently, wondering how long she had been out here. The last thing I wanted was for her to catch a cold. I slowly began to make my way over to her, and I stood next to her. She turned to look at me softly, and I smiled weakly.

"Pippa's worried about you." I spoke gently. "She said I may find you out here."

"I'm alright. Well, I am now. I find the ocean very calming...but exciting at the same time. Imagine the life underneath it all...lives we don't even know about..." She said sadly. I could see she was just trying to take her mind off how she felt. I used to do the same. I put my arm around her and pulled her close. Despite the cold weather, she was surprisingly warm.

"Pippa told us what you said." I started. "You got no reason to feel bad. You're doing so well! You and Pippa are great together. Plus, you're a brilliant mage. I tell you, there's no way I could cast magic like you can. Besides, I'm sure there's more things you can do besides that." As I spoke, Irina looked at me and smiled, her eyes lighting up a little.

"There is one thing..."

"Yes?"

"I can play the piano!" She said happily. "I've been playing since I was little. When I play...I feel lost. Lost in my own thoughts. It's just something that I love." She smiled. I smiled back, looking at her. I'm glad she was now looking a little happier, and I had been able to do something to cheer her up a bit.

"Well then, you'll have to play for me sometime!" I smiled.

"R-Really?!" She said in surprise, her face lighting up more. "I-I mean...I'd love to! So, Xanda...um...do you have anything you like to do?" She asked. As a matter of fact, I did. It was something I loved to do every winter and I was rather good at it. It made me feel strong and graceful at the same time, and a huge smile spread across my face just thinking about it. I turned to face her, and opened my mouth to speak.

Suddenly, we were both caught off balance as the ground rumbled! Irina yelped a little in surprise and grabbed a hold of me. It was quick, but it made a shudder spread throughout my body. My breath picked up pace, and I turned around to see what was happening. My eyes widened...this wasn't going to end well...

Before me stood the biggest Dragon I had seen thus far. He was shimmering gold in colour, and he had these eyes that shook you to your very soul. The rider was as equally intimidating. His long, mousy brown hair flew behind him as a strong gust of wind barged past. In one hand he held a spear, which glistened brightly as the rain fell upon to it. His dark, muddy eyes were narrow, and he stared down at us threateningly. I instantly stood in front of Irina protectively, feeling my heart pound rapidly against my chest. This wasn't good. I looked upon the armour that the rider was wearing...it was red. Dark red with a black Dragon draping over the left shoulder. The armour was from Brozanta, that much was clear. What wasn't clear was why a Dragon and rider from Brozanta were so close to the Gailoiyn capital. I had never felt fear like this before. It was like I was frozen to the spot as the Dragon craned its neck towards me, so close that I could feel his heavy breath on my face.

"Who...who are you?" I asked nervously, trying not to let them see that I was afraid. The Dragon seemed to take offense to this. He was the first to speak, his voice higher pitched than his partners.

"Who are we?! How dare you insult Brozanta's greatest knight, the most loyal and trusted to his majesty, King Stephan!"

"Nope." I said sarcastically. "Still doesn't ring any bells."

"Why you-!" The Dragon lunged forward, but his rider pulled him back. Irina and I jumped back in fright, but I tried my best to stand my ground.

"Enough, Adamski!" The rider cleared his throat. "I am Hendrix Montgomery, veteran knight to his majesty King Stephan. And this is my partner, Adamski Thorne. And we really don't care who you are." His voice was very monotone, but somehow that made him more terrifying.

"Good. Because I've no intention of telling you." I spat, which just seemed to aggravate Adamski more.

"Xanda!" Irina whispered, her voice shaky. "Please! Do not tease them so!" I looked back at her for a moment, and I saw the sheer panic on her face. I swallowed hard looking back at the intruders, my face as hard as stone. They weren't going to see me squirm.

"Enough child." Said Hendrix Montgomery. "I do not care what your intentions are. Just tell me what you know of Algora's defences, and I may just let you live." Spies...they were spies. But still...why were they here? I know relationships between Gailoiyn and Brozanta had been rocky since King Stephan succeeded his brother instead of Prince Lucas, but it's not like our countries were at war. I mean, as far as I was aware, people travelled between the two counties as if everything were completely normal. Were these two wanting a fight?

"I don't know anything about that." I said bravely. I suddenly let out a gasp of surprise as Adamski put his snout right in my face. I could feel my breath shaking, and I couldn't help but show the fear in my eyes.

"Don't lie to our faces!" Adamski said harshly, his breath feeling as hard as a tornado against my skin.

"I'm not!" I said desperately. "Even if I wanted to tell you I couldn't! I know nothing!"

"Liar." Said Hendrix sharply. "Kill her!" Those words made me freeze up. Was this truly going to be how I died?! Adamski leaped backwards, and I gasped seeing his large tail swinging towards me. I felt a rush of panic jolt through my body. Just then I felt Irina push me in the back, and I fell forward. I hit the sand, face first. It was everywhere...all over my clothes, in my face...I could barely see! I pushed myself to my knees quickly, and used my hood to wipe the sticky sand out of my eyes. I quickly looked around in a daze. Oh no...Irina had taken the hit for me! Her body lay on the beach quite a bit away, and the attackers were slowly stomping towards her. I was conscious, and she wasn't. She couldn't defend herself! I knew I had to do something...but what?! I looked around desperately for something to arm myself with, any weapon of some kind! After a few seconds, my eyes caught the glimpse of a rock sticking out of the sand. I wasted no time in reaching for it, taking it into my pale hands. I pushed myself to my feet and drew my arm back ready to throw. I knew I only had one shot at this. I knew that Pippa and Leon would have felt our souls in distress by now, so all I had to do was keep them away from Irina until help arrived! I trusted my partner. I knew he would come. Wasting no more time, I took the shot and threw the rock towards them. I watched as it flew, right towards its target. Just then, there was a yell of pain, as the rock scraped Hendrix's cheek. It went silent. A deadly silence. The only sound hearable was that of the howling wind as it became more ferocious. I watched as the attackers stopped, and Hendrix slowly lifted his gloved hand to his cheek. He then looked down at his own blood on his hand, staring at it as if he wasn't used to injury. He then slowly turned to face me, his eyes looking evil like he was possessed. I gulped, swallowing hard, feeling like there was a rock in the back of my throat. I whispered under my breath. "Balls..."

"Kill her!" Hendrix shouted angrily, showing any sort of emotion for the first time. I felt the fear in my heart spreading throughout my body. Adamski started charging towards me. Even now, I cannot explain the fear of having a Dragon charge towards you at full speed, especially with intentions to kill you. I clenched my fists. Yes...I was afraid. But I made up my mind that I wasn't going to die here! I had to protect Irina! I was going to fight in spite of my fear! Adamski stopped, and opened his gaping mouth. I dived to the side as a blast of fire shot out of his mouth. I could feel the searing heat on my back as I landed yet again, face first into the sand. Only this time I made sure to cover my eyes, as I knew I'd have no chance if I was blinded again. I quickly staggered to my feet, and turned to face my enemy. He had his jaws open wide, and he lunged for me. I quickly staggered backwards, keeping my feet shoulder width apart to have a better chance of staying on my feet, like Mr Davandrin had taught us. What I didn't think of though, is while I was off balance, Adamski turned and hit me with his tail. I let out a gasp of pain as I flew through the air like lightning. It wasn't long though before I hit the ground, landing on my back. I looked up at the sky, gasping for breath. My body began to ache all over, but I knew I had to keep going. I pushed myself to my feet, and watched as Adamski charged towards me with an open mouth. It was then I noticed...I was standing in front of Irina. If I moved, she'd die! I was the only thing between her and the deadly Dragon. I had a choice to make...it was between saving myself, or saving my friend. It wasn't a hard choice. If I died saving her...I'd have no regrets. I clenched my fists, standing my ground once more. I was scared, but I wasn't going to let them see that.

The next moment, I remember as clear as day. Adamski's jaws wrapped around my small body. I had never felt pain like this before. My body was

numbing, but in extreme agony both at the same. I was screaming...but the world around me was silent. The more I struggled, the more the Dragon's teeth sunk deeper and deeper into my flesh. I could see my blood...everywhere. He let go of me, flinging my body across the beach as if he were throwing away rubbish. I just lay there watching as my blood began to soak into the sand, staining the beach in a river of red. My eyes were open, yet I struggled to breathe. I refused to die like this. With every ounce of strength I had left in me, I used my hands to push myself to my knees. I gazed up, my vision fading in and out of a blurry sensation. The sky was dark. Adamski and Hendrix towered over me. Hendrix's expression was emotionless, as if he were about to kill a fly or an insect beneath his feet. He opened his mouth to speak...and at that moment, I knew it was all over.
"On your feet. I will not kill a girl on her knees."

I didn't really care whether it was on my feet, or my knees. Death was death, no matter how it happened. If it was for a good cause...that was all that mattered to me. I dug one foot into the ground, and pushed myself onto my feet. I took a deep breath, closing my eyes. I was ready. Just then I heard a roar, and the ground shook in front of me. I was so weak I fell backwards at the sudden movement, and my eyes shot open.
"Leon..." I whispered weakly, a small smile forming on my lips. He was here. Leon roared loudly at the attackers, as he shielded me from them in his Dragon form. Just then, a bright yellow Dragon landed over Irina's body. Pippa was here. Thank goodness! Then, Taz joined the party, landing in between us with Joey on his back, equipped with his bow. At last! Taz and Joey instantly started fending off the enemy, Joey firing his bow while Taz leaped around him, trying to get close. Pippa joined in every time they got close to Irina, but she stayed firm in defending her unconscious partner. Leon quickly turned to me.
"Xanda! Climb on!" He said hurriedly. I nodded, crawling over to him, barely able to see anymore. I reached up, and Leon helped me in any way he could. I don't even remember how, but somehow, I made it onto his back. I found myself clasping onto the spikes down his neck. I shivered, my body in a searing pain as my blood dripped onto Leon's green scales. The raging rain soaked into my skin. Just then, I was knocked about, and I found myself holding onto Leon for dear life! Adamski was attacking him, trying to get to me. However, Leon was not allowing it. He defended me bravely, not caring about any injuries he was taking in the process.

In a flash, appeared another Dragon. I had never seen anything like it before. The scale of this beast towered even that of Adamski Thorne. Its scales were as black as the night's sky, and the spikes around his neck were a deep purple. The mystery Dragon stood in front of Leon, and roared loud and threateningly. The roar just made me feel weaker, and I tried to stay awake as I watched the new beast battle ferociously with the enemy. Hendrix and Adamski were easily overpowered, and the last thing I saw before passing out, was the two flying away into the night's sky...

Chapter 5

Know your Enemy

It was dark, but faint colours danced around in front of my eyelids. My body felt completely numb and I struggled to breathe, feeling like a boulder was resting on my ragged chest. I grumbled, the world around me a daze as I heard familiar voices ring like a faint bell in my ears.

"Leo! She's moving!"

"Xanda...Xanda can you hear me?!" Leon and Taz...they were here. It was then I felt a warm, rough hand around mine. I tried so hard to open my eyes, but they felt as heavy as lead. Once again I groaned in pain and I heard Pippa and Irina speak to me.

"Xanda? C'mon talk to us!"

"Xanda...please be alright..." I felt my breath pick up, and I struggled to breathe again. I felt the hand around mine become tighter.

"Xanda?!" Said Leon worriedly.

"I'm getting the nurse!" I heard Joey speak hurriedly.

Just then, it went blank yet again...

I'm not sure how much time had passed before I regained consciousness again, but I assumed it was a while. I began to wake, properly this time. The first thing I saw were two emerald eyes shining down at me. The room was bright, and it took me a while to adjust to the light around me. The ceiling was white, as were the curtains around the bed I was lying in. It didn't take me long to realise I was in the school infirmary. The sheets were an eggshell cream colour, which I wasn't really a fan of. I was sitting up slightly in the bed, as it was tilted up behind my back. Because of this, I could see a wooden table near the end of my bed, with a few boxes of sweets placed onto it. Just then, a rough hand tightened around my own and I looked to my right weakly.

"Xanda..."

"Leon..." I smiled a little, not having much energy to do anything else. I just felt so weak and drained. My smile dropped however as I remembered how I got here. Adamski Thorne and Hendrix Montgomery were a force to be reckoned with. I remember clearly the exact moment his teeth sunk into my flesh. The pain had been nothing like I had ever felt before, and it was a pain I never wanted to feel again. It was unbearable and indescribable. Who would have known my first few days at Wyvern academy would have been so eventful? Leon was watching me with a worried look on his face. He leaned forward and spoke softly.

"Are you alright...?"

"I've been better" I replied weakly, my smile returning. I nodded towards the sweets on the table. "Let me guess...Taz and Joey?"

Leon chuckled softly. "Yeah. According to those two idiot's sweets cure everything." This made me giggle a little. Typical. Taz and Joey did like their sweets. They always had a packet of something or other in their pockets.

"That sounds like them." I chuckled. Then I watched Leon as his expression shifted to become more solemn. I looked at him, starting to get a little worried. I asked gently, "what's up?"

"I'm sorry. I really am..." He said hanging his head in shame.

"Leon..." I spoke sadly. "What for?"

"You're my rider, Xanda! It's my job to protect you!" He said looking at me sharply.

"Hey..." I said gently, squeezing his hand as hard as I could. "Stop that. You came, that's all that matters. I really would have been dead if you hadn't shown up when you did. So, no more beating yourself up over it, okay?"

"But-" He tried to protest, which was met by a stern look from me. He blushed brightly, and nodded. "Fine..." He said finally. I chuckled a bit and smiled again.

"That's better. Balls...speaking of the attack, how's Irina?! Is she alright?!" I added worriedly.

Leon nodded slowly. "Thanks to you, she's just fine. As is everyone else. You got nothing to worry about."

"Alright...just one more thing." I started. "Before I passed out...I remember this huge black Dragon..."

"Oh yeah." Said Leon. "That was my father." So, that Dragon that saved us was Leon's old man, Drevin Drogon. It's a good thing he had arrived when he did. I don't think I'd be here otherwise. I suddenly tried to move a little, and I grunted. My body was so stiff, and I closed my eyes in discomfort.

"Balls..."

"Are you alright?" Leon asked in concern.

"Yeah...just really numb, that's all." I smiled weakly.

"You should be!" Said a strong female voice. Just then a nurse walked in. She had enchanting white hair with orange eyes, and she wore a short skirt and a doctor's robe.

"Xanda, this is Mrs Ida McCoy, the head nurse." Said Leon, which shocked me a little. She looked quite young to be head nurse. She must have really known her stuff.

"You are lucky to be alive, Miss Sykes. I've had to drug you up quite a bit." Said Mrs McCoy. "But you have a good partner there. He's not left your side." She winked teasingly at Leon, and he blushed deep red. She chuckled and picked up a notepad from my bedside. "Call if you need anything." And then she left, as fast as she had entered. I blinked a few times, thinking about how lively and weird she was. But in a good way, of course! I mean she was pretty cool. I looked towards Leon.

"What does she mean 'you haven't left'?" I asked, and he just blushed deeper.

"I haven't left since that day a week ago..." A week?! I'd been unconscious for a week? Balls, I couldn't believe it.

"A week?! You've been here a week?! What about food? Lessons? Bed?!" I said, a hint of worry apparent in my voice. Balls, I was beginning to sound like Grandma.

"I've been sleeping here in this chair. It didn't seem right going to lessons without my partner...I needed to be here beside you helping you get better. And my father's been bringing me food."

"Leon..." I looked at him softly. Come to think of it, he looked so tired. Now it was my turn to take care of him. "Leon, I appreciate it all, but I'll be alright now. Go to bed and get some proper rest. You look like you need it." He thought for a moment, before nodding in agreement. He stood slowly and leaned over me, kissing my forehead gently. I smiled up at him.

"You rest up, yeah?" He said. "I'll be back soon."

"Take your time Leon...I aint exactly going anywhere..."

The sun was setting over the kingdom, and a few hours had passed since Leon had left. The infirmary was quiet, and I could hear the pitter patter of rain against the windows. Mrs McCoy had brought me some tomato soup for supper, which had felt soothing and warmed up my body. I couldn't eat all of it though, as I seemed to have lost my appetite. However, I wasn't too worried as I loved my food and I was sure it would come back. Mrs Madana had come to visit before supper, and she had given me a book to read to pass the time. Just lying here had been kinda boring, so I was grateful for the gesture. The book was very interesting, but it was a tale I had heard many times before. It was titled 'The Raven Queen', and this figure of legend was an integral part of our worlds history. It is said, that in ages past around four hundred years ago, life as we know it ceased to exist and humanity was on the brink of extinction. At the time, lived a girl and her twin, Alexzero and Pipit Raven. Pipit was taken by the evil and ruthless Queen Tmoria, and Alexzero set off free her. Along with the help of a group of heroes, Alexzero led a rebellion against the Queen and destroyed her, thus saving all of humanity. In my opinion...I don't think they were heroes to begin with. I think they were just people who wanted their lives back. Alexzero became known as 'The Raven Queen', and she ruled over Brozanta in Merdonex, which was the capital at the time but now it's in ruins. I'm not sure how much of her story is true, as there have been so many versions of it, but what is known is she is now buried in the Temple in the ruined city of Merdonex. She must have been a wonderful person, to put the world and its people before herself. If she had not done what she did all those years ago, right now, nobody would be alive. As far as I was aware, she was buried with her husband, King Luka. Also buried there I think is her father, her sister, and brother-in-law, along with their children. I know other members of her group were buried in an ancient Elven Shrine in the Brozantan village of Palmira. These heroes of old thus became our gods and goddesses. Raven herself is the Goddess of war, and her sister is the Goddess of Loyalty. Pipit's husband was an angel known as Edward Avalon, and he was the God of Wisdom. Edward had a little sister, and she was Lerai, the Goddess of Love. Luka was the God of Justice. It is said in many texts and manuscripts, that the Raven twins had a brother, but what happened to him is unknown. I must admit, his legend intrigued me the most, simply because it was shrouded in mystery and all we have to go on is pure speculation. However, the Raven Queen is someone who had inspired me my entire life, as I had grown up on tales of her adventure. What I wouldn't give to go to her graveside and pay my respects. But the way things were going between Gailoiyn and Brozanta right now, I don't think I'd get the chance anytime soon.

Speaking of which, the relationship between Gailoiyn and Brozanta was now at boiling point after the recent attack. At the time, however, I didn't know just how serious things were. It was at this point though, I was about to get a hint on that. As I was saying, I was still laying in my infirmary bed, the book now placed on the bedside table next to my sweets. The table had now been pushed up next to me so I could put the book onto it and reach the sweets, although like I said I really wasn't in the mood for them at that point. I let out a long sigh, my numb body beginning to ache all over as I stared at the ceiling. Just then, I felt myself looking over at the gap in the curtain as it began to slide open. To my surprise, Mr Drogon was standing there! He seemed even taller up close like this, and he had a small smile on his face. I remember thinking how kind he seemed at this moment, but I didn't ever want to see him in a bad mood, because I also remembered his appearance in the attack on the beach. When he had defended Leon, he was so aggressive and enraged. I could tell he loved his son and would do anything to protect him. Mr Drogon made his way over to my bedside. "Good evening, Miss Sykes. May I join you?" He asked gesturing towards the seat.
"Of course." I smiled weakly and watched as the tall man sat down in the seat next to my bed.
"I must say, Miss Sykes, it is nice to finally meet you."
"You too, sir." I said. "Although I wish it were under better circumstances."
"Indeed." Said Mr Drogon letting out a small chuckle. "You're going to be well looked after though. By Leon especially, I wager. He is rather fond of you."
This made me blush a little, and my chest began to feel tight. I was fond of Leon too. I'm just glad it was me in this bed and not him.
"He's a wonderful partner. We get on so well." I smiled brightly, just thinking about him.
"That's good to hear. I sense a strong bond between the two of you already. You will be a great team someday." He said proudly. "I'm glad Leon has finally found someone he feels compatible with."
"Me too. I was worried I'd go for ages without a partner." I chuckled. Then my expression shifted again. I had to ask him about the attack. I wondered what they had been doing there. I know they asked about the cities defences and all, but that couldn't have been the only reason they came here. "Sir, I was wondering...if I could ask about-"

"The ambush on the beach." He said plainly, as if he knew what I were thinking. There were a few moments of awkward silence before I nodded. "Yeah…" I said finally. He shifted uncomfortably, like he didn't want to talk about it.

"Well." He said clearing his throat. "Miss Rozanna said the Brozanta Knights asked you about the defences here. And she said you told them nothing, which I'm glad about." Well, that was short and sweet.

"I couldn't have told them even if I wanted to. I don't know nothing about all that. It's not like I'm in the army or on a king's mission." I said sarcastically. As we got further into the short conversation, the more uncomfortable Mr Drogon became. His face remained hard, but he twiddled his finger's nervously. I couldn't help but wonder if this was a nervous habit, like when I fiddled with the rings around my neck.

"Yes well…" He stood quickly. "I don't want you to think on it. It will all be taken care of. You must rest and get yourself back to normal. Goodnight, Miss Sykes."

"Oh…um…night?" I said raising an eyebrow. Well, that was brief. He really wasn't a man for deep conversations, that's for sure. And in truth, he left me feeling more confused than I had before as he left swiftly the way he had come in.

A few more days' past, and nurse Ida had said I was okay to go up to my room and rest. Leon had come to the infirmary to help me up, as I was still very unsteady on my feet. I had an arm draped over Leon's shoulders, and he helped me walk up to our bedroom. He took me during the time when the days first lesson began, so there weren't many people around and we could take our time. Balls, I felt like a granny. And a burden. I felt so useless having Leon help me along through the long halls and upstairs. One thing I hated was people nursing me. However, I couldn't really help it at this point. I was still high on medicine, which made me really drowsy. Despite this, I was starting to feel the pain all over my body as I dragged my feet along. After a long and agonising walk, we finally reached the room. Leon opened the door for me and I let go of him. I winced in pain, but was silent as I held my stomach and began to hobble towards the bed. Leon had turned to shut the door, while I began to sit down. As I sat, I felt my body go heavy and I practically fell onto the bed. This made me whine out in pain. Leon perked up and suddenly rushed over, holding my shoulders as he sat down next to me.

"Are you okay?!" He asked worriedly.

"Yeah…yeah I'm alright. Man, I can't wait to get some proper sleep…" I replied.

"Do you…" Leon trailed off, a little embarrassed. "Do you want me to help change you into your nightclothes?"

"Nah." I said rubbing my forehead. "I was gonna take a bath before heading to bed."

"Alright...then...I'll help you put your bandages back on afterwards."

"Yeah..." I looked down sadly, beginning to fiddle with my parent's rings again. Balls, I hated this. I was too independent for my own good. I decided I was going to turn the conversation to someone else. Someone other than me for a change. "Anyway, your old man came to visit me the other day. He was weird."

"He did?!" He said sounding surprised.

"Yeah. Sorry, I assumed he'd told you."

"No. Wait, what do you mean he was weird?" He asked curiously.

"Well, I asked him about those Brozantan knights that attacked us...and he just kinda avoided the conversation." I said remembering how Mr Drogon had just gone all quiet and then left. Leon just scoffed, but he didn't look surprised one bit.

"Pfft. That's just like him."

"What do you mean?" I asked curiously.

"Well...for years, I've been asking him about my mother. He says nothing but good things of her personality, but that's it. I know nothing of her other than that. He doesn't speak about how he knew her...how they met...how she died...nothing. He just clams up."

"I know how you feel." I said understandingly. What Leon described about his father sounded so much like my Grandma and Gramps when they talked about my parents. "Grandma and Gramps don't talk about my old folks either. I never knew why."

"Adults eh?" Leon smiled a little. "I'm gonna make sure that I'm honest with my kids, no matter what." I think at that point, the two of us both blushed. What he had said was so cute! He'd be a great parent one day. I'm sure mine would have been too...if they'd had the chance. "Speaking of the attack though" Leon continued, "it's been bugging father deeply. I've never seen him so anxious before. He can't put his finger on why they were so close to Algora." I admit this had bothered me too. Surely that was a declaration of war? I wasn't sure. But what I did know was this wasn't the end of the matter.

"I don't think we've heard the last of this Leo..." I looked at him slightly, and he simply nodded in agreement. I didn't know how, but I had a sickening feeling that there were worse things to come.

Balls. Having a bath probably wasn't the best idea I'd had all day. As soon as I had gotten in, the scars on my body stung to high heaven. You'd think been gnawed to death by a Dragon would be painful enough. A word of advice...don't get in the bath afterwards. I had sat up for a while, trying to adjust my body to the water. After a while I laid down, as I began to get used to it. I closed my eyes. I hadn't felt this relaxed in a long time. I lay still as the warm water rejuvenated my broken body, and opened my eyes to see bubbles floating towards the ceiling. I had been laying there for a while, just thinking things over and over. The attack, lessons, home, the legends I had learned about...a lot was happening right now. My life before was so routine. Y'know...I'd get up, have some breakfast, help Grandpa craft a few things, deliver the stuff that was ready, go home, eat and sleep. But now...things were so mixed up and so different. I admit I was struggling to get my head around it all. I didn't like change. But this, in a way, was a good change. It was good for me to finally get out and meet new people. Life is so secluded in such a small village, but now I was officially a girl of the big city. Well...an injured girl of the big city. While I was laying in the bath, I sat up, and I found myself just staring in a daze at the scars on my body. They were so red and inflamed, and they looked awful. Well, that was my model career over. Nurse Ida had said most of them would heal alright, but some may leave permanent scarring. That had been hard to hear, but hey, at least I wasn't dead. I let out a huge sigh before I held tightly onto the side of the bath and heaved myself up, climbing out. I was so stiff, and I cried out in pain as I moved, letting myself show my emotions now Leon wasn't around. He was going through enough already, I wasn't gonna burden him anymore than I already had. I put on my underwear, shorts and socks, with great difficulty I may add, and I wrapped my bra around my breasts. I slowly made my way back into the bedroom and sat down on the stool by my dressing table, grunting as I did. I felt so drained, and for a while I found myself just staring at the bandages on the side. I looked at myself in the mirror, and my skin was more pasty than usual, and my eyes were dull. Not gonna lie, I looked awful. Finally, I found myself reaching for the bandages and tried to apply them around my torso like nurse Ida had shown Leon. As I stretched to reach around my back, a quick shot of pain charged through my body, and I yelled out again. It was then the door swung open, and Leon barged in. I knew it was him because I could see his reflection in the mirror as he darted over to me. There were tears in my eyes because of the pain, and he came and held my shoulders worriedly.

"Hey! Slow down!" He said with a caring tone to his voice. "I told you I'd do that for you...stop being so stubborn and let me help you!"

"Sorry..." I sniffled, wiping my eyes. "I just...I don't wanna burden you..."

"Don't talk like that! That's not what I think of you at all" He said, and without another word, he began to help me cover my torso again with the bandages. Although his hands were rough, his touch was soft, and he worked carefully to make it as painless as possible.

"Thanks Leon..." I said smiling weakly.

"Don't mention it. Really, I'm happy to help. Besides, it's what partners do. We take care of each other. That's the whole point." He said looking at me finally after he had finished applying the bandages. "Listen, I don't have to go to last lesson if you don't want me too."

"No...no you go." I smiled at him. "Besides, I know you're still having some trouble bending fire in your human form. It'll give you a chance to work on it while I'm not there." I said knowing his last class was with Mr Davandrin. "Alright." He said. "You really need to get some rest. You look terrible. N-No offence!" He blushed.

"None taken." I chuckled, watching him squirm. Clearly, he wasn't used to dealing with girls. He was so cute when he became all flustered like that. Teasing him was going to be hilarious!

After Leon had left, I admit there was one thing that was now bugging me. It was what Mr Davandrin had said in my first lesson with him. Know your enemy. I had made two enemies. Hendrix Montgomery and Adamski Thorne. I know I've been mentioning the attack a lot, but I couldn't seem to get it out of my mind. It plagued me. And if it wasn't me, more than likely someone else would have been hurt. I remembered Irina's lifeless body as she lay on the beach. So still and defenceless, she was. I didn't want that to happen to anybody else. I wasn't gonna let this stop me. If I did, then that would mean that they've won. That wasn't an option. I had been lying in bed, staring at the clock on the wall, waiting for the right time. I waited until it was almost time for Davandrin's lesson to finish, before standing up, and taking my time as I staggered to the doorway. I had been dressed for a while, so I instantly made my way through the empty hallways towards Davandrin's indoor classroom. I was panting, completely exhausted even though all I had done was walk a short distance. My injuries were really weighing me down. I waited around the corner, as I didn't want to deal with awkward questions from my classmates. I didn't need the pity of people asking me how I was or how I was coping. Just then, I heard a babble of chatter as everyone started to leave Davandrin's lesson. I peered around the corner, waiting to see Leon...but he didn't show. Taz, Joey, Irina and Pippa came out and headed towards the great hall, but Leon didn't leave. After everyone had gone, I pressed my hand against the wall and walked towards the door, pushing it open slowly. Inside, there he was. Leon was sitting on the stage, as was Mr Davandrin, and they were talking. Leon's eyes widened as he saw me enter, and he instantly jumped down.

"Xanda!" He exclaimed. "I told you to stay in bed!"

"You did. I didn't listen." I replied. He pouted, and we walked towards each other. When we met, he put his arm around me and helped me towards the stage, and helped me sit on the edge. He lifted my legs up to take the strain off, and put them on the stage too. Davandrin just watched, putting on a weak smile.

"You are reckless, Miss Sykes. How are you holding up?" Davandrin asked.

"Not too bad, sir. I'm sure I'll be back in action again in no time."

"Good. That was very brave what you did. You're either a hero or a fool." He chuckled softly as Leon sat back down. He on the other hand wasn't finding it funny at all.

"Or both." I said. "Anyway, that's the reason I'm here. I'd like a word with you if you don't mind."

"Oh? What can I do for you?" He asked raising his eyebrows.

"In my very first lesson with you, you said 'know your enemy', correct?"

"I believe I did, yes."

"I want you to tell me about Hendrix Montgomery and Adamski Thorne." I said plainly, keeping a neutral expression on my face. I wanted him to know I meant business. Leon turned to look at me swiftly, and spoke with caution.

"Are you sure that's wise?" Said Leon. "I mean, it's still pretty raw."

"Yes, I'm sure." I said. Leon just nodded. He knew as much as I did we were a team now, and sometimes we had to compromise.

"Very well." Said Mr Davandrin. "Although I don't know how much help I can be. Hendrix especially is a very private person."

"Did you know him?" Asked Leon.

"Yes." Replied Davandrin. "I'm originally from Brozanta. I trained at Bloodbourne Academy. Hendrix was my classmate. Adamski was a few years younger but they paired up very quickly. We were never that close, they always kept themselves to themselves. Hendrix especially was very shy until he was on the battlefield." Jeez, I knew Hendrix was quiet, but I never thought he was shy. He had seemed so strong and self-confident. I guess deep down he was only human, just like the rest of us. He too, must have a family and people he cared about, just like everybody. Leon and I exchanged a look. Adamski was clearly the more outspoken of the pair, and the one most likely to get them in trouble. This was really all I got from Mr Davandrin, but it was definitely more knowledge than I had before. Hendrix Montgomery and Adamski Thorne. They were the first people that I knew had to be taken down.

Chapter 6
A Frosty Realisation

Time passed as it always does, and a few weeks had gone by since the attack on the beach. My scars were still healing, but I was managing to move around much better now. Slowly but surely, it was becoming easier. Leon had been great. He was a huge rock to me in my time of need. He was wonderful, and I was so grateful to him. I felt so lucky, knowing I had the best partner in the world! Just don't tell him I said that. So, life had moved on since that terrible day, and Leon and I were sitting at our breakfast table with Pippa and Irina. As I had suspected, I was eating a lot better now, and I was quickly tucking into my breakfast. It was just a few pieces of fresh fruit, but it tasted amazing. It reminded me of the fruit back home. On the trees in Lightwater, grew the most amazing green apples! Oh, how I loved my food. Leon was chewing on some sort of pastry, when he turned to me.

"Xanda, are you sure your feeling up to it today?" He said.

"Leon, you ask me that every morning, and every morning I tell you I'm fine." I chuckled.

"Awe, Leo!" Pippa grinned. "You're so cute when you fuss over her like that!" At this point we both found ourselves pouting, not quite knowing what to do with ourselves. A blush flushed both our cheeks red, and we looked away from each other awkwardly.

Irina let out a small giggle. "Don't tease them so, Pippa!" She smiled. "Although I admit, the way you two work together is adorable!"

"C'mon Irina! Not you too!" Leon and I said in unison. There was a moment of silence, and we looked at each other, realising how synchronised we were. The four of us then found ourselves laughing, finding the whole thing incredibly funny and awkward at the same time.

"Yo guys!" We heard Joey yell as he and Taz approached the table with a skip in their steps.

"Guess what?" Said Taz beaming.

"You've decided to be less annoying?" Leon said sarcastically.

"Nope!" Grinned Taz.

"The six of us are gonna be in Partner Bonding class together!" Said Joey.

"That's great news!" Pippa said excitedly. As mentioned before, Miss Wellworn and Miss Nebilia only take three couples in their classes, so they can work more intimately with people. I guess it makes sense...I mean, you can't really bond with one person with loads of people around. At least I know I couldn't anyway.

"Oh great." I chuckled, looking directly at Taz and Joey. "Why do I always get stuck with you two?"

"Is it just me, or are you getting as sarcastic as your partner?" Joey grinned.

"Yeah!" Said Taz. "Looks like Leo's a bad influence on you!"

"You idiots! I'll get you for that!" Leon laughed, and got up quickly. Taz and Joey started running out of the hall, followed by Leon. The three of them looked like three naughty little children. I swear, men could be so immature.

"Boys." Pippa stated plainly. We all started giggling again and us girls got up.

We started to walk out after the boys, who we saw playfighting in the hall. I suddenly froze, as something else caught my attention. My eyes widened in excitement as I charged through the boys. They stopped, wondering what was going on. I pressed my palms up against the frosty windows as I gazed outside. It was snowing! A blanket of beautiful white covered the grounds, and large snowdrops drifted down from the heavens. I loved the snow so much! My grandparents told me that I was born on a day like this. A wonderful, snowy day! We only had two lessons today. Partner Bonding first, then History of Dragons. After that, I was excited as I could go outside!

Partner Bonding class took place in the Western tower, well away from other classrooms. It was private and quiet. Inside the tower was a beautiful, relaxing jade green coloured room. It was small and circular, with a perfectly varnished wooden floor. Despite being in a tower, the room was surprisingly warm, but that probably had something to do with the burning log fire to the right. There were eight seats in a circle around the room, and a large, light pink crystal on the floor in the centre. Leon had told me that the crystal would be there. According to him, Miss Nebilia believed that crystals draw in positive energy. Well, most crystals anyway. I dunno how true that is. It just sounded like an old wives' tale to me. Light streaked into the room through the thin windows, and the whole place had somewhat of a calming aura. Miss Wellworn was the one with the green hair, and Miss Nebilia was the one that had those beautiful pink eyes. I bet she looked amazing in her Dragon form! Ivy Wellworn and Cassandra Nebilia sat in the chairs towards the back of the room. Cassandra smiled sweetly at the six of us, her pink eyes lighting up.
"Hello!" She said cheerfully, her voice soft and sweet. "Take a seat!" So, we did as she said, and we all took one of the remaining six seats. They were quite comfy to be honest, and they had these emerald green velvet cushions placed upon them. To me, the green interior was very calming. Green was my favourite colour after all. I never knew why, but it had been for as long as I could remember. Joey spoke up, a hint of confusion in his voice.
"Miss Wellworn. I was wondering, why is this room so...green?" Asked Joey.
The green haired lady looked over. She was taller than her partner, and more stern looking, but she did speak with a kind authority.
"I am a very spiritual person, Josef. I believe that the body can be split into sections, called Chakra's. Each section making up a part of who we are. You can sometimes see these Chakra's through colour meditation...we will have a lesson on this if you like at some point. Green is the colour of the heart Chakra...and represents our ability to love." She explained. Now that did sound interesting, and I admit, it intrigued me greatly. It was definitely something I would delve deeper into.
"That sounds very personal..." Said Irina quietly.
"These lessons are very personal." Cassandra said smiling reassuringly. "Which is why we don't have more than six people per class. Anything we talk about

in this room, stays in this room."

"You're all here because we have high expectations of you." Said Miss Wellworn. "We don't pick the classes at random. Your other teachers put you here depending on your compatibility not just as pairs, but as a whole group. The six of you have already battled together once."

"But we lost." I said simply, looking down. I hated being reminded of the beach attack. It made me feel like such a failure.

"Snap out of it Xanda!" Said Taz. "Were still alive, right? I don't think we can call that losing!"

"He's right y'know..." Said Pippa, smiling at me gently. I found myself looking back up.

I turned to look at Leon, who put his hand on my shoulder. "Just because you get beat up, doesn't mean you lost. You chose to stay. You coulda gone back to Lightwater and lived the rest of your life safe inside the smithy, and left us all here. But you didn't. You stayed. You stuck it out. And your carrying on, despite what they did. I respect you more for that. That's why you're such a cool partner!" As Leon finished, a grin spread across his face. I couldn't help but smile brightly as he spoke. I guess with everything that had happened, that was what I'd needed to hear. It meant a lot, what he said. I won't ever forget it. I really did have the best partner.

"Yeah." I said with a newfound determination. "Yeah you're right. We did the best we could, and we live to fight another day. I guess when you look at it like that, we didn't do too bad."

"And she's back!" Taz giggled.

"Ladies and gentlemen, Xanda Sykes has entered the room at last!" Joey chuckled.

I didn't think I had been acting too much unlike my normal self, but apparently, I must have been.

"It's good to see you all get along and support each other so well!" Cassandra exclaimed happily. "Right. Now, settle down. Ivy and I have been talking, and we want to work on an advanced technique with you six. Talking internally with your minds through your souls."

"Woah, Miss Nebilia!" Said Taz. "Isn't that like...really advanced stuff?!"

"Indeed." Miss Wellworn replied. "We have been observing you in other lessons, and we think, with some practice, you can all do it." I remembered that this was the technique Leon had said he'd always wanted to learn, and I could see the excitement flashing in his eyes. A pressure began to build inside me, as I really didn't want to let him down.

"Let's get straight to it then!" Said Miss Nebilia. "We'll see how far you all get today and then we can decide what to do to help you progress." We all looked between each other, then back at Cassandra Nebilia who was giggling. "Don't look so worried! It'll be fine. It will take time, but we'll get there in the end. Now, turn your chairs to face your partner." So, we did as she said, and Leon and I turned our chairs, so we were facing each other. I must admit, this was the first time I had noticed how good looking he was. Sure, he wasn't perfect...I mean that white strip in his fringe was kind of distracting...but something about him was compelling. Not just his looks, but his personality was intriguing to me too. Everything about him was drawing me in. I didn't understand the feelings coming over me, I had never felt so connected with anyone before. I was suddenly pulled from my thoughts as Miss Wellworn handed me and Leon a piece of parchment and a quill each. The other four were handed one too, and Ivy and Cassandra sat back down. "Now, I want you all to write one word upon your parchment. Something that means something to you." Miss Wellworn said. I stared at the parchment for a moment, the quill resting under my thumb. With the other hand, I fiddled with my parent's rings. Something important to me...I didn't have much in the way of possessions. My emotions meant more to me than material stuff. In the end, there was only one word I could write down. Leon and I began writing at the same time. Once we had all finished writing down the words, we were told to close our eyes and try and connect with our partners, and tell each other through our minds what word was written on the other person's parchment...

Let me tell you, I felt absolutely nothing. It was just black when I closed my eyes, and the entire lesson was literally just going nowhere. The others were just as frustrated as I was. Nothing was happening. No matter how long or hard I thought about Leon, I still couldn't hear his voice inside my head. And he couldn't hear mine either. After about an hour of trying, we were mentally exhausted, and I opened my eyes, rubbing my forehead. Leon seemed to have sensed my agitation, as he opened his eyes as well.
"I'm so confused...I don't know what were supposed to do!" I said in frustration, the others opening their eyes too.
"I agree." Leon sighed. "We've been here forever with no progress!"
"Yeah...nothing's happening!" Taz said gripping his white hair.
"I did say it would take time." Cassandra chuckled. "I'm surprised you all sat for this long though. Most students don't last ten minutes."
"We have been observing you, and I think I have an idea on how we can progress." Said Ivy Wellworn. "All of you seem to have the same issue. Your souls keep wavering in and out of sync. They are entwined, but not stable. We need to work on your stability. You have done well today though. Cassandra, if you don't mind, collect the parchments, please." She smiled at her friend and Miss Nebilia stood, coming around the six of us and taking our parchments back. "Do not tell your partner what's on your parchment out of class. Believe me, I will know if you do." As she said this she gave us a stern look, and we all knew she was telling the truth. I tell you, I wouldn't like to get on the wrong side of her. Cassandra put the parchments down beside her seat and sat back down.
"Miss Wellworn, do you really think we can do this?" Asked Pippa.

"I do." She replied. "In fact, I aim to have you succeed by your first lesson after the Winter Ball!"

"The...Winter Ball?" I said confused, since I hadn't heard of such an event.

"Yes!" Cassandra Nebilia said excitedly. "Tis a wonderful evening!"

"Does it celebrate anything in particular?" I asked curiously.

"The birthday of the Academy founders, is it not?" Irina said shyly, a worried look in her eyes fearing she was wrong.

"Yeah, that's it." Said Joey. "Some say, they also shared the same birthday as the Raven Queen herself! Coincidence isn't it? I mean, they're supposed to be of the same bloodline."

"When is it?" I asked.

"Ten days from now, dear." Said Miss Nebilia.

"Huh. That's my birthday." I said. Leon looked at me, his eyes widening. I looked at him curiously. "Um...is something wrong?"

"N-No! Just surprised, is all. That's my birthday too."

"Weird..." I said in shock. What were the odds? Of Leon, the Raven Queen, the Drago twins and I all sharing the same birthday? It may have just seemed like coincidence to some, but I on the other hand had a feeling there was more to it. Miss Wellworn had asked us to start meditating to calm our souls, before we did some deep colour meditation with her in class. However, I kinda glazed over that as I was too worried about this ball. Swirling dresses, music and candlelight...that wasn't really my thing. Besides, I didn't even own a dress! It would take place on my birthday, in the great hall. Great. I was gonna look like a fool. Not only did I have nothing to wear, but I couldn't dance either. Growing up in a smithy doesn't give you much call for all that regal stuff. And besides, I didn't really see the appeal. I wasn't looking forward to this at all...

The last lesson of the day was Miss Madana's history of Dragons class before lunch. We were all reading a book about the history of Gailoiyn. However, I wasn't really paying much attention to the book, or engaging in any of the conversations around me. My mind was wondering in other places. I couldn't stop leaning my arm on the window ledge, and gazing outside at the falling snow. Snow was so pure to me. I loved it, more than any other weather type. Somehow, it seemed to take my mind off things. I could watch it drift softly to the ground all day...it was so magical to me. My hair that day was in a side bun, and I suddenly became distracted as a piece of hair came out and fell into my face. I hadn't noticed it until now, and I thought nothing of it. Without thinking, I moved my arms to put the piece of hair back into place, still staring out the window. It was then my eyes caught something in the reflection. I felt my heart stop for a moment as I saw my sleeve had rolled up when I'd moved my arm, and a large scar on it became visible to me. It was in that moment I saw the teeth of Adamski Thorne around my arm, and I suddenly felt a flash of panic pulse through my whole body. I instantly found it hard to control my breathing. While the world around me spun slowly, the panic in my head became twice as fast. I just stared at the scar, flashes of memories appearing before me. I had suddenly snapped from feeling calm to incredibly anxious in the space of a second. I never thought an emotion could change as quick as the snap of your fingers...but it can. It was so instant, and so scary as it felt like my heart was running ahead of me.

"Xanda?" I suddenly turned my head rapidly to look at Leon, and his expression changed when he saw the fear in my eyes. He took my trembling hands and I swallowed hard. "Xanda, what's wrong?!" He asked worriedly.

"I need to leave." I said barely able to breathe, my heart feeling like a rope was being tightened around it. "I wanna go. Now!" I had spoken sharply, but quietly as I didn't want to draw attention to myself. That would have made me worse. Irina, Pippa, Taz and Joey looked on in concern. Leon simply nodded, not once questioning me, seeming to understand. He got up and took my arm gently, helping me to my feet. It was all muffled to me, but Joey turned to Leon and asked if I'd be okay. Leon told him that he would look after me and he pulled me out of the classroom. He took me into the hall, and sat me down on a bench against the wall, opposite a large window. Leon kneeled in front of me, and placed his gentle hands on my arms.

"Xanda...Xanda look at me!" He said. I had been staring at the floor until this point, but his words made me look at him slowly. "Deep breaths..." He spoke calmly, and started to coach me on how to breathe. At first, I thought he had lost his mind, but I went along with it and after a while my breathing slowed down. All through this, Leon had been rubbing my arm comfortingly with his hand, but I had been too panicked at the time to notice. I had however, been so focused on Leon I hadn't noticed Mrs Madana come into the hall and sit next to me. I felt her hand on my back, and I looked back down at the floor again in shame.

"I'm so sorry Mrs Madana..." I sniffled. "I'll...I'll come back in now."

"No. Don't apologise." She said softly. "I understand. It's still very raw, isn't it?" I just nodded slowly, trying hard not to think of the attack. I just wanted to forget the blasted thing ever happened! It made me feel powerless. Not to mention the nightmares I still had about it. "Go on." Said Mrs Madana smiling gently. "You and Mr Drogon get off. Go and rest, or do something to take your mind off things."

"Thank you Mrs Madana. I'll take care of her." Said Leon, as she patted my back.

She put her hands on her knees and stood. "Listen, if you need to talk, you know where to find me. I may not know how you feel...but I am always here to lend an ear."

"Thank you." I said in appreciation, managing a small smile before she made her way back into class. I then turned to look back at Leon, who was watching me supportively. I could feel tears welling up in my eyes. No...I wouldn't cry. I had promised myself I would not cry in front of my partner. But now...I kind of wanted to. It was a moment of madness, I guess. I gazed directly in to Leon's eyes, and spoke with a quivering voice. "Leon..."

"Yes?" He said softly.

"Leon!" I suddenly wrapped my arms around him and finally began to cry, letting out everything I had bottled up inside me. He seemed a little shocked at first, but it didn't take long for him to wrap his arms around me tightly, as I cried into his chest. He rocked me gently, just holding me as I cried. I suddenly felt like a weight was being lifted as I allowed myself to cry. There was no shame in still being scared about something that has happened. It's how you move on from it that makes you stronger. I realised by not crying and bottling things up, I was not allowing myself to move forward. Leon seemed almost relieved I was finally crying. He knew deep down that was what I needed. It was over now, and it was time to make our next move.

Leon had taken me back up to the room, where I had managed to get some sleep before lunch. He had then kind of forced me to go down to the hall to get something to eat. I hadn't eaten much for breakfast that morning, so I guess I needed it. I had eaten as fast as I could. There was something I wanted to do. Something I had been dying to do all day! Much to the confusion of my friends, I had hurried to finish my lunch and practically ran out of the great hall. I had gone up to my room, grabbing what I needed and shoving it in my backpack before flinging it over my shoulder. I made my way swiftly to the flying field, and down to the large pond, which was now frozen over with thick ice. Not many people in my world are accustomed to the winter weather, so the field was empty. I tossed my bag onto the ground and opened it up. I pulled out a pair of ice skates. They were designed a bit like sandals, designed to go over your normal shoes. I had two pairs. Simply because a few years ago, I had lost the pair I owned so Grandpa made me another pair because I had been so upset. Turns out, spring came and I found the old pair. Typical me. So, when I had come to the academy, I had brought both pairs of skates for fear that it would happen again. I sat down on a rock near the pond, feeling my behind becoming extremely cold. I was however used to this, and rather liked feeling the cold against my body. I put the skates on over my boots, and made sure they were fastened securely. I ran my fingers across the blades, smiling as I felt the familiar metal against my fingertips. I stood, and walked over to the pond without a problem. I placed one foot on the ice. It was stable. I felt a warmth within my heart, and I couldn't stop myself from smiling as I wasted no more time! I stepped onto the ice and began to skate with my heart. When I skated, it felt like flying. I could feel the wind in my hair and snowdrops float past my face as I performed spins and leaps, imagining a tune in my head. I had never actually skated to anyone playing music before, and I had always wanted to. At the time, I was lost in the moment. I had been skating for as long as I could remember, even though I couldn't actually remember how I first started. Every winter I would skate for hours on end upon the frozen Simmon river, and I was so glad the school had the pond I could skate on. Since the attack, this was the first time I had felt completely happy. Having a bit of normality I found was good for me. I could just skate and skate and forget about everything that was going on! I was in the middle of spinning, on one foot and leaning backwards, when suddenly I heard a round of applause. I suddenly snapped out of my trance, and steadied myself. I looked towards the side of the pond and saw Leon, Taz, Joey, Irina and Pippa all standing there! I felt myself flush red with embarrassment! How long had they been there?! I laughed nervously, starting to fiddle with the rings around my neck, not quite sure what to do. Pippa was the first to speak. "Wow Xanda, that was amazing!"

"Truly!" Leon smiled.

"You kept that quiet! Since when could you skate?!" Asked Taz.

"Um...since like...forever." I chuckled nervously, then became more mellow as I remembered something. I skated over to them. "In fact, one of my earliest memories is of my mother skating on the Simmon river, where I usually skate. It's weird...I can't even remember what she looked like...I just know it was her. My Grandma told me she was pretty good at it too."

"I'm sure she was." Irina smiled gently. I smiled back. Just thinking of my parents made me happy...all I ever wanted to do was make them proud.

"You bet!" I grinned happily. "Anyway, what are you lot doing here?"

"We were worried about you. Well, correction...Leo was worried about you. But, looks like he didn't need to be. You seem to be just fine." Taz laughed.

"H-Hey! I was just concerned." Leon blushed brightly, which made me laugh. "I must admit though, it was pretty cool watching you tear up the ice like that."

"Join me!" I beamed.

"What?"

"Awe C'mon Leo! There's another pair of skates in that bag! Don't be a wuss!" I giggled.

"Yeah, Leo, don't be a wuss!" Taz said egging him on.

"Now this I have to see!" Joey said with anticipation. Throughout this whole conversation, Leon's face just seemed to become redder by the second as he flushed with embarrassment.

"Do I have to?" Leon said rubbing the back of his head.

"You do." Pippa chuckled, pushing him towards my backpack. We were all laughing, for once forgetting about the dark things happening in the world around us. We watched as Leon pulled the skates out of the bag, looking at them.

"You must be joking! Look at how thin these blades are! I'll die!" Leon said looking terrified. We just laughed, and I couldn't help but once again think how cute he looked all wound up like that.

"Don't worry, I'll look after you!" I smiled brightly at Leon, who reluctantly sat down on the rock and fastened the skates to his boots. He pulled the straps tightly, and made sure they were fastened. His legs were visibly shaking as he stood up, and we instantly burst into laughter as Leon fell flat on his face. He wasn't even on the ice yet! He pushed himself up, and spat out some snow he had gotten in his mouth. We found the whole thing highly amusing, and after a while so did Leon. He laughed with us, as Irina hurried over and helped him to his feet. I watched him slowly as his face again turned to fear. I realised just how the tables had turned. He looked a lot like I had that day on the top of the tower. I thought how Leon had helped me conquer my fear that day...now I had to do the same for him. I held out my hand towards him. I saw him physically gulp as he put his hand in mine. I squeezed it tightly, and pulled him onto the ice. He suddenly froze up and gasped loudly, slipping. I swiftly grabbed his arms, keeping him upright. "Hey! Look at me. Just breathe...this aint nearly as dangerous as flying." I chuckled softly trying to reassure him. He looked at me like I'd told him to, and I just smiled as I explained. I began to skate backwards as I helped him forward. "Take it easy...it's just like walking. One foot in front of the other. Follow my movements...like I follow you when we're flying!"

"Y'know that's a completely different scenario, right?"

"Of course. And much more dangerous, so if you can do that, you can do this!" I smiled, and helped him skate into the centre of the frozen pond. I held both his hands so he felt safe, and after a while he began to look at ease. Slowly but surely, he was getting the hang of it. Leon's eyes widened as he realised this too, and they began to shine bright with pride.

"Xanda! Xanda look I'm doing it!" He said as excited as a child taking their first steps.

"Yup! You're a natural!" I replied as we picked up the pace. The others were cheering for Leon from the side, sounding impressed. I admit, I was impressed too. He was picking it up faster than I had expected.

"Well done Leon!" Irina cheered in encouragement.

"Awe, that looks like fun! I wanna go!" Pippa jumped impatiently. I let go of Leon's hands and skated backwards quickly, teasing him as I whisked around him.

"C'mon Leo!" I laughed as I jumped.

Leon stumbled, skating after me protesting. "That's not fair! This is my first time! Xanda!"

Upon the top of the tower, stood Mr Drogon. Unknown to us, he, Mr Ventus and Mr Davandrin were watching us from above. Drevin Drogon let out a laugh as he watched his son fall over on the ice, and he smiled seeing how much fun we were having. Jasper Ventus adjusted his dark red woolly hat, and beamed with pride.

"Kids eh." Said Ventus. "No matter how many times they get knocked down, they get right back up…just like my two."

"Two different scenarios, yet all eight of them have been to hell and still come back fighting." Mr Davandrin spoke grimly, folding his arms.

"Quite." Said Drogon, his face hardening. "I worry about my son every minute of every day. He's all I have. Yet this world is becoming more dangerous by the day, I fear that soon, things aren't going to stay peaceful."

Davandrin let out a large sigh at this, and scratched his head. "I should have listened to Alphonse and Kirani eleven years ago. Then maybe we wouldn't be here."

"Well, there's nothing any of us can do about that now, Zadlos." Said Jasper Ventus sadly. "Al was a good man. Kirani was a brave young woman. The best in our class. We all should have listened to them. But back then…it was impossible to believe."

"Not so much now." Said Drevin Drogon, not taking his eyes off us for a second. "Stephan grows stronger by the day, as does his madness. And the burden will land on their shoulders…"

"You think that the prophecy foretold by Fergo all those years ago, was referring to those two, don't you?" Said Ventus. Drevin Drogon narrowed his eyes, his vision fixated on us as we skated happily without a care in the world.

"Yes. I do."

Chapter 7
Family Ties

I was three years old that day. It was eleven years ago, but I remember it like it was yesterday. It was freezing outside, and the rain pelted the windows. The thunder roared in the sky above, and it sounded like an explosion in my tiny head. Even back then, the drab weather was fascinating to me, and I sat on the window ledge with my nose pressed up against the glass. I watched as the rain fell to the ground heavily. I had been waiting at that window every day since my mother and father had left. I didn't know where they had gone, but my father had promised they would come back soon before he'd left. So, every day I sat at the window, and waited for them to come home to me. "Xanda...sweetheart." I turned to see who had spoken to me, and it was Grandma. She looked like she had been crying, and Grandpa was behind her, his hand on her shoulder.

"Ganma...?" I said. Even at a young age, I could always tell when she was upset.

"Come and sit down with us, sweetheart..." She said sadly.

"Can't! I waiting for Mommy and Poppy!"

"Xanda...please, come and sit down darling..." My Grandfather said with a mellow tone, picking me up from the window. He carried me to the sofa, and sat me in between him and my Grandmother. As we sat down, I could tell something was wrong. It was just a vibe they were giving off, as they were both more sensitive than usual.

"Xanda...you know your mother and father love you very much..."

"Yup! They be home soon...and Mommy will have a baby and I be a big sister!" I said excitedly. Before they had gone, I had overheard my father telling my grandparents that my mother was in the early stages of pregnancy, or at least thought she was. I wasn't supposed to have known and as I mentioned this, I could see my grandparents turn pale. Knowing that I knew, only made the news they had that much more bitter.

"Xanda...your mother and father won't be coming home. They...they've gone missing." Said Grandma biting back the tears.

"Missing? But they can find the way home!" I teared up.

"No darling." Said Grandpa. "They had to go away, and now nobody can find them. It's very likely they have gone to heaven..."

"Heaven? So...I'll never see them again?"

"No sweetheart. But just remember, they'll always be with you. They won't ever truly leave. They'll watch over you from heaven and make sure your safe." As Grandma spoke, I burst into tears and they both hugged me, all three of us crying with each other. It was the worst moment of my life. All I wanted was for my mother and father to hold me and tell me everything was going to be okay. But that was not to be.

I was told they were missing, not dead. So, every day since then, I would look out of the window...and wait for them to come home. But they never did.

That was the first time I had dreamt about that day, but it did happen like that. As time went on, the time I had spent at that window became less and less, but I never forgot. Even until the day I left to come here, that morning, I had gazed out of the window, and imagined them walking up the path to come and wish me good luck. But they never did. To this day, I still didn't know why they left. I just hoped it was worth all this heartache. But, life goes on. And here I was. It was still snowing, and I was walking into town with Pippa and Irina, my boots trudging through the deep snow. I could see my breath fogging the air as I breathed. We were heading towards the Dragon's Eye pub, where the boys were waiting for us. I was deeply troubled by all these dreams I was having lately, and I thought about this as we walked. I did have dreams often, but recently they were becoming even more regular than usual.

"Xanda! You okay? You've been quiet." Said Pippa as we walked.

"Oh, yeah." I smiled back. "Sorry. Just lost in thought."

"I cannot wait for the Winter Ball!" Said Irina excitedly.

"Or me!" Pippa exclaimed. "Last year was so dull because everyone was boring. But this year, I got you two!" As she spoke, she put her arms around both of us, pulling us close. Irina giggled. I however, put on a fake smile. Not because they had upset me, I just wasn't looking forward to this ball. Not gonna lie, I was more nervous about this than I was before flying for the first time. It just wasn't my scene, and was completely out of my comfort zone. Besides, the girls would laugh if they found out I didn't own a dress. There was no point going shopping for one because I didn't know the first thing about fashion! After a short while, we approached the pub. It was made from stone, like the other buildings, but it had more of a rustic look to it. Over the front door hung a sign, with the name of the pub written below a picture of a red Dragon's eye. Pippa opened the dark wooden door, and wiped her boots on the mat. Irina and I followed in after her, and I looked around. It was very warm and cosy inside. It even had a beautiful log fire burning brightly in the corner. The tables were made from wood, like pretty much all the furniture. I scanned the room, and saw the boys sitting on a high table by the fire, sitting on high stools. There were six metal mugs on the table, filled with Dragonberry juice. Leon noticed us walk in and smiled. Taz waved to get our attention, and we moved over to them. We said hello and climbed up onto the stools. I sat next to Leon, and we smiled at each other again.

"Hiya! Hey, guess what! We got some gossip!" Joey said happily. I took a sip of my drink and raised an eyebrow curiously.

"What kind of gossip?" I asked.

"Ida McCoy is pregnant!" Said Taz.

"Oh my gosh, that's amazing news!" Said Pippa happily. Ida McCoy, you remember her, right? The young doctor that nursed me back to health. After what she did for me, I'd say she deserved some happiness.

"That's great!" I smiled. "Is she married?"

"Yeah." Said Joey. "She got married at the end of last year. She looked amazing! I mean, she's hot anyway."

"Joey! You shouldn't talk about women that way!" Leon said blushing.

"Why not? It's a compliment!" Said Joey, laughing. Just then, he froze up, and Taz waved a hand in front of his friend's face. Joey jumped down off the stool, and he grabbed the wrist of a random girl who was walking past.

"Mazei!" Joey said in desperation. The girl flinched, her brown hair flinging round as she turned. She looked startled. Joey looked at her face and he swallowed hard, letting go of her. Taz instantly jumped down off his stool and pulled Joey back. He turned to the girl, taking control of the situation.

"I'm sorry. He thought you were somebody else." I watched worriedly as the girl accepted his apology, and she left. Joey was breathing hard, and I began to wonder who this 'Mazei' was. Whoever she was, she was clearly important to Joey...he looked like he was gonna cry.

"Joey, do you wanna go?" Taz asked him quietly.

"N-No...I'm okay. I need to sit down." He said breathless. Taz helped him back up onto the stool, then sat next to him.

"Are you alright?" Leon asked in concern. Joey nodded, picking up his drink and taking a sip. I couldn't help but notice his hand shaking madly as he drank.

"Joey...I don't mean to pry but...what just happened?" I asked softly.

"I thought she was Mazei." He replied, a dull tone to his usual hyper voice.

"Your sister?" Asked Pippa, to which Joey nodded. "Oh Joey...I'm so sorry..."

"What happened to her?" Irina asked gently. Joey lowered his head, so we couldn't see the tears forming in his eyes. He was like me in that respect...he didn't like people seeing him cry.

"Its...why Joey didn't start school with me here last year..." Said Taz rubbing his friends back. "Mazei was a lovely girl. Sickly yeah...but bright and clever, and she always had a smile on her face."

"She was so proud when I got accepted here..." Joey wiped his eyes, smiling gently at her memory. "Then...just before I was due to come here, she got sick and collapsed. I nursed her with my folks, then...on this day last year...she died in my arms. Do you know what she said?! Her last words... 'live your life, big brother. Go out into the world and make me proud...and remember I will never leave you'. What was she thinking?! Oh Mazei..." He buried his face in his hands as we listened to him pour out his emotions. How tragic. Joey was always so happy, I had no idea he was going through something like this. Poor Joey...

"She sounds like an extraordinary young woman..." Said Irina smiling weakly, reaching over and placing her hand over his. Joey looked up at her, and their eyes met. He smiled back at her, nodding slowly.

"Yeah...she was."

"Joey, were all here for you." I said gently. "No matter what." The others all nodded in agreement, Taz still rubbing his back supportively.

69

"Thank you...all of you." Said Joey. "That means the world to me."

We had spent a few hours in 'The Dragon's Eye' before heading back. Joey had calmed down and was acting more like his normal self. I was glad, I didn't like seeing him upset. I had made my way back up to my room, and I started packing a bag. I wanted to go and see my Grandparents for a few days before my birthday. It was while I was in the middle of packing a small bag, when Leon walked in. He raised an eyebrow, confused. He laughed nervously as he sat on the bed next to my bag.

"What's all this?" He asked. "You're not bailing out on me, are you?"

"Of course I'm not!" I chuckled softly. "We don't have lessons for a few days before preparations for the Winter Ball starts, so I thought I'd go and visit my Grandparents."

"Let me fly you there." He said. I looked at him, a little surprised if I'm honest. I half expected him to ask me to stay.

"Really? I don't want to be a bother, Leon. Besides, there's no point you flying me there just to come all the way back."

"Can't I come and stay with you? I want to introduce myself to your Grandparents. It seems only right." He smiled. I couldn't help but think how old fashioned he sounded as he said this, but at least he was polite and had manners. My Grandpa would indeed like that.

"O-Of course you can stay!" I said surprised but happy. "As long as you don't mind sleeping on the sofa. My Grandmother doesn't like anyone sleeping in my parent's old room..."

"Not at all. I don't mind, and I completely understand. Gosh, I'm so excited now!"

"You sound like you've never been out of Algora before!" I chuckled, then looked at his face. He was smiling nervously. "You haven't, have you." I said in realisation. Leon smirked, and shook his head. "Well that makes two of us, I hadn't left Lightwater before I came here."

"Yeah, I think you mentioned it on the tower that night." He said, standing up. "I'm gonna tell my father, then come back and pack my bag!" And with that he left, practically skipping out of the room like an excited child. I laughed as he left, as I couldn't help but think how childish he had looked. He was brimming with excitement as he made for the exit, and it seemed like for once things were looking up.

I was sitting on Leon's back in his Dragon form as we flew through the air. He had been in a bad mood ever since we left. I didn't understand why his mood had suddenly changed, as he was so excited before. I had both mine and Leon's backpack on my back, and after a while it was becoming heavy. I leaned forward, resting on Leon's neck, gazing down at the world below. Finally, I plucked up the courage to strike up a conversation. "Leo..."

"Yeah?"

"Are you alright? You've hardly said a word since we left Algora." I asked.
"I guess so. My father didn't want me to come. He said it was dangerous outside the city walls. So, I said it was dangerous everywhere, and I told him I wasn't a kid anymore...then we just started arguing." He sighed.
"I see." I said pushing myself to sit upright again. "Well...I'm not surprised he's worried. He's bound to be shaken after the attack so close to the city walls. It could easily have been more than just me in the infirmary..."
"Hm. I guess you're right. He's always been overprotective of me. It gets quite annoying sometimes."
"Aint it weird how he never got re-married after your mother died? He must have really loved her..." I said softly.
"Yeah...he's never even come close to being in a relationship, and he still has a portrait of her on his desk. I often think that she's the reason he's so protective of me..."
"What was her name?" I smiled softly.
"Sera-Rose...simple, but...I like it." He said sounding a little happier.
"Me too." I patted his neck, smiling gently. "Anyway, do you mind if we land somewhere around here? It's just, the people of Lightwater aren't really used to seeing Dragons. The whole village turned up to see me leave, I don't want to attract any attention this time." I chuckled. Leon laughed back, agreeing with me. Seemed like neither of us were that good at being the centre of attention. I couldn't wait to see my Grandparents though, I had missed them so much.

"Woah!" Leon exclaimed as we walked into Lightwater village. He picked up speed as we entered, looking around in amazement. I smiled, watching some young kids playing around in the snow, throwing snowballs at each other, and people skating on the Simmon river. It appears Ice skating had become more popular this year, as there were more people than usual skating under the evening sky. Leon however, seemed more amazed at the building structure's. "Look at how cosy all these cottages look! And the Tavern looks so small!"
"It's the biggest building in the village, Leo." I chuckled. "Besides, it doesn't need to be that big. We don't get many visitors passing through, and not many people live here." Just then, a man walked out of the tavern. It was Mr Ackerman, the owner of the tavern. He had scruffy ginger hair and a beard, which hadn't been brushed, as usual. He brushed down his shirt as he shouted over to us.
"Sykes! Girl, is that you?!" He let out a loud belly laugh as he walked over. "Gawd, you look different somehow! It's a good different though!"
"Thank you Mr Ackerman!" I blushed nervously, fiddling with the rings around my neck. "Leon, this is Mr Ackerman, Miss Ackerman's Uncle. He owns the tavern. Mr Ackerman, this is my friend Leon."
"Ah! Your boyfriend?!"
"No way!" Leon and I said in unison, before looking at each other nervously

and blushing deeper.

I cleared my throat before explaining. "Leo's my partner. My Dragonbourne partner."

"Oh!" Ackerman laughed. "Well, little Leon, you'd better look after our Xanda!"

"I will, sir." Leon smiled, putting his arm around me.

"We'd best go, Mr Ackerman." I said. "Were not here for long, and I want to see my Grandparents."

"Of course! Say hi to Harry for me!" He said ruffling my hair. I pouted a little and rubbed my head after he did.

"I will. See you later." I waved a little as he walked back into the tavern.

"Hm. Seems like a nice guy." Leon smiled.

"Yeah, he is. Tell you what though, if you want any Lightwater gossip he's the guy to go to. He knows *everything!*" I chuckled.

"So, news of your return will be all around the village soon?" Leon laughed.

"Probably." I smiled, putting my arm around him too. "C'mon." So, I began to lead him towards the smithy, which was attached to the side of our home. There were no doors to Grandpa's working area, just wooden posts on the corners supporting the roof over his anvil, barrels and basins, and a table which held his equipment. Against the wall that adjoined to the house, was my Grandpa's forge, which burned brightly as we approached the smithy. Sure enough, there he was. Grandpa had a hammer in his hand and was pelting down on a piece of metal over the anvil. He looked like he was deep in thought, as he hadn't noticed me, and he usually did. He used his gloved hand to wipe the sweat off his brow, clearly working hard. I couldn't help but smile upon seeing him again...it felt like I had never left.

"Is that him?" Leon asked quietly.

"Aye...it is." I smiled brighter. Grandpa suddenly looked up, and his eyes caught mine. He let out a gasp and instantly stopped what he was doing. He put his work to the side, and started running over to me.

"Xanda!"

"Grandpa!" I shouted back to him, running towards him too. When he reached me, he immediately held me in his strong arms. Despite the chilly weather, his body was warm, and I closed my eyes as I rested my head against his chest. It was like nothing had changed. But of course, everything was changing. "Oh Grandfather...I've missed you so much!" I said finally looking up at him.

"Oh our sweet Xanda...we've missed you since the moment you left!" He smiled, placing a hand on my cheek gently. Out the corner of my eye, I then noticed a head pop up in the window. Grandma had seen me, and she instantly came running out of the house.

"Xanda! Xanda you're home!" She shouted happily, before wrapping her arms around me and Grandfather. We were there for a few more seconds, before we pulled away from each other.

She put her hand on my cheeks, smiling down at me. "Oh look at you! You look different somehow...but it's a good different! Oh, but it's good to have you home!"

"I'm happy to be home, I've missed you both! But I'm not here for long. Grandpa, Grandma, there's someone I'd like you to meet." I extended a hand towards Leon, and he moved over slowly. "This is my partner, Leon."

"How do you do." Leon bowed a little in respect, smiling politely. "It's wonderful to meet you at last! I've heard nothing but good things about you!"

"Oh, handsome and charming! Well done Xanda!" Grandma chuckled. Yet again, Leon and I found ourselves blushing and exchanging an awkward glance as my Grandparents took great delight in teasing us. Gramps chuckled at our reactions.

"Grandma! Please don't..." I covered my face with my hand in embarrassment.

"Oh sweetheart, you've gone all red!" She chuckled. "Don't worry, I won't tease you any longer. Come inside and get warm, you two. Dinner won't be too long, so get in and make yourselves comfortable."

"Thank you, Mrs Sykes!" Leon smiled gratefully.

"Oh please, Leon! Call me Beatrice." She smiled brightly, and began to usher Leon inside, practically talking his ear off. I shook my head and smiled. She seemed to have really taken a shine to him.

I watched three candles burn brightly as Leon and I sat up at the dining table. Our house was a typical cottage I guess. It was warm, comforting and homely. My Grandma took great pride in the home's appearance, so it was always tidy. My room was downstairs, while a spiral staircase at the back of the home lead up to Grandma and Grampa's room. My room was next to a small bathroom, but the rest of the house was all in one. That was except, of course, my parents old room...that nobody had entered since they went missing. The dining table was by the light, open kitchen area, and the lounge was on the other side of the cottage. The lounge consisted of a comfy three seat ruby red sofa, and my Grandfather's red armchair. Both were in front of a burning log fire.

Leon ran his fingers through the white section of his hair and smiled. "This is the smallest place I've ever stayed in. But it's also the nicest!"

"Is everything in the capital so big?" I asked.

"Pretty much. I actually really like this little place though. It's quiet, and away from trouble. Peaceful...that's the word."

"It's definitely been quiet without our Xanda." Grandpa chuckled as he shut the front door, and moved over to the kitchen sink to wash his hands.

"Oh c'mon, I don't make that much noise!" I pouted. "Anyway, what's for dinner Grandma?"

"Oh, just a stir fry, dear." She smiled.

"Sounds great, Mrs Sykes!" Leon smiled.

"Beatrice." I whispered to him, giggling.

"Sorry! Beatrice!" Leon said nervously. Grandma just laughed at how jumpy he was. I stand by what I said before. Leon really was cute when he became all flustered.

"Harry, could you get the cutlery, please?" Grandma asked Gramps. Once he had finished drying his hands on the towel, he reached into the cutlery draw and pulled out eight knives and eight forks. He placed them on the table next to us before sitting down next to Leon. Then, Grandma brought over the food and put a bowl of stir fry in front of me and Leon. She then went back and got her own food and Grampa's food, before sitting down between me and Grandpa. We were all starving, and instantly tucked into the food. It was lovely, and more like what I was used to. Not like the rich stuff in Algora, but just as tasty. Grandma always was a great cook. Me on the other hand, could burn a salad. Although I wasn't too bad at baking.

"Is everything alright with your meal, Leon?" Grandma asked.

"Yes, thank you! Its lovely!" He smiled.

"So, young man, tell us a bit about yourself." Said Grandpa striking up a conversation.

"Me?" Leon swallowed the food he had in his mouth, and took a sip of his drink. "Well, I'm from Algora. This is my first time out of the big city."

"I see. Do your parents not travel?" Asked Grandma.

"My mother died giving birth to me. My father travels sometimes though. He's the headmaster of Wyvern Academy."

"Oh, Drevin Drogon!" Said Grandpa. I narrowed my eyes, becoming curious. I looked at him. Of course, Drevin Drogon was well known, but my Grandfather had spoken like he knew him.

"Yes, that's right. Do you know him?" Leon asked, seeming to have picked up on what I had thought.

"Oh, I knew someone that knew him." He said looking at the food, trying to avoid eye contact with the pair of us. I saw Grandma shoot him a glare before continuing the conversation.

"So, how is school going?" She asked.

"Good. Although were struggling a little in partner bonding class." I sighed.

"Oh yeah! Miss Wellworn and Miss Nebilia set us this really hard task, because apparently were in the top class. Xanda and I both wrote down a word, and we have to tell each other what the word is without talking." Leon explained.

"Ah, the mind connection." Said Grandma.

"You know about that?" I asked raising an eyebrow.

"A little, yes. I was very into Dragon mythology when I was your age." She smiled. Something about how she said this though made me wonder. I finally realised how she knew so much. But she couldn't be...could she? I'd ask her about it later. The conversation went on to talk about other lessons, but I however was still deep in thought until we had finished eating. Leon pushed his plate forward and yawned.

"Boy, that was good! Thank you for your hospitality Mr and Mrs Sykes." Said Leon politely.

"Your very welcome, dear." Grandma smiled. "Are you sure you don't mind sleeping on the sofa?"

"Not at all." Leon replied.

"I'll make a spare bed to go in Xanda's room for next time you come." Said Grandpa.

"You don't have to, sir…"

"I know I don't, I want to." Grandpa smiled, standing up starting to gather our plates.

"I'll get you a blanket and some spare pillows." Said Grandma. "Is there anything else you need?"

"No, thank you. I'll be fine." Leon smiled. "Would you like help tidying up?"

"Oh, I really like you." Grandma chuckled. "No sweetheart, you both look tired. You should get some rest, leave tidying up to me. There isn't much anyway." I found myself yawning too, rubbing my eyes. I was tired. I'd sleep well tonight, that's for sure. There was a lot on my mind however, and these thoughts weighed heavily on my mind. Jeez, why did I have to be so absent minded? It was good to be home however, and I couldn't wait to be back in my own bed. Little did I know, emotions were about to run high.

Leon and I had sat in the lounge for a while. I had sat in Grandpa's armchair, and we warmed ourselves by the fire. We had talked a little bit, but I found myself drifting in and out of sleep. I woke up slowly, rubbing my brow. I stretched, sitting up in the chair and stretching. I smiled gently, seeing Leon fast asleep on the sofa. I stood, thinking it best I headed to bed before I dropped off again. I leaned over Leon and kissed his forehead, just like he had done with me while I was in the infirmary. I adjusted the blanket over him, before making my way to my room. I was so tired I forgot to close the door. I sat on my bed and pulled out a box of matches from the draw in my bedside table, and used the lighted match to light a candle. I kicked off my boots and let out a yawn. Just then, I looked up into the doorway, seeing my Grandparents enter the room. I wondered what they were doing here, since I had thought they'd already gone to bed a while ago. They were smiling down at me, Grandma holding a small paper bag. I smiled back at them. "What's this?" I asked.

"Your birthday present." Grandma smiled as she held it out to me. "We wanted to give it to you in person. And since we won't see you on your birthday, we wanted to give it you now."

"Happy birthday sweetheart." Said Grandpa. I took the bag and opened it up. Inside was a portrait in a wooden picture frame, and I pulled it out to see what it was. I felt my heart stop for a moment, and my eyes teared up in an instant. I covered my mouth with my hand, in complete shock. This was the first time I had looked upon my parents faces for as long as I could remember. My father had his arms around my mother, and he had a cheeky looking face. My mother looked so happy with him. My father had blue eyes, and my mother had dark, but piercing green eyes. I had one eye from both of my parents. I smiled, knowing there was a reason my eyes were so weird. My father had golden hair like me, but a shade darker and it stuck out wildly. My mother had long, flowing light blue hair, and she looked confident and strong.

"Where did you get this...?" I asked on the brink of tears.

"The original was painted many years ago. It's much bigger than this one...I asked a mage, an old friend to copy it onto this smaller parchment for you..." said Grandpa. My smile suddenly vanished when I listened to what he said. All these years, there was an original painting of them? I narrowed my eyes, looking at them sharply.

"Where's the original?" I asked.

"We...we don't know." Grandma stuttered.

"But you do. I know you do!" I stood, getting a little angry. "Just like I know you're a Dragonbourne!" They froze up on hearing that, which indicated to me that I was right. My Grandma was a Dragonbourne all along.

"How long have you known...?" She asked nervously.

"I've had my suspicions for a while, but honestly, just now at dinner." I took a deep breath, before speaking again. "Look, I am so grateful to you both for raising me. I couldn't ask for better Grandparents. You're amazing, both of you! But you gotta start being honest with me! I'm not a baby anymore! Why did you never tell me about you being Dragonbourne?! And what's more, why did my parents leave in the first place?! If they loved me so much like you say, then why did they go?!"

"Xanda please!" Said my Grandfather, holding my Grandmother close as she began to tear up. "You don't understand!"

"Then help me too! Alphonse was your son! Wouldn't he want you to tell me the truth?! Please...whatever the truth is, I can handle it!" It was then Grandma burst into tears, clearly thinking about her son as she ran out of the room. Grandpa didn't know where to put himself at first, but he took one look at me before running after Grandma. I sat back down on the bed, looking at the portrait. I found myself beginning to cry too, and lay down on the bed. I ran my fingers down the picture, then drew it close to my chest, hugging it tightly. I cried myself to sleep that night...and despite being home, I had felt more alone than ever.

Until that day, I had forgotten what my parents had looked like. I had missed out on so much...I wanted to see Alphonse and Kirani Sykes so badly, and it hurt more than anything in the world to know that would never happen...

Chapter 8
Xanda in a Dress

The winter sun was rising in the east, yet it was still freezing cold. I was up early, skating on the Simmon river like I had done many times before. The bitter air stung my fingertips, and my cheeks flushed a rosy red. I didn't notice how cold it was though, as I dug my toe pick into the ice and performed a triple loop jump. I felt the wind in my face as I twirled through the air, before landing steadily. I had been there for hours, yet I still wasn't tired. I hadn't gotten much sleep the night before though. I was too busy worrying about the altercation I'd had with my grandparents. I often did wonder why they refused to talk about my mother and father. Was it something they did? Or was it just too painful to talk about? I still wasn't sure. I wasn't sure if I'd ever know the answer. But I wanted to. I deeply wanted to know about them, even if what I heard was bad! At least I'd have some closure about where I came from. It wasn't fair, at least not in my opinion. The thought made me mad, and I carved up the ice with my blades as I began to skate faster. Just then I found myself coming to an abrupt stop as I saw a figure walking towards me. I sighed, skating over to the side as I watched Leon come over and stand on the bank of the frozen river. He smiled gently at me as we finally met each other.

"Morning." I smiled weakly.

"Good morning. You uh...look pretty fierce this morning. On the ice, I mean."

"Ugh...don't worry, I feel it." I stepped off the ice and sat down on a wooden bench on the riverside, and Leon sat next to me. I leaned down to unfasten my skates from my boots.

"Are you alright? I overheard your grandparents talking this morning about apologising to you or something..." He said softly. I stopped for a moment, sighing heavily. I reached down to the side of the bench where I had left my bag, and dipped my hand into it. Slowly, I pulled out the framed picture of my parents and handed it to Leon. He took it carefully and was silent, not quite knowing what to say. Not that I blamed him.

"They gave this to me last night." I stated, picking up my bag and putting my skates away. Leon just turned to look at me, a soft look in his eyes. It was a look of empathy.

"Is this..."

"Yeah." I said before he could finish. "I can't believe it took them fifteen years to give this to me."

"You've never seen this before?" he said a little surprised. "Wow, and I thought my father was secretive."

"I know they're only trying their best and trying to spare my feelings." I said sadly. "But it hurts more when they don't tell me anything!"

"Tell me." Leon said suddenly.

"What?" I looked at him in confusion.

"Tell me what you remember of them. I never knew my mother, considering she died giving birth to me. You knew your folks for three years. I know you probably don't remember much...but I'd like to hear what you do remember."

He smiled.

"Well…I admit this picture has stirred up some old memories." I smiled back. "My father used to throw me up in the air and catch me. I loved it, but it scared my mother half to death." We chuckled softly, and Leon put his arm around me. I found myself resting my head on his shoulder. He was warm, and I felt comfortable against him.

"He sounds like quite a daredevil." Said Leon.

"Yeah. He sure looks it on that picture…" I said, a hint of sadness in my voice as the two of us looked back at the picture in Leon's hand.

"I know, right! He looks proper cheeky!" Leon laughed, and I laughed with him.

"That's what I thought when I saw it! C'mon Leo, tell me about your father. What's he like away from the academy?"

"Believe it or not…he's really caring." Leon smiled gently. "I'd imagine the complete opposite of your father, as in he doesn't really joke around. He's serious when it comes to the kids' progression at the academy. He genuinely cares about every one of his students. I guess that's why he's so respected. He doesn't often crack a joke, but he cares about the people around him, and would protect them with his life." He sounded amazing, I admit. And it made me miss my parents even more. It made me sad to think of how much I had missed out on, but at the end of the day, I had a good upbringing. I couldn't fault the way my Grandparents had brought me up.

"He sounds a lot like my Grandfather." I said sadly. "We should head back. I need to apologise. Yeah, they kept this from me, but they gave me years of their life. I've been selfish…"

"That depends on how you look at it." Said Leon as I sat up straight. "But I'm your partner. So, whatever you wanna do, I'll support you. You and me, whatever happens from now on, the two of us do it together. Agreed?" With this he held out his hand, just like he had done when he asked me to be his partner. A grin spread across my face and I nodded confidently. I took his hand tightly and I felt a spark inside me, like our souls were connecting once again.

"Agreed."

So, we headed back to my Grandparent's house, where we could smell the sweet sensation of bacon wafting through the windows before we'd even got inside. Leon opened the door for me, and I smiled nervously walking in first. I had to hand it to Leon, despite his faults, he was a proper gentleman. I saw my Grandma at the stove, and she smiled gently as we came in. Grandpa was up the table already, reading a book of some sort. He looked up from the book nervously as we came in. One thing he hated was conflict, and I could see he was worried it would all kick off again.

"Morning, you two!" Said Grandma. "How does bacon sandwich sound for breakfast?"

"Wonderful, Mrs Sykes! It smells great!" Leon walked over to the table excitedly, followed by me. Grandma watched us, and her expression shifted to become more solemn as she spoke.

"Xanda, about last night..."

"I owe you both an apology." I said sadly. "You've both done so much for me, I shouldn't have pushed you like I did. I'm sorry." Grandpa sighed heavily and put his book down.

"Xanda...Leon...sit down." He said. Leon and I exchanged a glance before sitting down at the table. Grandpa cleared his throat before speaking again.

"We didn't mean to upset you, Xanda. It's just...very hard to talk about your parents. Especially for your Grandmother. We loved Alphonse with all our heart...and we loved Kirani too, so very much." He spoke with a quiver in his voice, and I could tell his words were true. I teared up, but tried to hide my emotions from them. I didn't want to upset them again more than necessary.

"Why did they have to go?" I asked slowly.

"They went to Eruznor." Said Grandma as she turned the bacon, not even able to look at me. "I don't know why. Alphonse wouldn't say. But he had this...strange look in his eye before he left. I knew it was important, so I didn't try and stop them. Kirani would never have taken no for an answer anyway." She smiled weakly. "So, they left. And they never came back."

"Do you think they ran away?" I asked as a tear trickled down my cheek. I wiped it away quickly.

"Absolutely not." Said Grandpa sharply, and I could tell he strongly believed that. "Your parents may have been young when they had you, a mere age of seventeen to be exact when you were born. But Kirani had suspicions she was carrying another child just before she left. And you...oh Xanda...your mother and father loved you more than life itself. You were their world. Everything they did, was for you. So, do I think they intended to come back? Of course I do. I may not know what happened to them, but I know my son. And my Alphonse wouldn't leave you without a father intentionally. I don't know if we'll ever find out what happened to them, but I hope it was worth it. I hope...I hope it was worth this pain I feel in my heart every morning knowing my son isn't in his bedroom. The pain I feel on his birthday, knowing I can't give him a hug and tell him how proud I am of him, and of you. He was a brave man. Foolish, but brave. And I love him. And I miss him, so very much."

"Grandpa..." I couldn't stop the tears from flowing as he spoke, and he was crying too. I reached over and threw my arms around him, crying into his chest. Grandma came over, and she held us both in her gentle arms. The way my Grandfather had spoken touched my heart fiercely. He was a true man. I had so much respect for him after speaking the way he had. It was clear to me that he and Grandma had adored their son, and couldn't understand why he didn't come home. And after hearing the story, neither could I. Alphonse Sykes didn't seem like the type of man to abandon the people he loved. I knew something had happened to them...the question is, what?

We had said a tearful farewell that morning. I knew my Grandma and Gramps needed some space, so we decided to head back to the academy. Besides, we all had things to think about. We were in our room, unpacking in silence. Everything my Grandparents had told me was just going around and around in my head. I finally pulled the picture of my parents out of the bag. I looked at it for a moment, smiling gently.

"Leo, do you mind if I put this on our dressing table?" I asked.

"Of course you can." He smiled. He watched me walk over to the dressing table, and I placed it on the right-hand side carefully.

"Hey, didn't you say you had a picture of your mother? You should put it on the other side."

"Yeah, I think I will." He smiled. "Say, you've been quiet since we left Lightwater. Are you still thinking about what they said?"

"Yeah. Its playing on my mind a bit..."

"Answer me this." Leon walked over and put his hands on my arms, making me look at him. I knew he wanted an honest answer from me. Leo could always tell if I was lying anyway. "Do you think your parents are still alive?" He asked. Now this I had given a lot of thought too.

"Honestly, I've no idea. If I had to guess, I'd say they were dead. From what Grandma and Gramps said about them, they had every intention of coming home. They didn't. I can't help but think the worst happened."

"It makes sense, but the circumstances are suspicious." Leon said scratching his head.

"What do you mean?"

"Your Grandma said they went to Eruznor, right? That was eleven years ago, the same time King Stephan came to the throne. The people loved the old king. When King Octavan of Brozanta died, the throne should have gone to his son, Lucas. And instead, Octavan's brother, Stephan came to power. Nobodies heard from Lucas since. And many think that Stephan is...slippery. Nobody had suspicions at the time, but after he ascended the throne, many started to wonder whether he assassinated his own brother."

"Grandma did say that my father was acting weird before he left." I said. "You're not suggesting that my parents thought something like that was going to happen?"

"I don't know. I'm just saying it's a possibility. We can't make assumptions like that until we know the truth. But yes, I do think your parents went there for more than just a holiday." Said Leon. It went quiet again for a moment, before the door burst open. We looked round to see Joey and Taz hurry in, followed by Pippa and Irina.

"Leo! Welcome home you wazzock!" Taz grinned as he grabbed Leon in a headlock and started rubbing his hair with his fist.

"What the hell is a wazzock?! Taz stop it!" Leon said struggling. The girls and

I just laughed as Joey poked Leon to torment him.

"That's just Taz's way of saying welcome home!" Joey grinned.

"We missed you two!" Irina said sweetly.

"Jeez Irina, we've only been gone for a day." I chuckled. "So, what have we missed?" Taz let Leon back up, and the boy ran over to the mirror desperately trying to sort out his messed-up hair.

"We've started putting up the decorations in the Great Hall! It's amazing!" said Pippa excitedly.

"I see you got some new decorations too." Said Joey as he looked at the portrait of my parents on the dressing table. "Who's the good looking blue haired gal?"

"My mother." I said, grinning a little as I could see him blush uncomfortably.

"Josef! What have I told you about talking about women so brashly?!" Leon said sharply.

"It's fine, Leo. Besides, she was very pretty." I smiled gently.

"Speaking of appearances, come and see our dresses for the ball!" said Pippa joyfully, grabbing my arm. Irina giggled softly and shook her head, following as her cousin dragged me out of my room. Irina turned to leave, her beautiful hair waving behind her as Joey's gaze followed her, his eyes soft and loving.

Irina and Pippa's room had all the things my room did, only it was laid out a little differently. Its colour scheme was also different to ours. While our room was decorated red, the girls' room was decorated in a beautiful deep shade of pink. I admit, it rather suited them. Unlike me, they were very girly. I walked over to their wardrobes, instantly noticing a beautiful dress hung upon each one of them. The first dress had a beautiful white diamond encrusted torso, which glittered majestically. There was only one sleeve, and the diamonds sparkled all the way down it. The dress skirt's colour softly changed from white to a fantasia purple as it reached the tip. The dress was short at the front, but long at the back. The other dress was short, only reaching knee length, and it was a beautiful shade of rose pink. The top rim was decorated with pure white roses, and there was a silky white sash around the waist. I could tell instantly the pink dress was Irina's. Somehow, I could just picture her wearing it. I smiled at how beautiful they looked. I had never seen such elegant dresses before, but as a child I had often pictured myself owning one. I touched the pink dress, feeling the silky fabric against my skin. I smiled brightly. "They're both beautiful…"

"That one is mine." Irina smiled gently. "I've only worn it once before, but it's one of my favourites!"

"I love them." I smiled weakly, stepping back.

"What are you wearing, Xanda?" Pippa asked. I swallowed hard. I knew I had to admit that I didn't have anything to wear. They both looked at me in anticipation.

"Um…I…don't actually own a dress…"

"What?!" They both exclaimed in surprise.

"I grew up in a smithy. I never had a need for one!" I said, blushing bright with embarrassment. "I've never even been to a ball before..."

"That's crazy!" Pippa chuckled softly. "C'mon."

"Where are we going?" I asked curiously.

"Where do you think?! Irina and I are taking you into town to have a look at some dresses!"

"What's the point?" I said. "I couldn't afford one even if I wanted to buy one."

"There's no harm in looking to see what type you like." Irina smiled brightly.

"You're coming whether you like it or not!" Pippa chuckled, grabbing my arm once again and pulling me out the room without a choice. She was starting to make a habit of that...

And so, yet again, we headed out into the snowy town as the girls led me towards the dress emporium. Jeez, I never thought I'd say that. They were walking a few steps ahead of me, deep in an enthusiastic conversation. Something else was on my mind though. As we passed several shops, I began to wonder what I should get Leo for his birthday. I tell you, he was a difficult person to buy for. I just had no idea what to get for him. Perhaps something he could wear at the ball? I didn't know what sort of things he liked. What do you get for the infamous son of Wyvern Academy's headmaster? I was instantly pulled out of my thoughts though as Pippa and Irina turned to face me.

"So, what do you think, Xanda?" Pippa said suddenly.

"What?" I had been so deep in thought I hadn't heard any of their conversation.

Irina just chuckled. "Were you listening? What's on your mind?" She smiled.

"Sorry. I was just thinking about what to get Leon for his birthday." I told them.

"Last year, Taz and I brought him a jack in the box. Obviously, they're not that common and it scared the living daylights out of him." Pippa laughed. I admit, I laughed too at the image in my head. I had only seen one once, when I was much younger. A traveller had one in Ackerman's tavern, and he had shown it to me. He only passed through our village once though, I had never seen him again.

"Here we are!" Pippa exclaimed excitedly. The shop looked pretty small from the outside, and it was situated on a corner. It had a bright rosy red door, and lovely wooden window frames. I craned my neck over to look inside, and saw all the beautiful dresses lined up on a wooden rack. From what I could see they looked exquisite! There was no way in hell I was gonna be able to afford any of these! What was the point in bringing me here? They knew I was only a blacksmith. I wasn't rich like them. Pippa and Irina's family's industry was fashion. In fact, it wouldn't surprise me if they owned the shop we were about to go into. Irina opened the door first and entered, followed by Pippa, and finally myself. The place had a weird smell to it, but it was a nice smell. It was sweet and very homely inside, and all the dresses were either neatly on a rack or displayed on a mannequin. They were all dresses for special occasions, and they were all brightly coloured and most were very regal and elaborate. The walls were covered in portraits of women wearing some of their dresses, and I must say they all looked incredible! I could never imagine myself looking that pretty. Irina and Pippa were in their element, already darting around the shop and admiring all sorts of dresses. I walked around the shop, sighing heavily. Irina turned to me and pulled a long, pink dress off a rack. The thing was hideous, and contained more ruffles than I even thought possible.

"Xanda! How about this?" Irina smiled.

"No offence, but no way. I wouldn't be seen dead in that! And don't you even suggest that one!" I said a little more frustrated, looking over at Pippa who held a very revealing dress in her hands. "I have no breasts as it is, I don't need the whole school knowing!"

"Chill!" Pippa laughed, putting the dress back. "Just relax! We have plenty of time. This is supposed to be enjoyable, not stressful!"

"I don't feel joyful. All of this feels really out of place...I mean, for me anyway..." I sighed. Irina smiled encouragingly, and placed a hand on my shoulder gently.

"So was joining the Academy, but you did that wonderfully! Now let's see...you wear a lot of blue. Maybe a blue dress? Hmm...what's your favourite colour, Xanda?" Irina asked.

"Green." I said simply. "Although I'm not sure green suits me."

"Nonsense!" Pippa grinned. "C'mon Irina. Let's focus on looking for blue or green dresses!" And with that, the two of them were hurrying around the shop, browsing through the dresses.

A while passed, and to be honest all I did was wonder around the shop completely aimlessly. I didn't know what to look for or even what sort of dresses I liked. I wasn't too keen on the longer ballgowns, even though I knew most of the girls in my class were wearing a longer dress. I didn't think a long dress would suit someone as short as I was. Irina and Pippa looked like they went shopping for dresses like this all the time, and their eyes were brimming with enthusiasm. Every dress they had shown me though, I hadn't liked at all. Just then, I found it. The perfect dress! It was at the back of the shop, on a simple mannequin. A beautiful, dark, royal red dress. It was short, the bottom reaching just above the knees. The sleeves were long, perfect to hide the scars on my arms from the attack. Fabric draped over the top of the arms and chest, and the edge of it was decorated in beautiful golden lace. There was another golden pattern in the shape of small leaves and roses running down the centre of the torso and wrapping around the waist magically. I just found myself staring at it, a little upset knowing it was way out of my price range. There was no way I had enough gold pieces to afford it. Pippa and Irina had spotted me looking at it, and the two of them came and stood behind me.

"Do you like this one?" Irina asked softly.

"I love it…" I smiled weakly, placing my hand on the soft fabric. "But… I can't afford something like this." I looked down sadly. Irina and Pippa started whispering behind me, but I hadn't noticed at the time. I took my hand off it, and began to head towards the exit trying not to look at the dress.

"Where are you going?!" Pippa asked.

"Out. Before I see something else I can't afford." I chuckled softly, trying to sound more light-hearted about the whole situation. I had never cared much for material things, but for some reason my heart sank. Part of me now wanted to go to the ball. I wanted to feel beautiful for once in my life…but alas, I knew it wasn't to be.

I let out a huge sigh as I breathed in the winter air. I had stepped outside the shop, thinking Pippa and Irina were following. It took me a few moments to realise they weren't, and I looked back through the window to see them both talking to one of the shop girls. I couldn't make out what it was about, but I didn't really care. I was pretty upset. I felt like the poorest person at the school, even though I knew I probably wasn't. I had always been so grateful for what I had, so for me to want something like this was very unlike me. I leaned against the wall, sighing once again as I watched the light snow float towards the ground. It was then I noticed a jewellers across the road. Now I know, I said I don't wear much jewellery, and I don't. But the particular piece I had seen in the shop window, I had in mind for someone else. I slowly made my way over to the window, and on display was a silver necklace, for just twenty gold pieces. It was in the shape of a flying Dragon with a female rider. The rider had her hair in a ponytail, and it reminded me of Leon and myself. I had noticed that there weren't many male Dragon and female rider partners at the academy. A lot were either the same gender, or a female Dragonbourne with a male rider. So to me, this necklace was instantly special to me. A huge smile spread across my face, and I had no hesitation that this was the perfect present for Leon's birthday.

We had gotten back just in time for supper, and the girls and I had headed straight for the Great Hall to have something to eat. After the day I'd had, I was starving! At least I had a present for Leo, so that was one thing off my mind. Pippa and Irina had cheered me up, and we were laughing happily as we entered the hall. The two of them made their way over to our table, but I had stopped. I found myself looking back up at the stained-glass window behind the teacher's table. Something clicked. The man riding the green

Dragon in the window…the man looked like my father.

Chapter 9

On a Winters Night

The day of the ball was fast approaching, and it wasn't long before it was only a day away. We had spent time around lessons helping with the ball preparations, but the day before we had spent the entire day helping. Classrooms had been transformed into places where food and drink could be placed, so the great hall could be free of tables. The tables hadn't been moved yet though, as we still all needed to eat supper. And that's where we were. We sat at our usual table, tucking into the food in front of us. I ate slowly, looking up a few times at the stained-glass window. The more I looked at it, the more the boy in the glass seemed to resemble my father. I hadn't mentioned anything to Leon about my suspicions though, although by the way he was looking at me he had probably figured it out on his own. We had stopped eating for a moment, when Mr Davandrin raised his voice and asked everyone if a few people would stay behind after dinner to help move the tables out of the hall so the band could bring in their instruments the next morning. People soon carried on eating after he had finished his announcement, especially Taz and Joey, who ate like a horse. Irina watched them and chuckled sweetly, gazing at Joey.

"Somebody's hungry tonight." She smiled at him. Joey swallowed hard, his cheeks flushing pink as he spoke nervously.

"Y-Yeah. Ventus had me, Taz and the twins climbing up ladders all day. You'd think he could just turn into a Dragon and do it himself!"

"I'd be terrified to transform in here in case I destroyed anything!" Said Pippa. "Then we wouldn't have a ball! Gee, I'm so excited!"

"Me too. Not so much about the dancing. I'm just going for the food." Taz grinned.

"That's it, now I'm gonna make you dance with me!" Pippa grinned back wider, to which Taz blushed even brighter than Joey. I just laughed at how awkward they could turn a conversation.

"Well, I hope you all have fun." I smiled weakly.

"What's that supposed to mean?" Leon asked.

"You're not coming?" Irina said sadly.

"No. I'm not. I...I got nothing to wear. Besides, it's not really my scene." I said, trying to sound like I wasn't bothered about going, although it was pretty obvious I was. The others just turned to each other and grinned, even Leon. This really confused me. Were they happy I wasn't going? That just made my heart sink more. They didn't protest about me not going either, which was very out of character for all of them. Did they know something I didn't? Leon covered his mouth as he yawned.

"Well, we all have a big day tomorrow. I'm gonna head to bed." Leon said standing.

"Yeah, we won't be far behind you." Said Taz. "I'm shattered."

Leon turned to me, running his hand tiredly through his hair. "You coming up now, or staying down here for a while?" He asked me. To be honest, my old wounds were starting to hurt after the day I'd had, and I was so tired. I stood too.

"Nah, I'll come up with you. Goodnight guys, see you in the morning." I smiled softly as the others wished us goodnight. Leon and I headed out of the hall, and once again, I found myself looking back at the window. Was I going mad? Or was the image Alphonse Sykes himself? If it was, what was it doing here? The hair colour matched the portrait. Even the eye colour matched. Was it just a coincidence, or was this who I thought it was?

Leon and I had made our way back up to our room, both of us exhausted. However, neither of us were able to sleep. Leon had climbed down off the top bunk, and we were both sitting on my bed, leaning against the wall with pillows behind our head to stay comfy. We had also draped ourselves under the blanket, making us feel warm and cosy. We simply sat there and watched the snow fall from the star filled sky. I rested my head on Leon's shoulder and he put his arm around me, pulling me close to keep me warm. I felt safe with him. We'd only been together a short time, yet we'd been through so much already. As cringe worthy as it sounds, it felt like fate had brought us together. I looked up at Leo, sleep washing over me. I began to feel drowsy, but I remember exactly what I said.

"Leo, have I ever told you how amazing you are?"

"What?!" He said, very taken aback. "What's brought this on?"

"Just the way you've stood by me even after getting beat up. Some people wouldn't have done that."

"Xanda, c'mon. I told you. We are partners. Whatever happens, we're in this together. Besides, I think your pretty awesome too." He said softly, looking down at me.

"Seriously?" I said, feeling a little more awake.

"Seriously." He replied. "Not many people would take a beating like that and choose to get back up. What you did was brave. And that's why you're such a cool partner."

"We are cool." I joked, giggling softly.

"That we are." Leon giggled back, very light heartedly.

"By the way Leo, I have something to give you. I don't think we'll have much time tomorrow so I wanna give you your birthday present now."

Leon's mouth turned into a soft smile as I reached under my pillow. "Oh, Xanda, you didn't have to get me anything."

"I know. I wanted to." I pulled out a small box from under my pillow and handed it to him. He took it carefully, and opened it. His smile widened, and he gazed down at the Dragon and rider necklace I had brought him a few days ago.

"Woah...I love it! Thank you!" He suddenly pulled me into a hug, which startled me as I wasn't expecting it. I let out a nervous chuckle and hugged him back before he pulled away.

"You're very welcome." I smiled, then my tone became rather mellow. "Leo..."

"Yeah?"

"We need to be ready, Leon." I said, suddenly turning serious. "I have a really bad feeling all of this will resurface soon."

"Alright. I believe you. We'll be ready. I don't know what Adamski Thorne and Hendrix Montgomery wanted last time, but whatever it is, I admit I've been wondering if they'll come back for it. I don't think the attack was random. They asked you about the cities defences for a reason. Jeez, I'm starting to sound like my father..." He chuckled softly, rubbing the back of his head. I had to agree, he was starting to sound like Drevin Drogon. They were definitely more alike than Leon had previously made out. He did have a point though. I hadn't thought about it until Leon had mentioned it, but it had seemed like the Brozantan attackers had been after something. The question was, what? There were so many questions unanswered, so many things we didn't yet understand. Leon and I had become silent, as we were both deep in thought about the conversation. I knew we were both on the same page, and we were thinking along similar lines. However, it wasn't long before sleep had beaten both of us, and we slowly drifted into a deep, deep slumber...

"Happy Birthday!!!" Leon and I bolted awake as the sound of our friends shouting rang in our ears. We sat up quickly as the others laughed at our shocked faces. Leon rubbed the sleep out of his eyes, and I ran my fingers through my golden hair.

"Awe man...!" I whined, also rubbing my eyes and yawning. It always had taken me a while to wake up in the morning.

"Rise and shine, Xanda!" Joey grinned, ruffling my hair roughly.

"Hey!" I smacked his hand off, adjusting my hair again. Jeez, I hated when people messed with my hair. Joey just laughed, and looked at Taz.

"You two looked cosy!" Taz grinned at Joey. The girls began sniggering between themselves, which just made Leo and I turn bright red. I admit, the situation did look suspicious, but we also knew what Taz and Joey were like. They weren't going to drop this anytime soon.

"K-Knock it off, you two!" Leon sighed heavily, a little wound up.

"Awe, cheer up, birthday boy!" Pippa giggled. "Todays a celebration! And allow us to be the first to give you your present!"

"Sorry, Xanda beat you to it." He grinned.

"Dammit!" Pippa said playfully.

"Just open your damn present!" Joey chuckled, handing Leon a medium sized box. Leon sat up straight, and took the box slowly. He looked cautious as he began to open it.

"If this is another jack in the box I'm gonna kill you all." He laughed a little as he opened the box. He smiled, sighing a little in relief as he looked down at a brand new, golden broach in the shape of a Dragon, with bright Emeralds in place of the Dragon's eyes. There were also some golden cufflinks, with emeralds perfectly inserted into the centre. Leo smiled and looked up at the others. "Thanks a lot guys, these are really cool!"

"Will you wear them tonight?" Irina asked politely.

"Of course!" Leon smiled at her reassuringly. "I really like them. Thank you all so much." Everyone then turned to look at me, and Leon smiled at me brightly. I felt a little uncomfortable, not sure where to put myself. "We got a special present for you." Leon said simply.

"M-Me?!" I blushed in surprise, my heart feeling light. I bit my lip, becoming very excited, like I was a little kid again.

"Yes, you!" Taz laughed.

"Come on! It's in our room!" Pippa said excitedly, pulling me off the bed by my arm.

"I can't wait to see your face! You're going to love it!" Irina said, grabbing my other arm as they pulled me out of the room.

"Guys, slow down!" I laughed happily, brimming with anticipation, wondering what it was they could possibly have gotten me. I hadn't expected anything, so it was a bit of a shock. Pippa giggled childishly, positioning herself behind me and covering my eyes with her hands. She pushed me forward, helping me into her bedroom as the others followed. She stopped in front of the bed, and I couldn't contain my excitement.

"What is it?!" I said impatiently.

"The more you whine, the longer you have to wait!" Joey teased.

"One, two…three!" Pippa removed her hands from my eyes, and I felt my heart rate pick up. I couldn't believe what was lying before me on the bed! I covered my hand with my mouth, as I gazed upon the beautiful red dress I had seen in the shop! There were also white tights with it, and some thick heeled, ankle high boots. They had gotten me an entire outfit for the ball! I found myself welling up, completely overwhelmed. I was lost for words, and the others began to exchange worried looks as they watched me just stand there gawking and in tears.

"I-I'm sorry Xanda…don't you like it anymore?" Irina asked nervously.

"No, I…I love it! I can't believe you all did this!" I turned to face them, and suddenly pulled Leo and Irina into a hug. "Thank you all so so much!"

"Group hug!" Taz grinned as he and Joey practically dived into the hug, as did Pippa. I was so happy! I had the most amazing friends I could ever ask for! This was so wonderful, and meant so much to me. I couldn't believe they would do this for me, and I felt like the luckiest person in the world! This was the best birthday ever! It seemed that I was going to the ball after all!

We spent all afternoon getting ready for the ball. Correction, I spent the afternoon just sitting there while Irina and Pippa helped me with my curlers and make-up. I had never done either of those things in my life. My Grandma had used curlers before, but I had never tried them. I'd never really had a need to. The curlers were tight and pulled on my head as my hair was wrapped around them. I looked in the dressing table mirror, thinking just how silly I looked. I was getting ready in Pippa and Irina's room, while the boys got ready with Leon in my room. To be honest I couldn't see why it would take lads long to get ready anyway. I mean, surely all they had to do is get dressed and maybe brush or spike their hair a bit? We could hear them laughing loudly next door. They sounded like they were having fun, whatever it was they were doing. I just hoped that they weren't making the room untidy after I'd spent ages the day before cleaning it. Pippa came over, and I turned to face her. Great, she had a make-up bag in her hand.

"Right, sit still!" Pippa grinned.

"C'mon, do I really have to wear make-up?" I protested.

"Yes!" Irina chuckled as she finished putting the curlers in her own hair.

"Fine." I sighed, giving up. I knew I wasn't gonna win. I watched Pippa as she put her make-up bag on the dressing table, and began to take things out of it. I hardly knew what any of it was, but she knew what she was doing so I just let her get on with it. She pulled out a soft pad and began to plaster this powder over my face. I closed my eyes, not being used to this at all. I had no idea what I was supposed to do.

"Just relax!" Pippa laughed. "It won't kill you."

"Sorry..." I smiled weakly, trying to calm down and release the tension in my body. I was becoming incredibly nervous. As I've said before, I'd never been to an event like this. I didn't know how to act or behave, nor did I know proper etiquette, and I was the most common speaking person at the school that I knew of. If I'm honest, I was worried about fitting in. But, why should I? I hadn't tried to fit in so far, and I was doing okay just being who I was. Maybe that was the solution, and I was just overthinking and overcomplicating things. It was my birthday, so I figured I should just focus on having a good night.

"So, what happened last night?" The girls looked at each other as they giggled. I swallowed hard and opened my eyes, feeling my stomach turn upside down.

"I-It wasn't what it looked like!" I stuttered. "We just got talking and fell asleep. That's all there is to it!"

"Riiiiiight." The girls said in unison, teasing me. I swear, they could be as insistent as Joey and Taz. They knew I was telling the truth. They were just sniggering slyly, like a sly fox trying to sniff out information. It was obvious they were just acting like this to wind me up.

"Well, if nothing happened, then answer this." Irina smiled brightly, pulling a chair up next to me. "Do you like him?" I took a while to answer. My throat felt heavy, like there was a rock in it. I wasn't sure, to be honest. Did I like him? Every time he was mentioned my stomach felt weird, like it was filled with butterflies. Was this how you felt when you 'liked someone'? Either way, I wasn't gonna tell them that. I didn't wanna admit the way I was feeling. I wasn't sure why at the time. I'm still not sure why. I guess I was just embarrassed.

"No. No we're just friends! And we're partners. I admit we are pretty close, but no…we're just friends. It's better that way…" I smiled sadly.

"If you say so." Pippa smiled. "Although I admit…you are cute together!"

"S-Shut up!" I blushed brightly as the two laughed. I wasn't sure if Pippa actually meant what she said or not, although it did make me blush. It didn't matter, I wasn't interested in romance. It never got my parents anywhere. No matter how much people say they loved me or loved each other, it still didn't end well for them, whatever had happened. Even if I did like Leon, I was so scared something would happen. I didn't wanna end up like my mother and father, having a family and then just breaking it. It probably sounds harsh and selfish, but that's how it felt to me. I was the only one in Lightwater without a parent. I would never want to do that to my own kids. Just the thought of liking someone stirred up these thoughts. I had decided long ago, I was gonna skip the whole dating thing. Life would be simpler that way. No hurt. No heartbreak. No feelings or emotions. Nobody letting you down. I was kicking myself for thinking this way, yet I agreed with myself at the same time! Clearly, I was heading into my crazy mixed up teenage years. I just hoped I wasn't gonna get too moody, like my friend back home had a few years ago when she was sixteen. I'm rambling, I know. But I remember this thought process like it was just yesterday. And I also remember the events that unfolded that fateful night…

I was finally ready. Pippa and Irina had left the room, thinking I was behind them. But I had to stop in front of the mirror. I couldn't believe how I looked. I hardly recognised myself! I smiled warmly, seeing my hair perfectly curled and flowing beautifully. The dress fit perfectly, and I couldn't help but think how much thinner my legs looked in those tights and heeled boots. It was the first time I had ever thought of myself as beautiful. It was the first time I had ever fully respected myself. And it was the first time I felt confidence in my appearance. I could have cried, but I didn't because I knew it would ruin my make-up. I heard Pippa call me from out the room, and I swiftly hurried out. I was filled with nerves, but now I was rather excited. I mean, what could possibly go wrong?

We made our way down the corridor, and to the grand staircase. I stopped behind the wall, watching Pippa and Irina go first. I heard Joey wolf whistle as the girls made their way down, Irina blushing brightly. Pippa giggled happily, Taz taking her hand as she reached him. Nothing had happened between the two of them, but they were very close. They often hung out together when they weren't with Irina or Joey. I have to admit, I thought they were good together. This didn't cross my mind at the time though. Right then, I was so nervous. What if people laughed at me? What if I didn't look as good as I thought I did? What if I looked fat? My heart began to pound against my chest, and my head felt heavy, like it was trying to tell me not to move. I suddenly froze, seeing Leon walking up the stairs to meet me. What should I do? Before I could retreat I found myself walking out towards him. It was then Leon who froze, and he just stared as he caught my eye. I swallowed hard, placing one hand on the railings at the top of the stairs. I didn't see the reactions of anyone else, for all I could look at was him in his deep green regal jacket. It was like the rest of the world was a blur, and only the two of us existed. It was then I heard Leon's voice in my head, and at first I thought I was imagining it! But I wasn't! Unconsciously, we had mastered the skill we had been practicing in Miss Wellworn and Miss Nebilia's lesson. It was like an echo in my head as he projected his thoughts into my brain. To be honest, I don't think it was intentional.

"{Woah...Xanda...you're beautiful...}" I heard Leon say. I was so shocked, I stepped towards him, my eyes wide.

"Leo...I heard that!"

"You did?!" He blushed brightly, coughing a little in surprise. I decided I would try it myself and I smiled gently at Leon, just trying to relax. He hadn't forced it, so I shouldn't either. I looked at him, projecting my speech into his head.

"{This isn't as hard as we first thought!}" I smiled.

"{Maybe not. So out of interest...what word did you write on that parchment?}" Leon asked. To be honest, I had been wondering what he had written too.

"{I wrote your name. I wrote Leon.}"

"{And...and I wrote Xanda.}" Leon chuckled gently. He reached out his hand and gently took mine. I looked down as he kissed it softly, and I felt a tingle surge down my spine. I gulped nervously, and he looked me in the eyes. I could tell he wanted to say something, but he was holding back.

"Leo...is everything alright?" I asked worriedly. He nodded, his lips tugging into a smile.

"Yeah. Yeah, everything's fine. I meant what I...accidently told you though. I...I think you look...incredible! I...I can't even get my words out!" My mouth gaped open like a fish. I had never thought anyone would ever say that about me. Oh gods...I was falling for him, wasn't I? With everything going on, that was the last thing I wanted. A bright blush filled my rosy cheeks and I responded, clearly nervous.

"Well, you're looking very hansom yourself. I especially like the hair, it looks the same as always." I joked, and we laughed a little.

"Well, do you really think I was gonna let Taz or Joey touch my hair? Besides, I did try and brush that stupid white stripe out of the way but it still shows!" I just smiled at him and reached up. His hair was rough like his hands, and it tickled my skin. I pulled the white section of his hair forward, grinning.

"I think it looks cute. I like the white bit." I said. He just laughed and extended his arm to me. I'll give him one thing, he had a lot of respect for me, and everyone around him.

"Very well" He smiled. "Now, will you let me escort you to the ball?"

"Jeez, Leon, you sound like an old man." I giggled, smiling brightly. He just blushed deeper. I wrapped my arm around his, not wanting to leave the poor lad hanging. We gazed into each other's eyes as Leon led me down the stairs carefully, and into the Great Hall for a great night...

As I entered the Great Hall, I was suddenly hit with the sweet sound of music from the band, standing on the raised section where the teachers usually sat. The room was filled with the swirling bright colours of bold dresses as couples danced around on the floor. There were people standing round the edges, talking with glasses of Dragonberry juice in their hands, and everyone was beaming with joy. The atmosphere was very uplifting, and my heart filled with excitement. I noticed the nurse, Ida McCoy, dancing with her husband. He was young like her, and I admit very hansom. He was a very thin young man, with slicked back jet dark blue hair. They looked so in love. I smiled watching them as Ida's husband, Seth, placed his hand upon her stomach. Soon, they would have a baby! They looked so happy! I hoped I could be like them one day. Mrs Madana was also dancing with a tall, brown haired man whom I could only guess was her husband. The other teachers were dotted around the room, chatting and mingling with the students. All except Mr Davandrin and Mr Ventus, who sat on the edge of the raised area watching the dancing while deep in conversation. Of course, with an alcoholic drink in their hands. I had never seen such a sight before. I felt like I had come such a long way, coming from such a small place, to now being in a grand ballroom. Pippa pulled a reluctant Taz to the dancefloor, and we chuckled as she began to lead him into the dance. Joey cleared his throat and looked at Irina. He glanced at Leo for a moment, who nodded. Clearly, they had had words about Joey's etiquette. Leon was like that after all. Joey held out a hand to Irina and blushed deeply. He tried to speak but no words came out. Irina giggled, but knew what the poor lad was trying to say. She smiled, taking his hand calmly. Her demeanour seemed to calm Joey too, and he stopped looking so nervous and managed to smile. Joey gently walked with her to the dance floor. I smiled watching them. They all seemed to know how to dance, and here was me. I had never danced in my life! Leon held out a hand to me, and I swallowed hard, shaking my head.
"No way, Leo!" I protested. "I've never danced before in my life!"
"And I'd never skated before, but you made me do that." He chuckled. "Come on. Try it...for me? Pretty please?" He tried to pout, pulling a cute face childishly. I rolled my eyes, and smiled weakly as I took his hand. He took my other hand, and pulled me onto the edge of the dance floor. He moved my left hand up and placed it softly on his shoulder, before letting go and placing his now free hand on my waist. My heart skipped a beat at his touch, and I gulped. He raised an eyebrow.
"Are you okay?"
"Y-Yes! Sorry. Just nervous, I guess!" I said sounding like a bumbling idiot. He

just rolled his eyes at me and smiled.

"Don't worry." He chuckled. "Just follow me. Think of it as Ice skating, without the ice!" Yeah, like that was gonna help! As the next song started, Leon pulled me further onto the dance floor and I looked down at my feet, not wanting to step on him. That would be embarrassing. "Hey!" He said, making my gaze snap up to him. "Don't look at your feet. Look at me, okay? Believe me, you've more chance of tripping by looking down."

"And believe me, that makes no sense!" I stated worriedly. He just laughed, and he twirled me around. I held back onto him tightly as I span back to face him, to which he just laughed again and told me to relax. Leon was wrong, it wasn't like ice skating at all! I didn't know what to do without blades at the bottom of my feet. I'm not gonna lie, I'm not the best dancer in the world but the more the night went on I seemed to get the hang of it. I honestly don't know what I had been so worried for! I was having the time of my life!

Zadlos Davandrin and Jasper Ventus had been chatting all evening. Despite an age difference between the two, they were extremely good friends. From what Seto Ventus had told me, his father had been taught by Mr Davandrin when he first came to school here, so they had clearly known each other a long time. It was then Seto came over to his father, and handed him a bottle opener.

"Here you go, papa." The young Dragonbourne said.

"Oh, thank you son!" Ventus smiled as he took it from Seto. "Now go on! I haven't seen you or your brother dancing with any girls yet!"

"Oh please! All the girls here are boring! Okay, Xanda and her mates are pretty awesome, but the rest are dull. Besides, I haven't seen you dancing with Miss Nebilia yet!" Seto pounced back.

"Oh, is there something going on between you and Cassandra?" Davandrin said prodding Ventus.

"No!" Ventus blushed.

"Oh, Seto, I think you just dropped him in it!" Davandrin bellowed, laughing loudly. Seto laughed, grinning widely.

"Oh, buzz off, Seto!" Ventus laughed. "Before you get me in even more trouble!"

"Alright. See you, papa. And lay off the drink a while, because I aint carrying you home!" Seto said, before walking away. When Seto's back was turned, Jasper Ventus grinned and opened another bottle.

"You not listening to your little one?" Davandrin grinned.

"Pfft, no! It's a party! And we don't get many of those." Jasper laughed, and then watched as Seto joined his brother across the room. He watched them sadly before taking a gulp from the bottle. "Y'know, when I think what those two have been through, it makes me so proud to know they call me 'father'..."

"Well, that man abused the hell out of poor Naia. He doesn't even have the right to have those boys call him father. You've done an amazing job with those two, Jasper. You've become a fine young man…"

"You think?" Jasper looked at him and smiled weakly. "I just want them to be happy. They deserve to be."

"They are lucky to have you. Not many get the chance to be happy…" Davandrin said, looking over at Leon and I dancing without a care in the world. Jasper took another big swig of his drink, and looked down before speaking.

"I miss them, so much. They should be here! Gods, why didn't I listen to them?!" He said, gripping his hair. Davandrin just watched him with a melancholy expression before he placed a hand on his shoulder.

"We should have had more faith in Alphonse and Kirani, it's true. But I fear it is too late for them. But look Jasper…" He pointed across the room, and Jasper looked up, his eyes transfixed on me as Leon led me across the dancefloor. "They left a very talented, beautiful and wonderful little girl behind. She needs us, Jasper. Alphonse and Kirani would have wanted us to take care of her."

"Yeah…yeah, you're right." Jasper smiled weakly. "Do you remember when Al and Kirani went to their first Winter Ball? Kirani's dress wasn't much different than Xanda's, and as Al tried to lead her into a dance, he fell flat on his face!" The two men laughed joyfully at the memory.

"Yes, I remember. He had a nosebleed afterwards, as I recall. And Kirani spent the entire evening cleaning it up!" Davandrin added, which just made them laugh more.

"Yeah. Al was a right laugh, wasn't he?" Jasper chuckled, taking another sip from his bottle.

"And he was a good father, even at such a young age." Davandrin smiled, watching me again. "Alphonse may have been the class clown, but he never did shy away from his responsibility to Xandario."

"Hmm. I have to admit, most men at that age would have run for the hills. I know I would have." Jasper smiled weakly. "But he didn't. He knew what he had to do, and he saw it through. Xanda's a lot like him in that respect."

"Indeed. Just like her parents, shouldering the worlds huge problems on her own tiny shoulders." Said Davandrin.

"Well, little Leon's like that too." Jasper sighed. "Besides, if the prophecy Fergo spoke of all those years ago really is about Leon and Xanda, they may not have a choice. They deserve more than this. All the kids here do! They deserve more than a world where a madman is trying to seize power over everyone and everything!" Jasper clenched his fists, and narrowed his eyes angrily.

"Jasper." Davandrin placed his hand on the back of Jasper's head, and ruffled his blue hair. "As you said, this is a party! A day will come where we dwell on such woe's, but just for tonight, let's just drink ourselves silly and reminisce on the good old days!"

"I can drink to that!" Jasper perked up, smiling once again as he raised his bottle as Davandrin picked his up. They hit them together gently, before both men tilted their heads back and walloped down as much booze as they could!

We danced all night! I was having so much fun, I didn't even know why I had been so worried in the first place! As the band finished a song, I curtseyed gracefully, and Leon bowed. I only knew how to curtsey because Irina had taught me earlier. Thank the gods she had too, or I would have looked like an idiot! We all turned to look at the band, as one member stepped forward and announced to the room with authority.

"Ladies and gentlemen! We would now like to play for you our latest song, 'Winds of Love'. It's time for a bit of romance!" With this, they all started playing the most beautiful, soothing song. Leon placed his hand on my hip again, and without saying a word, he began to lead me into a slow dance. I looked at him, my eyes wide.

"Leo, what are you doing...?!" I asked in surprise.

"Dancing with you. What does it look like?" He smiled weakly and I calmed a little, trying to compose myself. I took a deep breath, and slowly reached my hand up once again to rest my hand on his shoulder. I gasped as Leo lifted me up into the air, and spun me round! He held on for dear life, and he chuckled as he put me down again.

"Don't worry, I wasn't going to drop you!" He chuckled.

"Just warn me next time!" I giggled softly. He smiled, and lifted his arm to twirl me round. We were now dancing more smoothly, and our moves felt more fluent. I began to trust him more, and I let him lead me along. We had stopped talking, and all I could do was stare into the deep green of his eyes. He looked at me, and I could see he was breathing as deeply as I was. My heart was racing. At that moment, it was like nobody else mattered. It was just me and Leon. Leon and I. He pulled me closer to him, and he stopped dancing in the middle of the floor. I wondered for a moment what he was doing. The music was still playing, so why did he stop? I felt my heart pounding as Leon slowly leaned his face towards mine. I felt myself becoming compelled towards him. My eyes began to close softly, and I suddenly felt a shiver down my spine as his tender lips brushed my own. We were almost kissing, until...

The ground began to shake, and we all looked up in horror as part of the ceiling fell through! The stone roof showered the ballroom as blood curdling screams echoed throughout the castle. Leon grabbed my arm tightly, and he pulled me to the side as a large piece of rock came plummeting towards us. We yelled in fear as Mr Davandrin and Jasper Ventus jumped on top of us, saving us from being hit by the falling roof. Mr Ventus held me closely as I looked around, but the hall was smothered in rock and dust. Dragon roars could be heard screeching through the night sky!

We were under attack.

Chapter 10

The Battle at the Ball

The room was filled with a deathly silence. I sat up quickly. Jasper Ventus held me tightly in his arms, and I could feel him shaking. Seto and Naia hurried over, kneeling beside us checking that their father was okay. I panted hard, trying to comprehend what was going on. My heart rate was becoming faster and faster with every second that passed. Everyone was looking up at the hole in the roof. Just then, there was a burst of noise. Screams echoed through the room as Adamski Thorne plummeted into the hall. His huge wings knocked people over as he landed, and his roar was chilling to the bone. I felt like there was a rope around my chest, and it pulled against it tighter and tighter. I didn't scream. I wouldn't give Adamski Thorne or Hendrix Montgomery the satisfaction of hearing me scream. I narrowed my eyes as I pushed myself to my feet. Hendrix was sitting on Adamski's back, and he caught my eye. A smirk spread across his narrow face. He recognised me, that was for sure. As did Adamski. Even in his Dragon form, I could tell he was surprised to see me alive. Before any of us could say anything though, the teachers had shielded us from view. Leon stood in front of me, and pushed me behind him protectively. Suddenly, we all stumbled back as Brozantan knights began to jump down from the roof and into the Great Hall! Mr Davandrin gasped, pushing us back roughly. "Go. Now!" He yelled. "Get out of here!"

"But-" Seto began to protest, but Mr Davandrin and Mr Ventus soon yelled at us in a panic, and practically pushed us out of the hall. A lot of the students had fled, not knowing what to do, while others had rushed out to arm themselves. The teachers made sure all the students were out before the men slammed the huge double doors behind us, locking us out of the room! Taz, Joey, Pippa and Irina had been shoved out too by Mrs Madana and Ida McCoy, and the eight of us instantly started to bang on the door.

"Father! Father open the door!" Shouted Leon, his heart pounding as he smacked the door over and over.

"Papa! Papa!" The twins yelled, one of them almost in tears because of the fear of losing their father. We had to get in and help them! What if they were killed?! We were all hitting the door, trying to get back in, but to no avail. Mrs Madana had probably put a spell on it to try and keep all the students' safe. It was then it hit me...they wouldn't fight in the hall. Not if the Dragonbourne's in the hall wanted to change into their beast forms. They would have to take the fight out of the academy. Which is where we should go. Confined in here, we didn't stand a chance if the enemy managed to infiltrate even more of the castle. I took a step back away from the door, speaking to the others over the sound of the raging battle on the other side of the door.

"Guys!" I shouted, and they all turned to look. "We need to arm ourselves. Then we need to get out of here! The hall is too much of a confined space for them to stay in there for long! We need to get out of the Academy before were run through!"

"Xanda's right guys…" Joey said reluctantly.

"Yeah. If we stay here, and the enemy get in here we don't stand a chance!" Taz agreed. The others pulled themselves away from the door, and nodded in agreement. We took off down the hall, all of us running towards our rooms. "We'll get our weapons, then we'll all meet on the turret next to Leon and Xanda's room! We'll be able to assess the situation best from up there!" Said Naia as we darted down the hall. I nodded, and we began to run faster. There wasn't much time, and we all knew that.

Leon and I burst into our bedroom, and he rummaged through his wardrobe for a pocket knife that he usually carried with him in training. I however, noticed something glistening on my bed. I slowly walked over, and to my amazement, there was a sword! It was perfectly crafted from bright silver metal, and the hilt was gold, with a sparkling white metal swirling around it. It was unlike any blade I had ever seen, and believe me, I had seen a lot of blades. I slowly wrapped my fingers around the hilt and lifted the blade up. I gazed at my reflection in the shiny metal, and ran my fingers down the sharp edge. Leon's movement slowed too, and he looked at me as I lifted the sword. He moved over to me curiously.

"Where did you get that?" He asked. To be honest, I was wondering the same thing! Where had this blade come from? Who had placed it here? And who did it belong to? Part of me felt like I should put it down. I mean, it wasn't mine. Unless someone had given it to me. But then, why wouldn't they just give it to me in person? I admit, this was an odd situation.

"I dunno. It was on the bed when we walked in." I told him at a hurried pace.

"Well, can you fight with a weapon like that?" He asked curiously. "I mean, I know you normally wield a scythe." I quickly shoved the sword into Leon's hands, and made my way over to my wardrobe. I opened it and pulled out my boots, and began to change my footwear as I spoke. There was no way I was gonna be able to fight in heels.

"Yeah. But I used to fight with a weapon like that sword. Then I found out my father used to wield a scythe and um…I dunno. I guess I just wanted to be like him." I smiled weakly, throwing my heels into the wardrobe as I finished changing into my boots.

"Well, since somebody put it here, you may as well put it to good use." Leon said extending the sword out to me. He was right. However this sword had gotten here, I didn't think it was an accident. I felt like I had to use it. For Gailoiyn. There was also a strap on the bed, to attach the sword to my back. I reached for it and slung it over my shoulder before quickly taking the blade from Leon and sheathing it.

"All set?" I asked him quickly, knowing time was against us.

"Aye aye, partner!" He grinned, and opened the door for me. I sprinted out, and he followed. I don't think I had ever moved so fast before in my life than when I charged up the winding stairs of that tower.

Leo and I were the last people up on the turret. I felt the wind push against me fiercely as I ascended to the top. Despite it being a snowy night, a searing heat smothered the air. Dragon fire and clanging metal filled the night's sky, painting the air in a sea of red and silver. I gasped, running to the edge of the turret where the others were waiting. There was a sudden sense of urgency as I was finally able to see the battle raging on before my eyes below me.

"What's happening?!" Leon asked hurriedly.

"They're descending on the royal castle!" Seto announced. And he was right. I felt a pain in my chest as I watched Dragons swirling round the majestic structure that I had gazed upon in awe upon arriving in Algora. Now it was surrounded by flames and beasts of war fighting, trying to gain entrance. The Gailoiyn Dragon knights and riders were desperately trying to keep the Brozantan's out of the palace, but from where we were standing, it wasn't looking promising for us. I had never seen such chaos! People were being slaughtered in the street, and rivers of blood etched themselves between the cobbles. We couldn't just stand here and watch...we had to do something!

"So..." I began. "Has anyone got any bright ideas?!"

"Not currently. But if the castle falls, then Gailoiyn is done for!" Taz said, clenching his fists. I hated to admit it, but Taz was right. If the castle fell...if King Ricco and his sister died, then it was all over!

"I know what to do!" Irina perked up. The rest of us turned, a little stunned to be honest. Irina having an idea...now that was unheard of. Not in a bad way, she was just so shy she was never able to contribute anything in combat lessons! And trust me, I'm certain I wasn't the only one shocked that she had spoken up. I think I even saw Joey's jaw drop.

"Were all ears, Irina!" Naia said enthusiastically. "What do you have in mind?"

"The Brozantan's are trying to fight their way in. That's not our game. We create a path. An opening. Just for a split second! If we do, Xanda and Leon may be able to use that opening to get inside before they do!" She said, seeming to have a newfound determination.

"Woah, why us?!" I said nervously.

"Because you wield a combat weapon. You'll be able to fight inside the castle. I use magic, and Joey uses a bow. We may be able to use these long-ranged weapons to create the opening for you. Naia and Seto will back you up, and keep any attackers away from you!" Irina explained.

"Okay. Sounds good." Seto said in haste.

"Then let's go!" Pippa said.

"Yeah." Joey grinned. "They aren't gonna send us an invitation, so let's just crash the party!" Taz chuckled, and he stood on the turrets balcony, like Leon and I had when we first met. Taz jumped off, and in mid-air, transformed into his splendid purple Dragon form. He soared round to the side of the turret, where Joey hopped onto his friends back. Pippa did the same. Irina at first was a little reluctant to jump, but Pippa assured her she would be okay and she eventually mounted her Dragon. Leon and Seto jumped off the tower in unison, and I soon saw my partner hovering a little below the turrets edge so I could jump down. I wasted no time in vaulting over the side. I wasn't scared this time. I knew Leon would catch me if I fell. But I didn't. I landed on him, and I shuffled myself into position.

"All set?" Leon asked.

"Yeah. I'm good to go. C'mon Leo, to the palace!" I told him. He let out a confident roar that echoed in the wind. He flapped his wings ferociously, and soared through the air, directly towards the battle. We weren't running away. We would fight, or we would die.

We flew at great speed, and I clung onto Leo tightly. It seemed like the wind itself was trying to knock me off balance. We followed the others as they flew on ahead, and in the middle of the battle, we saw some familiar faces. Mr Davandrin was riding Mr Ventus! Davandrin pounded foes with his broadsword, making fighting on the back of a Dragon look easy! Trust me, it's not easy. Fighting just as good, were Miss Wellworn and Miss Nebilia. Pippa had been right when she said Cassandra Nebilia looked amazing in Dragon form! She had beautiful baby pink scales, that looked wonderful in the snow. I could have watched her all night, were there not people trying to kill us. It was then I noticed the huge black Dragon that had come to our aid on the beach. Drevin Drogon roared as he used his massive tail to swipe a Brozantan knight clean off his Dragon, and sent him plummeting into the ground! Just then, my eyes widened as we saw another enemy knight on his Dragon, swoop towards Mr Drogon from behind! A rush of panic shot through Leo, and he instantly zoomed towards his father, placing us between him and the attacker! Leon reared up, and I clung on tightly as I was thrust backwards. Leon dug his claws into the enemy Dragon, and I was thrashed about as Leon began to wrestle with him in the air. The rider glared at me, and tried to knock me off by lunging forward and trying to impale me with his spear. I reacted quickly, and drew the sword from my back. Our blades met in an instant, and Leon managed to gain the upper ground! I wasn't even thinking when I made my next move. To be honest, I don't know what came over me. I used one hand to steady myself, and I stood on Leon's back. I lined myself up with the knight, knowing I only had one shot at this. I leaped off of Leon, and I sliced the rider's chest as I fell past. The rider screamed in anguish as he lost his balance and fell off. His Dragon flew to catch him as he plummeted to the ground, but this gave Drevin Drogon the opening he needed to pounce on the other beast and destroy them both. Leon swooped underneath me and I landed on his back, panting hard as I clung to his neck.

"Are you okay?!" He asked me worriedly.

"Y-Yeah…" I gulped, sitting up straight. I suddenly flinched, feeling faint as I watched Drevin Drogon on top of the other Dragon. He swiped his huge claws across the Dragon's neck and swiftly ended his life. This was the first time I had watched someone die. His body transformed back into a human as he died, and a young man replaced the fearsome beast. He wasn't that old, yet he was led to his death by a madman filling his peoples head with rubbish. What a waste of a young life. I watched, a little pale as Drevin Drogon flew back up to us, hovering level with his son to talk to us.

"I owe you my thanks. But its dangerous out here, you must get to safety!" Drevin protested.

"And leave you lot to fend for yourselves?! No way!" Leon argued. Drevin became anxious as the battle raged on around us. He was desperate to know his son was safe.

"Leon, do as I command!"

"No, father. This is our fight too!"

"Xanda, talk some sense into him!" Drevin Drogon turned to me, and looked at me worriedly with his beady eyes. I looked back down at the fallen Brozantan knight. If someone didn't do something, our own people would end up like him. I looked back at the headmaster.

"Leon's right. This is our fight. We are part of this world, whether we like it or not." I spoke strongly, like a leader, although I hadn't realised it at the time. Taz and Joey zoomed past us, and I felt the force from Taz's wing's as they bolted past.

"Well said, Xanda!" Joey yelled.

"Were here to help, papa!" Said Naia as he and Seto began to fight alongside Jasper and Davandrin, who weren't far away from us. The two men didn't look surprised we had joined the fight, and Davandrin even managed to crack a smile.

"Leon! Xanda! Are you ready?" Irina asked as she and Pippa glided past.

"Yeah!" I shouted back.

"We'll try and open a path for you, so be ready!" Pippa yelled as they joined the fight. The end of Irina's staff began to swirl colourfully, and she cast spells on the enemy, making them dizzy and unbalanced. Leon and I tried to fly through, but when we did, we kept being blocked by enemy Dragons just like Irina had predicted. I was beginning to worry we'd never get through! It was then Taz spotted an opening. Two Dragons and their riders were flying towards us. If we evaded them, then we could get past. Taz knew this. And it took him a split second to decide to sacrifice himself.

"Joey!" Taz said to his friend as he began to soar towards us.

"Taz no!" Joey protested. "I know what you're thinking! If you do that you'll die!"

"I'll protect you from the fall Joey…" And that was the last thing Taz said before he came between us and the knights. The sky was washed with blood as Taz became impaled with the weapons of the two knights, and his shriek was paralysing as it rung in my ears. Leon didn't want to waste Taz's sacrifice, and he instantly flew over them, soaring towards the castle. Joey was screaming, not for fear of his own life, but his friends.

"Taz!" I was shaking all over, barely able to keep my grip on Leon as I watched over my shoulder. Taz began to plummet towards the ground, catching Joey as he fell from his back. I saw Taz hit the blood-stained cobbles as hard as a rock, and change back into his human form. He was dead, I knew it! His body was sprawled across the ground, and he wasn't moving! His white hair was now red, stained with his own blood. I couldn't take my eyes off him, I was so scared! Leon didn't look, but I could tell his breathing was unsteady. He just focused his gaze on the palace.

"What happened?" Leon asked, sounding like he wanted to cry.

"Joey's okay...but...Taz is down..." I said after a few moments, trying to compose myself.

"Gods, no!" Leon spoke like he was in pain, but we both knew we couldn't turn back. If we did, Taz's sacrifice would have been for nothing. I finally managed to prize my eyes away from the bloody scene, and look ahead of us. Leon was heading straight towards a large window on the palace! Balls, did he intend to enter that way? I was terrified, but I will admit, I give him points for entering in style.

"Balls, Leo!" I yelled.

"Brace yourself, Xanda!" Leon warned me. I quickly hid my face in Leon's neck, and held onto him so tightly my knuckles turned white. In an instant, the impact came, and glass shattered around us. I felt a sharp piece slice my finger, and I didn't dare think of the damage it was causing to my dress. Tiny fragments of glass shone in the moonlight, and we skidded to a stop as we fell into the palace throne room.

Leon skidded across the floor as he fell on his side, and I came flying off of him. I squealed as I hit the ground, and rolled across the floor a few times. I panted hard, trying to regain my breath. I quickly pushed myself onto my knees. The first thing I noticed was the blood coming from the cuts on my fingers, but it didn't hurt. Leon shook his head, and stood on all fours. He was growling. I staggered to my feet, looking around the very regal throne room. The room was dark. The only light illuminating the area were candles on the wall and the moonlight beaming through the shattered window. There was a royal blue carpet leading up to two royal thrones. I took a few steps forward, standing slightly in front of Leon. On the thrones, sat the young King and Princess. He looked so much younger than I had first thought. He was only twenty-five, but his face was as smooth as a baby. Both shared the same strawberry blonde hair. Princess Veronica was Dragonbourne, and her eyes were a piercing mix of pink and red, and King Ricco's were a muddy brown. The two were very similar in terms of facial features, and if you didn't know they were a year apart in age, you could mistake them for twins. However, this wasn't the time to dwell on their appearance. Both of them had a sword pointed to their throats by a Brozantan knight. As we had made our dramatic entrance, the four of them had turned to face us. I drew my sword from my sheathe, and prepared for battle. The one knight however, just laughed at my action.

"Well." He gloated. "Is this the royal rescue party? A little girl and her pet dog."

"How dare you!" Leon growled, becoming more angered.

"Calm down, Leo." I grinned, walking towards them slowly. The knights were unnerved by this, as I didn't seem afraid. I was afraid, but I wasn't going to let them know that. "He's only teasing us because he's insecure about himself." I placed the sword on the back of the knight who had spoken to me, and my grin widened. "Now..." I continued. "Give me one good reason why I shouldn't tell my 'pet' here, to rip your friends head off while I stick you like a pig."

"You're crazy!" Said the other knight. "She's possessed and-" It was then he started screaming. Leon had swiped him with his claws, and the knight squirmed on the floor in pain as Leon pinned him to the ground. While the other knight was distracted, King Ricco hit the sword away from him, and punched the enemy knight clean across the face. He fell to the ground, and I wasted no time in running my sword through his chest. It was an instant reaction, and I hadn't had time to think about it. I watched in horror as the life drained from his eyes. This was my first kill. His blood dripped from my blade, and I swallowed hard, just staring at the dying man as his soul was ripped from his body and his life drained from his eyes. Suddenly, my gaze was snapped away from him as Leon roared, raising his claws to deal the final blow on the other knight.

"No!" Princess Veronica stood with authority, and Leon froze. She walked over to the enemy, her eyes narrow. "We keep this one alive."

"Oh, thank you! Thank you!" The knight began to cry like a baby. It was quite pathetic actually.

"She didn't say you were getting away with this." Ricco spoke, and he reached for a pair of handcuffs hanging from his belt. Leon took a step back and changed into his human form. He hurried over to me as the King turned the knight onto his front and began to cuff his hands behind his back. Leon grabbed my shoulders, a worried look in his eyes.

"Are you alright?" He asked.

"Yeah. A bit shaken though..." I said. Leon and I looked at the dead knight as Ricco and Veronica forced their prisoner to his feet.

"You have a way with words, child." Said Veronica. "He won't miss you, that's for sure."

"I'm sure he'll miss his life more." I stated rather coldly. I hadn't intended to deliver it like that, but I was so scared. I couldn't stop my hands from trembling. Leon just gripped my arms tighter, trying to calm me down. King Ricco let out a chuckle. I hadn't intended that to be a joke either.

"Oh, now you, I like!" Ricco laughed. I admit, he wasn't anything like I had expected. He was very laid back, considering he was King. His sister, on the other hand, was more grounded and serious.

"Are you students at the Academy?" Veronica asked.

"Yeah. I'm Leon Drogon, and this is my partner, Xanda." Leon stated.

"Oh! Little Leo! Drevin's lad! Yeah, I remember you. Gee, you were still in nappies last time I saw you!" Ricco grinned. Leon blushed brightly with embarrassment.

"Enough, brother! Let us take this scoundrel to the dungeon! Then we must hurry to the vault!" Veronica said sharply.

"The vault?" Leon asked. Then it dawned on me...whatever was in that vault, was what King Stephan was after. That's why the city was being attacked.

"What's in the vault?" I asked.

"The Lightningstone." The knight growled, struggling against the King and the Princess.

"Of course! Now it all makes sense!" Leon said in realisation. He seemed to know the significance of the stone, but I had no idea what the hell it was.

"What's the Lightningstone?!" I asked.

"It's a long story. I'll fill you in later." Leon told me. "All you need to know for now is that it's a powerful artefact and we cannot allow a madman like Stephan to get his hands on it!"

"Agreed!" Ricco said. "We must protect the stone at all costs!"

"To the dungeon with you!" Veronica said as she and her brother began to shove the prisoner roughly towards the dungeon. Leon turned to me, taking my hand gently. I raised an eyebrow, a little curious. I could tell he was worried about me. And after what happened to Taz, I was worried about Leo too. And everyone else fighting outside.

"Are you sure you wanna go through with this?" Leon asked me. I nodded without hesitation. I...no. WE had come too far. I wasn't backing out now!

"Of course, Leon. We see things through together. Remember?" He just smiled as I spoke. His smile put me at ease, and I let go of his hand and pulled mine back. We high fived each other, just like we had when we had first become partners. We were a team. I didn't know what the Lightningstone was, but I trusted my partner. If Leon said we had to protect it, then we had to protect it. The two of us left the throne room, and we followed the King and the Princess, down towards the darkest corners of the castle.

After the prisoner had been taken to the dungeon, Ricco and Veronica led Leon and I to a secret part of the castle. In one of the corridors, was a large bookshelf. Veronica pulled out a rather small book, and to our amazement, the bookshelf began to move to the side! I had read about this old trick in books before, but I never thought it was used in real life. Veronica threw the book down, and grabbed a torch hanging off the side of the wall. The flame blazed in the darkness, and we could see that behind the bookshelf were hidden stone stairs, leading downwards under the castle. Veronica went first, followed by myself, Leon and then finally Ricco. As we descended deeper into the depths of the palace, I began to feel a chill. It was getting colder, and the stone began to become damper the further down we got. We suddenly found ourselves in a rocky area, light from the moon cracking through the rocks and lighting up the opening. Flowers of pink and purple grew around the water's edge, as a stream of clear water circled the centre of the vault. Large leaves were dotted about the room, and they seemed to thrive despite living in a cave. The air around us was fresh and clean, and there was a slight zephyr through the holes in the rock. But it was what was in the centre of the room that caught my attention. There was a pedestal made of white stone, with a swirling gold pattern wrapping around it from the ground. Placed upon it, was a bright yellow stone. It was shaped in a perfect triangle, which seemed odd to me. I began to wonder whether this was just one piece of another artefact. I was compelled towards it, and I started moving over towards the stone. My boots splashed in the water as I stepped across the narrow stream, the others following close behind me. I stood before the pedestal, and reached out my pale hand to take the stone. As I picked it up, I felt nothing. This was it? This is what all the fuss was about?! What people had died for? What did it do anyway?

Suddenly I froze. The room became chilly, and something didn't feel right. I was overcome with a sense of dread, and my heart began to pound against my chest. I looked at Leon, and we had both seemed to have sensed an unwelcome presence enter the room. We slowly turned around. The sound of heels tapping on the rock was heard before we caught sight of a woman stepping into the room. Her lips were as red as a summer rose, and her hair a wild, tangled, burgundy mess. She was however, very regal, and she walked with a majesty, like she was above everyone else. Her green dress flowed heavenly behind her, and it split down the middle to reveal her golden boots. Her very presence sent a chill down my spine. I could instantly tell that she was no ordinary foe. I gulped in fear as she spoke, her voice silky smooth and with an accent I didn't recognise.

"Give me the stone." She said simply.

"Who are you?" I queried, not trusting her one bit. She just laughed in a sickeningly sweet tone, making me feel even more on edge than I already did.

"Straight to the point. I like you." She said.

"You're popular today." Ricco joked, remembering he had said the same thing earlier. I just rolled my eyes at this.

"Shut up, and answer my question! Who are you?!" I said with more anger than last time. Her ruby red lips cracked into a smirk.

"I am Tenebris Magicae Ora. And I have come for the stone. Now give it to me." She held out her hand demandingly, and started walking over to us, not even worried about the odds being against her. Ricco and Veronica became concerned for our safety, and they rushed ahead of us, pushing Leo and I behind them protectively. I felt my heart racing ahead of me. There was only one enemy…yet I was terrified. Something about her seemed dangerous. Veronica swiftly put her free hand in the flame on the torch, and fire engulfed her palm, free for her to bend at will. Ricco pulled out his sword, and the two charged at the mysterious woman. Suddenly, Tenebris swiftly moved her hand, and a wave of purple magic shot across the room! Ricco and Veronica squirmed in pain as the two of them were thrown backwards! They hit the ground hard, and Leon and I gasped in shock.

"Princess!" I ran over to Veronica, and kneeled beside her. She was still conscious, but she was straining, like she was struggling to move. Leo knelt beside Ricco, and tried to help him to sit up.

"What's…happening?!" Veronica strained.

"I can't move!" Ricco panted, looking at the attacker in fear and panic. Balls, Tenebris had paralyzed them! I felt my heart skip a beat as Tenebris grabbed Leon by his hair, and yanked him to his feet. He let out a small yelp as he struggled. Ricco had fallen back over, and he was clearly frustrated that he could do nothing but watch.

"Leon! No! Let him go!" I stood, drawing my blade. My hands were shaking so badly. I was terrified I was gonna lose him! Tenebris just chuckled, which made me gulp. She pulled Leon's head back roughly, and she stared into his bright green eyes.

"Hmm…those eyes…you're my sister's son." She grinned.

"Oh, so you're the crazy one from the loony bin." Leon narrowed his eyes. Leon had mentioned before that his mother, Sera, had had a sister. He said he had never met her, but his father had told him she was crazy and spent most her life in the asylum in Palmira, a small town in Brozanta. Drevin had been right. She was off her head! When Leon had slated her, she became angry, and he gasped in pain as she pulled tighter on his hair.

"Shut it! Just because you're the perfect child of my perfect sister! Well, not so perfect, are you? You killed her…I bet she wrenched in pain as she brought you into this world…!"

"Shut up! Shut up!" Leon became angry, his face turning red. I'd never seen him so mad! He was losing it, becoming consumed by fear and anger. She knew exactly what to say to get under his skin.

"Leo, calm down!" I urged him, not wanting him to make Tenebris angry. I didn't know what she was capable of. "Please, Miss Ora, let him go, and I'll give you the stone."

"What?! No!" Leon practically screamed at me. I admit, what I had said was pretty stupid, but I didn't want to lose Leon! If he died because I refused to give her a stupid stone, I would never forgive myself!

"Xanda, don't you dare!" Veronica yelled. Tenebris held out her hand, her breath picking up the pace.

"That's it little girl…hand it over…" She said, her voice shaking a little. She may have been extremely beautiful, but she was completely insane. Her eyes were wide, and they stared straight through me. If I had a chance to get Leon away from her, it was now. I looked down at the stone in my hand. Why was there so much fuss over something so small? I looked back up at Tenebris, not taking my eyes off her as I slowly began to move my hand towards hers. As she reached for the stone, I swiped my sword towards her arm. She watched in horror, and in a flash her hand was drawn back! Leon used this moment to break free of her grip, and stand in front of me, pushing me behind him protectively. Tenebris stared at her arm, her breath picking up the pace as she was filled with rage. Her neck snapped, and she rapidly turned her head to look at us. She growled demonically, and scrunched up her face angrily.

"You little swine!" She screamed at me, her voice screeching.

"{Thank you.}" I heard Leon speak to me through my mind. It's a good job we were getting the hang of this technique, as it meant that we didn't have to talk in front of Tenebris.

"{Your welcome. We have to keep her busy until reinforcements arrive! We can't leave the King and the Princess!}"

"{I fear you may be right.}" Leon said back to me, our eyes fixed on Tenebris as she moved towards us. She pulled her hand back, and hurled another blast of purple magic towards us. We reacted quickly, spinning opposite ways so the blast hit the pedestal. I tried to remember everything Mr Davandrin had taught me. Don't take your eyes off your enemy. Fight as if your life depends on it. Well, in this case it did. I had no doubt at all that Tenebris would kill us without hesitation. We had to stay alive, and we had to protect each other and the Lightningstone. I didn't know what value it had, but it must have been important. Otherwise, none of this would be happening! I kept the stone tightly within my grasp, my sword in the other hand. Tenebris had her eyes fixed on me, and she hurled another blast of magic in my direction. I remembered when I had rolled over Leon's back in Mr Davandrin's first lesson, and I quickly did the same with the pedestal. I rolled over it to avoid the blast, and Leon caught me in his arms as I landed.

"{Are you alright?!}" He asked me through his mind.

"{I'm good. But we can't keep this up forever!}" I responded quickly, as Leon and I dodged another attack. I looked at his face, and he looked pained. He knew I was right. We couldn't just keep dodging, we had to do something! Magic sparked around the room, flaring up with all sorts of dark and mystical colours. We were running around like headless chickens, not knowing what to do! Tenebris was screeching at us to keep still. However, both Leon and I had a will to survive. But, we were growing tired. We'd had a long day, and a long fight, and we were exhausted. Our movements were becoming sloppy, and it was then I realised the magic around the room was draining our energy. We had to finish this soon before we collapsed and were rendered completely defenceless.

"{Xanda. Don't let this be a waste!}" Leon said. At first, I wondered what he was talking about...then it hit me. He was going to allow himself to be hit just so I had an opening. Just like Taz had done for us. Before I could protest, Leon charged forward towards her, and was soon hit by a bolt of magic. There was a sudden pain in my chest, but I couldn't let this opportunity pass! As Leon flew through the air, I skidded on the ground under him. As I stood before Tenebris, I swung my sword at her. All of a sudden, my heart began to race as Tenebris stopped my attack with her bare hand! She hit the sword away, and I heard it clang on the ground as Tenebris grasped me around the neck. For a moment, the room went silent. All the fighting had stopped. I felt my breath beginning to strain as her hand tightened around my neck. I tried to prise her off with my hands, but to no avail. The stone fell out of my hands and dropped to the ground. She let out a snigger, and her blood red lips parted as she began to speak. The Princess and the King watched on in fright, unable to do a thing. Leon lay behind me, out cold.

"You've lost, little girl. You may think he will always be with you, but he won't be. As he lies there now you are utterly alone. Nobody can save you. Nobody will answer your screams for help." She practically spat in my face, and terror filled my entire body. I wasn't going to scream though. She wouldn't have the satisfaction of hearing me cry for help, because I knew that was what she wanted. "Now...any last words? You will be the first to die." I didn't quite know what to say. I had never really given much thought into my last words, should I get to choose them. But I had to think of a way out of this mess! I couldn't die here. I was feeling faint as her hands squeezed around my neck, and my vision began to fade. I couldn't breathe. Just then, I saw somebody. No...two people! They were running over to me, and one drew a large knife from his pocket. He drove it through Tenebris's stomach, and she squealed out in pain, dropping me. My eyes shut tightly and I fell to my knees, beginning to cough as the man shoved Tenebris across the room. A woman kneeled next to me, and put her arms around me. Something about her touch felt incredibly familiar...and I slowly opened my eyes.

Grandma smiled gently at me, and my eyes widened. I looked up, and Grandpa was standing in front of us protectively, glaring at Tenebris. What were they doing here?!

"Stay away from my granddaughter." Grandpa snapped, and Tenebris scowled. She screamed in anger and torment. A huge, purple, magical ball began to form in her hands. The Lightningstone was resting on the ground beside me, and I saw it glimmering out of the corner of my eye. I picked it up quickly, and at that moment, Grandpa turned to look at me. He saw the stone, and instantly moved to my side, kneeling beside me. He grabbed my wrist, and pushed my arm out ahead of us. It was all happening way too fast for me to process any thoughts. Tenebris finally shot the magic spell straight at us, and a gust of wind blew against us heavily. Just then to my amazement, a large, magical shield from the stone protected all that was behind it. It shone bright yellow, and sparks of lightning surged from it. Tenebris's magic tried to break through the barrier, but it was just repelled like it was nothing. The Lightningstone was so powerful, and I could feel its energy flowing through me. Tenebris was becoming weaker by the second, and soon she had no choice but to stop casting her spell.

As we were saved the stone began to stop glowing, and the shield died down. I suddenly felt completely drained, and I saw glimpses of Tenebris running for her life as my vision faded in and out. I heard Gramps and Grandma talking to me, but it was all muffled and I couldn't tell what they were saying. I didn't even have the strength to sit up anymore, and my head was swirling all over the place. I lost consciousness, and fell back. I don't remember anything after that. I just completely blacked out, still holding the Lightningstone firmly in the palm of my hand.

Chapter 11
A Plan Revealed

I woke again days later, feeling the soft sheets under my fingertips as I groaned awake. I was so tired, and still felt drained. It was a real effort at first to open my eyes. I wasn't in pain anymore, just extremely exhausted and aching. I felt the warm, muggy, winter sun shine through the window and beam down onto my cheeks. The air was calm and peaceful, and all I could hear were the sounds of two soft voices talking quietly beside me. I recognised them instantly...it was Grandma and Gramps. I'd recognise their voices anywhere, and I was so glad that they were here. I slowly opened my eyes and saw the two of them chatting away, looking out of the window gazing at the ocean. I sat up quietly, and saw that Leon was lying on the bed too, his head resting on a soft pillow at the other end of the bed. My hands pressed into the sheets, and I pushed myself up properly, looking at him worriedly. Was he alright? I remembered the hit he had taken by Tenebris, and I began to panic. I placed a hand on his leg, which was next to me, and shook it.

"Leon?!"

"Oh Xanda!" Grandma and Gramps turned quickly upon hearing me speak, and they rushed over fretfully. Grandma sat on the bed next to me, and put her arm around me. I looked at them as Grandpa put his hand on my shoulder. "How are you feeling, sweetheart?" He asked, a look of concern on his face.

"I'm fine. Is Leon-"

"Leon is going to be just fine." Grandma reassured me. "His father just left, actually. We've all been really worried about you two."

"Is everyone alright?! How did you two get here?!" I asked quickly, wondering what had happened after I had passed out. Grandpa pulled up the stool and sat next to the bed as Grandma started to talk.

"Well...you figured out I'm Dragonbourne." Grandma smiled. "We flew here to see you in your dress for the Winter Ball, and we arrived as Algora was under attack. It looks like we found you just in time. Many students have been injured, I don't know any names though."

"We need to return home soon." Grandpa smiled gently. "Without us there, nobody is protecting Lightwater. And the army will need more weapons." I knew that Grandpa used to be a knight himself, and now I was certain that he had been a Dragon knight with Grandma. It was a theory I later found out to be true. But he was right...they needed to defend Lightwater. They were safer back home, and that's all I wanted. I couldn't bear the thought of anything happening to them.

"It's alright. I understand. By the way...what happened to the stone?" I asked curiously.

"The Lightningstone is safe, under the protection of the King." Grandpa smiled weakly. "You did really well keeping it safe from the enemy. The Princess gave you two high praise."

"I don't want praise. I just want all this fighting to stop!" I told them. I remembered the blood trailing through the city, and Taz plummeting to the ground while bodies littered the streets. I still didn't know what had happened to him, and that scared me. All this fighting made me feel sick. So many people had lost their lives in a single night. It had been pure carnage...all because of a stupid rock.

"Oh Xanda..." Grandma began to stroke my soft golden hair, as feelings of sadness welled up inside my heart. I knew they had to go, but I didn't want them to. I just wanted everything to go back to normal. But deep down, I knew that it never would. The world as we knew it was changing. Years of peace were crumbling into the depths of despair. But...who would be the one to put an end to it all? I saw nobody volunteering, not that I blamed them. Stephan was growing stronger by the day, as was his army, and soon his madness would engulf the entire world. Nobody was safe, not really. The first blow had been struck, and we had succeeded in protecting the Lightningstone. But to me, I felt like we had failed. I had to face everybody sooner or later and discover just how badly the city had been affected. I rested my head against Grandma's shoulder, and sat there in silence for a while. I just wanted to feel close to them once more. I just wanted some normality! I wanted to go home. But I was never going to do that. My place was here, with my friends and comrades. With Leon. We had made a vow to protect each other no matter what, and we would see this through to the end.

"Peace will come...one day." Gramps reached over and placed a gentle hand on my cheek. I smiled weakly, hoping what he said was true. I knew he was only saying that to make me feel better, and the way he had said it hadn't exactly filled me with confidence. Just then, there was a low growl, and I raised an eyebrow. Grandma chuckled, looking at Grandpa's stomach.

"Someone's hungry." She giggled.

"You should go and get something to eat before you head home." I told them, smiling gently. Grandpa smiled back, and rubbed his hungry tummy.

"I believe I will. The food here is exquisite!" He said. I couldn't agree with him more. The food here really was lovely, as I've mentioned many times.

"Go ahead. I'll be alright." I said.

"Are you sure you don't want to come with us?"

"No. I'm not hungry. You two go on." I smiled at them again, then looked down at the sheets. "There are people I need to see..."

Grandma and Gramps had left not long afterwards, and I climbed out of bed. I had been in my nightclothes before, so I got dressed into a casual attire. I wore a simple woolly blue jumper, along with my usual trousers and boots. They had been cleaned since the fight after the Winter Ball. I guessed Grandma had cleaned them for me, she always hated dirty clothes. I put my hair up in a quick ponytail before I exited the room. Leon was still fast asleep, so I didn't try and wake him. He needed his rest after all. I had to go and see Irina...I had to know how Taz was! Gosh, I was so worried about him. I just kept thinking about how he fell from the sky over and over until my head began to hurt. Plus, from what Grandma and Gramps had been saying, it wasn't just Taz who had been injured either. I was a little saw myself, but that was to be expected I suppose. I made my way to the room next to mine, and knocked on the door. Irina's familiar voice could be heard from inside.

"Who is it…?" She asked, sounding a little more withdrawn than usual.

"It's me, Xanda." I assured her. Just then the door swung open, and Irina burst out of the room. I was taken aback, as she suddenly wrapped her arms around me and squeezed me tightly. I hugged her back, clenching my fists around the soft fabric of her dress. She was warm, despite the castle being rather chilly due to the damage it had taken. I closed my eyes, just holding her close for a moment.

"Thank the gods…it's so good to see you again!" Irina said, pulling back and placing her soft hands on my arms.

"It's good to see you too." I smiled gently, looking at her. "And I'm glad to see that you're alright."

"How are you?" She asked. "You gave us all quite a scare."

"I'm good. Irina…please…tell me what happened after Leon and I got to the castle…" Irina froze as I spoke. She began to look terrible, like she didn't want to talk about it. Not that I blamed her, but I needed to hear this. Irina ushered me into the room, and shut her bedroom door sadly. She spoke in a soft, but melancholy voice.

"The battle was terribly bloody. Metal clashed and bodies fell. The streets were painted in a river of blood…and friends died right before our eyes. Morgan Ocrina in our class died too. Taz is still in the infirmary. He hasn't moved or spoken since!"

"Is that where the others are?"

"Yes." Irina nodded slowly, sitting on her bed trying to regain her composure. "Pippa and Joey hardly ever leave him." I sat next to her, silent. My mind began to wonder. Was all this bloodshed really worth it? I still knew next to nothing about the Lightningstone, but what I did know was that people had died for it. Our friend Morgan Ocrina was just one amongst many others, and it still wasn't clear whether or not Taz would survive. I'd be devastated if he didn't make it…as would the others. He was such a good person, he didn't deserve this! I had to see him. Part of me felt responsible for his injuries. After all, he did get hurt so that Leon and I could get past. Balls, I was so worried about him.

"I'm gonna go and see him." I said.

"I'll come with you, just let me tidy up a little first. I need some time to think…"

"Sure." I smiled gently, standing up. "I need to check on Leon anyway. Just knock on my door when you're ready to go." I began to leave, and my hand gripped around the wooden door handle. I opened the door, but stopped when Irina called my name.

"Xanda!"

"Yeah?" I turned my head round to look at her, curious as to what she was going to say. She had spoken rather suddenly, which had made me more alert. She sniffled, looking up at me with her big, brown eyes.

"Do you think we'll ever be at peace again...?" She asked. I swallowed hard, thinking back to the conversation I'd had with my grandparents not too long ago. I smiled weakly and nodded a little.

"One day, Irina...one day..."

I headed back to my own room. Just as I was opening the door, I heard a low moan from inside. I swiftly pushed the door wide open and looked over to the bed. Leon was waking up! I dashed over and sat on the edge of the bed next to him. Placing a hand gently on his shoulder, I shook him softly. I spoke his name quietly, and watched as his eyelids parted to reveal the shimmering emerald underneath. I smiled down at him, overwhelmed with happiness to see him awake. The white strip in his hair slowly fell into his face, and he instantly blew it away. I just chuckled. I don't know what he had against that small section of hair, but he really didn't like it.

"Hi." I giggled softly.

"Hello." He replied, smiling back at me. "Where are we?"

"In our room. Are you feeling okay? You took quite a hit..." I asked worriedly. Leon just nodded and tried to push himself up. His eyes closed, and he let out a groan of pain. I helped him sit up, holding him tightly to support him.

"Be careful!" I told him, sounding a little bossy. Balls, I was starting to sound more like my Grandma by the day.

"I'll be fine. Jeez, you stress too much." He chuckled.

"Hey! I care, that's all! I've been worried sick about you!" I snapped, then took a deep breath. "I'm sorry. I'm still trying to get my head around all this."

"Yeah...I know what you mean." He said solemnly. "The Brozantan's sure ruined a perfect night..."

"The only person to blame is King Stephan. None of this would be happening if he didn't have an obsession with that bloody stone!"

"What happened to the stone?" Leon asked.

"Grandma and Gramps told me the royal family have it again."

"Your grandparents are here?" Leon asked, raising an eyebrow.

"Oh, yeah. They came after you passed out. Tenebris got away, but so did we." I told him. He then ran his hand through his dark hair, huffing heavily. He looked like he was trying to take it all in. It was hard for anyone to comprehend what had happened. Even the teachers were still on edge. You could feel the tension throughout the city, and in the very air itself. I watched as Leon took a deep breath, and looked at me reluctantly. He didn't want to ask his next question, but he knew that he had to.

"Is Taz...did he..." He spoke quietly, not able to get his words out. I rubbed his arm comfortingly.

"He's alive...but he's badly wounded. Irina said he's in the infirmary. We were just about to go and see him." I answered gently.

"I'm coming with you." He said suddenly.

"Are you sure?!" I asked. "You've just woken up, you should rest!"

"I'm fine. Besides...I need to see him." He looked so concerned, I just didn't have the heart to try and stop him. He was close to Taz and Joey after all.

"Alright." I gave in, smiling weakly at him. "C'mon. You need to get dressed."

"Right." He smiled back at me, and climbed out of bed. I watched as he groaned again, stretching his arms and body. He looked really stiff and tired. I was worried he was pushing himself too far too soon. But I knew Leon wouldn't listen to me, not when someone he cared about was hurt. He was very irrational when people he loved were in danger, and cared little for his own health at times like this. I often wished he'd take better care of himself. I admired his desire to help others, but he didn't half worry me. The events of the other night were harrowing, and so many people had died. Leon and I could easily have been one of those people. Luckily, we weren't, but I feared this war was far from over...

The three of us headed down to the infirmary, and the scene before us was unlike any I had ever seen before. Every single bed was filled. Ida McCoy was ordering around a team of nurses, looking completely stressed out. I had never seen so many wounded people! Rain began to pelt against the windows, much like when I was in here. The raindrops patted the glass quietly underneath the sounds of groaning victims and panicked doctors. My attention was immediately drawn to the first bed on the right, where Taz lay unconscious. I felt a lump in my throat, and all I could do is stare in shock as he lay there. His skin was sickeningly pale, and he had tubes coming out of his nose. There was also a needle in his arm, attached to a drip. I shivered, feeling a little faint. I hated needles, and I tried my best not to look at it as I hugged my arms tightly. Joey and Pippa sat either side of him, Joey squeezing Taz's hand tightly while Pippa stroked his snowy white hair. I tried to speak to get their attention, but no words came out. Irina stayed behind us, her hands pressed nervously over her chest. I glanced at Leon, who seemed to be having trouble taking this all in, just like I was. Now I knew how they all felt when I was in the infirmary, only Taz looked ten times worse. Taz was usually so full of life and joy...I hated to see him like this. It was then that Joey looked up, and I could see the pain in his face and the hurt he was feeling. But, he looked more hopeful as he spotted us, and he instantly stood and charged towards us. Pippa looked round to see where he was going as Joey threw his arms around Leon and I. He didn't say anything, but he didn't need to. Leon and I both hugged him back.

"Oh my goodness!" Pippa stood, covering her mouth as she teared up. "Leo! Xanda!"

"Were alright..." Leon stated sadly.

"Were fine." I said, as we pulled away from Joey. Pippa came over and embraced me, also pulling Leon into the tight hug too. When she pulled away, she quickly wiped away her tears.

"We were worried sick about you two!" She said, looking distraught.

"Yeah. You gave us quite a scare." Joey said running his hand tiredly through his brown hair. I looked at Taz once again, and moved over to his bed. I sat down on the end of the bed, just looking at him. Balls, he looked so sick.

"Not as much as he has though..." I bit my lip, placing my hand comfortingly on Taz's leg. Joey and Pippa slowly sat back down where they had been, while Leon sat on the other side of the bed next to me. Irina stood behind Pippa, and hugged her from behind supportively. We were all around him, all there to help him through this. Part of me wondered whether Taz knew we were there, or if he could hear us. Either way, we all had to be there to help him through this. I'd never seen Joey cry before, but tears were streaming rapidly down his face as he gazed down at his sleeping friend.

"It's going to be alright, Joey..." Leon spoke softly, trying to reassure him.

"Yeah...I know." Joey sniffled. "Taz waited for me when I couldn't come here when Mazei died. He stayed loyal to me. So...it's my turn now to wait for him."

"You're from Kazura like Pippa and Irina, aren't you? Have you always been so close?" I asked gently. Joey just smiled a little, wiping his face with his sleeve. He nodded.

"Yeah. For as long as I can remember. Our birthdays are exactly a week apart. I'm forever teasing him about it since I'm older. My parents own the town's butchers, and Taz used to come with me when I'd go hunting. His family run the antique shop, y'see. Taz hates stuff like that, unlike his brother Alistair. Man, that guys a proper nerd." We all smiled weakly as Joey explained about their home life. It was nice that Taz had somebody like Joey who always looked out for him. They were more like brothers than best friends, and it was heart breaking to see Joey so upset about this. If I felt this bad about it, I couldn't imagine how he must be feeling. I looked up again and watched as the rain began to fall heavier on the window, thinking how such a wonderful night had led to all this sorrow. I suddenly found myself looking at Taz sharply as the boy groaned uncomfortably in his sleep. Joey was over to him in a flash, kneeling by the bed and grasping his friends hand again. He rubbed his arm comfortingly, looking pained once again.

"Shh...it's okay, bro. I'm here. Your gonna be okay." Joey said quietly, trying to comfort him.

"He's so lucky to have you..." Irina spoke softly, smiling gently down at the grieving Joey. The brunette looked up at her slowly, and a small smile passed his lips.

"Thanks." He said. "We're always gonna have each other's backs..." As Joey spoke, Pippa reached over and once again began to stroke Taz's hair. Her gaze didn't leave him, and she watched over him like a guardian angel. It was so obvious Pippa had feelings for him. Even a blind man could see that, no matter how hard Pippa denied it. She placed her other hand on Taz's arm, and she began to become really upset. She closed her eyes for a moment, and I began to wonder what she was thinking. She looked melancholy, but incredibly angry at the same time. She was experiencing a whole wave of emotions, and she could no longer contain her thoughts.

"By the gods!" She snapped, which made us all jump. "Why did this have to happen?! What did that creep Stephan want anyway?!"

"The Lightningstone." I answered simply. The others paused, and they looked over at me. Joey sat up straight, and raised an eyebrow.

"The Lightningstone?" Joey said curiously. "What's that?"

"I don't know. But you said that you did." I answered, and turned my attention to Leon. I remembered that when we had first met the King and the Princess, Leon had stated he knew what it was but didn't have chance to tell me back then. The others looked at him too, all of us now looking to him for answers.

"There's a story behind it. Not many people know it, but my father is one among few that do. He told it to me once, and its bothered me ever since." Leon said, running his hand through his hair.

"Well, we've got all day. And if that stone is why Taz is lying here, then I think we all deserve an explanation." Pippa said.

"The tale dates back four hundred years. It's about Ingus Raven, brother of the Raven Queen and her twin sister." Leon started. This immediately piqued my interest. As I had mentioned before, not much is known about the Raven Queen's brother, and I always thought that was strange. Our history is filled with tales of Alexzero and Pipit Raven...so why not their brother? We all listened intently as Leon told us the tale. "Historians tell us many things about Ingus Raven, but one thing they all agree on is that he loved his family, above all else. He was also an experienced and powerful mage, and used his magical ability to protect his family and his kingdom. But he grew scared that his family was in danger, and he craved more power so he could protect them. He travelled to the beach, now known as Siren's Bay, and he searched for the most perfect, crystalized stone. He finally found it, and he had it split into four pieces. Ingus then infused the four pieces of the stone with the magic of the different elements: Lightning, Earth, Water and Fire. After that, he fused the stones back together, creating the Elemental Stone. He attached the stone to his staff, and he became the most powerful mage in the world, wielding the very fabrics of nature. However the stone, infused with magic, began to get a mind of its own. The stone filled Ingus's mind with dark thoughts. Instead of Ingus mastering the stone, the stone began to master him. Ingus became brainwashed, and he became a tyrant under the influence of the stone. He turned on the very people he swore to protect. Finally, Pipit Raven managed to rip the staff from Ingus's hands. Finally, Ingus was free.

But, to make sure nobody else could be imprisoned by the stone, the Raven siblings tried to destroy it. They found that they couldn't, so they split the stones back into their separate elements. The Lightningstone, the Earthstone, the Waterstone and the Firestone were passed down through the Raven's descendants, until the Lightningstone ended up in the hands of the Gailoiyn royal family, and the other three became lost. Legend says that if the stones were reunited, the one who held the Elemental stone would have the power of a god." Balls. We just looked between each other, utterly speechless. We didn't need to say anything, we were all thinking the same thing. If Stephan got a hold of the Elemental stones, and fused them back together, he would be unstoppable. We knew now, that was his goal. World domination. At this moment, we all saw Stephan's plan crystal clear. He wanted to re-forge the Elemental stone, and use its power to dominate us all.

Woah. Well, that was a lot of information to take in. Now knowing what was at stake, I realised just how much trouble we were all in. If Stephan succeeded, it would be the end of life as we knew it. He would destroy everything the Raven Queen fought so hard to rebuild. I needed to clear my head, so I headed up to the turret by my room. This turret was becoming very sentimental to me. It was where I had first properly met Leon, and it was where we had taken off into our very first battle. I sighed heavily, leaning against the cold stone and gazing out to the ocean. The waves were rough, crashing up against each other like they were at war. The wind blew ferociously through my golden hair, and my fists clenched so tightly my knuckles turned white. My eyes narrowed, and for some reason I was overcome with an empowering rage. You'd think, after recent events I'd be scared into submission. I would have thought that too. However, it just gave me more determination to keep on fighting. Someone had to stop Stephan. And yeah, it probably wasn't gonna be me. But the way I saw it, I could still help bring his demise. I may have been a new Dragon rider...but I was a Dragon rider. I felt responsible for the fate of the world, which only a few months ago was a thought I would have considered stupid. I looked to my right slowly, as I saw Leon join my side. His hair waved harshly in the wind, and he looked at me with his cool, emerald eyes.

"Seems were not so different." He said. "I always come up here to clear my head too."

"Leo...we need to talk." I said simply. He shuddered, instantly becoming nervous. He fidgeted with his hair a little and looked out to sea.

"O-Oh?" He stuttered. "What about?"

"About when you took that hit from Tenebris to give me an opening."

"Oh...that." He let out a long sigh and ran his fingers through his hair. "What about it?"

"Please don't ever do that again..." I looked at him, a worried tone apparent in my voice. I reached over and gently placed my hand over his, which caused him to look up at me once again. "I thought she'd killed you."

"I'm sorry. In the moment, I feared that if I didn't do something then she'd kill you." He replied, his eyes soft and caring.

"Just...don't be so rash. Next time you might not be so lucky."

"C'mon, Xanda. You're my rider. It's my job to keep you safe."

"Oh, stop being so chivalrous!" I let out a slight chuckle, but I had spoken seriously.

"Sorry. It's just the way I am." He smiled softly at me, and then turned his head away to look at the ocean once again. I however, kept looking at him. His very presence was entrancing, and I thought just how much of a gentleman he was. He was kind, compassionate, and cool headed for his age. I then thought back to when we had faced Tenebris. I had rarely seen him lose his temper, but I remembered how angry he had seemed when Tenebris had said Leon had killed his mother. I mean, I completely understood why he would be angry at that, but I started to wonder whether that was why he had such respect for women. His mother died so that he could live, and he often told me how much he respected her. Tenebris and Sera must have been complete opposites. From what I knew about Sera, she was a quiet and caring lady. It was a shame I would never get to meet her. She sounded wonderful.

"Leo..."

"Hm?" He looked at me out of the corner of his eye.

"What do you know about Tenebris?" I asked.

"Everything I already told you." He smiled weakly, taking a deep breath. "She is my mother's older sister. Father said that gradually she began to dabble in dark magic, and it consumed her. She was thrown into the asylum, and father said she most likely escaped." I pushed back on the stone balcony, stretching out and sighing heavily.

"Balls...all this for a stone. Well...four stones." I said, standing back up straight.

"I know not where the other three stones are." Said Leon. "But I do know we cannot allow them to fall into Stephan's hands."

"Pfft. Stephan's a coward!" I snapped. "All he's done so far is hide behind his army. I bet he wouldn't be so tough if he himself fought on the battlefield!"

"Don't underestimate him." Leon told me. "He's the mastermind behind all of this...and I speculate that it won't be long until he reveals himself to us."

"Well, he's obviously going to try and either take the Lightningstone again, or locate the other three. The question is...where are they?"

"Alas, the legend gives us no clues...and nobody has seen them in years." Leo sighed, running his hand through his hair. "Except..."

"Except?"

"Well, you know I've been researching Fergo the Great Dragon a lot recently..."

"Yes...?" I raised an eyebrow, starting to wonder where this was going.

"Well, some say that he knew where they were."

"Oh, well that's helpful! We don't even know where he is, or even if he's still alive!"

"Yes, I know that. I've been looking for clues as to his location. Assuming he is alive, of course." He said. Well, I don't think I had absorbed this much information in one day before. I felt like my head was gonna explode! Stephan's plan was now revealed to us, and the only one that could help us was an ancient Dragon that may or may not be alive.

"Oh great…" I sighed heavily, huffing in frustration.

"Well, at least the Lightningstone is safe."

"For now." I added.

"Well, let's just focus on keeping it safe. And if we can, find the locations of the other three stones." I nodded in response. That was the main objective now. We had to keep our world safe, and if that meant finding the stones before Stephan did, then that is what we would do. Suddenly, we both jumped, hearing a voice from behind us. We turned swiftly to see who had spoken.

"But you can't do it alone."

"Naia?" I said in surprise. It was unusual to see him without Seto, and Leon and I both wondered what he was doing here alone. We watched as his dirty blonde hair waved in the wind, and we could hear the soft tap of his shoes on the cold stone as he walked towards us.

"Hey, Naia. Where's your brother?" Leo asked curiously.

"He's taking a bath. I'm sorry, I wasn't eavesdropping on you…I just came up here to clear my head."

"So did we." I smiled softly, a smile that soon faded. I saw a wound on his neck, a large gash going diagonally up the right side. I narrowed my eyes. The wound didn't look fresh, so it was clear he hadn't sustained it in the recent attack. Naia seemed to have noticed where I was looking, and he quickly adjusted his coat to hide the scar.

"I-I'm sorry!" He stuttered nervously. "I didn't mean to-"

"Hey!" I placed my hands on his arms comfortingly, and he looked at me in fright. Something wasn't right with him. He wasn't like his brother at all. Naia was so jumpy and cautious, and became incredibly anxious when I saw his scar. "Don't worry…it's alright."

"Please don't think badly of me!" Naia sniffled, looking like he was about to cry.

"Naia, calm down. We don't think badly of you at all." Leon smiled gently. "I happen to think you are very brave."

"R-Really?" Naia wiped his eyes with his sleeve. I began to grow more curious as to how he had gotten that scar, but I didn't want to upset him. I was worried somebody had done that to him.

"Who did that to you?" I queried worriedly.

"It was my father." Naia looked down sadly. I was taken back in shock. Jasper Ventus wouldn't do something like that, surely! Leon seemed to know what I was thinking, and he spoke quickly to set the record straight.

"His biological father. Mr Ventus adopted Seto and Naia."

"Papa and Seto saved my life!" Naia smiled a little proudly as he mentioned Jasper and his brother.

"Naia, you don't have to tell me if you don't want to..." I said.

"No. No I want to...I want to be strong like Seto."

"Well, if it will make you feel better, then Leon and I are always here to listen." I smiled gently, and Naia let out a sigh of relief. He seemed happy, but it was obvious a deep depression weighed him down, and after what he told me, I wasn't surprised.

"We grew up in Eruznor, the Brozantan capital. Our father was a noble, and a trusted friend of King Stephan. But what he was really proud of, is that generations of our family have always been Dragonbourne...until me. He hated me for it, and made me do things I didn't want to do. I couldn't have a home tutor like Seto, and I had to work with the servants. If I did the slightest thing wrong, he'd hit me...with anything. Mostly it was his belt, but sometimes he used harder objects...he even pulled a knife on me once. I was so weak, so hungry, and so bruised I could barely get out of bed. Seto was treated fine, but his loyalty to me is something I will always treasure. He hated our father, and begged him many times to stop hurting me. But he didn't listen. So, as soon as we came of age, Seto wrote a letter to Wyvern Academy, explaining our situation. He didn't write to Bloodbourne Academy because he wanted to get as far away from father as we could. The letter was answered, by none other than papa...Jasper Ventus." Naia smiled mentioning Jasper. I didn't interrupt him. His story was so mellow, and I couldn't believe what he had gone through. I just listened in silence as he continued his story. "After reading Seto's letter, he personally came to our home. Seto let him in, and my father was beating me around the back with his belt. Papa stopped him, and father went crazy. He grabbed his sword and began attacking not just papa, but me and Seto as well. Papa managed to stop him, and he took Seto and I away from there. I'm not going to lie, I was a shivering wreck. I wouldn't leave the house at all, because I was scared our father would come back for us. It wasn't long until we heard he had been killed in a brawl, and I didn't know what to feel...happy because he couldn't hurt me, or sad because he was dead. But I didn't feel sad. I felt nothing. He meant nothing to me. I began to wonder if that made me a bad person. Then one day, papa took us aside, and he asked if he could adopt us. He asked if he could have the honour of being our father. That...that was the happiest day of my life, and Seto's too. Finally, we felt like we belonged somewhere. Jasper Ventus didn't define us as Dragonbourne or Human. He defined us by who we were, and he wanted to keep us because of that. He truly is an amazing gentleman." I was almost in tears as Naia spoke, and it was now clearly obvious why the twins had so much respect and admiration for Mr Ventus. Naia was right, he really was a great man, and he had such a big heart. After Naia told his story, I also felt a growing respect for Jasper. It couldn't have been easy taking on two children that aren't your own and have had such a bad start in life. I slowly put my arms around Naia, and pulled him into a tight hug. Naia was a little confused at first, but he hugged me back and spoke softly. "W-What's this for...?"

"You just looked like you needed a hug." I pulled back and smiled at him, and he smiled back. I could see how happy he was that he finally had friends his own age that he could turn to. He was only a year older than us after all. "Thank you, Xanda. And thank you too Leon. It felt good to get all that off my chest..." He said.

"It's no problem, Naia. We stick together here." Leon smiled, patting his arm gently in support. Naia blushed a little, adjusting his coat again.

"That we do. So, if you need help finding the stones, you have mine and Seto's support. Although, I doubt our parents and grandparents will be happy about it."

"That don't matter now, does it?" I said leaning against the wall. "We're already part of this mess. We can't just turn our backs when things get difficult." Leon turned to look at me, and a grin spread widely across his face. "This is why you are the best partner ever!" Typical Leon. He never did back away from a fight knowing it was the right thing to do. That wasn't his style. Come to think of it, it wasn't my style either.

It was almost dinner time, and I had been reeling over what Naia had told me all day. He and Seto had gone off to visit Taz in the infirmary. Leon and I were going to go there too after we'd had something to eat. We hadn't eaten in days, since we were trying to take everything in after we had woken up. My stomach ached and groaned loudly through the hunger, and I couldn't wait to get something to eat. We knew we had to keep our strength up so we could be there for Taz. Balls, I still couldn't believe how bad he was. Seeing someone so strong looking like that was awful. It was a reality check however. This was really happening. This was real. A war was beginning, and Tazmin would be the first of many to be injured or even die. It was a sad thought, but a true one. How the hell did I ever end up in this situation? Leon and I were just about to enter the great hall when we stopped suddenly. Grandma and Gramps were walking out, and they smiled down at us.

"Leon!" Grandma beamed. "It's good to see you up and about again!"

"Thank you, Mrs Sykes. Its lovely to see you again." Leon said politely.

"We were just about to come and find you, Xanda." Grandpa said softly.

"We're about to head home." I suddenly felt a wave of sadness wash over me, and I rushed forward and hugged him. He smiled softly, and hugged me back. Grandma slowly put her arms around me as well. Balls, I had missed them so much before. Now they were here, it was hard to see them go again. I felt comforted in their arms, and for a moment it seemed like all my worries faded away like a dying fire. I closed my eyes, and allowed myself to be lost in the moment.

"Oh Xanda…" Grandma sighed softly, and began to stroke my hair.

"We'll see you again soon. I promise." Grandpa smiled down at me reassuringly. I was so lucky to have them in my life. I just squeezed them tighter, not wanting to let them go. I knew they had to go though. They were needed at home, and I was needed here.

So when they left Algora, I did not leave with them…

Chapter 12

Cooped Inside a Castle

On the other side of the Plain of Fire, King Stephan was in a rage about his loss. His army had been unable to retrieve the Lightningstone, and he was furious. The royal castle in Brozanta had been quiet for days, ever since the battle had been lost. The halls were dark and eerie and everyone was on edge, fearful that they should be on the opposing end to Stephan's wrath. One such boy feared this above all else. He was King Stephan's ward, as was his mother. The boy hadn't seen his protector in days, but he knew it was only a matter of time before he was summoned. He had never left the castle before, so the outside world was unfamiliar to him. He was only a few years younger than myself but he was wise for his age, yet timid. He would often stand on the balcony in his bedroom, gazing out over the city below him and dreaming what it would be like to be allowed out there just for one day. His deep green eyes scanned the horizon, as the wind blew his golden hair. He placed a pale hand on the stone balcony and closed his eyes, wanting to be lost in his own thoughts for a while. His mother had named him Cooper, a name the boy's father had always loved. Stephan however, said the boy should have a more appropriate name for a future king, as this was why Stephan had raised him. Stephan named the boy Julian. However, he was known as Cooper to all except the king. Despite Stephan's heavy influence the boy had his own mind, and he was beginning to question everything around him. Just then he opened his eyes, and turned around to see two of his friends walk into his room. The first was an elven girl. She was a slave of Stephan, whom was having a secret affair with his also enslaved nephew, Lucas. Her hands were loosely cuffed, and her pointy ears were bleeding. She had light pink hair in a long ponytail, and her fringe looked all messy like she had been ragged around. Her eyes were dark green like a forest, and she had a dark green leaf and vine tattoo over her right eye. Her name was Mahariel Rhonaa, and she was beautiful, yet timid like Cooper. She was afraid of most in the castle, except Lucas, Cooper and the other girl she had entered with. The other girl was no prisoner, and Cooper adored her with all his heart. Her name was Genevieve Farron, and she was simple looking, but pristine. She had gorgeous pink eyes that shone in the sunlight, and long, light brown hair that flowed behind her. She was the daughter of Stephan's advisor, yet she was treated badly like most in the castle. Her dress was short and loose, light pink in colour and tied at the waist by a rope. Cooper saw even more beauty within her, despite him being so young, he was completely in love. Mahariel moved over to Cooper's unmade bed, and began to tidy it hurriedly. The boy walked back into his room, and shut the door to his balcony behind him.

"Mahariel, please…you don't have to do that! I can make it myself!" He said nervously.

"Oh, it's alright, my lord. I don't mind cleaning up for you." She replied sweetly. Cooper just looked uncomfortable as she addressed him with such formality, and he shifted timidly.

"P-Please don't call me that…" He told her softly. "I've told you before, calling me Cooper is fine!"

"She just doesn't want to get in trouble with the King if he ever heard her address you so." Genevieve moved over to Cooper, and placed a gentle kiss upon his cheek. The boy blushed brightly and he raised his hand, brushing her cheek lovingly with the back of his fingers.

"I know. I'm sorry Mahariel...I'm quite tense myself. Say, do you both want to stay here for a while? We can play chess!" He beamed excitedly. Cooper and Genevieve often played chess, as it allowed them to forget the hardships they were enduring. However, this time, Genevieve looked at him sadly and shook her head.

"I'd love to, Cooper, but..."

"But?"

"The King asked me to come and get you. He wants to see you in his chambers." She told him. The boy turned paler than usual, and physically gulped. He hated seeing Stephan at the best of times, but he knew this time he was already in a foul mood.

"What now?!" Cooper turned his back to them, hugging his arms nervously. Gen placed a comforting hand on his shoulder, trying to give him courage.

"You have to go, Cooper...he is your protector-" Gen started, but Cooper swiftly turned around and cut off her sentence.

"But not my father! He will never be my father!"

"Who was your father?" Mahariel came over to them, speaking softly. "Its common knowledge that you were born here, and the king keeps your mother close to him. Are you sure he isn't your father?"

"I'm positive." Cooper stated. "The king has forbidden my mother of ever talking to me about him. He doesn't like my father being mentioned...but my mother did say one thing to me in confidence. She told me he wasn't of noble blood, but with him she felt like the wealthiest woman alive. She said he was a good, honest man. That's how I always pictured him..." Cooper smiled weakly at the memory, as did the girls. Gen leaned over and placed a small kiss on Cooper's lips, which made the boy turn deep red. She smiled at him.

"I'm sure he was a good man. But Cooper, you should head to the King now. You know he doesn't like to be kept waiting." She ran her fingers through Cooper's golden hair, and the boy nodded slowly.

"You're right. Please Gen...take care of Mahariel, alright? I don't want her to be whipped again." As Cooper spoke, Mahariel lowered her head.

"I will." Gen replied. "You're a good man, Cooper."

"That you are, my lord." Mahariel raised her head again and looked at the boy. "And...thank you, for keeping quiet about Lucas and I. I dread to think how the King would react if he knew."

"It's quite alright." Cooper smiled. "You two are great together."

"Please, be careful." Gen looked at him worriedly, and Cooper nodded gently before slowly leaving his room. The girls looked on in a panic, then at each other. They both knew this wasn't a good sign.

Cooper made his way through the winding halls, a fearful pain in his chest. The castle seemed darker than normal, and the darkness scared him. It was so unpredictable. He didn't like the winter. He liked the summer. The blazing sun often soothed his soul, but there was no sun that day. The castle grounds were covered in ice, and the air was chilly. He felt the cold more than most people, and he shivered as he made his way through the long halls. He began to wonder why his protector wanted to see him, especially while in such a bad mood. Stephan scared the poor boy, as did many others in the castle. Unluckily for him, he was about to bump into another. He had made his way to the ground floor, and was walking past the infirmary. That room had been busy for days, much like the one in the academy. As he passed, the large door suddenly swung open, and Cooper felt a figure bang into him. He gasped in surprise, and retreated into himself as the majestic mage Tenebris Magicae loomed over him. She was scowling at the boy, still in a terrible mood after her recent loss.

"Watch where you are going, boy!" She snapped at him. Cooper took a few steps back, his body physically shaking in terror.

"I-I'm sorry!" He stuttered. "I didn't mean it! Please...don't be mean to me..." He asked in an innocent tone. He hated Tenebris being uptight with him, as she could be so unpredictable at times. Tenebris just laughed at his question, which scared Cooper more. The mage grabbed the boy by his ear, and he gasped in pain as she led him to an empty corridor. His ear was throbbing in pain, but he knew better than to scream for help. He had done that once, and she had just shut him up using magic and hurt him ten times more. She loved torturing and toying with Cooper. She enjoyed it. And Cooper probably feared her more than he did King Stephan. There was no limit to her insanity. Tenebris shoved Cooper against the wall, and pinned him there by his hair. She was rough with him, yet the boy tried not to show he was in pain. He looked at her, desperate to not let her see he was afraid. He knew she hungered for fear, and it was what drove her to do wicked things.

"What are you doing...?" Cooper swallowed hard.

"Telling you the truth." Tenebris laughed. "You may think you are safe. You have been raised as the king's heir after all. But if he were to have a child...he would no longer need you. You would be cast aside like the son of the old fool king. Maybe you won't even be as lucky as him. Maybe you will die. And trust me...it would give me great pleasure to end your miserable life myself." Tenebris laughed, enjoying seeing Cooper squirming in fear as she spoke. He could no longer hide the fact he was afraid, and he began to struggle, tears forming in the brim of his eyes. He didn't want to die, but he didn't want to be King either.

"Get away from me!" Cooper squealed, and he pushed her away. He wasted no time in taking off down the hall, running as fast as his little legs would carry him. His heart was pounding as Tenebris's laugh echoed through the empty halls as the terrified child ran away from her twisted mind.

He dashed through the halls, not knowing where he was going. He just wanted to get away from Tenebris. Tears were streaming down his face. He had never been so scared. As much as he hated to admit it, Tenebris was right. If Stephan had a child of his own, he would be in danger, as would his mother. He would no longer be needed! And when that happened, Tenebris would kill him. He knew she had it in her, as he'd witnessed her kill people before. Death was something Cooper had become accustomed to, although no matter how many of his friends died under the king's influence, it never got any easier. A bringer of death was not what Cooper wanted to be, but he feared the longer he stayed there, the more inevitable that future became. He was suddenly halted to a stop as he turned a corner, as he found himself yet again running into somebody. He hit a large man, who didn't even flinch when the small boy pounded into him. Cooper gingerly looked up to see Hendrix Montgomery and his partner Adamski behind him. The mischievous looking Dragonbourne had a grin on his face, and the first thing Cooper noticed was that he had had a haircut. The sides of his ginger hair were shaved, and the top was thick and spiked upwards. Funny, he hadn't remembered him looking like that before the attack on Gailoiyn. He didn't dwell on it too much though, as he was still shaking madly from his ordeal with Tenebris. Adamski raised his hand at Cooper, who flinched, as he scolded him in his high-pitched voice.

"Hey! Watch where you are going!" Adamski said, swiping his hand towards the boy's face. Hendrix however, grabbed his friend's wrist and stopped Cooper from being assaulted. He looked down at the quivering boy.

"Enough, Adamski." Hendrix said, loosing his friend's wrist. He then placed a gentle hand on Cooper's shoulder, which made him feel more at ease. Hendrix must have been one of the only people in the castle that had never hit him or abused him. For some reason the knight had respect for the boy, and that respect was shared both ways. "Are you alright, little lord?" Hendrix continued.

Cooper nodded. "I-I'm okay...thank you, sir." Hendrix just simply nodded in approval, yet Adamski just laughed.

"What's ruffled your feathers?! Why are you crying?" Adamski teased. Cooper swiftly sniffled, wiping the tears away from his eyes quickly.

"I...I'm not crying!" The boy protested, trying to act tough.

"You so are!" Adamski laughed, and poked Cooper's cheek provocatively. Cooper squirmed, trying to shy away from him.

"Adamski!" Hendrix suddenly boomed, to which the other two flinched. Cooper cowered against the wall. Just for once in his life, he wanted to be left alone. He didn't want people prodding and poking and hitting him. Just for one day, he didn't want to be somebody's punch bag, or at the other end of Tenebris practicing her new spells. He was growing up, and he was changing. He didn't want this life. He thought about all this in such a small space of time as Hendrix moved over to him, and gazed down at him with his narrow, but soft eyes.

"Listen, little lord. I know I am not your father but if you ever need to talk to anyone, you can always come and talk to me." He said, very straight forward. Cooper raised an eyebrow, not expecting such an offer. He was grateful, but he knew Hendrix was a busy man and didn't want to bother him. So he just accepted the offer, not wanting to continue the conversation. He didn't want to feel like he was in the way.

"Thank you, Mr Montgomery. But I will be alright." Cooper said, smiling weakly. Hendrix again just nodded in approval, and began heavily walking down the corridor. Cooper watched after him, but jumped when Adamski yet again poked his cheek. He flinched, and watched as Adamski started laughing, following his partner. They disappeared around the corner. Cooper let out a huge sigh, leaning against the wall. He ran his fingers through his golden hair. Could this day get any worse?

Cooper began walking at a normal pace again, positive now that Tenebris was no longer following him. He hated that woman, with every fibre in his small body. Just thinking about her made him feel dizzy and nervous, and he wished she had remained in the asylum. If he ever lived to be king, he was sure the first thing he would do would be to send her back there. But he didn't want to be king at all. He wasn't a leader, and he knew that. He just wanted a quiet life in a small village with his mother and his friends...but he knew that was never to be. Just then, he came upon the grand staircase, which led up to a corridor where the king's rooms resided. However, at the bottom of the stairs, he saw his friend scrubbing the steps. His friend was none other than the nineteen-year-old missing Prince Lucas. Although he wasn't missing, he just hadn't been seen by anybody outside of the castle since Stephan assassinated his father. After that, he had been enslaved by his uncle and had been there ever since. His black hair was a mess, falling in front of his face and his rags hung loosely around his thin body. He was wearing cuffs around his wrists and his ankles, just like Mahariel. Cooper hated seeing him in such a state. He didn't understand why Stephan would treat anybody so badly, even if they did pose a threat to your crown. Cooper slowly walked over and sat on the first step, looking down at Lucas.

"Hey. Let me help you, Lucas..." Cooper said softly, but Lucas just began to scrub the steps harder.

"No, Cooper! Please...I don't want to get in trouble again. I'm already cleaning the steps as a punishment." He protested. Cooper just watched him sadly, noticing his friend covered in cuts and bruises.

"Have you been beaten again...?" Cooper asked quietly. Lucas began to scrub the marble stairs even harder, trying to block out painful memories.

"I don't want to talk about it, Cooper."

"They shouldn't be doing this to you!" Cooper said tearful. "You're the prince!"

"No! You're the prince!" Lucas suddenly sat up straight, and threw the scrubbing brush into his wooden bucket. He sighed, and sat on the step next to Cooper, continuing to speak to the boy. "I'm sorry I snapped, Cooper. Look. I accept my place. I am a prisoner of the king now. Now you must learn to accept your place, Cooper. You're going to be king one day."

"But I don't want to be king!" Cooper protested, looking at Lucas sadly. "We all know the king only raised me so you wouldn't be the rightful heir anymore. And even if I was the rightful heir, I still wouldn't want it! It's not me, Lucas. You're my best pal...and you...you are the rightful heir. Not me!"

"Shh!" Lucas hushed him, looking around the room nervously to see if anybody was listening. His heart was pounding fast. He knew this isn't what Cooper wanted. This wasn't what he wanted either. But he had to accept that it was going to happen. He gently placed a hand on Cooper's shoulder, whispering. "Don't say things like that. Talk like that will get us both killed. It's treason."

"But it's true, Lucas..." Cooper said quietly. There was a pause in the conversation, and both boys stared at the ground in silence, thinking on what the other had said. Lucas looked over at a ripped portrait of his father hanging on the wall. King Octavian was a good man, and he hated his uncle for what he had done. There was no conflict under his father's rule, and Brozanta and Gailoiyn were happy, and good neighbours. Stephan had ruined everything for the sake of power, and he was dragging poor Cooper down with him. He looked at Cooper sadly. He was so young and innocent. He didn't deserve any of this. He was in the middle of a war, when all he wanted was to live peacefully with his mother. Lucas knew the other boy's origins, and had also been forbidden from mentioning anything to him. But he did know Cooper had a chance at happiness, and he would make sure he got it, even if he lost everything.

"Go on, kiddo." Lucas smiled gently, finally speaking. "I take it you're off to see his majesty? You know he doesn't like to be kept waiting."

"Yeah, I guess you're right." Cooper looked up at him, smiling weakly. "I'll see you later though, right?" The blonde stood, and stepped up onto the next step. Lucas smiled, nodding his head.

"Just be careful, alright? Watch what you say."

"Don't I always?"

"No." Lucas chuckled. Cooper just blushed, knowing Lucas was right. He often didn't say the right thing when he was supposed to. He waved at Lucas, and began to make his way up the stairs.

"Okay, you win. See you later." Cooper smiled, turning his back on his friend and hurrying up the stairs.

"Hopefully..." Lucas trailed off as he said this, his face becoming mellow as he watched Cooper climb the stairs. He began to get more concerned, knowing first-hand what his uncle was like while in a temper. He silently prayed for Cooper, hoping to the gods he would be okay...

It wasn't long before Cooper was near the door to Stephan's office, but as he approached, he heard raised voices inside the room. The boy gingerly crept towards the door, and pressed an ear against the rough wood. King Stephan was in there, that was clear. He'd recognise his voice anywhere. It also didn't take long to figure out who else was in there either. He couldn't make out what they were saying, but Stephan and his mother were arguing ferociously. He heard his name mentioned a few times, which made him jump, terrified Stephan would discover him listening in. Suddenly, he heard a door slamming from the inside, and he could no longer hear his mother's voice. She must have left through the other door. Cooper could feel his body becoming tense, knowing for sure now that the King was in an argumentative mood. Cooper hated conflict, and every ounce of his heart warned him that he shouldn't go and see the king. But fear consumed him like a cage, and he worried that if he didn't go in, Stephan would come and get him himself. Cooper's entire body was shaking, from his head right down to his toes. He had a terrible feeling about this. He closed his eyes, and took a long, deep breath in. He let it out heavily, his breath quivering. Slowly, he knocked on the door.

"Come in." Cooper heard Stephan's sickeningly sweet voice respond to the sound of the ghostly knock echoing through the empty hall. The door creaked open, and the soft sound of Stephan's music box swept throughout the room. Cooper took a few steps in, the docile sound of the music doing little to calm his nerves. The study was decorated in royal red and glittering gold, flaunting the King's status to anyone who dare enter his domain. He sat at his golden desk, his chin resting on his hands as he listened to the pure sound of the music float to his ears. The silver music box rested on the desk beside him, and twirling in the centre was a small statue of a woman. Cooper's gaze slowly turned back to the King who's long, midnight black hair sprawled over his shoulders. His skin was as white as snow, and his black armour was shining in the candlelight. Cooper cleared his throat nervously, and Stephan opened his blood red eyes. Although soft, the music made this moment seem more eerie than usual. If he wasn't already on edge, he sure was now as the demon king stared right through the young child.

"Lord Julian." Stephan opened his thin lips, to address Cooper with the title and name he had chosen for him many years ago. Cooper couldn't stand the name Julian, which is why he had always opted to be called Cooper, his mother's choice of name. Stephan pushed himself back in his seat, and his hair shifted out of his left eye, revealing three distinct gashes down the side of his face. He'd had those scars for as long as Cooper could remember, but he never knew how Stephan had gotten them. The King had never told him about it, not surprisingly. Stephan was a very private man.

"G-Good afternoon, your majesty." Cooper stuttered nervously. Stephan once again rested his chin on his knuckled fist as he leaned back even further, his other hand grasping around the arm of the chair.

"How are you this fine day?" The king asked, his expression not even changing one bit. His voice was very monotone, nothing like the angry man he had been before Cooper had entered the room.

"I'm well, my lord..."

"I hear a 'but' coming. Spit it out, boy." Stephan said. Cooper averted his gaze, growing anxious. He wasn't going to say anything more, but Stephan could always tell when Cooper wanted to say something.

"W-Well..." Cooper swallowed hard. "I have been growing concerned about fellow members of the castle."

"What?!" Stephan, in an instant, flew into a rage! He stood, booming at the top of his voice as he smacked the music box off his desk. The music stopped playing, and Stephan stormed round the desk towards the shaking Cooper. "You are talking about that drat Lucas again, aren't you, boy?! You've been speaking to him again, haven't you?!"

"H-He's my friend, your majesty!" Cooper said stumbling backwards.

"Friend?! Friend?! He doesn't know the meaning of the word!" Stephan boomed. "I told you never to consort yourself with the likes of him! I warned you!"

"I'm sorry! I'm sorry!" Cooper squealed, but his pleas fell on deaf ears. Stephan grabbed the boy by his golden hair, and threw him over his desk. Cooper knew what was coming next...but he had no time to prepare himself for it. The King swiftly removed his belt, and started pounding Cooper's back with it. Cooper was crying, and screaming in agony. Tears streamed down his cheeks as the lashes swiped his back rapidly, one after another. Stephan was in a blind rage, gritting his teeth as he watched the small boy squirm under him. Cooper was just yelling, screeching from the back of his throat, begging him to stop. The stings were etching deeper and deeper into his skin and his whole body began to freeze up, unable to move. It took a while, but Stephan finally stopped, dropping his belt on the desk next to Cooper, panting hard. Cooper was frozen in terror, sobbing his little heart out. His hands were trembling, and he was unable to stop them from doing so. His breath was ragged and uneven as he slowly pushed himself up, crying out in pain and shock. He let out a groan of pain as he stood, his back aching, stinging and throbbing in agony. Stephan gazed down at the boy, and he was suddenly calm again as he moved over to him.

"Shhh..." Stephan said, trying to calm the boy down as he wrapped his arms around him. He pulled Cooper into a hug, and stroked the back of his head gently, becoming almost a different person. Of course, Cooper was used to this sort of behaviour from the King, but he still shivered as Stephan embraced him with his strong arms. Cooper sobbed into Stephan, wanting any sort of comfort he could get, even though what he really wanted was to get the hell out of there. "There there, child...it's all going to be fine." Stephan reassured him, pulling back a little and gently wiping the tears from Cooper's face. He smiled softly at him, and began to stroke his hair again.

"I...I'm sorry, my lord..." Cooper muttered quietly between his sobs.

"It's alright, Julian." He stated plainly. "How about we spend some time together...father and son bonding, eh? I'll teach you what it really means to be a man." Stephan smiled at Cooper, and the boy nodded in response, not having the courage to refuse him. Stephan walked over to his coat hanger, and pulled off his red cape. He draped it over his shoulders, and began to walk out of the room.

"Follow." He said simply, and Cooper began to obey almost instantly. His mind began to wonder, fearing what Stephan had planned. Did he genuinely want to spend time with him? Or...did he have something more sinister planned? As Cooper followed the King down the quiet halls, he couldn't possibly imagine what lay ahead of him...

Stephan led Cooper outside, and the chilly air did nothing to soothe the boy's aching back. Every step Cooper took was like running a mile, his wounds stinging like crazy as he walked hurriedly to keep up with the King. He had no idea where he was being taken, but he was starting to think that Stephan really did want to spend some time with him. If he wanted to hurt him anymore, he'd have done it by now, right? Wrong. Cooper was devastated when he saw where he was being taken. The gallows outside the barracks. Cooper froze, all the colour draining from his face as he stared at the ropes dangling in the winter wind. Stephan turned to face Cooper as the boy watched five people being led up onto the platform. He couldn't believe this...Stephan had brought him to watch an execution! Cooper just wanted to cry! He didn't want this...he didn't want any of this!

"Come now, child." Stephan said gently. Cooper just shook his head, petrified. He just wanted to go back to his room, and he didn't want the people in front of him to die, no matter what they'd done. "I said come on!" Stephan grabbed the back of Cooper's neck, and began to force him towards the scaffold. There was a man standing by the lever, wearing a black mask. Cooper just stared at him, whimpering quietly. He looked at the prisoners as another man began to place the ropes around the necks of the men. Cooper felt his heartbeat race ahead of him, realising that one of the prisoners was a young knight who had been a kind friend to him. His friend looked terrified, but poised and ready to die. Cooper fumbled backwards, biting back his tears.

"W-What have they done?!" Cooper asked.

"Deserters from the battle with Gailoiyn." Stephan said. "Turned tail and ran away. Cowards."

"I don't blame them." Cooper gulped. "Life is much more important than anything."

"Foolish boy." Stephan scoffed. "Deserting is a crime! Running away from your duty to me is treason!" He then grinned widely, having an idea. He slowly turned his head to face Cooper, and the boy physically gulped. Cooper knew he had an idea in mind, that was how Stephan always looked when he was planning something sinister. It was a look he dreaded, and there was a deathly silence as the wind rustled through the nearby trees. Stephan finally spoke, projecting his voice. "Executioner! Hold!" Stephan then grabbed a hold of Cooper's arm, and pulled him up onto the platform despite much struggling from Cooper. Cooper was panting hard, struggling to breathe. Was Stephan going to have him hanged too? He was terrified he was going to die. That however, was not what Stephan had in mind. What Stephan had in mind was much, much darker. He turned to the child, and placed a hand on Cooper's head, ruffling the boy's hair before speaking.

"Julian. You will pull the lever."

"What?! No!" Cooper instantly teared up, looking over at his friend quickly as the rope was tightened around his neck by the guard. His gaze met his friends, and his friend nodded slowly, knowing it would get worse for Cooper if he didn't obey. His head felt fuzzy, and he wanted to pass out. Surely he wasn't going to make him go through with this?! Cooper was in a panic, and he shook his head furiously, lost for words. "No, no no no no! No! I won't do it! I won't!"

"You will do as I say, or your mother will pay for your disobedience." Stephan said scornfully. Cooper just stared at him, open mouthed and lost for words. He knew Stephan meant what he said. He'd hurt his mother before, and that was the last thing he wanted. He was so scared...he didn't want anybody to be hurt because of him! He stepped up to the lever reluctantly, and placed a shaky hand upon it. He felt the smooth, damp wood under his fingertips, and his mind became blank. Stephan leaned his head over Cooper's shoulder and whispered into the boy's ear, which made him jump.

"Go on. Make me proud, Julian! You are not a true man until you take a life."

Cooper couldn't look at his friend...he just stared ahead of him, frozen. The world was silent, and the wind brushed his golden hair. He had to do this. For his mother. He just kept telling himself that he was brave, that he could do it. His fingers were shaking, as the bitter breeze swept across the ground. His heart was full of guilt. Cooper closed his eyes, as tight as he could...

...and he pulled the lever.

Chapter 13
The Forgotten World

A few weeks passed since that fateful day, and Algora was slowly coming to grips with the tragedy that had occurred. Winter had faded, and spring was just around the corner. The sky lightened, and beautiful baby pink blossoms were forming on trees all over Gailoiyn. It was getting warmer again, and the sun beamed down on the pitiful earth below. Life was becoming more stable, considering the magnitude of recent events. Slowly but surely, the townspeople were getting back to normal. However, an anxiety hung in the air. All of Algora was still very much on edge, afraid something like this may happen again. The good news however, was that Taz was recovering. He had been sitting up in bed and talking nonstop as per usual. It was good to know his personality was still intact, even if he did annoy the hell out of me. He was still pretty weak though, and he still hadn't been discharged from the infirmary. We visited him often over those few weeks, but he was showing signs of improvement with each passing day. I don't think he realised how lucky he was to even be alive. Anyway, you remember that sword that was on my bed as the siege started? Well it was still in my room. Nobody had come to reclaim it. It had served me well, so I didn't think twice about not getting rid of it. Maybe someone had left it there for me to keep? Whoever it was, I just wished I had known their identity, or where the sword had come from. It really was a mystery. Anyway, it was a lovely day, and the heat was warm but not muggy. I was sitting by the pond, gazing out to the water, deep in thought. Leon stood by the water's edge, with a lighter in his hand. He used his other hand to try and bend the small flame away from the lighter. He suddenly began to get rather excited as the flame moved away from its source, and hovered above his palm. Suddenly, the flame extinguished, and a rush of disappointment surged through him. I let out a soft chuckle and watched him try again. He was nothing if not determined. He had been practicing his fire bending so often since he had seen Princess Veronica do it so successfully. I did feel a little sorry for him, as I could see how frustrated he was becoming. Most of the Dragonbourne's in our class had gotten the hang of it, but Leon had told me once it was something he had always struggled with. He once again removed the flame from the lighter, and it hovered above his palm. His emerald eyes widened happily as the flame began to grow bigger. He turned to me, full of excitement.

"Xanda look! I did it! Uh oh…" He suddenly trailed off, screaming as the flame bounced back towards him and knocked him backwards. I covered my face as Leon plunged into the pond, feeling a few cool water droplets land on my face. I couldn't contain my laughter anymore, and instead of helping him, I was paralyzed with laughter. I placed one hand on the soft grass to steady myself, and I felt an ache in my cheeks as I smiled wider than ever before. I used my other hand to wipe my eyes as I felt tears of joy forming at the brim of my eyes. Leon however didn't look impressed. He stood, soaked to the bone as he waded through the water and back onto the bank.

"Oh gods…" Leon groaned.

"Oh come on, it wasn't that bad. I'll give you top marks for style." I giggled. Quickly I took off my jacket and threw it to him. He caught it swiftly, and began to dry his face with it.

"It's not funny, Xanda!" Leon said sighing heavily, sounding upset. "I'm never gonna be able to get this, am I?"

"Oh Leo…" I stood, and moved over to him. I took the jacket from him and gently wiped his face with it.

"Sorry. I'm not trying to make you feel sorry for me. I'm just so frustrated!"

"Don't worry, I get it." I smiled softly at him, and put my jacket back on, feeling the damp fabric against my skin. He smiled at me a little, and took off his own jacket, flinging it over his shoulder.

"Xanda. There's something I want to ask." Leon said.

"What is it?" I asked curiously.

"I've heard that it helps if the bond between Dragonbourne and partner is exceptional, then that can sometimes help the Dragonbourne to control the fire, as his or her soul is more stable. It's not just that though…with everything going on, the two of us need to be as strong as we possibly can. I was thinking about asking Miss Wellworn and Miss Nebilia about some extra lessons for just the two of us. But obviously, I needed to ask you first."

"All things considered, that's not a bad idea." I smiled at him gently. He had been struggling with fire bending for a long time, and he had been trying so hard. If I could help in any way I would. Besides, he did have a point about needing to get stronger. With all that was going on between Gailoiyn and Brozanta, we needed to be ready for anything.

"So, you agree?" Leon said happily.

"Yeah, why wouldn't I?" I chuckled. "Extra lessons aren't really my style, but you're right. We do need them."

"Thank you. I appreciate it." He smiled. "I'd better go and get some new clothes on before we head to the western tower."

"Oh that's a shame. I was beginning to think the damp look suited you." I teased.

"Oh yeah? Then you'll want a hug, won't you? C'mon, give me a hug!"

"Leon, get away from me!" I screamed playfully, laughing happily as I stumbled backwards. Leon held his arms out, trying to hug me while he was soaking wet. I wasn't falling for that old trick! He was also beginning to smell, the ponds odour perfuming the air. The last thing I wanted to do was touch him. I yelled at him as I began to run across the field towards the castle. He gave chase, insistent on catching me. All our worries faded away, and I realised that I was actually having fun. I'd forgotten what that felt like. It was also nice to see Leon not taking things so seriously for once. I liked it when he had a smile on his face and happiness in his heart. Joy rang in my laughter. I wished for more joyful times ahead, but I knew that was only a dream.

After Leon had dried off properly and changed his wet clothing, the two of us headed towards the western tower to speak to Ivy Wellworn and Cassandra Nebilia. We were just about to reach out for the door to the classroom when we were stopped by a familiar voice from behind.

"Hello, you two! You do realise you have no lessons today right?" We watched as the green haired lady strutted towards us. Ivy chuckled a little, and stopped in front of us. She looked happier than usual, and part of me wondered why. Out of the pair, Ivy was much more serious than Cassandra, but both of them could have a good laugh with you. We turned fully to face her.

"We realise that." Leon told her. "But we'd like a word with you, if that's alright." Ivy Wellworn raised an eyebrow at this, clearly intrigued.

"Very well. Please, come in." She said, reaching out for the door handle. She wrapped her long fingers around the golden iron knob and turned it, pushing the door open. Suddenly my jaw dropped open, as did Leon's. We couldn't believe what we were seeing! Ivy just stood there, and she physically facepalmed. I let out a laugh of shock as I saw Jasper Ventus and Cassandra Nebilia in the middle of a deep kiss. The two jumped as they heard us coming in, and both blushed deep red.

"So the rumours are true!" I laughed. "You two are together!"

"Oh...um...there's been rumours going around?" Cassandra blushed deeper, her face bright red.

"Well, Seto and Naia told us you two were getting close." Leon grinned.

"Why am I not surprised?" Jasper chuckled. Ivy put her fist to her mouth and cleared her throat.

"If you don't mind Mr Ventus, Mr Drogon and Miss Sykes would like a word with Cassandra and I."

"Of course." Jasper smiled and he kissed Cassandra on the cheek. "I'll see you later, my love." Oh jeez. They were so cute together, but they were so soppy. Jasper gave Leon and I a soft smile before he left the room, and Ivy walked over to her usual seat and sat down with Cassandra.

"Please, take a seat." Cassandra said gently. We followed her instruction, and pulled up a chair sitting opposite them.

"So, how can we help you?" Ivy asked.

"I've been having trouble with fire bending..." Leon said shamefully. "I've heard that having a stronger connection with your partner can help."

"That is certainly true, but it does surprise me." Cassandra put up a curled finger to her lips in thought, and gazed at the ceiling slightly. "You and Xanda have one of the strongest partnerships in your year. We are going to have to resort to drastic measures if we are to help."

"How drastic?" I asked, a look of confusion on my face. I mean, I'd do anything if it would help Leo, but did she mean drastic as in...dangerous? Ivy and Cassandra shared a look between them, as if they were both thinking of the same thing. They both looked over at two folded wooden beds by the wall, and then looked back at us.

"Help us move these beds into the centre of the room." Said Ivy, standing and starting to move the chairs out of the way. Cassandra followed immediately after her partner, as did Leon and I after exchanging a worried glance. Leon pulled out one of the beds, and he opened it up so it was straight. He took one end and I took the other, and we worked together to carry it to the centre of the room. Ivy and Cassandra did the same thing with the other table, and placed it next to the other one in the centre of the room. Ivy then told us to lie on a bed each. We were a bit apprehensive, but we did as we were told. I climbed onto one of the beds, feeling how cool the smooth wood was under my fingertips. It was more of a table than a bed to be honest, and I suddenly began to feel rather uneasy. I looked over at Leon once again, and he looked just as uneasy as I felt. A rush of panic began to shoot through me, and I took a few deep breaths as Ivy began to explain what was about to happen.

"We are about to cast a very...rare piece of magic. We are going to send you to a place called 'The Forgotten World', a dimension between life and death. We can send you there, but we won't be able to bring you back..."

"Then how the hell are we supposed to come back?" I asked, becoming even more nervous than before. If this place was between life and death...was there a possibility we would die? Surely the teachers wouldn't put us in so much danger.

"That depends on you two." Cassandra said softly. "Ivy and I have been there too, many years ago while in training. But it is a sacred place, one where the living does not dwell. Hardly anybody has ventured there while alive. The exit is different for everyone, and we cannot say for certain what will happen when you are there. This is very advanced training, so keep your wits about you." I did want to ask if there was a chance we would die, but to be honest, I didn't want to know the answer. Leon glanced over at me, and I looked at him worriedly. We weren't sure about this, but it was too late to turn back now.

"You ready?" I asked him quietly. He just nodded slightly, seeming nervous. I gave him a reassuring smile. He looked more at ease, my smile informing him that I was definitely up for this. I looked up slowly, as Cassandra stood over me. She gazed down at me, her rosy pink lips forming into a reassuring smile. Ivy stood over Leon and she placed a hand over his heart. He flinched a little, becoming worked up. I looked back at Cassandra, as she placed her hand over my heart also. As she did, I felt a strange magic rush into my body, and I felt my heart jolt. I couldn't process what was happening, as I felt myself falling deeper and deeper into a state of unconsciousness. The colours in the room began to fade, and my eyes slid closed...

I felt myself falling...floating...drifting into a state of unconsciousness as I entered a world entirely different than our own...

A strange sensation swept over me, and even though my eyes were closed, I knew I wasn't in Ivy and Cassandra's classroom anymore. Or at least, my soul wasn't. My chest felt heavy at first, but then it felt light in an instant, like a great emotional weight had been lifted from me. There was a chilly tingle trickling down my spine, and I was suddenly blasted with a rush of coldness. The very air around me was frosty, and I could feel a familiar coolness under my fingertips. It was something I had felt many times before. It was snow. I was lying in snow. I slowly slid my eyes open, and gazed up at the empty sky above. The sky however was a strange colour...a pale lilac, much like Irina's hair. I watched the snow drift in the air as soft as feathers. There was something very enchanting about it. It was then I noticed something strange...the snow wasn't landing on my face. In fact, it wasn't falling downwards at all. It was floating upwards, ascending towards the heavens. I adjusted my arms, and used them to push myself up into a sitting position. I gently reached out one hand, and I caught a snowflake in my palm. It was so delicate I barely felt it touch my pale skin, but I gently kept my fingers curled around it so it didn't float away. The pattern was like nothing I had ever seen before. It was so complex, just like everything in this place seemed to be. I raised my arm slowly and gracefully opened my palm, watching as the snowflake drifted upwards. It joined the other droplets of snow in the heavens, creating a white flurry in the lilac sky. I watched in amazement, knowing this was a magic far different from any in our world. Everything here seemed lighter...and free. But even I knew appearances could be deceiving. Suddenly, I heard a light shuffle from behind me and I whipped my head round to see what it was. Leon was lying just behind me. It was a wonder I hadn't noticed him until now. He was beginning to sit up. He too seemed in awe of the world around him, as his emerald eyes scanned the strange snow in the horizon.

"How odd..." He spoke slowly, his voice seeming to echo heavenly.

"Aye. It is aint it..." I said in reply, my voice echoing too. Part of me wondered why our voices were echoing, but I didn't dwell too much on it. It was beginning to feel like anything could happen while we were here. Besides, our voices were the least of our worries. We still had to find a way out, and I already knew that wasn't gonna be easy. Well, just sitting there wasn't going to help. So I pushed myself to my feet, and turned slowly to face Leon.

"I'm becoming quite sceptical as to how this will help us..." He said. I sighed gently and held out my hand to him. He just looked at it for a few moments before taking it. In one swift movement, I yanked my hand back and pulled him to his feet.

"Me too." I told him. "But we can't just stay here. You heard what Miss Wellworn and Miss Nebilia said. If we don't find a way out of here we'll be stuck here forever, and I don't fancy having my body hacked to bits in my sleep if Stephan ever attacked again."

"Yeah…that wouldn't bode well for either of us. So, which way?"

"How am I supposed to know? Besides…it doesn't look like there's anything for miles." We both looked on ahead, looking to see if we could see anything in the distance. But it was just blank. The snow ascended upwards for as far as the eye could see in every direction, and the lilac sky seemed to stretch on forever. Well, this was just great. It was freezing, and we had no idea where to go or what to do. I sighed heavily, before I noticed Leon beginning to walk. I instantly started to follow him.

"Hey! How do you know we have to go that way?!"

"I don't. But we don't have a plan right now." He replied as I jogged a little to keep up with him. I looked at him as I joined his side.

"When do we ever have a plan? Irina usually comes up with those." I chuckled softly. Leon smiled back weakly, but he suddenly stopped walking. He put his arm across me as a barrier, and I instantly stopped walking. I immediately knew something was wrong. Leon went as white as a sheet, and I swallowed nervously.

"What is it?" I asked.

"Didn't you hear that?"

"Hear what?" I was getting worked up now. I hadn't heard a thing! But clearly, he had. Then I heard it. A sharp cracking sound rang in the air, rising from the ground. Our gaze shot to the floor under us. The snow began to change, falling rapidly as the ground under our feet gaped open. We didn't have time to run! I screamed in a panic as I felt the floor under my feet disappear and we were swallowed up by the ground. We were falling once again, hurtling through the air as we plummeted through a lilac sky.

"Xanda!" As we fell, Leon called out to me in haste. He reached out his hand and grabbed my jacket tightly in his fingers. He thought quickly, and in mid-air began to transform into his Dragon form. He threw me upwards slightly, and I reached out until my fingers wrapped around the spikes on his neck. I grunted, pulling myself onto his back, catching my breath as I regained my balance.

"That was close…" I panted as I looked down below us. I saw nothing. There was no earth, just lilac sky as far as the eye could see. Then the colour shifted, and it slowly began to change from a soft purple to a blinding white. I put one hand over my eyes to try and see if I could spot some place to land.

"Are you alright?" Leon asked me after a moment.

"I'm good." I replied. "What do you suppose we do now?"

"I don't know. I suppose we just keep flying until we come across something." Okay, it didn't seem like the best plan, but it wasn't like I had a better idea. We hadn't been here long, but this place was already beginning to get to me. I wanted to get out. The very air around us just felt so unnatural. The fact that this was a realm between life and death weighed heavily on my mind. It occurred to me that perhaps spirits could pass through here, as well as the living. Perhaps this was the reason we were meant to be here...to meet someone. I honestly wasn't sure. To be honest, I wasn't sure why I agreed to come here in the first place. How could coming here possibly help anything?! What purpose did it serve?! This place was magical, but I knew it was dangerous. Cassandra said it herself, that the living don't usually come here. Most physically can't. So, why could we? I let out a huge sigh, scanning the horizon.

"This place is...abnormal." Leon said.

"Well, in most places, the floor doesn't just disappear from under you."

"That's certainly true." He replied. "I've heard stories of the Forgotten World. Some even say the Raven Queen came here. Of course, it's just a rumour. Nobody can really know what happened to her four hundred years ago."

"Well, if her time here was anything like ours has been so far, I bet she saw some weird shizzle." Leon chuckled a little at my response, but I hadn't intended to be funny. I could scarlessly imagine the things she had been through in her lifetime. Just then I snapped out of my thoughts, as something appeared in a hazy mist ahead of us. My eyes widened in amazement as I gazed upon a floating stone island forming in the mystical fog swirling swiftly amongst itself. I inhaled deeply, wondering where such a thing had come from. It had just appeared like magic! Honestly though, nothing about this place was surprising me anymore. First the floor collapsed, and now there was a floating island. Go figure.

"Xanda, look! Do you see that?!" Leon said with enthusiasm.

"Well, it isn't exactly hard to miss." I chuckled.

"That's certainly true. Do you think we should land there?"

"Yeah. We haven't come across anything else. Let's take a look around."

"Right!" Leon swooped down, and I watched intently as the island came into full view. Carefully, Leon lowered us down onto the rocky island. A low, thin mist draped the ground, and it dispersed like a parting wave as I jumped down from Leo's back. He changed back into his human form, and the two of us began to walk forward, examining the strange place we had ended up. The ground was rough and uneven, and my feet felt unsteady as I walked along the cold, grey stone. A few pillars of jiggered rock spiked up from the ground, giving this small island a more eerie feel to it. Apart from that, there didn't seem to be anything else here. It was empty, and quiet...almost too quiet. Suddenly, there was a voice behind us. It sounded much like my own, but there was a sense of cockiness and playfulness to her tone. We both jumped, and Leon and I spun round quickly upon hearing it.

"Finally! I've been waiting ages for you two!" Said the mysterious girl. I found myself looking at a young woman, appearing not much older than myself. In fact, she looked very similar to myself. She was short and pale, but not as pale as me. Her hair was golden blonde, and in two braids. I looked into the deep blue of her eyes, and even at first glance, I noticed how similar they were to my own. Not just in the colour of my right eye, but in the shape too. Leon seemed to have noticed the similarities also, not that they were hard to miss. He was glancing between the two of us, clearly thinking the same thing I was.

"I...I'm sorry...do we know you?" I asked in confusion in response to her greeting towards us. What did she mean she had been waiting for us?

"Yes! Well...no. I know you, but uh...you probably don't know me. Although you've probably heard of me. Wow, this is awkward!" She giggled nervously as she began to move closer towards us, rubbing the back of her head. I couldn't help but notice this was something Leon always did when he felt nervous. My suspicions were becoming aroused, as now she was showing traits of the both of us. Leon however, hadn't seemed to notice that little detail. I guess if you have a habit of doing something, you don't realise you do it until somebody points it out to you.

"You can start making sense any time now." I said.

"Okay, okay! Jeez!" The girl chuckled. "It's like this, I'm an ancestor of yours. Of both of yours. You two are direct descendants of me and my sister. My sister visited this place once in her lifetime, and ever since my death I've come here often. But I didn't meet you here to bore you over our family history."

"Woah, slow down!" Leon scoffed. "One, this is a lot to take in all in one go. Two, we came here to get stronger!"

"Oh c'mon." The girl laughed. "If you think you're here because of some dumb training exercise, your stupider than I thought."

"Then why are we here?" I asked. "Can you help us?"

"With your training, no. But with the Elemental stones...maybe."

"You know about the stones?!" Leon gasped. The two of us quickly found ourselves looking at each other. "Where are they?!"

"Hey, I said 'maybe'!" The girl let out a long sigh, moving her hair out of her eyes before looking back up at us. "I don't know exactly where they are. But I can give you a clue. There's a rhyme. A rhyme I heard from a Dragon in your world. He also doesn't know where the stones are, but Dragons can hear things...sense things...and their prophecies are usually quite accurate." This Dragon she mentioned...I couldn't help but think she meant Fergo. But maybe she meant a Dragon from her time, or a Dragon of the past. There was no way of knowing for sure, and I wasn't going to ask her because she was confusing me enough already.

"How does the rhyme go?" I asked softly. The girl looked at us intently, as if to make sure we were listening, before taking a deep breath and speaking lowly and clearly.

"A stone has sunk where the sirens sing,
A lightning bolt strikes the man who is king,

In an ancient home, a stone resides there,
And the last changed hands, in haste and despair."

So, that was the true reason we were here. But why us? Surely there were more capable people she could have told this too. Unless there was more to this prophecy stuff than she was letting on. Speaking of her, it had only just occurred to me that I still didn't know her name. She had dropped it on us that we were related but neglected to tell us exactly who she was. In my heart, I knew who she was, but at the time I just didn't believe it.

"A stone has sunk where the sirens sing…" I began to repeat it slowly, until the girl cut me off.

"Yeah. Try saying that line ten times faster." She said.

"Do you know anything else?" Leon asked.

"No. I'm sorry I can't be of more help." She said. "I wish we had more time, but our time here is growing short. I can't linger here for too long, and neither should you. This place isn't for the living or the dead. It's kind of weird, isn't it?"

"I…guess so." Leon said awkwardly. "How do we get back home?"

The girl thought on this for a few moments before answering.

"You could try going back the same way my sister did all those years ago." The girl pointed out towards the sky, and Leon and I instantly looked away from her, our eyes following the direction she was pointing. "Go that way. You'll come across another island. In the centre is an old oak tree. It's an ancient gateway between worlds. Farewell. Until we meet again."

"Thank you. By the way, what's your name?" I began to ask, but as we both turned back to face her, she was gone as quickly as she had appeared. I swallowed hard. If I wasn't confused before, I sure was now. "Weird…did we just imagine all that?" I asked Leon, wanting to double check that I hadn't gone insane.

"I don't think so. Should we believe what she told us?"

"I don't think she had any reason to lie. I mean, she's already dead. We can talk about this when we get home. Right now, I think we need to focus on getting out of here." I told him. Leon nodded in response, and we found ourselves once again looking out towards the distance in the direction the girl had told us to go. I don't know what awaited us on the other island, but it couldn't be any stranger than what had already happened…could it?

We had set off flying again. We had been flying for quite some time before we came across the island. We had both been wondering whether the strange girl had been telling us the truth, or whether she was just leading us on a wild goose chase. Turns out, she had been honest with us. As we flew, another floating island appeared before us. This one was bigger than the last island, and it was much greener. Soft moss draped over the grey stone, and ivy twirled up the sides of two larger rocks. In the centre was the tree the girl had told us about. It was a tall oak tree, larger than any oak tree I had ever seen before. Its branches were as thick as Davandrin's arms, and ruby red flowers bloomed around its trunk. This island was much more beautiful than the last, but that only made me warier. Beauty was entrancing, but that's what can make it dangerous. However, I knew we had no choice but to land there. The tree was apparently our way out. So, Leon swooped down towards the island and landed gently. I jumped down off of his back and he turned back into his human form. I must admit, I still wasn't quite used to riding a Dragon. The idea of it still seemed unreal. But I was adjusting to it, and getting used to Leon changing his state of being from human to Dragon. I still found it amazing though, I do even to this day. This time however, I didn't watch Leon as he shifted back into his human form. I looked dead ahead of me, instantly walking slowly towards the tree as if my feet were moving on their own. It was like an instinct to move towards it, and something about this place seemed familiar. It was like I had seen the tree somewhere before, but I didn't know where. I gingerly stood before the tree, and placed my hand on its trunk. The wind around me seemed to sing, chiming mystically through the air. I felt the softness of the moss on the trunk under my fingertips, and something within my heart awakened. It was like an ancient spirit surged through me, and I knew that this place was far older than I could ever have imagined. Leon walked towards me, and gazed up at the tree's branches looming over us like a giant.

"Does something about this tree feel...familiar to you?" He asked me quietly.

"Aye..." I replied in no more than a whisper. I pulled my hand away and took a few steps back until I was level with Leon. We looked at each other, not saying a word. We didn't need to speak. We knew full well what the other was thinking, and it scared us. If that girl was who I thought she was, then this tree would mean that this was the tree depicted in so many of the Raven Queen's stories, although nobody ever knew its significance. But that would also mean that Leon and I were both descendants of her royal bloodline, as the girl had stated. As this realisation hit us, there was suddenly an eruption of light. The ground flashed white right before our eyes, and a gust of wind shot upwards as it began to snow once again. The snow began to fall this time, fluttering towards the ground in a magical flurry across the island. My skin began to tingle with a cool sensation as the snow drifted past me. Leon's gaze lowered and he gasped in surprise, seeming to notice something.

"Xanda...your hand!" He said. I quickly looked down to my right hand, and I was shocked to see that there was a long, thin, silver light glowing around it. My eyes widened in surprise as I lifted my hand. Strangely, I wasn't afraid. The light didn't seem or feel threatening. Just then, a solid object began to form in the light. It was the sword! The sword that had been on my bed during the attack at the Winter Ball. As the sword merged together within the light, I moved my hand over the top of the sword and wrapped my fingers around its hilt, gripping it tightly as the light died down.

"This sword again..." I said, a little curious.

"If this place truly is about our heritage, then perhaps it belonged to that girl, or...another ancestor." Leon speculated. I must admit, as crazy as it sounded, he did have a point. I didn't think it belonged to that girl though. If she was who I thought she was, in her lifetime she wielded a bladed staff, not a sword. The Raven Queen on the other hand was known to use a sword, but she was often depicted as wielding a bow.

"I don't think this sword belonged to that girl, but I think you may be right about it belonging to somebody else significant to us." I told him. He raised an eyebrow and looked at me curiously.

"Do you know who that girl was?"

"I have an idea." I said. "Obviously I can't be certain, but I did have a gut instinct."

"Who is she?"

"I think...I think she may be Pipit Raven." As I spoke, Leon's eyes widened in surprise. It was just a hunch, but it all added up. In paintings of her, she often wore her hair in two braids, wore green, and was known for being rather sarcastic. Also, she had mentioned to us that she had a sister, which would have been the Raven Queen, Alexzero Raven.

"The Raven Queen's sister?!" Leon gasped. "That's incredible!"

"Indeed. It also won't mean a thing if we can't get back home. She said this tree was our gateway, right?" I said turning my attention back to the tree. Leon followed my gaze, and he rubbed the back of his head nervously. It had occurred to me as I watched him do this, that I hadn't fiddled with my parent's rings for a long time. It wasn't that I had forgotten about them, far from it. But lately I hadn't felt the need to constantly fiddle with them when I was anxious or scared. Was I getting stronger? Or...was it because of Leon? I just watched him in silence as he began to examine the tree, and I thought about everything we were going through. He'd never given up on me, and he'd always been there when I needed someone to talk to. Perhaps this was part of growing up? I dunno. Whatever it was, I couldn't have asked for a better friend and partner.

"It just seems like a regular tree to me...as in, there's no way through it." Leon said taking a step back. I was starting to get a little worried now, considering this was our only known way home. I stepped up to the tree and started to look around it. My hand brushed against the rough bark as I made my way around the tree. Alas, like Leon, I found nothing. No way to get us home. He was right, this just seemed like a normal tree. I made my way fully around it before crossing my arms and standing next to Leo once again, staring at the tree.

"Okay...any more bright ideas?" I bit my lip, starting to feel rather frustrated now. As pretty as this island was, I was still worried we'd never get home. Leon shrugged, and he reached forward to place his hand on the tree. At the exact same time, I also reached forward, and our palms touched the trunk at the same time. We let out a huge gasp of surprise as we were blown backwards by a sudden gust of wind emitting from the tree. I yelped a little as I hit the ground. Leon grunted, having fallen next to me. He let out a low groan of pain as he forced himself to sit up. I sat up too, eager to see what had just happened. The tree was now arched, and swirling lights coloured white and green mystically swirled between the trunk. I blushed a little, knowing the gateway had appeared when Leon and I had touched the tree together. The colours magically dancing before us was truly a sight to behold. I pushed myself to my feet slowly and turned to face Leon. I smiled down at him and extended my hand towards him.

"Ready to go home?" I grinned. His black hair swayed in the breeze, his white strip becoming more visible. His lips broke into a smile and he nodded, gently reaching up and taking my hand. My heart skipped a beat as our palms touched, and I instantly pulled him to his feet. I was about to let go, but his grip around my hand tightened which just made me blush more. We turned our heads in unison towards the magical gateway. It was time to go home.

My eyelids felt heavy, but I forced them open. I felt like I was awakening from the deepest sleep of my life. I was tired, but I felt at peace. And strangely...stronger. My hand still felt warm. I looked to my side, seeing that Leon and I were still holding hands. I quickly let go, and pushed myself into a sitting position. Leon sat up too, rubbing the back of his head. He was a little paler than normal, and he looked incredibly tired. I must admit, I felt the same. I looked up, seeing Cassandra Nebilia and Ivy Wellworn sitting across from us. They stood in a hurry and came over to us seeing that we had awakened.

"Here." Ivy came to my side, and handed me a glass of water. Cassandra gave Leon a glass also. I nodded in thanks and took it gently, drinking a sip. The water was cool and refreshing, and it woke me up a little as I felt the cold liquid trickle down my throat.

"How are you both feeling?" Cassandra asked gently.

"Good...although, it wasn't what I was expecting." Leon said.

"How so?" asked Ivy.

"There was no fighting." I started. "But...things appeared before us. Things we've only heard about in stories. We did find out some useful information while we were there though."

"Sometimes, knowledge is power." Cassandra said smiling gently. "You can tell us another time. For now, you need to go and wake yourselves up properly, and adjust yourselves back into this world. You've done well today, I knew you two could make it back!" She spoke excitedly, but her expression dropped when the classroom door opened. We all looked over as Joey walked in hurriedly, speaking much more loudly than he had probably intended. Although, this is Joey were talking about.

"There you are, Xanda! I've been looking everywhere for you! O-Oh...sorry...were you in the middle of something? I can...come back later if this is a bad time." Joey now fidgeted nervously, slightly embarrassed about barging in without thinking.

"No worries, Mr Danaris." Ivy rolled her eyes a little, but smiled. She knew what he was like. "We are all done here for today."

"What is it, Joey?" I asked in confusion. Whenever Joey came looking for me, he usually wanted to know where Leon was. But this time, he seemed different. He looked at me strangely, like something had happened.

"There's something I think you need to see." He said simply.

"What?"

"Please, just come with me." Leon and I exchanged a glance, and we got off the beds. I was beginning to feel anxious now. What was so special about it that he couldn't just tell me now? Leon and I hastily thanked Cassandra and Ivy for their help, and hurried out of the room following Joey, deeper into the castle.

Chapter 14

The Boy with the Brains

I was becoming increasingly nervous about what it was that Joey had to show us. He had this weird look on his face as we wondered through the castle...the look of a man that wasn't sure whether he should be showing me whatever it was. We soon found ourselves in a part of the castle that was unfamiliar. It was a long, wide corridor, the walls painted in a shade of deep red. Small, golden chandeliers hung from the ceiling, lighting up this otherwise dark hallway. There were no windows, just large portraits lining the walls, all of which were displayed inside regal golden frames that glittered in the candlelight. We stopped at the top of the corridor, and as I looked down it I instantly felt that something wasn't right. I had never been to this part of the castle before, as it was situated high in the castle not far from Drevin Drogon's office.

"Where are we?" I asked quietly.

"The Hall of Heroes." Leon replied. "I've only been here once, but this is where they hang up portraits of past students. Although, you have to have done something pretty extraordinary to have your painting featured here."

Without a word, I took a few steps forward, examining the detailed portraits of past students and their Dragonbourne partners. I noticed that much like my year group, most of the past partners were of the same gender. Of course, there were a few male/female partners hung up here. Leon turned to Joey, confused.

"What were you doing here in the first place?" Leon asked.

"Well, I went to see Taz but he was asleep." Joey replied. "So I thought I'd go exploring. It is a big castle after all."

"So why are we here?" I turned to face Joey, a serious look in my eyes. He looked down for a moment, seeming a tad nervous. He put one foot in front of the other and began to walk, brushing past me softly. I followed him quickly, Leon trailing behind. Joey took a deep breath as he began to speak.

"I remembered that picture you have in your room, y'know...the one of your folks. And I came across this..." Joey stopped in front of one of the paintings, and I actually couldn't believe what I was seeing. The original painting of my parents...it was right here in front of me! It was much larger than the copy my grandparents had given me, and the detail was incredible. I could see a mischievous sparkle in my father's deep blue eyes, and the way my mother's cheeks were flushed in a gorgeous pink glow. My mother was holding something in her hand. It looked to me like it was some sort of red crystal. It must have been a keepsake of hers or something. One thing I was certain of, is that they both looked so happy together. They looked made for each other. My father looked like he had the world at his feet as he embraced my mother. I felt tears sting my eyes, and I reached forward and gently touched the frame, gazing up at their faces in disbelief. It was almost like they were here with me. But then, I began to realise why the painting was here in the first place. They had attended this school too. They had walked these very halls, sat at the same desks, ate in the Great Hall and slept in this very castle. But why had nobody ever told me? Surely, I'd had a right to know! Just then, I began to get that weird feeling you get when you think you're being watched, and I knew we were no longer alone. I stepped back, and saw none other than Jasper Ventus and Zadlos Davandrin staring at me down the hall. Both of them looked as white as a sheet. Then it hit me. So that was the reason Mr Davandrin knew who I was when I first came here. He knew my parents, and I began to suspect Jasper Ventus did too. None of us could find any words to say to each other, and there was a long period of silence as the men shifted awkwardly. Joey and Leon just stood back, silent, not sure what to say. It took me a while, but I finally plucked up the courage to speak.

"I think you owe me an explanation." I said simply.

"Yeah..." Jasper said, sounding ashamed.

"Let us take this conversation to my office." Mr Davandrin spoke in a low voice.

"How will this conversation be any different there?" I scoffed.

"It is more private." Davandrin said, turning and beginning to walk on ahead of us. Jasper looked at me for a moment, his eyes flashing with a hint of remorse before following Zadlos Davandrin.

"I'm gonna go and see Taz..." Joey said softly. "Y'know, so you can have some space. If you wanna talk about it later then...um...you know where I am."

"Thank you, Joey. I appreciate that." I smiled weakly, and was a little shocked when he moved forward and hugged me slightly.

"Good luck..." He pulled back and walked down the hall and around the corner without another word. Leon on the other hand stayed, looking at me worriedly as Joey left. I turned to look at him as he placed a gentle hand on my shoulder.

"I can go too, if you'd like. It's up to you." He said. No way. No part of me wanted him to go. I needed him. I wanted him with me, supporting me. Just like he was when I spoke about my parents with Grandma and Gramps. I quickly placed my hand over his, a nervous shiver running down my spine. He later told me that he could feel me shaking at that point, but at the time I honestly hadn't noticed.

"No. I mean...I'd like you to stay with me. If you would..." I gulped nervously. He just smiled softly at me, and nodded a little. I found myself smiling again as I saw him do the same. Something about him always seemed to put me at ease. I guess that was why I wanted him with me. Now I had met him, I couldn't imagine life without him.

Zadlos Davandrin's office was small, but cosy. He had soft drapes over the wooden chairs, and a light red cloth over his desk. Next to the wall was a tall wine rack, with bottles of red wine displayed on them. There was a pile of books on the floor behind the desk, covered in a thin layer of dust. Leon and I were sitting on one side of the desk, while Jasper Ventus sat on the

other side. Mr Davandrin stood beside us, pouring the wine into four glasses.
I raised an eyebrow a little in curiosity.

"Are we even allowed that?" I asked.

"It doesn't contain that much alcohol." Davandrin said, looking at Leon. "Just don't tell your father."

My partner chuckled a little and nodded. "Sure." Davandrin smiled at him and screwed the lid back on the bottle before walking back over to the wine rack to put the bottle away. All through this, Jasper sat there in silence, seeming nervous and agitated. He reached over for his glass quickly and suddenly took a large swig of his wine. Davandrin sighed and sat down, resting his hands on the desk, clasping them tightly. I couldn't take my eyes off them, and I watched intently at every move they made. Jasper couldn't look me in the eyes, and Davandrin's hands fiddled uncomfortably.

"So?" I began sharply. I just wanted them to get to the point and tell me what they knew. Davandrin inhaled deeply, and rubbed his face with both hands before clasping them together once again.

"We did know them. Your parents. In fact, we...knew them very well." He said. So I was right. They had known Alphonse and Kirani Sykes. I sat forward in my chair, completely intrigued as to what they had to say.

"They came here, didn't they? To Wyvern Academy." I asked.

"Yes. I was their teacher. And Jasper was in their class." Davandrin answered.

"More than that!" Jasper put his glass down, his sudden outburst making me jump a little. I wasn't sure, but I swear I could see tears in his eyes.

"Were you in love with Kirani?" Leon asked. But before I had time to question this theory, Jasper jumped in and corrected it.

"No! Gods no! I'm her cousin."

"Were related?!" I couldn't believe what I was hearing. I was related to Jasper Ventus! Why had he never mentioned this before? Jasper cupped his hands over his nose and mouth, taking deep breaths as he simply nodded. Suddenly, the anger I felt began to melt away like the sun shining on glittering snow. I felt...sympathy for him. Kirani was my mother, but she was also loved by Jasper too. I wasn't the only one that missed her. My heart began to soften, and I reached out and placed my hand gently on his arm. I allowed a reassuring smile to form across my face. After a few moments of silence, I finally spoke.

"Tell me about her."

"Oh gods...she was incredible." Jasper wiped his eyes before he started crying, sniffling a little. He began to smile as he thought of my mother, which made me happy. It made her seem...more real, and not like she was just a dream. "Kirani and I were from noble families, but I couldn't tell you anything about them."

"Why not?" I asked curiously.

"I simply don't remember. We were very young, and my entire family gathered at my mansion for a party. There was a fire. Our whole family died, except Kirani and I."

"I'm so sorry…"

"Don't be." He smiled weakly. "Like I said, I was too young to remember. With no relatives to take care of us, we wound up in the orphanage here. It's not as bad as it sounds. Kirani and I had a good childhood."

"Were you close?" I asked curiously.

"Very. Kirani was wild, bright and vivacious. But she was also clever, smart and level headed. We were both Dragonbourne, so naturally we were offered a place here. We didn't think our lives were going anywhere, so of course, we accepted the place here. When we came here, it was like a dream. We had never known a place like this before. And that, dear Xanda, is where we met your father." Jasper smiled again once he mentioned my father, and I began to wonder what relationship they had.

"Did you get on?"

"Yeah." Jasper laughed softly. "He was the class clown."

"Understatement." Davandrin chuckled. I laughed too. It was nice to hear my father mentioned in such a light-hearted way. Whenever my grandparents spoke of him, they were always so serious. Upon hearing that he was a bit of a rebel made him seem…better than I could ever have imagined.

"Al was a cheeky sod. But he was also brave, and he never did shy away from responsibility." Jasper said.

"He was also very talented." Davandrin said. "When I saw you with that scythe in our first lesson, you reminded me so much of him. He and Kirani were a force to be reckoned with. Top of the class in fact, just like you two."

"Seems trivial now, doesn't it?" Jasper looked down once again and I moved my hand away, once again fiddling with their wedding rings around my neck in order to feel close to them.

"How so?" I asked.

"None of that matters anymore. I loved Kirani like she was my sister, and Al…he was the best friend I ever had. He had a sharp tongue, and was loyal to a fault. Just like you. When we were seventeen, Kirani got sick. Not long after, she discovered she was pregnant. Your Gran went ballistic at Al, but your Gramps soon made her see sense. Kirani was…vulnerable. I'd never seen her like that. She was terrified she wouldn't be a good mother. So, she said to Al that if he wanted to walk away, she wouldn't hold it against him."

"He didn't….did he?"

"No. He didn't even consider it." Jasper smiled weakly and looked at me once again, wiping his eyes. "He stood by her. Then, the winter came…and you were born here."

"Wait…here? As in, Wyvern Academy?" I looked at them, shocked. I had always assumed I was born in Lightwater.

"Yes." Davandrin smiled. "You were born here. I was one of the first to hold you. You were so tiny. I'd never held a new born child before, and I was so worried I was going to break you." I looked at Davandrin softly. I knew he'd recognised me as soon as we met, but I didn't realise that our paths had crossed so many years ago. Davandrin seemed to be getting emotional too, and he reached out for his wine, stirring it a little before taking a sip. "What then?" I asked after a short period of silence.

"Harry and Beatrice offered to look after you so your parents could finish school." Jasper started. "But both of them missed you so very much. They picked you up almost every week and you'd stay here a while before going back to Lightwater."

"What about lessons?" I asked curiously.

"Well, as you know, you and young Leon here were born on the same day." Said Davandrin. "After Sera-Rose passed away, Drevin became a single father. He was…devastated over Sera's death so much that he threw himself into his work. He had a corner in his office full of toys, and he would sit at his desk and work while watching Leon play. He offered to watch you too while Al and Kirani went to class. I can't count the amount of times I walked into his office and you two were in the corner hiding in the toy box." Now that I hadn't expected. Leo and I slowly turned to look at each other, both of us seeming utterly shocked. Leon and I had met before. I began to wonder if this was why we had instantly had a strong connection when we first met. I was also surprised that Drevin Drogon had offered to look after me, despite what he was going through at the time. He really was a generous man deep down. I gulped a little and looked down at the floor, leaning back in my seat. I let out a long huff and rubbed my mouth with my hand, trying to take this all in. After a long pause, I looked up at the two men.

"I want to know about the time they left." I said finally. I watched closely as Jasper and Davandrin looked at each other, Jasper turning as white as a sheet.

"They…had not long been married." Zadlos Davandrin said quietly, looking at me.

"It was a lovely ceremony." Jasper said. "The sun was shining. It was by the Simmon River. It was small, but it was the happiest day of Kirani's life. The wedding was attended by the late King Alfred."

"King Alfred? You mean, the father of King Ricco and Princess Veronica? What was he doing there?" I asked, raising an eyebrow.

"King Alfred had met your parents many years before that." Said Davandrin. "They met at their first Winter Ball, and the king was teasing Alphonse about his dancing skills. Anyway, he would often come to the school and watch the students blossom into young warriors. He regarded your parents very highly, and at their wedding, he asked them if they would consider ever going to be his generals."

"Did they say yes?"

"They never got chance to. Al was excited, but Kirani said they'd think about it. But she did say that they'd be available to help out with whatever he needed. They did get on with the King rather well." Said Jasper. "This…is where things get complicated."

Davandrin sighed heavily and leaned forward, resting his elbows on the desk. He looked deeply into my eyes, and I made eye contact with him, ready to listen to what he was about to say.

"Alphonse and Kirani came to myself, Jasper and Drevin Drogon not long afterwards. They were talking about a rumour they had heard. A rumour saying that Prince Stephan of Brozanta, was going to kill his brother and take the throne for himself. We disregarded the rumour."

"Why?" Leon sat forward, his eyes narrow. "They were completely right!"

"At the time, Stephan wore a mask." Jasper said sadly. "He was nothing like the monster he is today. He was well liked, as much as King Octavan in fact. Nobody suspected a thing. I don't even know where Al and Kirani heard this rumour!"

"Is that why they left?" I asked sharply. "Did they go to investigate it by themselves?!" I began to feel an anger burn inside of me once again. This is why they kept it quiet! They were ashamed. And rightly so!

"I am so sorry!" Jasper said, covering his face. He rubbed his eyes a little then removed his hand, looking at me once again. "Kirani was so angry with me…and so insistent that she and Al go to Eruznor just to be on the safe side. I went to Lightwater, and to your Grandpa's smithy. In your house, I walked in on Kirani and Beatrice talking. They went quiet when I came in. I told Kirani I was worried about her and Al, and that I wanted to go to Eruznor with them. She told me to forget it. She asked me to leave. So, I did. I never saw them again. I know my apology means nothing right now, Xanda. But I want you to know that there isn't a day that goes by where I don't think about them. If I could go back in time and stop them from going, I would."

"Why did I never see you again? You knew where I lived. Why did you never come and visit?" I asked sternly.

"I…wanted to protect you." He said, taking a deep breath. "After what happened to Al and Kirani, I wanted to keep you away from this life. From all the fighting, and the Dragons and political issues of this world…and King Stephan. I wanted to protect you from him, just like I wish I'd protected them from him. But look at you…you're here anyway. You're just like them. I must have been a fool to think that the daughter of Alphonse and Kirani Sykes would just walk away from a world she is meant to be a part of." I looked over at Leon and he reached out, taking my hand gently. I found myself squeezing his hand, taking deep breaths, trying to take this all in. A certain question burned within my heart. What exactly happened to them once they got to Eruznor? Jasper Ventus may have angered me, but I respected his honesty. Not many people would admit that they made a mistake. I just hoped that one day, I could live up to my parents…they sounded like amazing people. No, they were amazing people. Hearing about them only made me want to put an end to King Stephan's reign even more than I already did. He was a tyrant, a madman, and somebody needed to take him down.

I didn't sleep too well that night. So much was going through my head that I found myself tossing and turning and bolting awake at the smallest sound. I just kept going over and over everything in my mind. There was more to my past than I ever knew, but I began to wonder about the future. Still, the question on everyone's lips was simply: what happened to Kirani and Alphonse Sykes? Were they killed by Stephan? Or were they alive? What happened to their baby? Was she even pregnant? Were they off living somewhere in obscurity with the child? Or were they killed eleven years ago? There was still so much left unanswered. I tossed the sheets off of me in a huff, frustrated that I couldn't sleep but not wanting to sleep either. I was so confused by it all. The world was changing...and so was I. I wasn't the same person that left Lightwater Village at the beginning of Autumn. I felt stronger, and much more...well, much more me. I know that probably doesn't make any sense, but hey, none of this did. I pushed myself up slowly, wiping the sleep out of my eyes before walking over to my window. I sighed gently, placing my hand on the cool glass as I gazed out towards the ocean. It looked different at night. The waves were calm and black, but it glistened a soft silver in the pale moonlight. It looked like diamonds floating on the water's surface, and something about it seemed rather magical to me. I sighed again, feeling incredibly tired now but knowing I wouldn't sleep while so much was going on inside my head. The stars looked so beautiful at night. I know there's that old cliché that they 'twinkle', but they really did. I wondered if my parents were alive, if they looked up at the same stars and wondered about me. I wanted to go to Eruznor, to investigate myself. But I knew there was little hope of finding anything out about them. It all happened eleven years ago, and with our two countries in high tension it wasn't the safest place to be right now. But saying that, neither was Algora. I had a really bad feeling things were going to get worse. A war was coming, that was obvious. The last thing I wanted was to find myself in the middle of a war, but I also knew there was nothing I could do to stop it. I was just a child. Someone like me could never put an end to a war. But still, I couldn't just sit ideally by and watch the people I loved and cared about suffer. My parents, Taz, Leon...all of them had been hurt some way or another by this war. By Stephan. He was no King, he was just a usurper. From what I heard, he was raising some puppet to be his successor. How naive must that boy have been not to see through him. I'd never met the bloke and even I knew he was bad news. I suddenly felt a wave of dizziness wash over me, and I began to feel tired once again. I felt like my head was about to explode. I couldn't contemplate the world more than I already had, and that was just over the space of one night. I yawned, and stretched my arms out as far as they could go as I made my way back over to my bed. What a day...

The next morning we had been in Mr Davandrin's class for combat training. I barely spoke to him, and people in our class were starting to notice the tension between us. I couldn't care less. It was none of their business anyway. I knew I wouldn't stay mad at him forever, but right now I just needed some space. Although, the class wasn't a complete failure. Leon was now growing much better at throwing fire around the place. I was proud of him for not giving up with it. He was so excited and proud he was practically skipping down the hallway after class as we headed towards the infirmary. With any luck, Taz was going to be out soon. Lessons had been so quiet without him, it didn't feel right. I was actually looking forward to having him cracking jokes in the middle of classes again. Leon and I were walking down to the infirmary, and before we even got there we could hear Taz talking rather loudly. He sounded frustrated and embarrassed. I raised an eyebrow and looked at Leon before we entered through the infirmary's open door. Inside, Taz was sitting up in bed, his face bright red. He hid his face in his hands, groaning in embarrassment. Joey sat at his side, laughing. There was another boy at Taz's bedside, who was fiddling intently with the medical equipment. He looked very much like Taz, with those deep purple eyes and snowy white hair, but I could tell he was a little older. He wore thin glasses resting on his nose, and he rolled up the sleeves on his yellow jacket as he began to tap on the equipment completely captivated. He was very quirky, and if you ask me, a little odd. His hair was spiked up all over the place, even more of a mess than Taz's hair...and that's saying something.

"Fascinating! Absolutely fascinating!" The boy said, holding up the equipment high to view underneath it.

"By the grace of the Raven Queen, put that thing down, Alistair!" Taz cursed. So, that boy was Taz's older brother, Alistair Periwinkle. Not that I was surprised, the two were the spitting image of each other. It turned out that Alistair had been here on business and had heard that Taz had been injured and had come to visit him. Although, he had seemed much more interested in messing with the medical equipment by the side of his brother's bed. Alistair sighed and put the thing he was holding back down on the bedside table.

"Oh, Tazmin. You must appreciate such contraptions! They are truly-"

"Fascinating. Yes, Alistair, I've heard it a thousand times before. And please don't call me Tazmin! Gosh, you're so embarrassing!" Taz growled, almost sinking under his bedsheets.

"I...hope we haven't called at an inconvenient time." Leon chuckled as we stepped forward.

"So, this is Alistair, is it? It's great to meet you!" I smiled politely. Alistair immediately turned to Taz, pointing at him sharply.

"Ha!" Alistair grinned. "So you do talk about me to your friends!" Taz simply rolled his eyes, his skin turning bright red. I giggled a little, thinking he looked rather cute all wound up like that. Alistair flicked his hair, a wide smile across his face showing his shiny white teeth. "Yes! I am Alistair. Alistair Periwinkle, at your service!"

"I'm Xanda, and this is Leo. Were in Taz's class." I said.

"Hm. Well, you're a blunt one." Said Alistair. "Straight to the point."

"Is that wrong?"

"No. Just an observation, not a judgement." Alistair smiled.

"Stop cross examining Xanda, Alistair! She isn't one of your machines!" Taz said in annoyance.

"I thought you specialised in antiquities, Alistair." Leon stated, rubbing his hair.

"I do. Antiquities, relics, contraptions, new machinery, it's all interlinked. See, many antique dealers only look at the old things. But I believe that so much of our past shapes our future! We must learn about new machines, new magic, new spells, new items, new designs! We must look at this as well as the old things!" As Alistair spoke, there was so much passion in his voice, I couldn't help but admire him. He was a nerd like Taz and Joey had said, but he was pretty cool.

"Which do you prefer?" I asked him curiously.

"Oh, historical artefacts, definitely." He answered. "Our worlds history is incredibly fascinating to me!"

"Then...if I asked, would you take a look at something for me?" I said. The others went quiet, listening closely to what I was saying.

"Um, sure." Alistair said, a little taken aback. "Anything for a friend of my brother." Without another word, I reached out for my back and pulled out the mystery sword from its sheathe. I'd just come from combat training so naturally I had it with me. I handed it out to Alistair, and he took it carefully. Joey and Taz exchanged a look, before their eyes fell upon Alistair.

"Where did you get this?" Alistair asked.

"I don't know. It was left on my bed the night of the attack."

"These engravings on the hilt are fascinating! Perhaps...elven? I'm not sure." Alistair said, running his bony fingers along the hilt and narrowing his eyes to try and get a better look.

"Can you translate it?" Leon asked with enthusiasm.

"I should be able to, given an hour or two." He said, looking at Joey and Taz. "May I use your room to conduct my research?"

"Sure." Joey said looking at me softly. I could tell he and Taz wanted to know where this sword came from just as much as I did. If Alistair could translate the writing on the hilt, then maybe that would solve another mystery...

I sat in the infirmary, watching a flurry of pink and white blossoms float past the window. It had been a while since Alistair had left, and since we had no more classes that day Leon and I had stayed in the infirmary with Taz and Joey. Pippa and Irina had joined us, and they sat on the end of the bed with Taz as we waited for him to be discharged. They were talking about a trip our class was taking the day after next, to a small town called Roseosh to the south of here. I must admit, with all the commotion going on I had totally forgotten about it. To be honest, I didn't really want to go. What use was a school trip when there were bigger things at steak? We were only going for a culture trip to see the Fairy gardens anyway. Oh yeah...did I mention fairies lived there? Many people in my class had never seen fairies before, considering most of them lived in Algora or Kazura. But me, I'd seen fairy traders many times, as merchants of all races would pass through Lightwater. They were pretty cool to be honest. All fairies had magic, unlike the other races where only select people had the ability. They were proud creatures, but shy and never got involved in politics. If a war were to come, I doubt very much that the fairies would get involved. The others had been talking about this for a while before Taz turned to me.

"Xanda! You're been quiet." He said, and they stopped their conversation to turn to me. I smiled weakly, looking back at them.

"Sorry, I was just really deep in thought."

"What's on your mind?" Leon asked in concern. I sighed a little, clenching my hands together and resting my chin on them, my elbows resting on my knees.

"About what happened in the Forgotten World." I replied.

"About Pipit Raven?" Pippa asked.

"No...well yeah. But more specifically about that prophecy rhyme thing she told us. Y'know, about the locations of the stones." I said. The others went quiet, realising this was something we had neglected to talk about.

"Remind us what she said, Xanda." Irina spoke softly. I didn't even need to think about it. The rhyme had been ingrained in my brain from the moment I'd heard it.

"A stone has sunk where the sirens sing,
A lightning bolt strikes the man who is king,
In an ancient home, a stone resides there,
And the last changed hands, in haste and despair." There was a short moment of silence after I had spoken, each one of us processing the rhyme once again. Joey sat up in his seat, and he was the first to speak.

"Well, the second line is obvious." He said. "Lightning bolt...king...it's a reference to the Lightningstone being in possession of the Royal family."

"That sounds about right." Said Taz. "So...maybe the first line is suggesting a stone is in Siren's Bay? Or in the ocean? Or...in the ocean by Siren's Bay?"

"It's possible." Said Leon, rubbing the back of his head.

"In an ancient home...well, that could mean anywhere that's old! Kazura, Palmira, Merdonex, the Plain of Fire, the Frostbitten Mountains...take your pick!" Said Pippa in frustration.

"The last line is the most puzzling to me." Irina piped up, bringing one hand to her cheek as she thought aloud. "The last changed hands, in haste and despair. That would suggest to me that it is owned by somebody, or was and then was passed to somebody else in a hurry."

"That could be anyone!" I said in frustration, running my hands through my golden hair.

"Xanda!" Called an excited voice from the doorway. The six of us looked up curiously to see who it was. Alistair hurried over to us, an exhilarated gleam in his eyes. He held the sword carefully in his hands as he stopped before me. Everyone's eyes turned to him, all of us eager to see if he had managed to translate it.

"Did you manage it?" Leon asked in anticipation.

"Indeed! My findings are fascinating!" Said Alistair.

"Is it engraved in elvish like you thought?" I asked.

"No! In fact, it's written in ancient Dwarfish!"

"Your serious? So...it belonged to a Dwarf?"

"Again, no." Said Alistair, balancing the blade on the palm of his two hands so I could see the engravings. "Quite literally, it translates to: *'Sword of Astrid Drago, descendant of the Raven Queen, and hero of Utopia'.* I believe...this is the sword she used to kill Figro the Great Dragon. It has been lost for decades! That is, until now." I couldn't believe what I was hearing. If Astrid Drago was a descendant of the Raven Queen like I was, then I was related to her also! But, that wasn't the first thing that came to my mind. The first thing was, how did such an important blade end up in my possession? Who gave it to me? We found ourselves looking round at each other, silent and shocked. I reached out and wrapped my fingers around the swords hilt. I gazed into the silver blade at my reflection. A sense of empowerment washed over me, and I felt like I could conquer the world. Astrid Drago had once wielded this sword, and now, it belonged to me.

Chapter 15

Xanda Hates Flowers

A day passed, and it was now the morning of that stupid school trip to Roseosh Town. I still didn't really want to go. The Kingdom was on the brink of war! In my opinion, this was a stupid time to go on a trip. Don't get me wrong, Roseosh was an important town. I'd never been, but it was common knowledge it was full of fairy gardens where they grew crops that supplied most of Utopia with its food. We were going to learn about this today. Balls, I hated gardening. Grandma loved it. She used to grow strawberries, tomatoes, lettuce and other stuff I couldn't remember in our garden back home. Home...it seemed like such a long way away now. I couldn't remember the last time I was there, even though I knew it was just before the Winter Ball. It didn't seem real anymore...none of this did. I was so lost, I didn't know what I should do anymore, but then I knew what needed to be done. My head was all over the place lately. And knowing I was to spend the day around flowers just made me grumpy. Don't get me wrong, I like nature. I like trees, mountains, grass, rivers...but flowers can bog off. They looked pretty, but they all just smelled the same to me and then made you sneeze. Flowers are abominations. Anyway, enough about my personal war with pansies. Leon had persuaded me to get in one of the carriages that morning, after much protesting. I was in a foul mood. I was so tired and it was so hot that I just passed out and went to sleep. The muggy heat shot through the window, covering my body in a sticky sensation. See, that's why I hated the summer. I had fallen over, and my head was resting in Taz's lap. My eyelids were so heavy I just couldn't stay awake, but I couldn't sleep properly either. I was half asleep when I heard my friends having a conversation, although at the time I was too out of it to comprehend what they were saying.

"Leo, looks like you're gonna have to look for another partner, dude." Taz joked as he put his arm around me to stop me from falling off the seat. Leon chuckled softly.

"No way, Taz. Xanda and I are solid." He replied.

"That is true." Irina smiled softly. "But...is she alright? She's been falling to sleep a lot recently."

"Yeah." Leon said sadly. "She hasn't been sleeping too well at night lately. She either tosses and turns in her sleep, or she can't sleep at all and goes and sits on the balcony."

"Perhaps this is all getting to her..." Said Joey. "Not just the whole issue between Gailoiyn and Brozanta, but all this about her folks too..."

"Yeah, she hasn't spoken to Mr Davandrin or Mr Ventus in a while." Said Pippa.

"To be honest, I think she's just trying to get her head round it all." Leon spoke softly, reaching over and gently moving a piece of hair out of my face.

"So, while she's out...what do you think, Leo?" Taz asked, a serious tone in his voice. "Alphonse and Kirani Sykes. Do you think they're alive?"

"Probably not." Leon sighed softly. "We all know how ruthless King Stephan can be. But...since our chat with Mr Davandrin and Mr Ventus, I can tell that's all Xanda is thinking about. I hear her sometimes…just going over and over it inside her head. It's exhausting…"

"I think the carriage is stopping. Should we wake her?" Joey asked as our carriage began to slow down, and the sound of the horse's hooves began to fade away to a halt.

"Yeah." Said Pippa, reaching over and placing her hand on my arm, beginning to shake me. "Xanda! Sweetie, wake up. We're here."

"What…? Already?" I said groggily, opening my tired eyes slowly. I pushed myself up and rubbed my eyes.

"Well, you've been using my lap as a pillow for over an hour." Taz chuckled.

"I-I have?! Balls, I'm so sorry!" I stuttered nervously, my face flushing bright red with embarrassment. The others laughed, seeming to find my embarrassment amusing.

"It's cool. Although its lucky you're awake, cos Leo and I were about to trade partners." Taz grinned, clearly trying to wind Leon up. And it seemed to work. Gosh, Leon could be so gullible sometimes.

"N-No we weren't! I can explain!" Leon said flustered.

"Leon, he's joking, you idiot." I chuckled weakly. "C'mon, when have you ever known Taz to be serious?"

"Pfft, never." Joey laughed as he pushed open the carriage door. He jumped out, raising his arms and stretching them out as far as he could as the sun beat down upon him. The others stepped out ahead of me. I sighed softly, wiping the sleep out of my eyes before following the others. When I stepped out of the carriage, the sun practically attacked me, slapping me in the face as soon as I stepped foot on the smooth, cobbled ground.

"Balls…" I cursed under my breath, raising my hand in front of my eyes to stop myself being blinded by the sun. I huffed infuriatingly…this was gonna be a long day. I looked around at the pretty little town. The buildings were painted a deep shade of baby pink, and all the shops had dainty wooden signs hanging above them. In the centre of town was a tall, stone statue of a female fairy watering a flower. Don't ask me what type of flower it is, because I don't have a clue. To the right, there was a small hill, with a small church resting at the top. The stone of the church was a pale brown and ivy grew up the wall, draping itself over the wooden door. To the left were small cottages with thatched rooves. Each cottage was painted in a different colour, but each one was a pale shade and perfectly painted. Each one also had a lovely, small garden out front. But past the houses, down the hill, was the biggest allotment I think I have ever seen. In the centre was a small lake, the water as clear as a crystal. The sun made the place seem brighter and more welcoming, and the leaves on the crops were of the brightest shade of green I have ever seen. It was beautiful to behold. Despite me not liking flowers, if Lightwater didn't exist, I think I'd have loved to have lived here. Although there was a drawback. Roseosh Town wasn't that far from the Plain of Fire, the ancient battleground. I had a feeling that it wouldn't be ancient much longer...with the tension between Gailoiyn and Brozanta being so high, I sensed another battle would take place there again very soon. My class gathered in front of the fairy statue, and Mr Davandrin and Mr Ventus ushered everyone over. Mrs Madana stayed at the back, and I hadn't noticed her keep glancing over at me. When we were all there, Zadlos Davandrin spoke up.

"Ah, we're all here! Alright, kids. So, were going to head down to the allotment now to help the fairies out this morning. Then, after lunch you'll have a few hours to walk around the town and have a look around. All set?!" The other members of my class answered him in a sort of unison mumble, I however, remained silent. I still couldn't concentrate. I was suddenly snapped out of my thoughts however when a couple of fairies flew over our heads. There was a gasp of awe amongst my class as we all gazed up to watch them fly towards the allotments. Their pale wings fluttered in the breeze, and they flew effortlessly. They really were magical. I smiled a little watching them, not noticing that the class had begun to follow Mr Davandrin and Mr Ventus as they started walking. Suddenly, I felt a hand on my shoulder, and my heart skipped a beat. I looked round quickly to see Mrs Madana there, smiling down at me gently. I let out a sigh of relief.

"Balls...Mrs Madana, you made me jump."

"My apologies. I was wondering if we may have a word while we walked." She said softly. I raised an eyebrow, curious.

"Sure..." I said. She began to walk slowly behind the group, and I slowed my pace to keep level with her.

"It has come to my attention that certain members of staff are worried about you." She said. I rolled my eyes, sighing heavily. I knew exactly who she meant.

"Mr Davandrin and Mr Ventus. Yeah, I know. I'm not exactly on good terms with them right now." I said.

"May I ask why?"

"To cut a long story short, they knew my parents. Balls, Mr Ventus didn't just know them...my father was his best mate and my mother was his cousin! For years, I blamed myself for what happened to them...and they kept what really happened from me all this time."

"I see. Well, that must be very hard to fathom. I have studied history for many years. If there's one thing I have learned, is that humanity has a tendency to just bury their heads in the sand and pretend it never happened. Sometimes, it's because it will ruin their reputation. But sometimes, it's simply because the past is too painful to face again. No matter how brave Jasper and Zadlos may appear to be, no matter how strong, they are still only mortal, like all of us. They have feelings, emotions, and a past."

"So...you're saying that I should just forgive them?" I asked. I was extremely interested in what she was saying, and it did make some sense to me.

"Yes. Whatever their reasons, they must have believed it was the right choice at the time. I think you should forgive them. They care very much about you. That said, I don't think you should forget. Not about your anger, anger rarely helps one move forward. Whatever they told you about your parents, don't forget it. Hold onto it. What matters now is that they told you. What you do with the information, is now up to you. But also, don't forget Jasper and Zadlos must also feel pain. I know a little about your parents, and I know they meant a great deal to those two. It must have been very painful to relive. It must have brought up many memories, good and bad, upon seeing you." I listened, silent. She was right. I felt a pain burn in my chest, and I instantly felt so guilty. I did need to apologise.

"You're right." I said sadly. "I've been so horrible..."

"I don't think they see it like that." Monica Madana said, rubbing my back gently in comfort. "They completely get your reaction. They are worried about you, you know. You should talk to them." She smiled gently.

"Yeah..." I said nervously.

"Don't be scared." She chuckled. "Zadlos's bark is worse than his bite. But, I can tell from talking to him, he isn't angry with you. Not in the slightest. Now, stop worrying about everything!" She stopped walking, and she placed her hands on my shoulders, and I looked into her deep brown eyes. She was smiling down at me, reaching up with one hand and patting my head like Mr Davandrin often did. "Today is a day where you can relax and do something different for a change. Forget about fighting, and conflicts of the past. Just be a child and go and have fun!"

Now that was easier said than done...

So, we walked past the cottages and made our way down to the allotment. Fairies fluttered above the crops tending to their every whim. They all seemed very happy, and content with life. Or, as I thought at the time, oblivious to the problems around them. See, that was the thing with fairies. All the ones I knew that used to pass through Lightwater didn't care about the problems the world faced, they just cared about whether or not their business was protected. But you didn't want to upset the fairies, either. As I mentioned, the fairies in Roseosh Town grew most of the crops used to feed everyone. Business...politics...money...it's all corrupt if you ask me. Balls, what was wrong with me? I used to be so carefree, but everything that morning just seemed to annoy me. Perhaps that was just part of being a teenager. One of the fairies fluttered over, and he welcomed us to the Fairy Gardens and told us we could look around and try any of the produce we wanted. There was a small brook trickling through the gardens towards the lake. The water seemed to shimmer in the sunlight, and I became entranced by it. Pippa and Irina were more interested in the flowers growing at the brooks side. The two were kneeling beside them, breathing in deeply to take in their sickeningly sweet aroma.

"Xanda! Smell these flowers!" Pippa said excitedly.

"They smell divine!" Irina said.

"No thanks." I said sharply. "Flowers are just...evil."

"Jeeez. Someone got out of the wrong side of the bed this morning!" Joey chuckled.

"Isn't her bed against a wall?" Taz laughed back.

"Very funny." I said turning to face them. I really wasn't in the mood for anything.

"So, Xanda's stroppy today, eh?" We heard a familiar voice say. We all looked to our right, and we saw the Ventus twins walking over. Seto had a grin on his face as he spoke, and Naia looked at him in annoyance to what his brother had just said.

"Seto!" Naia said. "If she's upset, don't wind her up!"

"I'm not upset. I'm just not feeling myself today, that's all. Wait, what are you two doing here? You're not in our class." I asked, turning to face them fully.

"Well, we were bored." Seto grinned, running his hand through his strawberry blonde hair. I had only just noticed, but their hair looked much brighter in the sunlight.

"So, we asked papa if we could tag along." Naia smiled.

"I guess that's a perk of havin' your old man as a teacher." Joey said.

"Yup. Anyway, what's up with you?" Seto asked turning to me. I sighed.

"Oh nothin'." I said. "I just don't think this is a good time to have a school trip with everything that's going on."

"Well, maybe that's the best reason to have it." Said Naia. "Some normality may be just what we all needed. I know I could certainly do with a break from training."

"Yeah...I guess you're right. I'm sorry, guys. I've been a right cow this morning." I said, feeling really silly about the foul mood I had been in.

"That's alright." Said Irina, smiling sweetly. "We all have off days. Days when we don't feel ourselves."

"Come on. Let's go and help the others. I've never picked fruit before!" Leon said, taking my hand. He looked so excited, I instantly believed him when he said he'd never picked fresh fruit. I giggled softly as he began to pull me deeper into the gardens, the others following. Perhaps today wasn't going to be so bad after all...

About an hour past, and the sun was getting hotter and hotter by the minute. I couldn't remember the last time the weather was this warm. After my talk with the twins, I had cheered up a little. Leon was happily kneeling beside the strawberry plants, picking them carefully and placing them in a bowl. I say placing them in a bowl, but in reality he placed every other one in a bowl...and ate the rest. Pippa was with him, and she was just as bad as Leon for eating the strawberries. Irina and I weren't far. We were in the orchard by the lake, picking fresh apples off of the trees and putting them into a bucket. I hadn't seen the twins, Joey or Taz in a while. No doubt they were off causing trouble somewhere. I was beginning to enjoy myself. It had been ages since I'd helped Grandma pick her fruit in the garden back home, and this brought back some happy memories.

"It's a lovely day, isn't it?" Irina said smiling at me as she placed an apple in the bucket I was holding.

"If you like the hot whether it is, yeah." I smiled back.

"Well, it's nice to see you relaxed for once." Irina said.

"Yeah. Well, my Grandma grows fruit in our garden so I used to help her pick it. This brings back some nice memories."

"I can imagine. Naia was right. This trip was a good idea...I haven't thought about the conflict in ages." Said Irina. I looked at her once again and smiled.

"You remember that day on the beach? Before we got attacked. We were talking. It just occurred to me that I still haven't heard you play the piano." I said.

"Oh! I'm sure you will one day." Irina smiled, blushing a little. I opened my mouth to reply to her, but I was suddenly chilled to the bone...literally. I gasped as a gush of water was thrown at me. I was soaked through, my mouth wide open as drops of water dripped off the end of my nose. I looked round slowly and saw Joey and Taz standing there with a bucket, laughing hysterically. Those little swine's! Luckily for me, the idiots were standing in front of the lake. I stormed over to them, and before they could comprehend what was happening I placed my hands on their chests and shoved them roughly into the cold water. The boys didn't know what hit them as they broke the surface, treading water. They laughed, starting to splash water at me from inside the lake.

"Xanda!" Irina happily shouted to me, laughter apparent in her voice. I turned sharply to see the twins running towards me with a bucket each. As they threw the water I moved out of the way, and the cold fluid instead landed on the heads of Taz and Joey in the lake. They cursed, and I grabbed my bucket, running to the lake to fill it up. The boys climbed out, and soon the six of us were engaged in a full-on water fight. The cool water was so refreshing in the burning heat, and I couldn't remember the last time I had had this much fun! Soon, other members of our class began to join in. For once, all the troubles in my life just washed away. I dipped my bucket into the lake and threw water over Leo and the others, as well as ducking out of the way from them throwing water at me. I had just been hit by some water thrown by Seto, and I retaliated by throwing water from my own bucket back at him. The only thing was, Seto moved and I hit someone else. Balls...I watched, frozen to the spot as Mr Davandrin stood there, drenched by the water I had thrown intended for Seto. The water fight stopped, and I covered my mouth with my hand. It seemed like in that moment everyone held their breath for fear that we were in trouble. I swallowed hard, watching as Zadlos Davandrin stomped over to me and loomed over me like a giant. In a flash, a grin spread across his face and he pushed me backwards, just enough for me to lose my balance. I squealed as I tumbled backwards into the lake, my body becoming devoured by the water. I quickly breathed out of my nose, as I didn't want to get water up it. I quickly swam to the surface, gasping for air when I immerged above the water. I wiped my eyes while treading water, and looked at the others. I'd never heard so much laughter in my life, and it was rare to see it in such a dark time. I laughed too. I hadn't expected Mr Davandrin to push me in like that. Nobody else saw because they were all looking at me, but I saw Jasper Ventus creeping up to the group. He moved fast, putting his finger to his lips as he stood behind Zadlos Davandrin. I suddenly laughed hard as Mr Ventus shoved Mr Davandrin into the lake, and I covered my face as the water splashed over me. I laughed as he broke through the surface. The look on his face was priceless! He didn't know what had hit him! Jasper looked at me, literally crying with laughter. I looked at him, and for the first time since his revelation I didn't feel angry. Mrs Madana was right...he was only mortal, like me. He had feelings, emotions, and the ability to not only be sad, but happy too. Mrs Madana watched on happily, hoping that for now, the feud between the three of us had been resolved. In my mind, it was. There was too much fighting in this world to start fighting with the people that cared about me. My friends jumped into the lake, and they all started splashing each other without a care in the world. Jasper leaped in, and slicked his soaking blue hair back. He swam over to me, and smiled down at me.

"I'm sorry..." He said simply. I just looked at him, and I could see the sadness in his eyes. I sighed softly, and quickly reached forward to wrap my arms around him, hugging him tight. He quickly hugged me back, placing a hand on the back of my head. We said nothing more...we didn't need to. We were family, and we needed to stop avoiding each other.

It was such a hot day, that we dried simply by just staying outside. The muggy heat burned against my skin, and my clothes soon became bone dry. We'd sat down that afternoon in the apple orchard, and all had some lunch together. Lunch that mainly consisted of the fruit we had picked. It was so refreshing, especially the strawberries. Now I understood why Leon and Pippa had constantly been stuffing their faces with them. It had been a lovely morning, and a pleasant afternoon. Straight after lunch, we headed into town to take a look around. To be honest though, there really wasn't much there in the way of shops. In the end, we ended up sitting on a table outside the tavern in the town centre. It was named 'King Alfred's Tavern', clearly named after the father of King Ricco and Princess Veronica. I often wondered how they were doing. I hadn't seen them since the night of the Winter Ball, and it looked to me as if they were keeping a low profile. So as I was saying, we were sitting outside the tavern, each of us enjoying a mug of thick Dragonberry juice. Taz was talking intently to Pippa, and Joey was trying to impress Irina by showing her that he could lick his own elbow. Yeah, weird I know. Leon and I were talking to Naia and Seto, and we were chatting away about strange habits that people around the academy had. Seto swore that one girl in his class would smell a book before she read it. Like, how weird is that? I was still laughing, finally relaxing and just having a good time as I listened to the twins' rattle on while sipping my drink. Then I saw someone...someone that when I laid eyes on them, made me almost spit out my drink. I swallowed my drink down, and stood abruptly. The others immediately stopped their conversations, and looked in my direction. It was that Brozantan knight! The one that we had encountered in the throne room. The King and Princess took him as a hostage, so he must have escaped! His clothes were torn and tattered, and he stayed in the shadows clearly trying to slink back to his homeland. Leon stood too, seeming to have noticed him as well.

"That's him...!" He said in shock.

"Damn right it is! Hey! Stop right there!" I yelled at him, and he noticed me. He recognised us instantly, as a look of fear swept across his face. He instantly took off running down the side streets, and I found myself giving chase. The others got up and followed, running as fast as we could to try and catch him. Despite me being smaller than the rest of them, I somehow managed to keep ahead of them. We entered the alleyways. I crashed into walls as I turned corners, but I refused to stop running. He picked up the pace, sprinting for his life. Faster and faster. There was no way that rat was going back and leaking secrets about Gailoiyn to King Stephan! I'll give him credit though, he was very quick. We finally came to the edge of the town, and the Brozantan soldier began to scramble up the pristine white walls. I growled, clenching my fists tightly as I sprinted towards him.

"Stop!" I yelled, desperate to not let him get away. He turned, gritting his teeth. Suddenly, fear struck through me like a lightning bolt. He looked at me sharply, and I couldn't comprehend what was happening. Before I could slow down, he pulled a knife out of his pocket and hurled it in my direction. My eyes widened as the realisation hit me that I was moving too fast to stop in time. The dagger headed straight for me as I tried to skid to a halt. The fear was rising inside me, a flame of anxiety burning in my breast. Just then, I felt a forceful hand push me aside, and I gasped as I hit the wall, falling to my knees. The sound of clanging metal rang through the air, and suddenly time around me seemed to slow down. I looked up slowly, my body shaking a little as I tried to comprehend what was happening. My friends were standing behind me, all of them seeming as shocked as I was. A man had blocked the knife with a large dagger. Wait...no, not a man. It took me a moment to realise it, but my saviour wasn't human. I had to lower my gaze substantially before my gaze met his. He was a dwarf! He was short and stocky, and the sides of his light brown hair was shaved short. The top of his hair shone in the sunlight, and as he turned his head to look at me I could see my reflection in the pale green of his eyes. The Brozantan soldier didn't attack again. As we were distracted he leaped over the wall and got away. I was frustrated, but I focused my attention on the dwarf. I recognised him. He was a merchant. He used to travel through Lightwater sometimes on his travels. He stomped over to me with his hefty boots, and extended a chunky hand towards me.

"You alright, cupcake?" He said in a low, raspy voice. I took his hand, and I felt the sheer power in his beefy arms as he yanked me to my feet. Leon joined me at my side, and placed a hand on my arm. He looked at me worriedly. It took me a moment to answer, but finally I replied.

"Yeah...yeah I'm fine. Thanks."

"No problem." The dwarf replied, looking at me curiously. "Say...don't I know you from somewhere?"

"Um, yeah..." I said nervously. "I'm from Lightwater."

"Oh, I know you! You're Harry's little granddaughter. How is he?" Said the dwarf gleefully.

"Uh...yeah, he's good." I said, confused as to how he could be so cheerful after having a knife thrown at us.

"Sorry, who are you?" Asked Seto, narrowing his eyes suspiciously, still not sure if he could trust the dwarf. I wasn't surprised, Seto wasn't exactly a trusting person, but after his past I couldn't blame him.

"I'm a simple merchant. The names Bernard. Bernard Tarrick."

"Simple? You expect me to believe you're just a merchant after deflecting that knife the way you did." Seto scoffed.

"Well, nobody is simply one thing. For example, there's two of you." Bernard grinned looking at Naia. The other twin blushed, looking away shyly.

"I'm not my brother!" Seto stepped forward, looking rather offended. "He's much stronger than I will ever be..."

"Seto!" Naia said, gulping a little. Bless him, he always hated being the centre of attention.

"Well, you should all watch each other's backs from now on. No more running into trouble, cupcake." Said Bernard looking at me again. "Things are...about to get ugly."

"What's that supposed to mean?" asked Taz. We were all thinking the same thing. What Bernard said had shaken us to the core. Did he know something that we didn't?

"Well, I've not long come from a trip to Palmira, and let me say, things are going downhill in Brozanta fast. Palmira is now a slavers den. Women are being forced into marriages or servitude, and the men are being trained to fight to the death. It...wasn't a pretty sight. I dunno what Stephan's up to, but I sure hope this is all just one big joke." Said Bernard. Balls...it seemed like things in Brozanta were far worse than we feared. Stephan wasn't just ruling people anymore, he was dominating them. We all shared a worried glance between ourselves. We all knew that if Stephan wasn't stopped soon, then the same thing would happen to us. Not me. Never. I refused to live that life. I was never going to bow to anybody. And I was starting to feel like I didn't want to serve anybody either. I wasn't going to take sides, I was going to do what was right...and that meant stopping King Stephan at all costs.

"Then that settles it..." I said slowly.

"We need to find the four pieces of the Elemental stone before he does." Leon spoke, finishing my sentence.

"C'mon, you're just kids." Said Bernard. "Besides, the Earthstone is safe." We all suddenly felt alert, looking at him sharply.

"How safe?!" Joey stepped forward, desperation in his voice. "Where is it?!"

"It doesn't matter, what does is that King Stephan won't find it."

"How do you know that?!" Pippa said angrily.

"She's right!" Irina said cupping her hands over her heart nervously. "We need to find the stones...we can't risk anybody else getting hurt!"

"People get hurt every day, cupcake. Emotionally, physically...it doesn't matter. With or without Stephan as King, there will still be hurt in the world." Said Bernard.

"Even so, our world was at peace before he took the throne!" Naia said, clenching his fists. "Now look...Gailoiyn and Brozanta are on the brink of war. Brothers are fighting brothers. Sisters are fighting sisters. Good people are being enslaved or going hungry, and King Stephan does nothing to help them! And it seems to me like King Ricco doesn't even understand the gravity of the situation! Where has he been since the night of the Winter Ball? Nowhere! He's done nothing! At least Princess Veronica has her head screwed on! King Ricco is just sweeping all of this under the carpet and hoping it will go away! Well it won't!"

"Naia...easy." Seto said, taking his brother's arm gently. Balls, I'd never seen Naia like that before. He rarely spoke his mind, but now he was just letting all the anger pent up inside of him blurt out without thinking. Naia looked at his brother, and his hardened facial expression softened again, looking scared like a child about to get into trouble for saying something wrong.

"I can't argue with you there, kiddo." Said Bernard after a short period of silence, finally putting his daggers away. "You kids look out for each other, alright? I'm sure this won't be the last time we meet." And with those words, Bernard began to walk away, soon disappearing around a corner. Joey ran forward a little, shouting after him.

"Hey, short stuff! Don't just leave us hangin'! Where's the Earthstone?! Come back!"

"Just let him go Josef..." Leon sighed, then turned his attention to Naia. "Are you okay?"

"Yes. Sorry for my outburst. I didn't mean it." Said the nervous boy, looking down at his shoes.

"Don't apologise." Pippa laughed a little. "In my opinion, you were bang on."

"At least now we have a lead on the Earthstone." Said Irina hopefully.

"Yeah." I smiled weakly, turning to face the group. "It's almost time to go. We should head back. We can talk about this tomorrow after we've slept on this information and had time to think about it."

"Pfft, what information?" Seto said as we began to walk back towards the centre of town. "All we know now is that a random dwarf knows where the Earthstone is. And that random dwarf is a travelling merchant, which means it could be anywhere!" I hated to admit it, but Seto had a point. Bernard must have travelled all over Utopia, so the stone could still be anywhere. Just when I thought we had a lead, it looked like we were back to square one.

Balls...it had been a long day, and we arrived back in Algora rather late. Except the part where we chased a rebel through the streets, it had been a really nice day. Thinking back to the moment where we had that water fight in the fairy gardens, I realised that I hadn't smiled that much in ages. It was so nice to feel like a child for once, and not having to live up to responsibility. But the day was drawing to a close, and the sun began to set across the earth. As soon as we had gotten back to the Academy we had all headed straight up to our rooms. I dunno about anyone else, but I was ready to go to sleep. As I opened the door, I threw my bag onto the floor next to my wardrobe and stretched, extending my arms as far as they would go. I let out a huge yawn, and practically threw myself onto my bed. Leon walked in behind me and shut the door gently. He rubbed his eyes tiredly, and walked over to our bunkbed. He sat down on the bottom bunk next to me, and gazed down at me. He rubbed the back of his head.

"Well...that was weird." He said, sighing softly.

"What was weird?" I asked, raising an eyebrow.

"You know...the whole thing with that dwarf. He's a strange little fellow, isn't he?"

"Leo." I laughed a little, sitting up. "We live in a world where people can turn into Dragons. That alone is pretty messed up if you ask me."

"I guess you're right." Leon chuckled softly.

"Leon. Can I just say...despite what happened with the Brozantan and Bernard...I've really enjoyed today. It was nice to see you chilling out for a change." I smiled.

"I could say the same about you." He replied, smiling back at me. He then stood up, and stretched out his arms like I had done. "Well, I'll see you later. I won't be long."

"Where you goin'?" I asked, raising an eyebrow.

"To see my father. I haven't seen him in a while with everything going on. I'm just going to check that he's okay."

"Want me to come?"

"You can if you want to." Leon smiled.

"Sweet." I replied, which made Leon laugh. I couldn't figure out why. I mean,

I didn't think I had said anything strange. "What?"

"Oh nothing. It's just you country folk can speak very strangely sometimes." He chuckled.

"Alright, rich boy!" I let out a short laugh and punched his arm as I stood up. I just looked at him and smiled. He made me so happy for no reason, but I had noticed he had changed since we had first met. "Y'know, you've become a lot cheekier recently."

"Well, that's because I've been hanging around you too much."

"See what I mean?!" I shook my head, but I couldn't stop smiling. Balls, I must have looked like such an idiot.

"Come on." He said, taking my arm gently. My heart skipped a beat as his hand touched me, and I caught my breath. Oh gods...I wasn't falling for him, was I? Surely not. Damn it...what was wrong with me?

So, we headed to Drevin Drogon's office. I thought back to what Mr Davandrin and Mr Ventus had told me, that I used to play in there with Leon when we were little. It was so strange to think I was born in the Academy. As I've said before, I had always assumed that I was born in Lightwater. Leon opened the door to his father's office, and it wasn't anything like I had expected. The room was light, the evening sun shining through a large, open window. In front of the window was Mr Drogon's desk, which had a wooden panel at the front with Dragons carved into it. On the other side of the room was a large bookcase, and a table in front of it with a weird looking plant on it. However oddly enough, there was no sign of the headmaster.

"Father?" Leon said, a little worried. We stepped into the room and looked around, but there was definitely no sight of him. "I don't get it...he's always in here."

"Leon, he is allowed to leave his office, y'know."

"Yes, but...he's always here. Like...always. He's work crazy!" Leon ran his fingers through his hair, in a complete panic. I realised that this must have been very out of character for Mr Drogon. Leon looked beside himself, and he began to get me worried too. I slowly made my way around the back of Drevin Drogon's desk. I tilted my head to the side, seeing something rather curious behind the desk. I pulled his chair back to see what was there.

"Leo...look at this." I said, and he rushed to my side. There was a secret doorway in the floor under his desk, some stone steps leading downwards into a cavern of some sort. There was a holder on the side of the wall that was supposed to hold a torch, but it looked as if it had already been taken.

"I've heard about this!" Said Leon. "Apparently it was built by Astrid Drago as an escape route for her if she ever needed it. My father has mentioned it but I didn't know that it actually existed."

"Do you know where it leads?" I asked curiously.

"Under the Limping Cliffs."

"Your joking!" I said surprised. "Leo, that's right next to the Crossroads, one of the only two points where Gailoiyn and Brozanta meet that isn't half way across the Plain of Fire! What the hell is he doing going down there at such a dangerous point in time?!" I admit, now I was worried. As I mentioned, there were two points where Brozanta and Gailoiyn met that wasn't the midway point across the Plain of Fire. The crossroads, a pathway atop of the Limping Cliffs were one of them. The other was the peak of the Frostbitten Mountains, at the other end of the Plain of Fire.

"I don't know!" Leon replied worriedly. "But I need to find him!"

"Leo! Wait for me!" I said sharply as Leon began to sprint down the stone steps. I followed him in haste, and the sound of our footsteps echoed throughout the cavern as our boots touched the cool stone. I placed one hand on the wall to steady myself as we neared the bottom. The air was beginning to become salty, to the point where I could taste it. We were nearing the ocean, that much was clear. As we hurried deeper into the caves, we started to hear voices echoing in the distance. The one voice was Drevin Drogon. The other was harrowingly familiar. I hoped and prayed it wasn't who I thought it was...

"Is that-... no...it can't be!" Said Leon quietly as we got nearer the voices. "Yeah. It sounds like your aunt!"

"Tenebris is no aunt of mine!" Leon hissed. We slowed down a little as we came to a large opening. There were some larger rocks to the side, and Leon faced me with his finger to his lips as he began to crouch lower behind the rocks. I followed him, and placed my hands on the damp rocks as I peered over the top. Standing there was Drevin Drogon and Tenebris Magicae Ora, shouting at each other ferociously. I hadn't seen Mr Drogon angry before, and he was so intimidating. Tenebris bit back hard, practically screaming in the headmaster's face. There was a large opening in the cliffs behind them, and I could see the weather was turning nasty. The sea was crashing up the sides of the rocks, and splashing into the cavern. Just like the weather, this argument was about to get worse...

Chapter 16

Promise Me

"You are nothing but a liar!" Tenebris growled.

"Sera came with me! Nobody forced her to!" Drevin countered, clearly trying to reign in his temper. It was obvious that despite how much he hated Tenebris, he didn't want to fight her.

"She died giving birth to your brat!"

"Leave my son out of this! This is not his fault!"

"No! It's your fault! It's all your fault! You took her away from her home and impregnated her! You murdered her! You murdered Sera-Rose! Now make this easy, Drevin. Give me the boy! It's what Sera would want!" She spat. Leon and I looked at each other worriedly, still concealing ourselves behind the rocks. If Tenebris wanted to take Leon, we both knew this argument wasn't going to end well. Mr Drogon stayed silent for a moment. He run his hand through his hair, and sighed heavily.

"No." He said sharply. "I was with Sera on her deathbed. She made me promise that I would raise him. That is what I have done, and that is what I will continue to do!"

Tenebris's face turned as red as her hair, and she was overcome with rage. She started to scream from the bottom of her lungs, and she ran towards Drevin. He really didn't want to attack her, so Drevin Drogon took a step backwards as she lifted her hands to attack him. Before I could stop him, Leon leaped over the rock and put himself between his father and his aunt.

"Stop it!" He yelled, pushing her back. Tenebris panted, trying to catch her breath as she stared down at him with an insane look in her eye. I leaped over the rock after him, and watched them in fear. Drevin looked between myself and Leon, probably wondering what we were doing there. I hurried over to Leon and pulled him back by his arm, and I could feel my heart racing as the tension rose in the air around us.

"Leon! Xanda! What are you doing here?!" Drevin boomed. "Did you tell them to come to?!"

"I did nothing of the sort!" said Tenebris angrily.

"It's true father. We were coming to see you and we found the passage. Come on, let's just go home!" Leon said, desperately grabbing his father's arm and trying to pull him away.

"Leon! Come with me!" Tenebris reached out her claw like hands to grab him, but I wasn't going to allow that. I put myself between them and smacked her arm away, beginning to lose my temper now too.

"Hey, back off! You heard him! He wants to go with Mr Drogon, not you!" I spat.

"How dare you touch me you little-!" Tenebris became enraged, and she pulled her hand back as a pulse of magic began to form in her palm. I panicked. In a flash, Drevin Drogon grabbed me and pulled Leon and I behind him protectively.

"I'm warning you!" Drevin said sharply. "Stay away from them!"

"Never." She scowled. "You think that I don't know who she is? Did you think

I wouldn't figure it out?! My lord would very much like to know of her existence!"

What was she talking about? Her words made no sense to me!

"That is not why I'm protecting them, and you know it!" Drevin said darkly as two balls of fire began to form in both of his hands. A sudden heat washed over us, and the chilly cavern started to become warmer. I could feel the heat of the fire burning my skin despite being a safe difference from it. It was then I realised the fire was closer than I thought. I gazed down at Leon's hand, and he too had a fireball formed in his palm.

"Do you trust me?" Leon asked quickly.

"Always."

"Then stay behind me." Leon suddenly reached around his father, and sent a bolt of fire hurdling towards Tenebris. She stumbled back a little, clearly not expecting it to be Leon that would attack first. She blocked the attack with magic from her palms. She didn't take kindly to that at all. Tenebris began to fly out of control, and rapidly began throwing bolts of magic at us. I'm not gonna lie, I was terrified! I had nothing to defend myself with! I couldn't use magic...I'm not a mage or Dragonbourne! If there was ever a time when I needed to be one of those things, it was now! I couldn't do anything except run around behind Leon like a headless chicken as we did our best not to be hit by one of Tenebris's attacks. Mr Drogon was desperately trying to keep her attention away from us, firing attack after attack at Tenebris. Although, she seemed deadly focused on me and Leon. She knew I was the weakest link in the team, having no way to defend myself. Dammit, if only I'd brought my sword! Tenebris was chasing after us like a wild animal, and I could see no sign of sanity in her eyes. My heart was thumping against my chest, and I was so scared I could barely breathe. She was trying to get closer to us, and Leon tried desperately to force her away. Then, we hit a dead end. Tenebris had forced us between her and the cliff opening. A rush of adrenaline surged through me, as I knew we were done for! Mr Drogon was sprinting over, shouting at Tenebris in utter panic. I clung onto Leon, petrified. I kept looking between Tenebris and the rough ocean crashing up the cliffs behind us. Suddenly, a black mist began to drape around Tenebris, and her cackle seemed to echo throughout all Algora. Leon turned and wrapped his arms around me, wanting to shield me from the blow. Drevin Drogon was almost near us! But...he was too late...

The blast made the sound of a hurricane. The headmaster was thrown backwards, his head smacking on the side of the rocky cavern. That was the last thing I saw before it went dark. We were engulfed by a huge wave of dark magic. I could see, but only because of these weird purple magical ropes that were glowing around us. Leon pulled back a little, but he kept his hands firmly on my upper arms as we gazed upwards to look at the ropes swirling above us. It was almost like we were in a trance like state, the glowing ropes seeming to move in slow motion. Suddenly, the ropes darted towards us, and Leon gasped as one of them wrapped firmly around his wrist. There was a complete look of panic on his face. My eyes widened as one of the magical ropes wrapped itself around my ankle. Just then, the ropes began to tear us apart, separating Leon from myself. More and more of the magical bonds began to wrap themselves around our arms and legs, and soon it was impossible to move! My body was completely overcome with shock, and I couldn't do anything other than desperately struggle against the ropes and hope that somehow, I would break free. The more I struggled, the more the bonds squeezed around me. Tighter and tighter. Leon was groaning in pain, he too trying to free himself. The ropes were beginning to hurt now, and the searing pain weakened me with each passing second. I didn't know what to do, it seemed as if there was no way out of this! Just then, it went silent. Leon was staring at me, no longer struggling. Had he given up? He had a strange look in his eye, almost melancholy. Just then he spoke to me, clearly in immense pain.

"Xanda...promise me. Promise me, that you will never stop fighting! Never...never let Stephan win! Promise me, Xanda!"

With those words, a white light surrounded me, pushing away the darkness shrouding me. That idiot...he was using the last of his strength and the last of his magic to save me! I tried to call out to him to tell him to stop! But it was too late. The bonds around me snapped open, and I was thrown out of the darkness and back into the cavern. I hit the side of the rocks as I was thrown out, and bounced off the wall straight through the cavern opening.

I fell rapidly towards the ocean, not even being able to prepare myself before I found myself crashing into the waves. There was blood rushing from the side of my head, and it stained the grey waters around me. I used my tired body to swim towards the surface, taking a huge breath when I broke through the top. I had placed a hand to my head, and pulled it in front of my face. I cursed under my breath, not even realising I had hit my head on the way down until now. I didn't have time to dwell on that though. I couldn't stay here or I'd be shark food! I began to swim, knowing that if I kept swimming west along the cliffs I'd eventually reach the beach by the Academy. Unfortunately, that proved to be much harder than it sounded. The water was so choppy and the sky was becoming darker, making it more difficult to see. I tried to swim forwards, but the waves washed up against me pushing me back. The water lapped over my head, and after a while I struggled to stay above the surface. The waves just kept forcing me under the water, and my chest felt heavy as the air was beginning to drain from my lungs. My arms were flailing around desperately as I tried to break through the ocean's surface again, but I just felt myself sinking deeper and deeper. I couldn't breathe any longer, and I was beginning to lose control of my body.

My muscles were burning, and I was struggling to stay awake. My eyes began to close. I was passing out, sinking deeper and deeper into the depths of the ocean. But then, something strange happened. There was a figure swimming towards me. I could make out flowing green hair and a pale, slender face as she reached me. Her hands felt rough as she grabbed me. I somehow felt a glimmer of hope, and I allowed my eyes to close.

I awoke slowly. I wasn't sure how much time had passed. My vision kept fading in and out, becoming clear and then blurry again. The dazzling aqua blue light from clear water reflected off a rocky ceiling above me. I was in some sort of cove. The area was small but warm, despite being near the water. I could feel a softness under my fingertips as I lay on a bed of lush, green moss. I was lying next to the water's edge, where a few colourful koi fish kept on bobbing up to the surface. Small, purple flowers blossomed out of the moss, and specs of light seemed to float upwards from their delicate petals. It wasn't long before I noticed the woman that had saved me. Her skin looked like silk, nothing like how it had felt while in the water. Her eyes and long, braided hair were as green as seaweed. It was then I noticed something odd about her clothing. She wore a dark green material draped over her breasts, but nothing more. I couldn't tell what the material was, but it looked very strange and foreign to me. She parted her blood red lips and spoke softly to me.

"Hello. Are you alright?"

"Ugh…" I groaned in pain, using my elbows to sit up slightly. "My heads banging…" No word of a lie, I had never had a headache like this before. I looked at the lady, and it was then that I noticed her bottom half was…green and…scaly. At first, I thought I was hallucinating. Then I realised that I wasn't. Part of it was in the water, but there no mistaking it. She had a tail! I suddenly felt my eyes widen in shock, and I began to freak out. "Holy Raven's nickers! You're a fish!"

"Well spotted." She giggled softly. "I'm a mermaid. Wait…your eyes! Xandario?!"

"Y-Yeah? That's me." I swallowed hard, not quite knowing what to make of this. First, she was a mermaid. Second, she knew me! She quickly got over the shock and shook her head.

"Forgive me, I am Annalise. I have close connections with the Academy, and have for many years. I knew your parents. They saved me once, when I was a little girl. My fins were trapped between some rocks, and they set me free. You were barely walking the last time I saw you." She smiled softly. I just found myself looking at her, and began smiling when she mentioned my parents. There was still so much about them I didn't know. Just then, I felt a searing pain shoot through my skull, and my head instantly became heavy again. I fell back to the floor, holding my head in my hands. Annalise became panicked, and she placed her hands on my arm in comfort, looking at me worriedly.

"Shh…It's alright, Xandario. I sent for help. You'll be out of here soon." Said Annalise. Out of here…but to what? It was then that it hit me…Leon was gone. What did I have to go back for? My partner was gone. I failed. I felt guilt burn inside my heart like an uncontrollable fire. I just kept apologising to Leon over and over inside my head. It felt like forever, but it wasn't long before I heard people enter the cove. The sound of hurried footsteps raced towards me, and I recognised the two voices instantly.

"Annalise!" Said Mr Davandrin as he knelt beside us.

"Xanda!" Jasper Ventus covered his mouth. "Oh, thank goodness!" Mr Davandrin helped me sit up, and I lay in his strong arms. My body was still burning, and I felt so weak. I could barely stay awake.

"She has a head injury." The mermaid told them. "It needs tending to right away." Mr Ventus knelt beside me, and I looked up at him pitifully as he moved my hair out of the way to take a look at the bump on my head. His fingers brushed my head gently, and he winced when he saw the wound. I didn't know how bad it looked. I hadn't seen it. But apparently, there was blood everywhere.

"Dear gods…she needs stitches. C'mon Zadlos, we need to get her back to the Academy. You're going to be alright, Xanda. I promise." Said Jasper with a worried look in his eyes.

"Annalise, you should go and warn your people." Mr Davandrin said, cradling me in his arms and picking me up gently.

"Thank you…" I spoke quietly, looking at the mermaid. She smiled softly at me, and nodded.

"For you, anytime…" She replied. With a small, graceful leap, she entered the water and disappeared below the surface. I groaned in pain, and grabbed onto Davandrin's shirt with my shaky palm. My head was reeling, and it started to throb as Davandrin briskly carried me back towards Algora.

Thunder roared in the sky above. Lightning crashed into the earth below. The sky was dark. Rain smacked into the ground like daggers, and pelted against my window. Once again, I had passed out on the way here and now had no concept of how much time had passed. I felt like someone was inside my head, constantly banging on a drum. A throbbing pain burned inside my brain, and even lying down I felt so unfocused and off balanced. I awoke in my own bed at the Academy. As I looked around, the room was spinning wildly. I wanted to be sick. I reached up and grabbed a hold of the wooden bars of the bed above me, and heaved myself up into a sitting position. My body slumped, and I tried to catch my breath. A part of me hoped this was all a dream…but it wasn't. Leon was gone. He wasn't in the top bunk where he usually slept. He wasn't here. My heart felt heavy, but I continued to try and control my breathing. I knew that I had to get up and find out what was going on. Leo needed me. I took one final deep breath and swung my legs around. My feet touched the cold, wooden floor, and I stood slowly. I wobbled a little, but quickly grabbed onto Leon's bed to steady myself. My vision faded in and out for a moment, and I knew I probably should have stayed in bed...but if our roles were reversed, I knew Leon would come for me. I shifted my gaze slightly to my wardrobe, and I began to stagger over to it. I placed a shaky hand on the wardrobe handle, and swung open the doors. With great difficulty, I started to get dressed. I could hear the storm roaring outside, so I made sure I dressed warm. Finally, I knelt down to tie up my boots, which was extremely difficult as I could barely focus on what I was doing. With my nightwear thrown onto the floor in a heap, and my outerwear gear on, I was ready to go. I tried to stand, but I became dizzy once again and I immediately fell back down. The room was spinning in so many different directions. I felt like I was drunk. I cursed under my breath and began to crawl over to my dresser. I groaned in agony and determination as my hands gripped the side of the dressing table, as I used it to hoist myself to my feet. As I finally steadied myself, I noticed that I was eye level with the mirror. In that moment, I barely recognised myself. I remembered when I had first come into this room and looked into the mirror. I had seen a naive, nervous little girl with no worries in the world apart from stressing about school life. Now, I looked a mess. My golden hair fell at the sides of my face, and my ponytail was spiky and windswept. My face was a little dirty, and there was dry blood swept over my nose. My eyes were not as innocent. I had a harder expression on my face. I was not the same person I was back then. So much had happened...so much had changed. But one thing remained the same...I was still Xandario Beatrice Sykes. My legendary sword lay on the dressing table, and I rested my hand around its hilt. I curled my fingers around it, and I felt like my arm was whole again. I took the sword into my right hand, and turned slowly to face the door. I let out a short cry of pain and began to hobble towards the open doorway. As I turned to leave down the corridor, my foot caught the edge of the door frame, and I fell face first into the hall. The sword clanked loudly as it skidded across the floor ahead of me. I moaned in annoyance, and felt tears of frustration forming in the brim of my eyes. It was then I heard Leon's voice in my head for the first time. It wasn't really him...but it was a memory. When I was in the infirmary after the attack on the beach, I remembered him saying:

"Not many people would take a beating like that and choose to get back up."
He was right. Giving up wasn't my style at all. Those words rang inside my head, and they gave me a strength that I didn't even know that I had. I growled in determination, and used my newfound strength to push myself up to my hands and knees. I slowly crawled over to my sword, and once again took its hilt into my hand. I quickly placed one foot on the ground, and used it to push myself upwards. I could barely see, as there were no candles lit in the hallway like there usually was. The castle was dark, and quiet. All the doors were shut, and there was something rather eerie and sinister about it

all. I slowly made my way down the hall, becoming more focused with every step that I took. Ahead of me, at the end of the hall, was a large window. I could see how bad the weather was outside, and I thought how unusual it was to have a storm at this time of the year. I didn't think on the weather for long though. As I walked slowly down the hall, I just kept remembering the last words Leon had said to me.

"Xanda...promise me. Promise me, that you will never stop fighting! Never...never let Stephan win! Promise me, Xanda!"

Promise me. Promise me. Promise me. That was all that kept going around and around inside my brain. I burned those words into my mind, never allowing myself to forget them. Promise me. Finally, I reached the window, and I placed my left hand on the ledge to support myself. The window overlooked part of the city, and I couldn't quite believe what I was seeing. The royal army were marching through the streets, armoured to the teeth. Their weapons looked as if they had been sharpened to the max. Surely Leon's capture hadn't started the war?! If it had, the reason behind it puzzled me. The Brozantan's had attacked us several times, yet Gailoiyn refused to fight back. So why now? Just then, I felt my heart skip a beat. I jumped as someone forcefully grabbed my shoulder!

I gasped in surprise, turning around swiftly. I breathed a short sigh of relief when I saw Drevin Drogon standing before me. He looked...odd. He seemed different than before, and incredibly on edge. His grey eyes looked mellow, yet angry at the same time. He was clearly hurting from the loss of his son. He once again placed his hand on my arm, and his long fingers began to dig deep into my skin. He had a firm grip, but it was a grip that hurt.

"M-Mr Drogon?" I said, becoming rather nervous about the way he was acting. He suddenly started to pull me back down the corridor. "Mr Drogon! Stop it! That hurts!" I started to struggle, wondering what on earth was going on. He just looked directly ahead as he practically dragged me down the hall. "You need to stay in your room." He spoke sharply.

"Have you gone mad?! I need to find Leon!"

"Don't be stupid!" He boomed as he threw me roughly back into my room. I stumbled backwards but stayed standing, looking at him nervously. "I've just lost my son! Do you really think I want to lose you too?! We need you both alive!"

"What are you on about?!" I scoffed. "I need to save my partner!"

"No. No, you stay right here! I don't want you anywhere near the battlefield!" And with those words, Drevin Drogon slammed the door in my face. I felt a rush of panic surge through me, and I dashed over to the door.

"No!" I yelled, trying to pull the door open. I heard the lock click shut, and the sounds of Mr Drogon stomping down the corridor. I started hammering on the door, banging loudly hoping that somebody would hear me, or Mr Drogon would come back and let me out. "Mr Drogon! C'mon, this aint funny! Let me out!" My heart was pounding against my chest, and all I wanted to do was scream! I ran over to my balcony, swinging open the glass doors and darting out into the pouring rain. I placed both my hands on the wet, stone balcony, immediately becoming soaked through as the rain pelted against my clothing. I looked down, hoping to see some way that I could possibly escape. But I soon realised I was way too high up, and there was nothing to grab onto. I couldn't contain my scream any longer, and I shouted and cursed from the bottom of my lungs. I felt an anger burn in my breast, an anger I hadn't felt in a long time. I fell to my knees against the stone wall, keeping my hands grasped onto the side of the balcony. I allowed the rain to soak me through. The thunder roared once more, later followed by another bolt of lightning in the distance. These sounds however, seemed to fade away almost instantly as I once again heard Leon's voice echo inside my head...over and over...

Promise me. Promise me. Promise me.

Chapter 17

The Plain of Fire

I was now more awake than ever. I desperately wanted to get out there and save my partner! Damn that Drevin Drogon! I just remember being so angry and frustrated and worried that all I could do was pace up and down my room. All that I could think about was that Leon needed me and I wasn't there for him! I tried to calm down and think rationally. There must have been a way out! If this had happened to me at the beginning of my story, I would have been on the ground sobbing right now. But I wasn't going to cry. Crying wouldn't change anything. I needed to get out of here and get my partner back! Just then, a gush of wind came surging into my room. I stumbled back a little, and realised my balcony door had been opened! When I looked over, I couldn't believe my eyes! Suddenly, I felt so happy and sighed deeply in relief! My friends came in, dripping wet from the storm. Pippa, Irina, Taz, Joey and the twins all hurried in and rushed towards me. I found myself running towards them automatically, and they all wrapped their arms around me in a group hug.

"Xanda! Oh, thank the gods!" Irina cried, squeezing me tightly.

"We thought you were dead!" Said Joey.

"Sorry to disappoint you." I smiled, laughing with happiness. "Balls, it's so good to see you all! How'd you get in here?!"

"Duh. We flew and landed on your balcony, obviously." Taz grinned. We all pulled back, and I looked at them. As ecstatic as it was seeing them again, I knew I had to get back to the situation at hand.

"Of course." I said seriously. "Right. Can somebody please tell me what the hell is going on?" The others went silent for a moment, looking at each other as if wondering how to tell me what had happened. Seto put his hands in his pockets and spoke slowly.

"You, Leo and Mr Drogon went missing after we got back from Roseosh Town. There was so much talk around the school the next morning. News travelled fast. Then...Ida and her husband, Seth McCoy were seen helping Mr Drogon to walk through the school. There was blood all over him! It was horrible!"

"He did look awful..." Irina said sadly. "But we got worried when he didn't return with you two."

"So we followed him in." Said Taz. "Davandrin and Ventus was there. Mr Drogon just kept on babbling that you and Leon weren't coming back. Then Mr Davandrin and Mr Ventus got a message and they left. When they came back, Mr Davandrin was carrying you. Honestly, you looked like you were dead."

Pippa placed her hand on Taz's shoulder and continued. "Things got worse. Mr Drogon woke up. He took one look at you and flipped. He was so angry."

"Because of Tenebris..." I said quietly.

"Tenebris? She did that to you?!" Naia asked softly. I nodded in response.

"She tried to take me and Leon. She said it was more than just because Leon was her nephew. I don't understand why she wanted me too. When Leo refused to go with her, she went crazy. She cast this weird spell on us to take us back to Eruznor...but Leon used the last of his strength to free me."

"We heard the Brozantan's had Leon, and we thought they had you too until you were found." Said Seto. "King Ricco and Princess Veronica instantly sent a message to Eruznor to meet the Brozantan army on the Plain of Fire. King Ricco hopes to get Leo back without further bloodshed."

"Like that's going to happen." I scoffed. I walked briskly over to my dressing table and picked up my sword quickly, staring at my reflection in the blade. Naia looked at me a little worriedly, swallowing hard.

"Xandario...would you-"

"Naia, please don't try and talk me out of this. Mr Drogon's already tried." I said.

"I wasn't going to." Naia smiled a little. "I was going to ask if you would ride with me."

"O-Oh!" I said in surprise. Well, this was a new Naia. He was changing. Had this been the Naia I first met he would have told me to stay put and stay safe.

"I doubt our teachers will be happy we crashed the party." Joey grinned widely.

"Look at how disobedient we are." Seto chuckled. "It makes me wonder if we are actually related, Xanda."

"Wait...you know?!"

"Yeah. Papa told us." Naia smiled. "Its fine. Were cool with it."

"Papa didn't tell us the details, but from what he said about Kirani...if she were here now she'd want us to go and save our friend. And she'd want you to save your partner."

"Yeah...yeah she would." I smiled brightly, a look of determination in my eyes. I put my hand out to them. "For Leon."

As I spoke, the others wasted no time in putting their hands over mine. We were so in tune, and so determined. We all spoke the following line at the same time. This was it. The second Wyvern War had finally begun.

"For Leon!"

The Plain of Fire. It is unlike any other place on this earth. It was dry and dusty, and the very air seemed choked with pieces of ash floating around. There were lines in the earth, each filled with a lava like substance trickling through them. The rain had lightened, but the thunder and lightning still roared heavily in the sky above. The sounds of stamping feet could be heard as two fully armoured armies marched towards the centre of the battlefield. At the front of the Gailoiyn army was the King and the Princess, both dressed in regal armour that glimmered as the rain fell upon it. Young King Ricco was clearly out of his depth, but he stood tall, trying not to let it show. Close behind them was Mr Zadlos Davandrin, Jasper Ventus, Cassandra Nebilia, Ivy Wellworn and Monica Madana. Leading the Brozantan army was none other than Hendrix Montgomery, closely followed by his partner Adamski Thorne. Behind them, Tenebris walked proudly, her arm draped around Leon. She looked different. For one, her clothes were different to what she normally wore. Her robes were draped, and golden in colour. Her boots shone silver, almost like they were made of metal. She looked and walked like a queen. Mr Drogon arrived in his huge Dragon form, wanting to inflict fear into the enemy. As he landed the ground shook, and he turned back into his human form. His eyes were narrow, and he gazed upon his son. Leon's eyes were glazed over, and much darker than before. Drevin was sickened by this. Leon's bright, emerald eyes were the same as his beloved Sera's. He feared he would lose his son that day, just like he had lost Leon's mother all those years ago. King Ricco took a deep breath, and he walked forward alone to meet Hendrix Montgomery in the middle of the battlefield. The two men stood there silently. Ricco must have been so intimidating right then, as Hendrix was much taller and much rougher around the edges than he ever was. Both armies held their breath, still not sure whether or not they would have to fight. It was Ricco who spoke the first words on the Plain of Fire on that fateful day.

"Mr Montgomery. We do not wish to fight. I swear by the gods the Gailoiyn army will stand down if the child, Leon Drogon, can return to his father." Hendrix was silent. He just stared down at the enemy King with those narrow, beady eyes of his. When Hendrix finally spoke, his deep voice sent a shiver down Ricco's spine.

"You know why we cannot do that." Hendrix answered.

Tenebris stepped forward to Hendrix's side confidently. She started speaking in other language. "Una Puella, Unus Puer, Caeruleosque implexae animabus illorum, Draco et Sedebat, Unum pro Pugnans. One Girl, One Boy. Their Souls entwined. Dragon and Rider, fighting as one. The prophecy as foretold by Fergo the Great Dragon of the two that will end the reign of our Lord, high King Stephan."

"And yet you have no proof Leon Drogon has anything to do with that prophecy!" Mr Davandrin spat across the battlefield.

"Oh don't be an idiot. We both know it is. If we want our world to stay at peace, then we must keep them apart! The girl and the boy must not meet again!" Tenebris growled back.

"Peace?!" Veronica scoffed, and she stepped forward next to her brother. She was becoming filled with rage, and she could not avoid the situation like her brother did. "Look around you! We stand on a battlefield! If we were truly at peace, we would not be here! Look at what your so called 'Lord' has become. A tyrant, exploiting his people until they have nothing left. His people are starved, while he sits at his table and eats until his stomach is full. How many have died under his command? From your kingdom, and ours! Perhaps our world would benefit the prophecy coming true!"

"Why you-!" Tenebris started to hurry over towards the princess threateningly, but Hendrix held out his arm and stopped her.

"I've heard enough!" Drevin Drogon pushed his way forward, desperately watching his son just stand there defenceless. "Give me back my boy! Give him back right now!" He was so full of emotion, and fearful that his son would never come home. He began to run towards Leon, wanting nothing more than to hold his son in his arms once again. Tenebris however, had a very different idea. She would keep Leon and I apart even if it killed her. She reached over Hendrix's shoulder, and sent a hurl of dark, purple magic towards the headmaster. Drevin let out a short scream as he was hit, and he found himself being lifted into the air by the magic. Magical bonds wrapped around his wrists and ankles, and he hovered in the air with his arms outstretched. Drevin struggled, his heart racing ahead of him as he was unable to free himself. He looked over at Leon, not noticing the look of panic on the faces of the Gailoiyn army.

"Leon! Son...snap out of it! Leon listen to me! Leon!" He screamed. But Leon didn't move. He didn't even look in his father's direction. He was completely under Tenebris's spell. As Drevin struggled, Jasper Ventus and Zadlos Davandrin stepped forward in haste.

"Miss Ora!" Jasper pleaded. "I beseech you! Put him down! He has done nothing!"

"Never!" She spat.

"Enough!" Hendrix said abruptly, raising his hand sharply. He then took a deep breath and slowly lowered his hand. "My lord Stephan has need of the boy. Alas, I too, do not wish any bloodshed this day. I shall command Miss Ora to release Mr Drogon if you will hand over the Lightningstone to me."

"Don't, Princess! That stone is more valuable than I will ever be!" Drevin Drogon shouted to her. I hated to admit it, but he was right. That stone was more powerful than an army, and it had to be protected. King Ricco stayed quiet, unable to make the tough decision. Don't get me wrong, Ricco's a great guy...but he's about as much use as a chocolate fireguard. In the end, it was Princess Veronica who took charge.

"Over my dead body."

The rain pelted in my face as we flew towards the Plain of Fire. My clothes were soaked through, which made my clothing heavy and uncomfortable. I couldn't afford to think about that right now though. I'd just have to endure it, as it didn't look like the weather was going to change any time soon. I was flying on Seto's back with Naia. I sat behind him, my arms tightly around Naia's waist. I'd never ridden on a Dragon apart from Leon before, so riding on Seto's back felt a little strange. His scales were different to Leon's, and not just because they were blue. They had a different feel to them. I guess each Dragon form was unique, in its own way...just like every human. Joey and Taz flew at my side, as did Irina and Pippa. I hoped and prayed that a war hadn't started...that negotiations didn't get out of hand! But the closer we got to the ancient battlefield, the noisier things became. Despite the raging storm, the sound of metal clashing together could be heard singing with the raging wind. The rain pelted on heavy armour, and the thunder rumbled in tune with the cries of people fighting for their lives in a haunting symphony. It was finally happening…Utopia was at war. Hearing the battle rage on was harrowing, but seeing it was even worse. We flew high over a tall, brown rocky formation. As we glided over, the war came into view. I had never seen a place like the Plain of Fire before. It was dark, and the red flowing lines running through the earth looked magical, but…not in a good way. The luminous red lines were blinding to look at, and were made brighter by the rain turning the brown soil into an icky black colour. Seto, Taz and Pippa swooped down, flying just over the battlefield.

"Here's your stop!" Seto said loudly above the noise.

"Got it!" I replied.

"Go get that idiot back!" Joey grinned, clenching his fist around his bow.

"Be careful, Xanda!" Irina said. I nodded back to her, and leaped off of Seto's back while he was still flying. I rolled onto the ground not too far from the fighting. I rolled onto my feet, and scanned the area. The wind was blowing my hair fiercely into my face, but I could see the soldiers battling with all their might. The sound was deafening, and the blood of the people ran through the earth and into the strange lines on the Plain. The rain slapped me in the face as I looked up, watching my friends fly towards the Dragonbourne's battling in the air above. I reached behind me, and drew my sword. The silver metal shone brightly as drops of water fell upon it. My brows furrowed, and I narrowed my eyes as I focused on the battle ahead of me. I was a good fighter, but I wasn't the best. I knew I wouldn't last long on my own…I had to find Leon! I didn't stand a chance on my own. I charged towards the battlefield, gripping my sword tightly in my hand. I wasn't prepared. I had no plan. But I also had no choice.

Mr Drogon had never felt so helpless in his entire life. Tenebris's spell was still binding him, and all he could do was watch as the people he loved and cared about fought and died on the battlefield below him. And it wasn't just below…Dragonbourne's and their partners dominated the sky above, and plummeted into the ground like bombs as they fell. Mrs Madana had tried to get close to him to use her magic to free him, but she couldn't get close enough. Drevin struggled more intensely, desperately wanting to join the battle and find his son. He even tried to turn into his Dragon form, but Tenebris's magic seemed to prevent him from doing so. He scanned the battlefield, trying to see if he could spot Tenebris. He thought, maybe he could reason with her. As much as he hated it, she was his sister-in-law, and both of them had loved Sera dearly. It was Sera that made him fight more and more to free himself, as he thought about the promise he had made to her on her deathbed. The promise to protect her son no matter what. Failing

Sera was not an option. Just then, his attention shifted as he noticed more Dragon's flying into battle. He recognised them immediately as Taz, Pippa and Seto. His grey eyes widened, and a sudden panic consumed him. He had specifically banned his students from joining them on the Plain of Fire. But when my friends showed up, he wasn't surprised. Worried, yes, but surprised, no. He also knew that I had come with them. His vision was blocked though, as Adamski Thorne flew towards him. Hendrix rode his partner, his spear poised and ready to snuff out the life of Drevin Drogon. They knew killing Mr Drogon would decrease the morale of the Gailoiyn army. Plus, bound like he was, he was an easy target. He squeezed his eyes tightly shut, ready to take the hit. But there was none. Drevin was shaking, certain that he was going to die. But when the spear never pierced him, and the loud cries of Dragons pierced the air next to him, he slowly opened one eye. He then opened the other upon seeing his friends and fellow teachers, Zadlos and Jasper viciously fighting the head of King Stephan's army. Zadlos repelled Hednrix's attacks with his sword, as Jasper and Adamski were fiercely gnashing out for one another.

"Zadlos!" Mr Drogon called out to his friend.

"Just sit tight, Drevin!" Mr Davandrin shouted back. Hendrix pulled his spear back a little, and Adamski snarled.

"Zadlos. My old friend." Hendrix said sternly. "Tis a shame we should meet in such a way."

"You don't have to do this, you two! The Hendrix I know would never fight for such a man as Stephan!"

"My loyalty's lie with my king!"

"Your King is wrong!" Said Jasper. "Join us!"

"It isn't too late to change allegiance, Hendrix." Zadlos pleaded. "Stephan is a madman! Deep down, I know you're a good man!"

"I am. I keep my vows, Zadlos! I vowed to protect my King! And that is what I intend to do!" Hendrix suddenly lunged forward again, and pierced Jasper's front leg. The purple Dragon let out a roar of pain, and began fighting back once again as his blood began to trickle down his scales. All Mr Drogon could do was watch, which infuriated him. He hated being so helpless. Their fight was becoming more intense by the second, Hendrix blinded by the fact that he thought he was doing the right thing. Hendrix was in a rage, and he swung his spear fiercely towards Zadlos and Jasper until he and Adamski were in the air above them, practically smashing them towards the ground. It wasn't looking good for Davandrin and Ventus, but they refused to back down and fought back with all their might. They could only do so much though, and their chance of winning became weaker as they neared the ground. Adamski wasted no time in pouncing on top of Jasper, pinning him to the dirt. Zadlos Davandrin held on for dear life, as he watched Hendrix pull back his spear to finish him off. Jasper squirmed, trying to free himself. The more he struggled, the harder Adamski dug his claws into Jasper's flesh. Just then, Hendrix gasped as his spear was knocked clean out of his hands! Seto charged past, and Naia had used his shield to smack the weapon from Hendrix's grasp. While distracted, Jasper reached up and clawed the side of Adamski's face, and managed to push the pair off him. He hovered back into the air as Adamski growled in pain.

"Naia! Seto!" Jasper said in surprise as the twins flew over next to him.

"Hey, papa!" Seto grinned.

"What the hell are you doing here?!"

"What do you think? We came to help! And to find Leon!" Naia said, worried they were in trouble.

"Is Xanda here?!" Mr Davandrin asked.

"Yes." Naia replied. "So is Taz, Joey, Pippa and Irina." They were going to reply, but they soon stopped talking as Hendrix and Adamski began to take off once more and fly towards them.

"Gee, do they ever give up?!" Seto scoffed.

"Not a chance. Since you're here, you may as well fight at our side!" Davandrin smiled at them. The boys looked at each other, then at their father. Jasper nodded towards them in acceptance, and the boys smiled brightly at this. They knew their father trusted them enough to fight alongside him, and that made them beyond happy. Naia grinned like his brother often did, and brandished his sword, staring down at Hendrix and Adamski as they flew towards them.

Tenebris was a ruthless fighter. She did not hold back one bit as she sliced down her enemies with dark waves of magic. The blood of her victims splattered all over her golden robes, but this did not phase her...if anything it made her feel more empowered. Her dark red hair whirled around her as she turned to stab a knight running towards her. There was no emotion in her eyes as she drove the knife into his chest, and she took pleasure in watching the red liquid seep out of his body. As Irina and Pippa flew over, the girls instantly recognised the savage necromancer. They had never seen her before, but they knew who she was from mine and Leo's description of her. Irina narrowed her brown eyes, and gripped her wooden staff tightly between her shaking fingers. Pippa flew towards Tenebris, and Irina raised her staff backwards. She threw down a white, magical beam at Tenebris. Unfortunately, Tenebris noticed the girls and quickly countered the attack with her own dark purple wave of sparkling magic.

"Irina!" Pippa screamed in alarm. Irina lost her balance, and she was hit by the magical wave and forced off Pippa's back. She yelled in pain, and hit the ground a few times before stopping. She was panting hard, her purple hair sprawled around her. Her chest felt heavy from the direct hit, and she struggled to breathe. She was lucky she wasn't dead. Pippa instantly changed back into her human form, and ran over to her cousin's side. She knelt next to Irina and helped her sit up. They were unlucky...as Tenebris had now turned her attention to them. The girls held onto each other tightly as they watched the tall woman strut over to them. Pippa narrowed her bright amber eyes, and she helped Irina to stand. If she was going to die, she was determined to die fighting.

"Oh girls...you really should have picked an enemy that is more on your level." Tenebris chuckled.

"Where is Leon?!" Irina asked innocently. Her question was answered by a sinister cackle from Tenebris, which just angered Pippa more.

"She asked you a question!" Pippa growled in retaliation.

"My my...you're not very patient, are you?" Tenebris grinned. "No matter. I have no intention on answering your question. But, I do have a question of my own...how would you like to die?" The girls looked at each other, swallowing hard. They seriously thought that was the end, but they weren't going to die without fighting first. Irina kept a hold of her staff, and stood in a fighting stance. Pippa stood beside her, creating a ball of fire around her entire hand. Tenebris laughed once again, finding their feeble enthusiasm to fight back rather amusing.

"Well, I can't tell whether you're brave, or foolish." Tenebris smirked, not even phased that the fight was two against one. Her magic was much more powerful than Irina and Pippa's put together...and they all knew it.

"A bit of both I imagine." Pippa said, throwing a blast of fire at Tenebris. The necromancer easily deflected the spell with her own. Usually, (with the exception of Dragonbournes), mages needed a staff to cast spells...but Tenebris wielded magic with her bare hands. She was something completely out of this world. Despite being completely crazy, I had to admire her magical ability. Irina and Pippa were sweating in fear, but the girls were not going to back down. I had to admire Irina's bravery. I mean, there's no way she would have stood up to someone like Tenebris a year ago. Tenebris stared down at the girls with an uncomforting glare. Her hands began to spark with magic, and dark thoughts began to cross her twisted mind. Irina stepped in front of her cousin, and blasts of magic hurdled back and forth between the two. The magical colours swirled through the air. Irina knew she was outmatched, but she fought with the strength of a lion. Pippa fought alongside her cousin, shooting fire rapidly at Tenebris. The strong-willed girls managed to keep Tenebris at a distance, but she was slowly becoming closer and closer to them. The battle raged on around them. The screams of people drawing their last breath rang in their ears, but they couldn't afford to let it distract them. But it did...and Pippa and Irina soon lost their concentration as a body hit the ground in front of them. They let out a yell of surprise as they watched the young soldier die face down in the dirt before them. They looked back up again, terrified when they saw Tenebris looming over them. Her piercing eyes bore a hole into their souls. She raised her hand to strike the final blow, and sent a blast of magic towards the girls. Irina was terrified, knowing there was nowhere to run. But Pippa...Pippa wouldn't allow it. Without hesitation, she shoved Irina aside, and was caught up in a huge, magical blast.

The dust flew up in the air around them, and the soldiers caught up in the blast were thrown off balance. Irina covered her eyes with her arms, staying close to the ground as the bright white light surrounded her. She was panting hard, her whole body shaking in fear. She pushed herself to her knees, scraping them in the wet dirt as she adjusted herself. She looked around, and the soldiers were staggered but continued to fight. The people caught up in the blast however...they were all on the ground, and Irina couldn't tell whether they were dead or unconscious. Her eyes suddenly widened, and she looked around to see if she could find Pippa. Just then, her eyes fell upon her cousin's body.

"Pippa!" Irina cried, instantly getting up and running over to Pippa's sprawled body. Pippa was just lying there, her body splattered in blood. Suddenly, Irina felt a cold hand on the back of her neck, grabbing onto the back of her dress collar. She gasped at the touch, and was whirled around to face Tenebris. The tall woman grabbed Irina around the neck with both hands. Irina panicked, and brought her hands up to Tenebris's wrists to try and prise her off, but to no avail. Tenebris squeezed and squeezed Irina's neck, feeling no emotion as she squeezed the life out of the quivering girl. Irina whimpered, trying to prise her fingers away, but Tenebris's grip was firm. Irina let out short cries of pain, trying to breathe as she slowly felt the air leaving her body. Just then, Tenebris let out a cry of pain, and she suddenly let go of poor Irina. The girl fell to one knee, holding her neck and coughing as she tried to regain her composure. Tenebris reached for her back and pulled out an arrow. The tip of it was dripping with her blood, and she spun around to see who had shot it. Irina looked up, a small smile forming across her lips as she saw Joey standing a few feet away, his bow raised and eyes narrow. Taz stood behind him, a ball of fire in both of his palms. Neither of them were in the mood to mess around, and they certainly didn't take kindly to Tenebris battering the girls.

"You stupid boy!" Tenebris screeched. "You have made a huge mistake!"

"Really? Shooting you has been the highlight of my day. Perhaps I could see you more often and I could use you for target practice." Joey snarled, as he reached for his quiver and pulled out another arrow. He placed it on his bow and pulled back the string. The usually sarcastic boy didn't sound like his normal self...there was a dark tone to his voice. I tell you, you don't want to mess with Joey when he's angry. Nor Taz for that matter. His light purple eyes turned dark with rage when he saw Pippa lying on the ground. The fire within his palms began to grow, becoming brighter as his eyes became darker.

"Step away from my friends." Taz spat.

"Joey...Taz...no! She'll kill you!" Irina whimpered.

"Hush Irina. Mummy and Daddy are talking with the bad lady." Joey grinned, his sharp personality seeming to come back as a newfound confidence surged within him. All he did was take one look at the girls and realised that he needed to protect them.

"I still don't see how I'm the woman in this relationship!" Taz rolled his eyes. Irina looked at them as if they were idiots. Okay, they were idiots. But if there was ever a time for Joey's wise cracks, it wasn't now. Tenebris started laughing again, not even seeming phased about the arrow that had penetrated her. She didn't even seem to be bleeding anymore! And when the boys noticed this, they were unnerved by it.

"You fools." Tenebris scoffed. "You boys are in way over your heads. Now, how about I teach you a lesson in manners? Didn't your parents ever teach you it was rude to disrespect your elders?" Joey and Taz grinned, more determined than ever to take Tenebris down. Joey pulled back on his bowstring, and Tazmin raised his flame filled fists.

"They did." Joey replied sarcastically. "But you're a lunatic, so it doesn't count!"

To my surprise, a newcomer joined the battle. Remember that Dwarven merchant, Bernard? He was dashing across the Plain of Fire as fast as his little stocky legs would carry him. He saw the war raging ahead of him, and he drew out his duel daggers from his sheathes. He dived straight into the midst of the battle, taking down the Brozantan soldiers like an assassin. He was a ruthless fighter, slicing down the enemy as he scanned the battlefield. Just then, he saw people he recognised. Princess Veronica was in her Dragon form, her pinkie-red scales glistening as the rain fell upon them. Her brother, King Ricco, sat on her back. He was wielding a sword and shield, fighting with his sister. Veronica spun round and smacked some incoming attacks with her strong tail. Bernard was almost caught in the assault, but he quickly rolled underneath the tail before it could hit him. He stood quickly and shouted up to Ricco and Veronica.

"Watch it, Princess!"

"Bernard!" Veronica said in relief, noticing him. "Thank goodness you're here!"

"Look out!" Bernard shouted, noticing a Brozantan Knight running towards them. He turned swiftly and threw one of his knives at the Knight. The blade flew so fast through the air that it pierced his armour. He hit the ground as hard as a rock. Dead. Bernard hurried over, and ripped the knife out of the knight's frozen body.

"Good shot!" Ricco grinned. Bernard turned to face them, and moved over to them to talk.

"Where is she?!" Veronica asked quickly.

"Here! She's come here!" Bernard replied.

"What?!" Veronica said a little angrily. "I told you to watch her!"

"I was!" Bernard protested. "Those other kids snuck her out the window. I'm trying to find her!"

"Maybe this isn't a bad thing, Veronica..." Ricco interrupted, to which his sister gave him a death stare out of the corner of her eye.

"What?!" She spat.

"Well, if she does find little Drogon, then maybe she can snap him out of it." Ricco stated. They looked at each other for a moment, realising that maybe the King had a point. After a few moments of silence, Bernard spoke once again.

"I'll find the kids, don't worry."

"Hurry. And Bernard...keep them safe." Veronica said. Bernard nodded in response, and he watched as she flapped her strong wings and lifted herself into the air. The dwarf watched as the King and Princess ascended into the sky above, fighting alongside other Dragon Knights and their Riders. Bernard nodded silently, accepting her order. He then took a deep breath, and started looking for Leon and myself.

Killing people wasn't something that came naturally to me, but when it was either kill or be killed...there was no other option. That said, I took no pleasure in it. As I struck people down, my heart was pounding, through fear and guilt. But the more lives I took, the easier it became. In fact, it was scary just how easy it was. I remember this one knight. He was charging towards me, shouting from the bottom of his lungs like doing so was going to help him. He swung his huge sword at my head, and I naturally ducked out of the way. But then, without hesitation, I drove my blade deep into his gut. He screamed in agony, but I felt...nothing. I ripped my blade out his side, and watched the life drain from his body as he lay there choking on his own blood. It was then I recognised him...it was the one from the castle. The one that had escaped from us at Roseosh Town. He killed my friends in the Battle at the Winter ball. And he was the one that killed my classmate, Morgan Ocrina. He looked up at me, fear in his eyes.

"Please...make it quick..." He rasped weakly. I hadn't known Morgan for very long, but she was a nice girl. She was clever, kind, a bit up herself...but she was a good person. She didn't deserve to die. I narrowed my eyes at him, and I pointed my sword at his throat. He flinched a little as the cool metal brushed against his skin.

"Is that what you said to Morgan?" I asked coldly. "Probably not. You probably don't even remember her. But I do." It didn't sink in at the time, but at that moment I had the power of a god...I had the power over his death. He was going to die anyway, so did I let him suffer? Or did I give him a quick death? I hated him, but as I looked at him, I couldn't help but feel sorry for him. He was squirming in pain, his breath ragged and uneven. He couldn't breathe anymore, and my heart began to drown in guilt that I had done this. Balls, my emotions were so conflicted! I closed my eyes for a moment, then opened them. "See you in hell." I said darkly as I drove my blade through his neck. I kept eye contact with him as he took one last breath, and died. I pulled out my sword and stood over him, the rain battering me in the face. I slowly knelt down and used my pale fingers to close his eyelids. I let out a soft sigh, looking at him sadly. What was happening to me? I'd changed, and I knew it. I wasn't naive anymore, and I didn't feel like a child. I wasn't someone to be messed with. I stood again and looked around, keeping my sword tightly within my grasp. Blood dripped off the tip of my blade, but I didn't care. I had to find Leon. I'd wasted too much time already. As the thought of him crossed my mind, I felt our connection grow once more. It felt strange…like the time when we first met, and I felt our souls entwine. I suddenly felt like I was in a bubble, and the sound of the world around me began to numb. I was being drawn to an area on The Plain of Fire that was enclosed by tall, spiky rocks. Having no other lead, I decided to head over there. I didn't look back at the war going on behind me.

My feet began to move faster and faster, until I found myself running towards the rocky formation. I was panting hard, my clothes feeling heavy because of how wet they were from the rain. I placed my hand on one of the slippery rocks, and saw there was a ditch below. I vaulted over and fell into the ditch, landing on my feet. I stood upright and gazed ahead of me. He was there. Leon was at the other end of the short ditch, sitting on a rounded rock at the end. I immediately felt a sense of dread. His eyes were different. The eyes I knew were a brighter shade of green than anything I had seen before. But now…they were so dark, almost black. I swallowed hard, and took a few steps forward towards him.
"Leo…?" I gulped, speaking quietly. My heart suddenly skipped a beat as an evil smirk spread across my partners face. He looked directly into my eyes and spoke to me. His voice sounded different, like it was doubled over. He was under a spell.

"There you are." He said darkly. "I've been waiting for you."

Chapter 18

Burn

"What do you mean? You knew I was coming?" I asked as I stared at my partner. Just then, my heart began to bang against my chest as fire began to stem from Leon's palm. He jumped down off the rock and pointed one of his hands at me, the reflection of the fire blazing in his dull eyes.

"Stay back! She said you were coming. She said you'd hurt me, and turn me against them!" Leon said darkly, but I sensed a tinge of fear in his voice. I took a step back and raised my hands. This was awful. I just wanted to cry! Not only had she kidnapped him and put him under a spell, but Tenebris had brainwashed him too!

"Leo...it's alright!" I spoke to him calmly, desperate to try and get him to snap out of it. "I'm not here to hurt you!"

"I don't believe you! You're still holding that sword!" He shouted back. I swallowed hard, looking at the bloodstained blade in my hand. Balls! I knew I had to put it down if I wanted to gain Leon's trust again and release him from the spell, but if he attacked me the sword was the only thing I had to defend myself! I looked at him again, and I knew that my partner was still in there somewhere. So, I slowly bent down to my knees and placed the sword on the ground, before standing slowly once again.

"There. Now you put that fire out, eh? Let's just talk about this." I spoke softly, trying to reason with him. The last thing I wanted to do was fight him, but deep down I knew it might come to that. I started to walk towards him again, but he just got more uptight and the fire within his hands grew brighter.

"No!" He shouted. "Stay away! I'm warning you! Stay away! She told me not to trust you!"

"It's her you shouldn't trust!" I snapped back. "Leon...I'm your partner! We've been together through thick and thin, remember?! You said whatever happened, we were going to go through it together! That's what you said! So no! I won't stay away! I won't! I won't leave you! Not now, not ever! Please...our friends want you to come home! They're waiting for you! So's your old man! Yeah, he can be an idiot at times, but he loves you! And so do I, Leo! I want...I need you to come back to us! Please!" I'd started crying as I practically screeched at him, begging him to come back to me. Tears were streaming down my face, and began to hit the ground as they became mixed in with the rain. Whatever it was that Tenebris had said to Leon, it had worked a treat. What I said just seemed to make him angrier and he suddenly lunged at me, screaming from the bottom of his lungs. I shouted his name desperately as he grabbed my hair with his other hand, and started to bang my head against the rocks. He held me so tight that it felt like he was ripping the hair out of my scalp. I could feel sharp bolts of pain bounce around inside my brain as he repeatedly shoved my cranium against the jiggered rocks. It was then my instincts kicked in, and I knew if I was going to rescue him, I'd have to fight back. I was no use to him dead, after all. There was blood pouring down the side of my face, and I started to feel dizzy. But I knew I couldn't let that stop me. The way he was, I knew if I passed out he'd kill me in a second. I did the only thing I could, and I used my whole-body weight to elbow him in the stomach. He let out a cry of pain and stumbled backwards. I jumped at the opportunity, and punched him across the jaw. He lost his balance completely and fell backwards. I bent down quickly to try and pin him to the ground, but he reacted fast and grabbed my shoulders and threw me across the floor. I grunted in pain as I hit the ground, and rolled a few times before I stopped myself. At this point I was lying on my stomach, and I pushed myself up with my arms. To my horror, Leon was already back on his feet and rushing over to me. He suddenly kicked me hard in the stomach, and I let out a cry of agony. He grabbed my hair once more and dragged me to my feet. He was so fast! I didn't have time to process what was happening, and before I knew it he had a fire burning in his hand. He suddenly pressed his hand roughly against my stomach, and I felt a searing pain engulf my whole body. I couldn't hold it in any longer...and I screamed louder than I've ever screamed before. The pain was so bad, it's hard to find words to describe it. It was like...sharp bolts of searing heat mixed in with shots of lightning pounding through every cell in my body. I had never felt pain like this before...even Adamski biting me was no match for the sheer suffering I experienced at this moment in time. The pain was made worse knowing that it was somebody that I loved whom was inflicting it. The fire burned within my body, and I honestly thought he was going to kill me. But I soon realised it was just pain...I wasn't dying. Leon was still in there! And that part of him must have held back, because the fire was just hurting me, not killing me. I gritted my teeth, and fought back despite the pain. I lifted my knee and kept booting him in the stomach as hard as I could. Finally, he let me go, and I kicked him away from me. I used what little time I had to catch my breath, but never once did I take my eyes off of him. I brought a shaky hand up to my stomach, trying to compose myself. Leon lunged for me again, but I ducked out of the way and pushed him backwards. As fast as lightning, Leon pounced on me, forcing me to fall backwards. I let out a startled gasp as I hit the ground once more, feeling my head bang against the soggy dirt. Leon was immediately on top of me, trying to put his hands around my throat. I fought back ferociously, wrapping my fingers tightly around his wrists to keep his hands away from my neck. Just then, something fell from around his neck. The Dragon necklace I had brought him for his birthday fell out of his green jacket, and swung in front of my eyes as it hung from his neck. Leon seemed to have noticed where my gaze was heading, and he slowly looked at the necklace too. His whole-body actions slowed down, and he carefully pulled away from me. The pace of his breath began to quicken. He stood, staggering a little. He held the necklace in the palm of his hand, and started to look rather distressed. I sat up slowly, swallowing hard.

"You're still wearing it..." I stated, no louder than a whisper. It hit me that he hadn't truly forgotten me. Just then, he began screaming as purple magic began to surround him. The light was blinding, and I covered my eyes with my arm.

"Leon!" I screamed worriedly, but I couldn't get close to him even if I wanted to. I stood quickly, trying my best to stand my ground as the magic tried to push me away. I remembered the promise I made to him, that I wouldn't leave him. So, I stayed. No matter how hard I felt myself being pushed back, I stood firm. Just then, the magic began to die down, and I saw Leon standing there. He was swaying, and he looked like he was going to faint. As the purple magic faded away, I rushed over to him. Leon collapsed, falling to his knees. I shouted his name once again, catching him in my arms before he hit the ground. I lay him back and cradled him in my arms, shaking him worriedly, calling out his name to him. He just lay there, unconscious, his eyes closed. I shook him roughly, begging him to wake up. But he didn't. He was completely out of it.

"Leon! Wake up! Leon!"

While the fight between Leon and I had been happening, Naia and Seto were still at arms with Hendrix Montgomery and Adamski Thorne. Jasper and Zadlos were defending Mr Drogon, whom was still trapped by Tenebris's spell. The four of them were desperately trying to keep the enemy General and his pet away from Drevin Drogon, but it was clear their fatigue was dropping considerably. Despite just hanging there, Drevin was now in serious pain. His arms were burning from being stretched out, and his whole body was aching because he couldn't move. He hung his head, at this point seeming to have completely given up. Mr Davandrin kept glancing over at him, shouting words of encouragement. But none of those words seemed to reach Mr Drogon's ears. He was exhausted, from the pain but also from constantly worrying about where Leon was. It was clear Hendrix and Adamski weren't giving up though, as they kept trying to batter their way through. I honestly don't know where Adamski got his energy from, but he never seemed to get tired. He wasted no time in flying forward every time he saw an opening, and gnashing out at his foes with his giant jaws. He descended upon Seto, and grabbed him with his sharp claws. The boy Dragon screamed in pain as Adamski's talons dug into his flesh.

"Seto!" Naia yelled, grabbing onto his brother for dear life. Jasper wasn't having any of this, and he immediately soared forward, digging his own claws into Adamski and forcing him away from the twins.

"Stay away from my boys!" Jasper demanded, snarling through his sharp teeth. Seto managed to stay in the air, but his front leg was bleeding heavily, and it was clear he was struggling to stay afloat. As Jasper and Zadlos pounded Adamski and Hendrix, Seto tried to fly higher.

"Seto! What's up?!" Naia asked.

"I think my arms broken...I can't stay balanced!"

"We need to land, Seto! You can't fly anymore!" Naia said in concern for his brother's safety. "We have to go down!".

Seto panted hard, watching his father get beaten by the General as Hendrix began to pierce through Jasper's thick purple scales with his bladed staff. Seto growled, knowing Naia was right. But going down wasn't his style.

"You're right." Said Seto. "But that doesn't mean we can't take them down with us!" Seto had guts, I'll give him that. He flew upwards, as high as he could go. He glared down at his enemy, before turning his gaze slightly to his brother. Naia didn't even need to ask what Seto's plan was...he knew him too well. "You ready?" Seto asked.

"Yeah!" Naia scrunched up his face, and gripped his blade as tightly as he could. With his brother's word, Seto zoomed down towards Hendrix and Adamski, heading straight for them. Seto bashed into Adamski, which was followed by a roar of surprise from the amber Dragon. Seto growled loudly as he plummeted the pair towards the ground. Just then he swirled through the air, giving his brother an opening. Naia angrily drove his blade through Adamski's side. Hendrix shouted his partner's name as Adamski screeched in agony. Adamski squirmed as he plummeted towards the ground. Naia gasped as he was hit by Adamski's thrashing, and came tumbling off his brothers back!

Jasper shouted in fear, being too far away to catch his son. Adamski brought down Seto with him, and the two smacked into the ground. Naia was still falling, rapidly descending towards the dirt not far behind his brother. Just then, he felt a large Dragon claw wrap around his thin body, stopping him from falling. Looking at the scales, he saw that they were pink...and he knew immediately who it was.

"Miss Nebilia!" He said in relief looking up at her. "Miss Wellworn!" Jasper Ventus and Zadlos Davandrin watched from a distance, and sighed in relief as they saw their fellow teachers save Naia from the fall.

"Hop on, Naia!" Cassandra Nebilia said, as she lifted him up towards her back. He was met by the familiar face of Ivy Wellworn, who extended a hand out to him and helped him climb onto Cassandra's back with her. Ivy sat Naia in front of her.

"Are you alright?!" She asked quickly.

"Yeah, but Seto fell! We have to land!" Naia replied, panicking as he scanned the world below for his brother.

"Not now, Naia, it isn't safe!"

"It isn't safe up here either!" He fought back.

"Naia!" Cassandra said abruptly as she flew over to Jasper and Zadlos, determined to keep at least one of the boy's safe.

"Naia!" Jasper said worriedly as they approached. "Thank the gods! That was reckless!"

"It wasn't my idea!" Naia protested.

"We never thought it was." Zadlos spoke, smiling weakly.

"Cassandra, Ivy." Jasper started. "Look after Naia for me...and take over keeping the Brozantans away from Drevin! Zadlos and I need to find Seto."

"Alright...and Jasper...please be careful..." Said Cassandra softly, looking into her lover's eyes. Jasper nodded slowly, before soaring down to the battlefield with Zadlos. All Naia could do was watch them. He was so scared, not knowing if Seto had died in the fall. Adamski and Seto had changed back into their human forms as they hit the ground, like Taz had done when he was injured. Because of this, it made it harder for Naia to spot his brother. He gazed off into the distance, wondering where Leon and I were. He bit his lip nervously, and then spoke in a whisper.

"C'mon Xanda...we need you!"

I needed Leon. I had sat with him for a while, cradling his body in my arms. The rain soaked my blood into my clothes, and I was beginning to feel incredibly cold. I was shaking, feeling a chilly sting as the wind rushed through my body. I felt so helpless! All I could do was sit there and hold him. I was beginning to worry that he'd never wake up. But just then, he started to stir. He groaned weakly, and his eyes began to tighten.

"Leon...?" I spoke gently, not wanting to startle him. Just then, I felt the heavy burden on my heart flutter away as he opened his eyes. Balls, I can't tell you how comforting that was. His bright emerald eyes were once again present, and they shimmered as his eyelids parted to reveal them. I let out a gasp of happiness, and I couldn't stop myself from smiling.

"Xanda...?" He said weakly, still coming around from his slumber. I suddenly pulled him tightly into my arms, forcing him to sit up so I could hug him. I squeezed him tighter than I ever had before. He seemed a little taken back, and confused. He wasn't entirely sure what was going on. After a moment, he slowly hugged me back. It felt so good to have him back. Slowly, Leon pulled away from me and looked at me as he rubbed his head.

"What happened to me?" He asked slowly. My expression mellowed, as I remembered what had happened to him. Part of me still felt responsible. I did tell him the truth though...I wasn't going to lie to him.

"You sacrificed yourself so that I could escape Tenebris's spell. I'm so sorry, Leon."

"Yeah...that makes sense..." He said slowly, rubbing the back of his head. "It's hazy, but I remember some of what happened."

"You do? Do you remember anything after that?" I asked curiously.

"No. But um...thank you...for saving me."

"It's fine, don't worry about it." I said. He smiled gently, and looked up at me again. His eyes widened.

"Xanda! You're bleeding! What...what's going on? Where are we?" He asked in a panic, suddenly realising that we weren't anywhere familiar to him. He reached up to the wound on my head and touched it gently. I knew I'd have to tell him what was happening, but I decided to leave out the part that he was the one that made me bleed. He'd been through enough already, I didn't want to freak him out.

"The Plain of Fire." I answered. "Leo, the war's started. Everything's such a mess!"

"Are the others here?" He asked calmly.

"Yeah, they're here. Balls, Leo, you have no idea how worried we've been about you!"

"Wait...you came for me?" He said with a guilty look on his face.

"Of course we came for you, you idiot! Your father was here in a second. Listen, we have to go. People are dying out there!" I said worriedly. I slowly stood, helping him up carefully.

"Go where...?" He asked.

"Well...the way I see it, we have two choices. We can either go home and hope this passes over, or we can go and fight alongside everyone else." I replied. A small grin spread across Leon's face, and he took a few steps backwards. I watched intently as he changed into his Dragon form, his green scales glistening in the rain. He roared loudly, which made me smile brightly. I was so glad he was back. He looked at me with a determined grin on his face. Clearly, he had no intention of backing down either.

"Is the first choice even an option?" Said Leon. I bent down and picked up my sword from the floor. I looked at the blade shining as the raindrops fell upon to it, and then turned my gaze back to my partner.

"Not really."

Chapter 19

I Am Xandario

I wish I could tell you that somehow the fighting had stopped...but it hadn't. To be honest, things weren't going well for Gailoiyn. We had been outnumbered from the very start, but our people were being cut down like lambs to the slaughter. Much blood had been spilt already, and there was much more to come. Worst of all, my friends weren't fairing too well against Tenebris.

"Ngh!" Joey was beaten to a pulp, lying on the ground just staring up at the stormy sky. He groaned in pain as Irina and Taz dashed to his side, helping him sit up.

"Joey!" Irina said worriedly, placing her hand on his bloodied cheek. The three of them looked up terrified as Tenebris swaggered over to them. They shuffled backwards, trying to stay as far away from her as they could. They had all taken a beating, and were battered and bruised. Joey tried to stand, but he couldn't! Tenebris was descending on them, and they could tell she was readying a spell to finish them off. They couldn't shuffle back any further, so they just held onto one another as tightly as possible. As she neared them, Tenebris raised her hands as if she were ready to cast a spell at them. It was then Pippa awoke. She sat up quickly, and her eyes were wide with fear. Her heart was racing, knowing she was too far away to help. All she could do was watch as Tenebris's magic around her hands began to grow brighter and brighter. The necromancer was so focused, and never once glanced away from them. Pippa quickly stood, wanting to shout for her to stop, but no words came out. She didn't know what she could possibly do to help, so she started running towards them as fast as she could. She knew she wouldn't get there in time, but she didn't know what else she could do! The spell was all set, and Tenebris let out an insane laugh as she thought about the oncoming damage she was about to inflict...

But it was then everything changed. There was a deafening roar that swooped over the battlefield, drowning out all other noise. Tenebris swirled round, lowering her hands at the sheer shock of the sound. The battlefield went silent, and everyone looked round in the direction that the roar had come from. Just then, Leon and I soared into the sky. I raised my blade high into the air, and a bright white light emitted from it. A rush of power raced through my body, and I began to tingle all over. My friends jumped to their feet, an excited and relieved look on their faces. Joey fist pumped the air, and began to cheer. The others joined him, and soon there was a huge rallying cry from my people. Pippa ran over to the others, laughing happily as they watched Leon and I ascend into the stormy skies. Naia held onto Cassandra's neck and gasped in surprise, hearing Ivy whisper as she grinned. "Xanda. Leon. About time." She said to herself.

Veronica and Ricco had noticed too, and the young royals beamed happily. Bernard stopped running for a moment, and gazed up at us. He shook his head, despite a small grin forming across his lips.

"There you are. Guess you didn't need my help after all, cupcake." He chuckled.

Mr Davandrin and Mr Ventus were also relieved to see us, both of them cheering in happiness with the rest of the Gailoiyns as my sword lit up the sky. Mr Drogon was the most surprised of all. He slowly raised his head, and his tired eyes widened as he saw the familiar figure of his son in his green Dragon form swoop into battle. He started shaking, the light shining from my blade blinding him. He clenched his fists once more, his biceps burning in pain. Drevin's breath was uneven and shaky, but he managed to crack a small smile when he saw us. Although we didn't know it, he was beaming with pride.

"Leon...Xanda..." He said weakly under his breath. Tenebris on the other hand was not at all impressed to see us. She knew that me riding on Leon's back could mean only one thing...that I had broken her spell. Her face dropped, her expression turning between a mix of shock, anger and frustration. My sharp eyes spotted her immediately, and seeing that she was by my friends just made a wave of dread wash over me.

"Leon!" I shouted loudly at my partner. Reading my mind, he knew instantly what I was thinking and he nodded. I gritted my teeth, and felt the cool wind push against my face as Leon darted quickly towards Tenebris. For the first time, I saw Tenebris physically frightened, and all the colour drained from her face. Leon growled ferociously. Tenebris let out a blood curling scream as Leon simply swiped her with his claws. My friends yelled at us encouragingly as the necromancer went flying through the air, landing somewhere in the midst of the fighting. I couldn't help but feel rather smug as she was sent plummeting across the battlefield. It served her right for what she did to us. It was rare that I hated people, even people that I didn't like. But Tenebris...I hated her with every fibre of my body. As we continued to fly, I didn't see where she had ended up, and frankly I didn't care. I turned my attention to my sword. The blade was still glowing a faint white, and I couldn't tell why. Leon seemed to have noticed it too, and he swooped closer to the ground. There was a group of Brozantan soldiers charging towards King Ricco, and Leon's chest glowed a faint red. He breathed fire over them, a searing heat escaping from his gaping jaws. The inferno engulfed the soldiers, and they screamed in agony as their bodies were burned to a crisp. Leon had never been able to breathe fire so profoundly before, which shocked me.

"Leon..." I said in confusion, and he answered before I even had chance to ask the question.

"Your sword." He said. "I sense a strange light magic coming from it. It seemed to enhance my ability!" I thought on this for a moment, and I then turned my attention back to poor Drevin Drogon, whom was looking over at us worriedly. Cogs began to turn inside my brain, and I suddenly had an idea.

"Light magic, you say? Leo, fly over to your father! Maybe the sword's magic can break Tenebris's dark magic spell containing him!" I said with enthusiasm. "Okay, let's try it!" Leon said as he flew round in a circle to face his father, and began to fly towards him. "Oh, and Xanda, try not to chop his hand off in the process." He added.

"I'll do my best!" I replied with a nervous chuckle. I focused my eyes on the purple magical bonds around Drevin's wrists, and I narrowed my eyes to focus in on it. I took a deep breath, and pointed my sword forward as we neared him. I didn't look at Mr Drogon, because I knew that if I did I'd lose my concentration. According to Leon, Mr Drogon closed his eyes shut as tight as he could, realising what we were about to do. I tightened my fingers around the hilt of my sword, and I somehow felt all my strength flowing into my blade. The purple bonds glowed before me, but I wasn't going to let the mystical hypnotic swirls of the magic distract me. As Leon passed his father, I swiftly swiped my blade across the magic hoping and praying I hadn't cut off Drevin's arm. There was a loud noise when the two substances hit, and I felt a shock through my body which made me unbalanced. I held onto Leon tightly and looked back at Mr Drogon. The white light from my sword was now engulfing his bonds, and we watched in anticipation to see if it had worked. The restraints around him suddenly snapped, and Mr Drogon fell. We gasped, but we should have known better than to worry about Drevin Drogon. Despite his aching body, he used the last ounce of his strength to change into his dark grey Dragon form. He lowered himself safely down to an open clearing, and looked up at us immediately after landing. I smiled down at him and to my surprise, he nodded towards me in respect. I was a little shocked, but I nodded back to him. Leon was relieved that his father was okay, and knew he was now more than capable of taking care of himself.

"C'mon Leo." I said determinedly.

"Right!" He nodded, a small grin spreading across his scaly snout. Leon took off once more, and the two of us left to find our friends on the battlefield...together.

For some reason, seeing Leon and I had given the others newfound strength. Taz, Joey, Pippa and Irina were pushing their way through the troops, running in the direction that Leo had hit Tenebris. The necromancer was still conscious, and struggling to stand. She managed to push herself to her feet. Tenebris surveyed her surroundings, her face pale with a mixture of dirt and blood resting on her cheek. Taz growled, seeing her in a small clearing as he led the group towards her. He bent down and picked up an abandoned sword from the ground, and charged at her without thinking. He sped up, running much faster than the others.

"Taz, stop!" Pippa shouted in fear, knowing he still hadn't fully recovered and he didn't stand a chance on his own. But her cries only made the situation worse, as Tenebris heard her. She turned around swiftly, but Taz wasn't going to stop. He gritted his teeth and swung the sword down on her. Tenebris screamed as her blood splattered upwards, and was rapidly swept away by the wind. She grabbed her shoulder and stumbled backwards, crying and screaming loudly, her eyes wide with madness.

"Agh!" She growled, staring at him in a pained rage. "To your knees, boy!" She spat. She quickly fired a purple bolt of magic from her palm, and before Taz could react he found the magic forcing him to his knees.

"No! Not my partner!" Joey yelled as he sprinted towards them. He suddenly jumped on Taz's back, and leapt off of him towards Tenebris. Her eyes widened as she saw the glistening arrow in his hands, soaring down towards her. Joey forced the arrow into her arm, right into the wound Tazmin had already made. She shrieked and squirmed, pushing Joey back roughly. Josef tumbled backwards, landing beside his partner. While they were both on the ground the girls stood behind them, determined not to allow Joey and Taz's attacks be in vain.

"Pippa!" Irina planted her staff firmly into the ground, and a swirl of rainbow colours emitted from the staff's head. Pippa placed her hand tightly over Irina's, and a fiery ball encircled Irina's magic. Their majestic purple and royal red hair blew violently in the heavy wind, as they sent their combined magic hurdling towards Tenebris. The necromancer didn't know what hit her. The spell smacked her so hard that the arrow impaled in her arm was immediately ripped from her flesh. She hit the ground as hard as a rock and for once in her life, she had nothing clever to say. She knew that she had been beaten. Her only options were to lay down and die quietly, or run away. She let out gasps of air, short pants passing through her blood red lips. Tenebris glared over at the others, watching as the girls helped the boys back onto their feet. Luckily for Tenebris, she didn't have to use her legs to escape. Before my friends could finish her off, she used the last bit of strength to conjure up one final spell. Joey, Taz, Pippa and Irina quickly looked over at her as they once again noticed Tenebris's dark purple magic at work once more. This time, the magic surrounded her entire body. Taz felt an anger burn inside of him, not wanting her to get away after what she did to Leon. His heart raced, banging against his chest.

"No!" He yelled at her, starting to sprint over as Tenebris began to fade away.

"Taz, stop!" Joey shouted in fear, as he ran after his partner. Before Taz could reach Tenebris, Joey grabbed Taz's arm and yanked him back. He panted hard, still reeling at the thought that Taz could have been caught up in the spell. "You idiot!" Said Joey, more out of worry than anger. Taz's purple eyes turned softer, a whole wave of emotions washing through him as he watched Tenebris fade away and her magic die down. He fell to his knees, trying to stop his hands from shaking. Joey watched him sadly, and placed his hand on Taz's shoulder in an attempt to comfort him. The girls exchanged a nervous glance...knowing that this wasn't the last they would see of Tenebris Magicae Ora.

Seto hadn't been found. Luckily, he wasn't dead. He was lying on the soaked soil, his blood trickling down his arm. He began to wake up, his blue eyes opening slowly. He grunted quietly in pain, his vision fading in and out for a moment. He used his other arm to push himself up, and a sharp pain shot through his entire body. His head suddenly felt incredibly fuzzy, and he closed his eyes for a moment to try and stop the dizzy sensation he was feeling. Seto slowly opened his eyes once more as the sounds of metal clashing rang in his ears. He suddenly gasped, noticing that he was sitting next to the unconscious bodies of Hendrix Montgomery and Adamski Thorne. His heart skipped a beat, and he painfully scrambled to his feet. He held his arm, his body shaking all over as he stared at the enemy General and his partner. Adamski was covered in blood, and he was incredibly pale. Seto couldn't tell whether or not he was dead. He began to panic, his breath racing ahead of him as he quickly scanned his surroundings. Where was his brother? Naia not being with him seemed to heighten his anxiety, and he began to stumble around.

"Naia?! Naiaaaa! Naia!" He screamed, tears brimming in the edge of his crystal blue eyes. He was starting to stress out even more, his palms becoming sweaty as he became more and more worked up. He didn't know what had happened to Naia, and the thought that something bad had happened to his brother scared him more than anything. Suddenly, Seto found himself being thrown back to the ground by a strong pair of hands. He suddenly felt more awake, yet paralyzed in fear as Hendrix Montgomery kneeled over him. His mousy brown locks fell in front of his face, making his dark eyes look narrower and more intimidating than usual. The rain dripped off the tips of Hendrix's long hair, and splattered onto Seto's bloodied face. The General looked possessed with anger as he clenched his fist and pulled back his hand. Seto was so scared he couldn't find the strength to fight back...that and Hendrix was physically much stronger than Seto was. Seto grunted as Hendrix punched him across the face, crying out in pain as Hendrix's fist met his jaw. Leon and I saw this, and my heart burned with anger. There was no way I was going to let Hendrix hurt my friend the way he had hurt me! I shouted Leon's name, and he instantly knew what to do. He swooped down lower, and before Hendrix could land another blow on Seto, Leon grabbed Hendrix's raised arm in his tight claws. Leon only flew a couple of paces before he dropped Hendrix roughly. Leon skidded to a halt, landing. He turned swiftly and stared down at Hendrix, who was pushing himself up to his knees. When Hendrix looked at him, Leon practically forced his snout in his face and roared loudly from the bottom of his gut. The roar was so strong that it made Hendrix's long hair blow madly behind him. There was a furious and spiteful look in Leon's eyes, as he remembered what Hendrix and Adamski had done to me all those months ago. Ironic how the tables had turned, eh? That day on the beach, it was Hendrix sitting high up on his Dragon while I cowered on my knees. Now the roles were reversed, and I honestly had no sympathy for him. For the first time Hendrix became nervous, and he staggered to his feet. He turned to run, but he had nowhere to go. He couldn't believe what he was seeing. His men were fleeing! Abandoning him! And not all of them were heading towards Brozanta. Not only that, but the Gailoiyn army was surrounding us. He stood still, physically panicking as he spun around on the spot. Jasper and Cassandra rushed over to Seto in a hurry. Jasper picked him up in his arms and hugged him tightly as he carried him back to the crowd.

"Oh, son, thank the gods!" Said Jasper.

"Papa!" Seto cried, hugging his father back in tears. Naia, Ivy Wellworn and Zadlos Davandrin pushed their way to the front of the crowd on the opposite side. Naia sighed in relief when he saw that his father and Miss Nebilia had Seto safe and sound. Taz, Joey, Pippa and Irina had also made their way to the front, following behind Princess Veronica and King Ricco. Leon looked around for his father, but Mr Drogon was nowhere to be seen. I couldn't see him either. I jumped down off of Leon's back, and my partner wasted no time in turning back into his human form. He was glaring at Hendrix, his fists clenched tightly at his sides. The King and the Princess took a few steps forward ahead of the Gailoiyn army, and Hendrix reluctantly turned to face them.

"This battle is ours." Ricco declared. "Surrender now, and no harm shall come to you or your partner." The air was silent. The only audible sound was that of the rain tapping gently on metal armour. There was a tension in the wind, one that made everyone on the Plain of Fire uncomfortable and curious as to what Hendrix would do next. Just then, he turned to face Leon and I. The look on his face sent a shiver racing down my spine, and I caught my breath for a moment.

"This isn't over!" He sharply raised his arm and pointed a long, bony finger at us. "You challenged me before, and I thought you had lost. Yet here you are! Alive! So, this battle is far from over! Fight me! Fight me!" Hendrix shouted. I swallowed hard, quickly glancing over at where Adamski had been lying, seeing that he had been detained by the soldiers and taken to the back of the crowd. My heart was beating faster than it ever had before, and I struggled to breathe through the swirling feelings of shock and panic. Leon reached over, and he suddenly grasped his hand in mine. My heart was racing ahead of me, and I sharply turned to look at him as he tightened his grip. Veronica tried to step forward to stop this, but Ricco put his arm out to stop her! Was he seriously gonna let this go ahead?! Jasper on the other hand wasn't going to keep his mouth shut, and he yelled over in disgust.

"You lost, Montgomery! There's no need to fight anymore! Especially not those two. They've been through enough!" Jasper said in anger.

"No." Said Leon, stepping in front of me protectively. He stared at Hendrix, looking him directly in the eyes. "We'll fight."

"What?! Are you insane?!" I said in shock. It was official, he'd gone crazy. Nobody in their right mind would have agreed to that! But Leon wasn't in his right mind. He was angry. A rage burned in his breast, as the memory of me in the infirmary bed latched onto his brain. Mr Davandrin wasn't far behind me, and he loudly whispered my name. I turned my head around to face him quickly, and he nodded towards me. I was gobsmacked...surely, he wasn't okay with this?! I looked back at Hendrix, who had walked over to his spear. He bent down and picked it up quickly, facing us with a face like thunder. His spear was poised, pointing at us. With a shaky hand, I reached for my own blade, slowly pulling it out of its sheathe. I stood beside Leon once more. He erupted a ball of fire in his hand, and turned sideways. I did too, and we both stood back to back as we stared Hendrix down.

"{Xanda...}" I heard Leon's voice in my head. It sounded soothing, with a hint of nerves.

"{Yeah?}"

"{Do you have my back?}" He asked softly. I didn't even need to think about my answer. I smiled weakly.

"{You know I do.}" I said to him adjusting my stance, ready for a fight. I was so confused. Somehow, I had gone from winning the war, to been thrown right back into another fight. But I knew I couldn't allow that to distract me. I'd come too far to die now.

Hendrix was the first to move, and he charged towards us. Despite his bladed staff being covered in blood, I could see how sharp the blade was. I knew that if we were stabbed by it, we wouldn't stand a chance. My sword wasn't anywhere near as big as my scythe was, so I knew immediately that I was at a disadvantage. Not to mention that Hendrix was wiser, taller and much stronger than me. Leon pushed me behind him, and threw a ball of fire towards Hendrix. Of course, the General had to evade the attack, so he stumbled to the side. While he was off balance, I switched places with Leon and went on the offensive. I soon found myself being caught up in a ferocious duel between myself and Hendrix. The sound of our blades clashing together seemed to harmonize with the wind itself. I was holding my own, but his weapon was much longer than mine, so I couldn't really get close to him. I had to think of something...but what?! If I could just get close to him, I could disarm him. Hendrix wasn't that great at fighting at close range, and that was really my only advantage. I racked my brain trying to come up with some way to beat him, but it was hard to think when there was a 6ft trained man trying to beat the crap out of you. Just then, I heard Mr Davandrin shout to us, but I didn't turn to face him. If I had, Hendrix would have struck me down. I kept on fighting as best I could.

"Leon!" Zadlos Davandrin called.

"Bit busy for one of your lectures right now, sir!" Leon said as he backed away from us a little, trying not to get hit by Hendrix's staff.

"Just listen, Drogon!" Davandrin said sharply. "You know how Mr Ventus tells you that it's okay to make mistakes, because that is how you learn?"

"Yes? What's your point?!" Leon asked desperately.

"Well you can also learn from things you did well!" As Mr Davandrin said this, it suddenly hit me what he was trying to say. Leon just seemed more confused, and scrunched up his face at our teacher. I shouldn't have glanced at Leon, because it made me lose focus. Hendrix broke through, and he knocked my hand away! I didn't let go of my sword, knowing I couldn't afford to be disarmed now. He dug the end of his staff into the ground and kicked me with his metal plated boots. He hit me right in the gut, and I screamed as I tumbled. I felt like my insides were turning up-side down as I was forced backwards, rolling across the ground until I finally came to a stop. There was a gasp from the crowd, but many held their breaths wondering what was going to happen. I groaned in pain as I forced myself onto my hands and knees, looking down at the blood-stained ground below me.

"Xanda!" Leon exclaimed, rushing over and kneeling beside me.

"Leo." I said sharply, trying to hide the pain I felt. I had to tell him quickly what Davandrin meant, as I knew Hendrix wouldn't waste any time in attacking us again. "Remember our very first class with Davandrin? Remember what you did?!"

"I joined you on the stage and- oh…now I get it!" He said in realisation. Quickly, Leon took my arm and pulled me back onto my feet. As expected, Hendrix was making his way towards us. We knew what we had to do. For the first time since this duel started, I actually believed that we could win.

"{Xanda. If this doesn't work, I want you to know that…I'm proud to call you my partner.}" I heard Leon's voice in my head once more, and a small smile spread across my lips.

"{Back at ya, Leo!}"

We only had one shot at this, and I was determined to make it count. Leon charged towards Hendrix, the two males staring each other down. Since Leon had no weapon, Hendrix became smug, thinking he would strike him down with ease and he was only charging to protect me. How wrong he was. Leon had no intention of fighting him. Hendrix skidded to a halt, and brandished his bladed staff to the side, ready to swing it at Leon's head. My partner had amazing reflexes, and he quickly sussed out what Hendrix was going to do. Just before the blade reached Leon's neck, he suddenly stopped and fell to one knee. Now it was my turn. I wasted no time in sprinting to my partner, and barrel rolling over his back. I raised my sword as our backs touched, and my blade skidded along the hilt of Hendrix's staff. The General's narrow eyes widened, as I pushed his staff clean out of his hands! As I landed on two feet, I instantly brought my blade up to his neck. Leon scrambled to the side and picked up Hendrix's staff so he couldn't arm himself again. There was a deathly silence. I stared him down. The look on his face was priceless. He was so embarrassed, and ashamed. He was a very proud man, but in that moment, he just seemed a shell of his former self. I slowly glanced down at the ground, and then back at him. It was a silent indication by myself that he should just surrender. And that is exactly what he did. I saw him physically gulp, and he raised his hands up and placed them behind his head. He slowly knelt, feeling the cool metal of my blade against his throat. The rain had stopped lashing down, and the wind was no longer howling. It was so quiet you could have heard a pin drop. Ricco and Veronica took a few steps forward, and Veronica spoke with authority.

"Hendrix Montgomery, your life is ours." She said.

"No." He replied, which surprised Veronica. She hadn't expected him to answer back. "The girl bested me. My life is in her hands." He spoke softly, and glanced up at me. I was seeing a different side to him. He sounded nothing like the man I had first met. I was shocked, and I felt my heart skip a beat…but I didn't let that show. I didn't want to show him any weakness.

"But-" Veronica tried to protest, but her brother raised his hand to stop her. King Ricco looked down at me, a serious look in his eyes.

"He is right. The battle is yours." Ricco said to me. I suddenly felt a huge weight of responsibility. His life was in my hands, and I honestly didn't know what to do!

"Girl." Hendrix spoke up, snapping me out of my thoughts. I looked at him once more, swallowing hard. "Despite my first impression of you, you have grown into a fine young warrior. Kill me, or let me live. It's your choice, and I will honour it."

One by one, my friends stepped forward to give me their advice. I didn't look at any of them, I just kept my gaze firmly fixed on Hendrix as they gave their opinions. I remember vividly what each of them said that day…

Naia said:
"It's not my decision. But if it were, I'd let him live. I know Seto would disagree with that, but his death does not need to be added to the amount already piled up. But whatever you decide, Seto and I will be here."

Leon said:
"Xanda, listen to me! You know what I think about this war, and that I don't believe in it. But this man did not even think of sparing your life on the beach that day! Why grant him the chance to live when he wouldn't do that for you?"

Taz said:
"But don't you think enough blood has been shed today? I'm tired of all this fighting, Xanda. We both know there will be more to come. That said, I still

don't see what we would accomplish with his death."

Joey said:
"I do! And I agree with Leo. This guy wouldn't think twice about killing any of us, and he's so blinded by his loyalty to Stephan he's a danger to everyone here! Just kill him and be done with it!"

Irina said:
"No! Xanda, please. I was on the beach with you that day...but more violence isn't the answer! Taz is right...enough blood has been spilt this day. Just step away, I beg you."

Pippa said:
"It's not often I agree with Joey, but he's right, Xanda! Hendrix Montgomery is a monster, just like his master!"

There was so much to think about, and not much time to do it. Pippa's words hit me when she called him a monster. This man had almost killed me, yet when I looked down at him...I didn't see a monster. I don't know what I saw, but my mind was made up. I pulled my sword away from his throat, and raised it high into the air ready to strike him down. Hendrix looked a little nervous, and called out to me.
"Wait!" He said with a sudden urge. "At least tell me your name..."
I swallowed hard, gripping the hilt of my sword tighter.
"I am Xandario Sykes."
He looked at me for a moment, his eyes hollow. Something about his reaction to my name didn't seem right. It was like he had heard it before. He slowly lowered his head in acceptance. There was a rock on the ground not far from us, and to my surprise he crawled over to it. He placed his shaky hands on the side of the wet stone, and lowered his head onto it like it was a chopping block. I stepped towards him, feeling next to no emotion as I placed my blade on the back of his exposed neck. He closed his eyes, seeming to have accepted his fate. I raised the sword with both hands. I took a deep breath, and brought the blade down swiftly.

But then something happened that I did not expect...at the last second, I changed my mind.

I threw my blade to his side, and it stabbed into the ground before him. He visibly flinched, his breath instantly picking up the pace. He looked up at me sharply, his eyes full of shock. I closed my eyes for a moment, swallowing hard. I composed myself, and looked at him softly.
"I am Xandario. And I am not like you. Enough people have died today." I took a few steps backwards, before starting to walk away. The people

219

cheered, but their sounds were drowned out in my ears. I heard Veronica shout orders to her men to arrest Hendrix and take him back to Algora. I ignored everyone and pushed my way through the crowd. People patted me on the back and congratulated me. I didn't care for that. In my opinion, there was nothing much to celebrate.

Jasper sat Seto on the ground and knelt beside him. The boy held onto his father, but looked around desperately towards his brother. He smiled in relief, not being able to stop the tears from streaming down his face as Naia sprinted over.

"Naia!" Seto called out to him happily.

"Seto! Father!" Naia shouted back, suddenly falling to his knees beside them and hugging them both. The twins couldn't contain their happiness, and cried as Jasper put his arms around them both. Cassandra knelt beside them, smiling as she placed a comforting hand on Naia's back.

"Oh my boys!" Said Jasper, completely overwhelmed. "Don't you ever scare me like that again!"

"I'm so glad that you're both okay!" Cassandra smiled softly, starting to stroke Naia's hair. The boys just sobbed into their father's chest, unable to control their emotions any longer.

"Hey, c'mon...don't cry!" Jasper said squeezing them tighter.

"Papa...you won't...you won't disown us for disobeying you...will you?" Naia sniffled.

"What?! No!" Jasper just held onto them tightly as he cradled them in his arms, showing them all the love they needed as a child. "I would never even consider giving you away. You are both so important to me. You're my sons! My boys! I couldn't disown you even if I wanted to. I love you both so much!" Jasper couldn't hold his emotions in check either, and a few tears trickled down his cheeks. He wasn't ashamed of crying, despite being a man. He didn't care what anybody thought of him. He was just so overwhelmed that his sons were safe and sound.

Zadlos Davandrin watched Jasper from a few feet away, and was beaming with pride at his former student. He couldn't help but think on how much Jasper had grown, and how he had turned into a fine young man. Ivy Wellworn was at his side, watching Cassandra comfort her new family. She was happy for her, thinking on how Cassandra deserved to finally have some happiness in her life. Mrs Madana walked over to them, wiping off the dirt from one of her spell books.

"By the gods..." Monica Madana said sadly, closing her eyes. "What a mess..."

"That's certainly an understatement." Said Ivy, letting out a heavy sigh. "So many wounded...so many dead...this couldn't have been worse."

"It can always be worse." Zadlos snapped, his blue eyes scanning the corpses scattered across the Plain of Fire. "This isn't the end...tis just the beginning."

"Xanda?! Father?!" Leon stepped over the bodies of the fallen, trying to find me and his father. He didn't have to look for long. Leon twirled around, feeling a shaky hand on his shoulder. He turned to see his father standing before him, his dark eyes full of sorrow, yet relief at the same time.

"Son…" He said softly, unsure of what to do. Leon teared up and suddenly wrapped his arms around him, hugging his father tightly.

"Father!"

"Oh, Leon…I'm so sorry!" Drevin quickly hugged his son back, holding him tighter than he had ever held him before. He placed his hand on Leon's head, and stroked his son's hair. Leon closed his eyes, resting his head against his father's chest.

"You have nothing to apologise for, father…" Leon said softly. Drevin slowly pulled away and knelt before his son. He placed his hands onto Leon's arms. Leon stared into his father's eyes, and he had never seen him so upset.

"I thought I'd lost you." Said Drevin biting back his tears. "You are the most precious thing in my life. I don't ever want to lose you again! I love you so much!"

"I love you too, father…" Leon replied, smiling weakly. Drevin slowly raised his hand and placed it softly on Leon's cheek.

"Look at you. You look so much like your mother."

"Do you think she's proud of me…?" Leon sniffled, tearing up himself. Drevin laughed a little and wiped his son's eyes, smiling through his own tears.

"Of course she is. And I tell you something…I couldn't be prouder of what you did today. My strong, brave, fearless little man…"

"I'm not fearless, father." Said Leon. "I was so scared today. And not of dying. I could cope with dying. But I was scared I'd lose you and my friends and…and Xanda."

I'd heard that. In truth, I wasn't so far away. I'd been walking towards them, but kept my distance as they shared that moment together, not wanting to intrude. I froze when Leo said this, not sure whether I should go over or not. Luckily, I didn't have to decide. Drevin saw me out the corner of his eye, and turned to face me. Leon followed his gaze and a wave of relief washed over him.

"Xanda…!" He exclaimed.

"Hi…" I smiled weakly, not being able to say much else. Drevin smiled softly at me, and extended a hand towards me.

"Come here, Sykes." Said Mr Drogon. I hesitantly made my way over, not sure if I was in trouble or not for disobeying him. He stood slowly as I neared him, and suddenly pulled me and Leon into a hug. My eyes widened in surprise, and I looked at my partner. "I'm so proud of you…the pair of you!" Said Drevin Drogon. I don't know why, but his words hit me, and I found myself hugging him and Leon back tightly. I closed my eyes, wanting in that moment to forget about the world around me. The battle was over, but the

221

war had only just begun.

It had been a while since then but we were still on the Plain of Fire, waiting to march back. There were too many dead to carry back to Algora, so their bodies were being prepared to be burned in a dignified way before we left. We weren't just burying our own people, we were going to bury Brozanta's too. They deserved some sort of a funeral just as much as our people did. I was tired and worn down that all I could do was watch as the bodies were laid side by side. I was sitting on the ground leaning against a rock, resting my elbows on my knees. Seto sat next to me. Miss Nebilia had made a makeshift sling for his injured arm until he could receive proper treatment from Ida McCoy when we returned. We'd been sitting in silence for a while...I tell you, he'd never been so quiet.

"How's the arm?" I finally asked him. He turned to look at me and smiled weakly.

"This? Oh, it's nothing. It looks a lot worse than it feels." He replied, trying to act tough even though it was obvious that he was in pain.

"Whatever you say." I chuckled softly.

"You know, Xanda...when we didn't see you for ages after you went to find Leo...I really thought you were dead." Seto said to me, a sad look in his eyes. I smiled at him weakly and turned to face him.

"So did I." I replied. "Y'know, when we decided to come here, I didn't actually think that we'd make it out alive."

"Jeez...what the hell is happening to Utopia?! Our whole world is becoming a battlefield." Seto sighed heavily, and stood up slowly. He looked in pain, so I stood with him and carefully took his arm to help ease him up. Just then we looked up as Leon walked over with Naia, Pippa and Irina trailing behind him. Leo sighed and rubbed the back of his neck.

"The bodies are almost ready to be burned..." Leon told us.

"There's so many of them..." Irina said sadly, crossing her hands over her chest and looking at the ground.

"What a waste of life..." Pippa sighed, turning slightly to look at the lines of bodies in the distance behind her.

"Yeah..." Naia added, with a weak voice.

"Guys, c'mon!" Just then, we all heard a more upbeat voice. Joey and Taz were strolling towards us, their usual grins painted onto their faces. "What's done here is done. We can't bring back those we lost." Said Joey.

"Many more will die tomorrow, and the day after, and the day after that." Said Taz, his purple eyes shining brightly. "But that just gives us more reason to keep on fighting. We started this thing together. So, what do you say we end it together?" With Tazmin's words, our small group of eight seemed more upbeat and determined. Leon nodded intently.

"I think we can do that." He said.

"So, what do we do now, Xanda?" Naia asked, and all eyes turned to me. I felt a little nervous when he mentioned my name.

"What?! Why are you asking me?! Do I look like some sort of benevolent leader?!" I asked in shock. Taz and Joey just looked at each other, and chuckled.

"Not really." Said Joey. "But you act like one."

"And wherever you go, we will follow." Irina smiled, and the others nodded in agreement. I didn't want this at all...I didn't like it. But our goal remained the same as it always had. They parted as I walked through them, stopping to look into the distance at corpses being prepared for burial.

"Stephan will need time to gather his forces. So, we go home and we rest ourselves. Then we'll meet at my place in Lightwater." I turned to face them, my face strong. I then continued to speak. "Pack your walking boots. We need to find the fragments of the Elemental Stone before Stephan does."

Leon moved over to my side, and he took my hand in his. His skin was warm and soft for once. I looked at him, and he smiled. Suddenly, the bodies were set alight. A huge fire began to rise towards the star filled sky. The flames looked magical as they danced around with each other. It was strange...I didn't feel sad at all. I knew those people had gone to a better place now. They didn't have to fight on this hellish earth any longer. Leon squeezed my hand tightly, which made me turn my head to look at him. He looked at me too, and smiled once more as the flames swirled into the air gently in front of us.

"We can do this, Xanda. Together."

I then thought back to my first day at Wyvern Academy. I remembered the three simple, but powerful words that Drevin Drogon had said to us. Embrace the Fire. And hell...that is what I intended to do.

Chapter 20

The Great Dragon

Remember Cooper, King Stephan's ward? The boy he had been grooming to be his heir? Well, he has a much bigger part in my story than I first suspected. Cooper had been changing by the day. Both he and Naia had similar upbringings, and as we know, Naia never challenged his father. But that is what Cooper was starting to do. He was changing, and was finally starting to become less timid as he realised the state that the world was in outside of the castle walls. His mother had warned him not to mess with Stephan, but Cooper had taken so many beatings from him already he didn't see how things could get worse. Since Stephan had forced him to hang his friend, the young lord had been filled with rage and thoughts of vengeance. Cooper had never known anything different, but surely a King who murdered his own people was a bad king. That's the way he was starting to think. He was growing up, and developing a mind of his own. He had started keeping a knife under his pillow, one that he had stolen from the palace kitchen. There were whispers around the castle that the boy was going insane...but his friends didn't see it like that. Lucas, Mahariel and Genevieve were growing more and more concerned about him, as was his mother. Deep down his mother was glad her son was finally seeing things for what they were, but was scared of what Stephan would do to him if he spoke out of line. She was right to be afraid. Cooper was sitting on his bed, fully clothed. He now seldom wore nightclothes, for he was growing more paranoid that he would have to defend himself in the middle of the night. He wasn't tired, as he'd slept most of the day. He just sat there, twirling around the knife in his hands. He turned his head to look out of his window at the starry sky. Genevieve had not long gone home, and he knew that as long as her father stayed Stephan's most trusted advisor that she would be safe should something happen to him. He had thought that Mahariel had gone to the servant's quarters, and that Lucas had gone back to his cell in one of the towers...but he was wrong. He jumped in surprise, standing instantly as the two snuck into his room quietly, quickly closing the door behind them. He let out a heavy sigh, clenching the knife hilt firmly between his fingers.

"Balls, you two! You nearly gave me a heart attack!" Said Cooper still trying to calm himself. He instantly knew something was wrong, when Lucas hurried over to him and put a finger to his lips.

"Shh!" Lucas said hurriedly.

"What's going on?! What are you doing here at this time of night?!" Cooper asked worriedly, quietening the tone of his voice.

"It's Tenebris...she's returned!" Said the shivering elf. Mahariel looked terrified as she moved over to him, and Cooper placed a hand on her arm in comfort.

"What...? What's happened?" Asked Cooper.

"Stephan lost!" Replied Lucas. "We lost the battle. My uncle's gone mad! We have to get out of here!"

"And go where?!" Asked Cooper, flustered.

"Algora of course! You were right, Cooper...my Uncle has to be stopped!"

Lucas said, sounding like a born leader for the first time in his life. Cooper nodded in agreement. He didn't want to spend another minute in that castle. "Okay. What's your plan?" Cooper asked.

"There's a prisoner, well hidden in the dungeon. He's been there as long as I can remember. I don't know much about him, but I heard that he is from Gailoiyn. I'm going to free him. Hopefully with his help, we'll be able to pass into Algora safely. We're going to Merdonex first. The Dwarves live underground there, so we should be safe there for a while to gather supplies. Genevieve is going to meet us there." Cooper liked the plan, apart from one aspect of it. After a short moment of silence, he spoke up.

"I can't go without my mother."

"My lord, she is with Stephan and Tenebris now in the War Room." Mahariel stated.

"We have to go now, Cooper. Or we'll be seen!" Said Lucas desperately.

"We'll be seen anyway!" Cooper protested. "Has it escaped your notice the number of guards that patrol this castle?!" Once again, the conversation fell silent. Lucas and Mahariel looked at each other, realising Cooper had a point. The boy looked down at the knife in his hand, swallowing hard. He placed it in his pocket slowly. He knew what he had to do. "You need to go."

"What?!" Lucas said, eyes wide. "You can't expect us to just leave you here!"

"You must! Listen to me, Lucas. You are the true Prince of Brozanta...not me! I never have been, nor did I want to be. I'm going to the war room, and I'm going to try and escape with my mother. If we get out, great! If we don't...then your life is still much more valuable than mine. My mother has risked everything to keep me safe. I need to save her, or die trying. And you need to get to Algora. If I try my escape in full view, there won't be much focus on you. If anybody is a symbol of hope right now, it's you, Lucas. You know I'm right..." Cooper smiled at them weakly, and for once in his life, he felt like he had a purpose. Prince Lucas teared up, looking down at his friend beaming with pride. He suddenly hugged him tightly, and the boy hugged him back.

"You'll be okay, Cooper. You're a smart boy. You'll get out...I know you will!" Lucas smiled and pulled back.

"I'll try my best, and Mahariel..."

"Yes?" She said.

"If I don't make it, tell Gen that I'm sorry." Said Cooper sadly. The elven girl suddenly wrapped her arms around him, and the boy blushed as her pink hair fell into his face.

"Oh Cooper! You will make it! Please don't talk like that!" She said worriedly. Cooper smiled as she pulled back. He said nothing, but that was the first time she had ever called him by his name. It made him happy to hear it. He was no longer a Lord to her...he was her friend. He blushed deeper, and fiddled with the knife nervously in his pocket. However, his expression soon shifted as he realised the gravity of the situation. He knew he could die that night, but he also knew that this was his last shot at freedom.

"Enough talking. We need to go. Now." Said Cooper with a sense of urgency. With one last hug from the other two, he bid them farewell he left the room. He wasn't sure if he'd ever see them again, but he hoped he would. Cooper closed his eyes as he made his way down the corridor, and imagined Genevieve smiling at him. She just smiled, nothing more. The thought made him happy, and gave him the strength to do what he needed to. He knew he would either finally leave the castle tonight, or likely be killed inside the walls he had spent his entire life.

Cooper had never been so afraid in his whole life. He knew he only had one shot to get out of that place. He also knew he only had one shot to distract the Guards from Prince Lucas's escape. So much was resting on his shoulders. He felt the heavy responsibility weighing him down. His skinny legs wobbled violently with every step that he took as he came ever closer to the War Room. From all the way down the corridor, he could hear raised voices. That alone put him on edge. He could tell straight away whom the voices belonged to: Stephan, Tenebris and his mother. As Cooper neared the door, he pressed an ear up against the rough wood, trying to listen in on their conversation. Well, I say conversation...it was more of a screaming session.

"You fool! How dare you allow my Generals to be captured! And the boy! I told you specifically not to take him to the battle! What the hell did you hope to accomplish?!" Stephan boomed. "We needed him! You stupid, STUPID woman!" There was a thud from inside the room, like Stephan had shoved Tenebris into something. Cooper jumped, his heart racing ahead of him.

"I'm sorry, My Lord!" Said Tenebris, seeming genuinely scared. "I did it for you! Everything I did, I did it for you!"

"Does that include harming my son?!" Cooper's mother shouted, her voice becoming stronger. "You are evil! Both of you are pure evil! You tear me away from my family, abuse my son, try and kidnap my daughter! And you expect me to stay quiet?!" Daughter? Cooper couldn't believe what he was hearing...he had a sister?! But there was no time for him to comprehend the thought, as he heard his mother scream in pain.

"SHUT UP, SHUT UP, SHUT UP!" Stephan screeched. Cooper couldn't stand listening to this any longer! Without thinking, he pushed the door open and burst into the room. He froze at the scene he saw. Tenebris looked a mess, sitting by Stephan's desk which had been shoved onto its side. Her dark red hair covered her face, and her once majestic clothes were in tatters. She was also covered in blood. However, Cooper's eyes soon left her and focused on the King. Cooper clenched his fists, upon seeing his mother on her knees, with Stephan's hands clenched into fists like he had just hit her. Her long, blue hair was falling out of its braid, and her shirt was becoming loose. She looked at her son nervously with her green eyes, and adjusted her shirt with her shaky hands to cover herself up once more.

"Cooper…!" She said quietly, clearly worried.

"What are you doing here?!" Stephan boomed angrily, storming over to him. "You know the War Room is off limits to you!"

"With all due respect, my lord, I couldn't give a damn." Said Cooper, standing his ground. "I no longer wish to live here. I'm leaving. Right now. And I'm taking my mother with me." Stephan's reaction was not what Cooper had expected to say the least. There was a short, uneasy moment of silence. Cooper held firm, but deep down, he was bricking it. He physically gulped, when Stephan suddenly broke into a sinister laugh. The boy just watched him, terrified as to what he would do next.

"I'm sorry…" Said the King amongst his dark laughter. "I must have misheard you. I thought you said you wanted to leave."

"You didn't mishear me, sire." Cooper stated, his voice starting to quaver a little now. He knew it was only a matter of moments before Stephan would burst. He could see the boiling anger rising in the King's eyes. Stephan's hands were clenched so tightly, that his nails began to dig into his palms. But it wasn't him that erupted first. Tenebris was already on her feet, and storming over to the boy. She spoke harshly to him, her voice raised.

"How dare you even suggest that, you little runt?!" She spat. "He raised you as his own, even though you didn't deserve it! You deserve to die you little-" Tenebris neared him, leaning over him like a hawk about to attack its prey. This was all becoming too much…he couldn't handle this any longer! Tenebris raised her hand. He had no idea if she was going to hit him or cast a spell on him, but there was a sudden rush of panic that raced to his head. For the first time in his life, he didn't think on what he was going to do. Cooper pulled out the knife from his pocket, and stabbed her. He dug the knife in deep, right into the wound she already had on her shoulder. Tenebris let out a cry of pain, stumbling backwards. Stephan lunged forward, and reached out for the boy…but his mother wouldn't let him! The blue-haired woman practically leaped on Stephan, keeping the King away from her son.

"Cooper, go!" She shouted.

"But-" The boy tried to protest.

"Go!" His mother yelled again, and Cooper soon found himself racing out of the room. This was all happening so fast! He had no idea what to do, or where to go from here, but there was one thing he did know…he had to escape!

Cooper ran through the dark, castle halls. All he could hear were the sounds of his mother screaming as she struggled to hold back the King. He tried to drown out the deafening noise, but even after turning the corner he could still hear it bouncing around inside his head. Something kept telling him not to look back, but he couldn't resist it. To be honest it was probably a good thing that he did, because Tenebris was hot on his heels. A rush of adrenaline surged through him, and he began to panic. But then he started to think differently…almost logical.

"Okay, Cooper, calm down!" He thought, trying to control his breathing. He knew the castle like the back of his hand. He also knew that Tenebris was much faster than him, for no other reason than her legs were longer. He had nothing to defend himself with, or no magical ability. He had a strategy in mind…do everything in his power to stay ahead of her. She hadn't cast any spells at him yet, so he speculated that her magic may have been weakened by her injuries. All these thoughts passed through Cooper's mind in a matter of seconds. He didn't look back again, but he could hear that Tenebris was getting closer to him. Her heels digging into the floor was like a knife to his tiny ears, and he immediately turned a sharp corner into the grand hall. Tenebris skidded a little, bumping into the wall. She soon regained her balance. Cooper heard her once again getting nearer to him, and he knew he had to ditch her somehow. It may have been a rush of blood to his head, but he had an idea. It was a stupid idea, but still, it was an idea. He saw Tenebris's hand reach out for him out of the corner of his eye, and he panicked realising just how close she was! Cooper reacted quickly, and suddenly leaped over the railings and landed down onto the tall, grand staircase. Tenebris let out a roar of frustration as the boy's shirt slipped through her bony fingers. She quickly began to run around towards the top of the stairs. Cooper tried to land safely, but his legs gave way. He cried out, beginning to roll down the stairs. His body smacked into the edges of the steps as he tumbled down, faster and faster until he hit the bottom. He landed roughly, rolling onto his back. He was in so much pain, he just wanted to lie there on the cool floor and hope that none of this was happening. However, he knew he couldn't afford to think like that. Cooper slowly looked up at the grand staircase, and saw Tenebris darting down the stairs towards him. The adrenaline suddenly hit him, and Cooper fought back against his aching muscles and pushed himself upwards. His golden hair fell into his face, as sweat began to drip down his brow. He was so tired and winded from the fall that he could barely breathe. As he forced himself to carry on running, he let out gasps of pain as he realised that he had injured the left side of his torso. He placed his right hand over his left side as he moved trying to support it, but it didn't really make that much of a difference. He seemed to have lost Tenebris…for now. What I mean by that is he could no longer hear her close behind him. Cooper turned a corner, staggering to the first door he saw and pushed it open. He hoped he could hide in that room for a while so he could figure out what to do next. He just hoped Tenebris wouldn't find him there…

Cooper took a few cautious steps away from the door, his shaggy breath racing ahead of him. He just stared at the door, his mind going blank for a moment. It was quiet. Almost too quiet. He whirled his head around, seeing he had arrived in the Grand Dining Hall. There were long tables stretched out almost the whole length of the room, and black drapes hung from the walls with images of red Dragons sewn into them. He swallowed hard, taking in his surroundings. He had only been in that room a few times before. Stephan never ate in there, as he had most of his meals taken to his study or the war room. Cooper often ate in his room, too. Just then, the silence was broken. Cooper heard faint, hurried footsteps racing down the hall towards him. "Balls..." He cursed under his breath, and sprinted to the back of the room. He held his side, wanting to cry out in pain. He bit his lip, trying to hold it in. He had to stay quiet. Tenebris was like a hawk, and he knew she always hunted down her prey. He ducked down behind the chairs and table at the back of the room and stayed still, trying to catch his breath. He closed his eyes for a short moment, before instantly becoming more alert. The door had opened. He lay on his front, looking under the tables. He'd recognise those ridiculously high heeled boots anywhere...they belonged to Tenebris. To be honest though, he knew it was her anyway from the way her boots tapping on the tile sent a shiver down his spine. He watched with a shaky breath as Tenebris began to walk around the room. Cooper didn't understand how Tenebris could have more injuries than him, and still be able to walk around okay. He was just barely able to move!

"Cooper darling...I know you're here. Do not hide from me." Tenebris said in a calm, yet darkened tone. As she said his name, Cooper's heart seemed to stop in alarm. He repeatedly told himself to calm down...well, he thought it as obviously telling himself aloud wasn't the best idea. Anyway, he knew he had to come up with some sort of plan to get out of this one...and he had to come up with it fast! Just then his eyes fell, not upon the open door, but what was behind it. A large cabinet. The cogs in his mind started to turn. He realised that if he could just get out, he may be able to use it to barricade her in! She knew he was in the room, so Cooper knew he couldn't hide any longer. If he tried to move, she'd hear him...so he decided to play along with her little game.

"I'm scared of you, my lady..." Cooper said to her, still concealing himself behind the table. As soon as he spoke though, he watched as Tenebris began to walk closer towards him. It was obvious to him now, she was going to use the sound of his voice to locate him.

"Oh, do not be afraid of me. Were friends, are we not? You're such a good boy, helping me with my experiments...why don't we go back upstairs, and we can forget all about this!" She said, a sickeningly sweet tone to her voice. As she talked, Cooper used the opportunity to crawl across the floor around the edge of the room.

"Do you promise you won't hurt me? Or mother?" He asked, a little more quietly than before. He then shimmied under the table, and waited for Tenebris to be out of sight before quickly shuffling under another.

"I promise." She was obviously lying, and Cooper wasn't falling for any of it. He knew he had to make a run for it soon, but he wanted to be as far from

Tenebris as he possibly could. She was nearing his first hiding place at the back of the room, and Cooper kept on glancing nervously at her feet as he shuffled ever closer to the door. Just then she began to walk around the tables, and back towards him. It was now or never. He had to make a run for it! He neared the end of one of the tables, taking a deep breath. This was it.

"Liar!" Cooper screamed, and he scrambled to his feet. Tenebris's beady eyes locked onto him immediately.
"Get back here!" She shrieked from cross the room, and rapidly began to form a wave of magic in the palm of her hand. Cooper glanced back at her as he darted towards the door. She threw a bolt of dark magic towards him! The magic propelled through the air, and Cooper dived back onto the ground to avoid it. He let out a sharp cry of pain, holding his injured side as he wasted no time in scrambling back to his feet. He scuttled through the doorway, and saw Tenebris racing towards him when he turned round. She looked like she was possessed! Cooper quickly slammed the door, and turned to face the cabinet. The side of his torso began to burn as he used every ounce of his strength to push the cabinet over. It crashed against the door, barricading her in. Cooper couldn't believe it...his strategy had actually worked! He didn't have long to admire his work though, as Tenebris was soon hammering against the door trying to escape. He wasn't sure how long it would hold her for. He knew he had to leave immediately if he wanted to escape. For the first time, a small yet satisfying grin was formed on his lips, as he took one last look at the door before he ran off deeper into the castle.

Cooper just kept on going, staggering through the halls holding onto his side. He began to wonder why he hadn't come across any guards...where were they? Had they found Lucas? Perhaps they were protecting the King? Or were they somewhere else? However, he didn't question his good fortune. He just hoped that the others were okay. Soon enough, he found himself in a very strange part of the castle. He'd limped down several sets of stairs, and had come to be in a place he didn't recognise. He had been banned from going into certain areas of the castle, and this had been one of them. He didn't think anything of it though, he just wanted to put as much distance between him and Tenebris as he possibly could. Just then, he came across a strange, barred door. He was nowhere near the dungeons, so he began to wonder what a cell was doing here. As he placed his hands on the bars and gazed through, he saw that the walls inside consisted of purely natural rock. Plus, there was a cold breeze whistling through. Perhaps this led outside? Knowing this was the only lead he had, he opened the door and stepped through. He didn't even think of shutting it behind him...he just wanted to get out. He took deep breaths, trying to calm his nerves. Finally, he took a few steps forward, feeling the area around him becoming chillier. He took a few more steps, and noticed that there was a spiral staircase hidden in the darkness. He hesitated for a moment, wondering if he should go down there. Something in the breeze seemed to call out to him, and he realised he had no other option but to go down there anyway. He took a deep, shuddering breath, and placed one foot on the top step. Without hesitation, he continued to descend further down the steps. As he travelled further and further into the depths, it began to become increasingly colder, and his body started to shiver. Finally, he reached the bottom. Cooper found himself in a huge, open cavern. He gazed around in awe, having no idea a place like this existed under his home. He looked upwards, and beams of moonlight shone through the cracks of boulders blocking the ceiling. There was a drop below, with huge rocks sticking up from the ground like perches. It was then, Cooper noticed that there was a huge clamp resting on one of the perches in front of him, attached to the thickest chain he had ever seen. He swallowed hard, wondering what on earth Stephan was keeping down here.

"Hello?" Cooper called out. No answer. So, he called out again and this time, he got a response. "Hello?!"

"Who goes there?!" Said a loud, grumbling voice. Cooper was startled, looking around quickly to see where the voice had come from. He gulped nervously, before answering.

"My name is Cooper."

"And why are you here, Cooper?"

"I'm trying to flee from the King!" Said the boy, beginning to shake all over. Just then, Cooper's world changed forever. A humongous gust of wind blew him back like a hurricane, as a Dragon emerged from the ground. He flapped his huge wings, ascending upwards before sitting on the large rocky area in front of the small boy. Cooper was too shocked to move, and he found himself practically glued to the spot. The Dragon was the biggest creature he had ever seen, with wings that looked so strong that it could carry him into the heavens. His scales were of the purest white he had ever seen, and his eyes were a soft red like the sunset. Cooper's jaw dropped open, trying to come to terms with the sheer magnificence of the beast before him. He seemed perfect...except one rather large scar covering his left eye.

"You're...not Dragonbourne...are you? You're...a real Dragon!" Cooper said in amazement.

"Indeed, child." The beast spoke. "My name is Fergo. I have lived far longer than anyone alive today."

"What are you doing down here...?" Cooper asked.

"I was captured by Stephan many years ago..." Fergo answered. As he said this, Cooper turned his attention to Fergo's front right leg, and saw that the chain was attached to him. Cooper couldn't help but feel sorry for the poor creature...surely, a wonderful beast such as Fergo needed to be free. But so did he. He looked around at the stairs once more, his paranoia beginning to take hold.

"That's awful...really. But like I said, I really need to get out of here or he'll kill me!"

"That's certainly believable." Said Fergo. "I'll make a deal with you, boy. Unchain me, and I will help you escape." It was a tempting offer, but Cooper didn't know if Fergo could be trusted. But then again, what choice did he have? Just then, Cooper jumped out of his skin, hearing footsteps hurrying down the steps behind him. He turned quickly, his eyes widening in panic. Tenebris was racing down the stairs, shouting commands at some of the guards. Cooper whirled back around to Fergo, and seeing no other way out, he agreed. The boy vaulted down from the platform he was on, shouting out in agony as his torso began to ache once more. He rushed forward, and grunted through the pain as he began to climb the rock that Fergo was perched on. The Dragon glanced at the stairway, before reaching down and helping Cooper climb the best he could. Finally the boy neared the top, and he grabbed onto the edge. Moaning loudly he pulled himself up onto the ledge, and staggered to his feet. He was starting to feel a little dizzy, but he knew he had to stay awake. He knelt beside Fergo's leg, and examined the chain closely. Suddenly, his eyes fell upon a tiny latch, which he instantly clicked. As the chain snapped open, Fergo let out the loudest roar he had ever heard. Cooper covered his ears, looking up at the Dragon in fear. He hoped he wouldn't turn on him and eat him. Fergo looked down at Cooper, and nodded in gratitude.

"Hurry child! Onto my back, the enemy is near!" Fergo told him. With those words, Cooper felt some sort of relief. He did what Fergo said, and started to climb onto the back of the huge Dragon. Fergo twisted slightly, and used his long talons to help him onto his back. Cooper looked down at the ground below him, grabbing onto Fergo's neck as a wave of nausea washed over him. "Oh, balls, that's high!" The boy said in fear. But right now, he had bigger problems. Tenebris had emerged from the stairway, a group of guards behind her. Fergo and Cooper both stared at her, as Tenebris screeched.

"You insolent boy! Get back down here!"

"Never!" Cooper shouted back. Never again did he ever want to obey her. Fergo growled at Tenebris, which just seemed to make her more dangerous. She began to conjure up another spell, this time in both palms. The purple magic grew bigger with every second, and Fergo glanced up at the ceiling.

"Stay close to me, boy!" He said. Before Cooper could even question this, Fergo flapped his wings, and lifted himself into the air. Tenebris threw the magic at them, but it missed Fergo by an inch. Cooper lost his balance, and grabbed onto Fergo even tighter. The cavern shook madly from the impact of Tenebris's spell, and the boulders blocking in the open ceiling began to shudder. It was then Cooper realised what Fergo was doing...he was heading straight for them! He quickly shut his eyes, and buried his head into Fergo's scaly neck, bracing himself for the impact!

Cooper's entire world began to shake, as Fergo bashed through the boulders. His strong wings carried him through the rocks, knocking them aside. Tenebris and the guards started to retreat as the cavern began to crumble inwards. The sound was as frightening as an explosion, and it spread throughout the kingdom. It didn't last for long though. When the noise had subsided Cooper slowly raised his head, and found that he was floating amongst the stars. He had never seen a more beautiful sight. He was no longer afraid of Fergo, and he sat upright. The boy smiled, and laughed in the joy he felt finally being free. He raised a hand, and watched as the clouds melted around his fingertips. He didn't know where Fergo would take him from here, but there was one thing that he did know. His life was just about to begin.

This part of my story ends with a discovery like no other. Prince Lucas had ordered Mahariel to flee ahead of him, so it gave him and the mysterious prisoner less chance of being seen. Nobody knew who this man was, or where he had come from, but he was from Gailoiyn...so he would be vital in their attempt to get into Algora safely. Lucas was walking to the deepest, darkest part of the dungeon, where Stephan held his most valuable prisoners. He had already stolen the cell keys, and was carrying a simple torch to see in the darkness. Finally, the young prince reached the last cell. The bars were thick and sturdy, and there was nothing inside the cell apart from the prisoner, and some chains. Lucas swallowed hard, hoping this man wasn't a danger to him. He took a deep breath and unlocked the door, stepping into the cell. The prisoner didn't even look up at him. Lucas looked down at the skinny man, and saw how underfed he was. His rags were practically hanging off his bony body, and his dark blonde hair was all scruffy and dirty. Looking at him, Lucas didn't think he was very old at all...maybe around thirty. The prince took a deep breath, and pointed the torch at him so the prisoner was in the light. His ankles were cuffed to a chain bolted into the floor. Lucas looked over him one more time, before speaking to the prisoner.

"Who are you?" Lucas asked simply.

The prisoner finally raised his head, and stared at the prince with his hollow, blue eyes.

"Alphonse Sykes."

To Be Continued

...

Credits

Author
A. N. Attebery

With Thanks To
Illustrator
Adrian Davies-Ratcliffe

Amazon Publishing

About The Author
A.N.Attebery

A.N.Attebery (Alexandra Nicole Attebery) is a young author from the UK. From a very young age, she has always been interested in fantasy novels, such as 'Harry Potter' (J.K. Rowling), 'Vampirates' (Justin Somper) and 'The Lord of the Rings' and 'The Hobbit' (J.R.R.Tolkien). Alexandra is also a huge fan of George R.R. Martin's 'A Game of Thrones'. She was born in Walsall, England in November 1997. She first discovered her love for writing at primary school, where she would write stories and poems in her free time both in and after classes. At around the age of ten, she wrote her very first story. It was not very long, and never published, but she knew she wanted to continue writing fantasy

stories. When she went to secondary school, Alexandra's great grandmother began to develop dementia, and Alexandra was diagnosed with depression. Alexandra used her grief to start writing the very moving and emotional novel 'Broken Soul: The Forgotten World'. Between her home struggles and school exams, it took her five years to complete the book. She dedicated the novel to the memory of her great grandparents, whom she loved dearly and inspired her to start writing again. 'Dragonbourne: The Wyvern War', is Alexandra's second book that she has published, and is even bigger and better than the last one. She is incredibly proud of what she has achieved, and she hopes that her stories give people some escape from their realities, as it has done for her. She is currently at university, continuing to explore her passion for creativity. She has stated that a second instalment of Dragonbourne is on the cards, and she is very much excited to continue writing about Xanda and Leon's adventure.

Want to know the true story of what happened to The Raven Queen 400 years ago? Her story is now available to purchase on Amazon! Don't miss out on ordering your copy of

'Broken Soul: The Forgotten World'

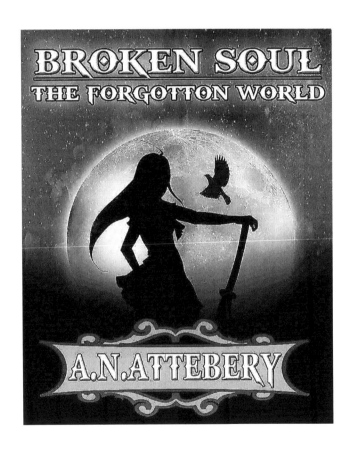

Printed in Great Britain
by Amazon

40440371R00144